Choestoe Book 3

Spirit of the Rabbit Place

J.R. Collins

W & B Publishers
USA

W & B Publishers

For information:
W & B Publishers
9001 Ridge Hill Street
Kernersville, NC 27284

www.a-argusbooks.com

ISBN: 9781635541564

Book Cover designed by J.R. Collins and Melissa Carrigee
Printed in the United States of America

Prologue

A season had come to the valley of Choestoe in 1829. A valley whose name to the settlers meant "land where the rabbits dance." They said it as Cho-E-sto-E. The Indians said it a little different, "Cho-es-tee." The folks what lived in the valley could not understand this new season. It was a time of change. A change none wanted. The expected harvest of this new season was profit. Finding gold brought greed through the strangers what come to Choestoe in large numbers lookin' for said profit. Many searching for the dream of riches in the creeks and streams of a most beautiful, and to the Indians, a most sacred place. This mass invasion brought with it this season of change. Certain hardship and unnecessary danger beset the folks what called the valley home. Jebediah Collins, a young man of Irish descent, and his best friend in life, Wolf, a natural-born full-blood Cherokee, lived in the valley through this change. Saw the pain and hurt of what folks can do to one another that live outside the Will of the Great Creator. Considered the one true God by most settlers, and many Indians alike. An invasion, as the settlers seen it, being that the mountains and valley was a frontier when they first come to it. A frontier filled with natural wonders they never would've imagined to the sense of family and home. It is a perfect land for life. Good weather mostly. Hot in the summer and cold in the winter with plenty of good, clean, cool water.

The time of falling leaves and the time of flowers filled the days between winter and summer. A paradise for those who figured it for so, at least until the leaders of the U.S. Government found out about its resources. What they did in 1838 made the Cherokee cry. The hated change finished their natural way of life. The Indians knew it in the end as the "Trail where they Cried." The settlers knew it as "The Trail of Tears ." Me and Wolf called it "The Rabbit Place Lost." We hurt for all the loss folks come to when the soldiers came to end the Cherokee living in the mountains. It drove many deeper into the mountains to live what most would consider a hard way 'a life. No, not hard for them. It was more natural, so they survived. It does not escape wonder that now they thrive from the settlers' losses. Life is a circle.

Chapter 1: To Fetch the Ol' Black Angel

I'd never shot no folks before, but I was meanin' to shoot this 'un. He'd done crossed up with me and mine. We owed him his due. A Choestoe family was sufferin' on account 'a what him and his friends had done. Un-rightful killin' weren't to be tolerated in the mountains where I lived. Folks had rights. 'Sides, he was aimin' to kill me. Done shot at me twice. Near hit me the second time. Close enough I could hear the air burnin' as the lead ball sizzled by my ear. Four inches left would 'a sent me across the Great River to be with the ancestors. "Praise God he missed" was all the prayer I could muster as I dove behind a huge white oak for cover. The same tree my rifle was now braced against pointed back at him. He was comin' on full out. Drawin' his short guns and screamin' wild threats like a mad man. His flintlock rifle now abandoned, standin' dark against the poplar tree from where he'd last shot at me. Not sure why he was wantin' to pull my tongue out or tie my guts in a knot, but that's what he was yellin'. I allowed he was took by ol' Satan his self, or at the very least, one 'a the fallen.

My rifle's bead was dead center his chest, a little ways below the shoulders. I held the long barrel steady against the tree. Dad always said, "If you're gonna kill a body, hit it right in the middle above the belly. Hold still when aimin'. Don't flinch while pullin' the trigger." As I looked down the barrel, I remember thinkin' it weren't much different than shootin' food meat. A little taller was all.

I'd come to the understandin', shortly after my young adult reckonin', that the day would come when I'd be forced to drop flint on a fellow human. Killin' was serious business to a person of my faith. One had to be positive 'fore strikin' out. Accordin' to the Good Book, what Jesus did for us on the Cross made every soul have worth, so takin' life without strong purpose was one 'a the ten worst in God's eyes. I figured a body better be sure they was in the right 'fore sendin' a lead ball at a man's chest to fetch the ol' Black Angel. That kinda doin's could tempt the Almighty, and that's not good for the soul. I was sure on that.

Shootin' folks is a tough chore. It's worrisome thinkin' on it. I had no doubt throughout my life I'd better be ready to drop flint on a body havin' Wolf, the son of a battle-hardened Cherokee Warrior and Tribal Elder as my Blood Brother. My lifelong best friend. What we faced as threats weren't much different than what all folks in the Choestoe Valley faced most every day that Old Man Sun rose, maybe a little more deadly for us, bein' we lived Cherokee a good part of the time. Anymore, the mountains had become a dangerous place with all the greedy strangers in the woods lookin' for gold. I wondered if I was ready to kill now that the day had finally come. I had no choice as it was. The one to die was comin' hard. Mad all over his face. It had suddenly become him or me. I was intendin' fer it to be him.

I commenced on instinct, 'cause I know'd my life depended on me hittin' the varmint solid 'fore he got too close. The trigger felt perfect as I let out my breath while pullin' back smooth as I could. The pressure familiar. I'd been shootin' the Harpers Ferry .54 caliber for a while, so I know'd when it would go off. It all felt normal as the flint dropped makin' the powder flare. I figured the outlaw for dead as the heavy rifle's butt slammed against my shoulder. At least his charge never broke the soft, gray cloud 'a burnt black powder smoke slowly risin' to the sky in front of me . . . and . . . I'd heard a hard, slicing thud from what I figured was fast movin' lead hittin' homespun, meat, then bone. That would not be good for him as close as he was. The shot seemed good. Timed as his right foot hit the ground not ten 'a Dad's paces short from where I was squatted beside the white oak. I'd know soon if I'd become a killer, it would be fine if I had. Right was on my side. Evil struck first.

"Jeb, we must move," hollered Wolf as he grabbed my arm pullin' me away. "The evil ones will be on us if we stay here. Death is all around, stay low. I will lead. Reload your rifle as we travel. You may need to fire again before we can reach safety. This thing has turned bad for us."

I'd also learned in my short life that plans don't always turn out like you first figure 'em. This was one 'a them times. Wolf and me studied over our recent efforts for several hours 'fore makin' the trail to follow our fathers, after, of course, they'd told us with strong talk to stay home. They weren't a flaw to be reasoned over that we could foresee. But, our little adventure had turned sour without us wantin' it to. It'd become clear as creek water in a drought that the Great Spirit had pushed us down a trail we didn't even know was there. We'd not planned on doin' no killin', know'd they'd be some, but didn't allow it to be by our hand. The trail started out like we figured, then quickly slid sideways like a snake with its blood up. The Almighty'd done laid a bigger purpose to our cause what took us a while to figure out. I guess that's why He's in charge. I never liked gettin' shot at, though. I wished He'd not allowed that.

Our only way out from the fix we'd got ourselves in was to run, so run we did. It seemed we'd been doin' a lot 'a that lately. Crouched low. Movin' fast as possible. Rifle held firm in our right hand, so our left was free to signal. I'm sure I heard a couple more rifle balls sizzle over our heads as we made our way east toward Panther Cave. It weren't really our fault folks was shootin' at us, but that makes no difference when evil ones get killin' in their mind. Most often means good folks like myself and Wolf or one's family end up squarin' things for balance. I'd learned to live with that. It was part 'a growin' up mountain. You looked after your own and theirs; friends, too. Wolf stopped us to talk.

"We must split up, Jebediah. Go to a safe place. I will climb high on the Blood Mountain. You circle low into the valley. Make your way to Panther Cave from the east. I will come from the south. I counted five more to face our fathers. The two Indians with them are Cherokee. I do not know them. I believe them to be from another place. They are trackers, so mind your trail. Leave no sign. Meet at the cave when you are sure no one is following. Good luck my friend. If by the grace of the Great Creator any of these evil men get by our fathers, do not let them shoot you. I know your family would be very sad."

I saw the slight grin touch the corners of his mouth as he slipped away into the woods. I never got to say a word durin' our little stop. That was common for this type a' happenin'. I turned, leavin' no less quick headin' east. I'd need to move that way for 'bout an hour 'fore turnin' south a while then back west toward Panther Cave. All the time checkin' my back trail for any followin' company. Trail savvy I'd learned from Wolf and his family. My folks, too.

Things that probably saved my life a few times durin' my growin' up years in Choestoe.

My friend was most natural when movin' through the mountains. I trusted his every thought. Listened to his every word, especially when my life depended on it. That weren't a lot, 'cept for sometimes. His clan called it a gift; considered it spiritual. I believed it was givin' all the things I'd seen him do when we was out on trail together. Cherokee stuff most folks never even heard of, probably wouldn't believe and for sure didn't understand. I thought, as I kept movin' east, on how we'd got foul in our latest comin' together. Ended up runnin' for our lives from a bad bunch 'a folk. That should not 'a happened. I'd rather been hog huntin' on Rattlesnake Mountain than fool with all we was havin' to fool with, but that weren't my decision. The gold lookers should 'a stayed away.

My life in the Choestoe Valley began when my grandfather, James, Dad's Dad, settled there with my ancestors. All come from Ireland. The Mother Land they'd tell ya. He and his wife, my dear sweet grandmother Cathleen, settled in a most beautiful valley the Cherokee called Cho-E-sto-E, meaning "Place Where the Rabbits Dance", layin' to the east side of the southern tip of the Appalachian. It was my home. This area come to be part of the great State of Georgia after the U.S. Government took the Cherokee's land. Give it to folks what didn't earn it -- never could come to know it proper. Took by soldiers at the end of a gun paid for by greedy money folk what influenced the dishonest elect in Congress. Fortunately, not all folks think like that bunch.

I was born in the mountains. Raised a farmer and mountain man, but near lived as a Cherokee, even more after word got out about the gold bein' found. My dad,

Thompson Collins, kept a farm what grow'd mules for coin or trade. Them was good mules, too. King Jacks bred straight up with Draft mares to give a solid frame what worked perfect on the slopes and steeps of the big mountains. My brother Cain and I near lived with the Indians. Know'd 'em well. Farmed with 'em. Traded with 'em. Hunted with 'em. Fought alongside 'em. Loved with 'em. Worshipped with 'em. Married into their tribe. Become family in several ways, so we didn't like folks comin' in tryin' to claim what they'd called home for many generations. The place where their folks was buried. Stealin' the land given by the Great Spirit what was handed down through the ancestors. That's in part how our most recent trouble got started. Good folks homsteadin'. Followin' God's Will for what would hopefully be a better life.

History talks about "Gold Fever." How it can be a stronghold of a man's conscience; a nation. Consider then, in all fairness to the Cherokee and the settlers, how this fever for riches took hold of a young, growing nation durin' the first ever gold rush. A nation left in debt from a long war fought purely for freedom and a better way to live. A nation with folks eager to get their share of what the mountains had to offer. Gold, hides, timber, minerals, property . . . Cherokee scalps . . . slaves . . . all to be sold for profit. Didn't matter who or what got bent, broke, took or kilt along the way. Shame is terrible company when it finally comes. The problem is, it don't usually show up till after history has been written, or the guilty parties come to recompense. With common folk, mercy is typically applied as time helps heal the hurt. Not true with the Indian. Revenge can be a lifelong quest. I've never seen anything like it. Self-control with a taste for warm blood kept close to the heart for the sake of honor.

The Cherokee did not take kindly to the mass intrusion of the 1829 Gold Rush to their lands. I couldn't blame 'em after seein' it firsthand. Shameful behavior was all it was. Behavior what caused anger to burn red hot in the hearts of many Cherokee warriors. You could call it . . . an invasion. That's the way the Cherokee took it. They would fight for their home and what it held. I, Jebediah Collins, son of "Thompie" and Celia Collins of the Choestoe Clan, never doubted their will to live and die where their ancestors walked. My heart was with them. Their effort was my effort.

It was near dark when me and Wolf met back up at the entrance to Panther Cave midway up the north side 'a Blood Mountain. He was there waitin' for me. I didn't expect no different. He had less ground to cover sure, but that would not matter. He'd got there first. Cherokee understand things as they see it. He got there before me, so in his mind, he was the better traveler. I weren't gonna let all that worry me none 'cause I know'd he was a better woodsman than me. Fact was, outside 'a my dad and Wolf's father, Dancing Bear, or maybe his uncle, George Black Oak, the biggest Cherokee you'd ever see, or maybe his brother, Moon Shadow, or my brother, Cain, or Wolf's other uncle, Red Hawk, he was the best woodsman in Choestoe. Of that he could be proud, 'cause that was some mighty fine company to be raked in with.

"My brother. You travel like a little sister," Wolf said with a curious look on his face. "Where have you been? Why has it taken you so long to come here? I was thinking an evil one shot you. Left you for dead. That I would need to come find your body. Take you home to Ben's Knob. I have been here for a long while waiting on you, worried. I am glad you made it with all your blood still traveling through your body. It is good there is none leaking out. Are you sure you weren't followed?"

"Wolf!", I said kinda sharp like. "You couldn't 'a been waitin' that long. It ain't took me but a couple hours to get here. Are you sure you been waitin' that long, Wolf? And yes, I know I weren't followed. How 'bout you? Are you sure you weren't followed?"

He looked at me like he'd just got caught hawkin' a penny from the offering plate at Sunday meetin'. Near took faint, even. "I am sure my friend, and you are right, I've only been here but a short time. I looked around some but have not gone inside Panther Cave. I've found no sign of anyone being here now or anytime recent. The sign of old still shows since we've had but little rain the last few moons. Let us sit among the boulders for a time and watch. Make a smoke. Say a prayer of thanks that you were not killed. Wait to see if any of the bad men made it past our fathers, then was lucky enough to cross any sign we might have left on our way here. What say you on this, Jeb Slow Like the Turtle?" he finished with a smile in his eye.

It weren't all like Wolf the way he was funnin' around with me. He had a sense 'a humor, sure, but didn't usually speak so much when we was dodgin' danger. Then it come to me. He was bein' a true friend. A trail savvy Cherokee. Distractin' my thinkin' so maybe I'd not get to studyin' on bein' a fresh birthed killer till later, when the threat we was facin' would be over. Always the true warrior thinkin' like that. Hopin' to delay the deep gut bustin' punch you get when it finally hits you you've taken life. For me, it was layin' still by the warm fire we'd built inside the cave later that night. Wolf had already taken life. Know'd the sickness I'd face when the thinkin' on it come to my body. We'd only be turnin' fifteen 'fore long, me and him share our birthday, and he'd been forced to take a man's life near a year to the day earlier. He'd had no choice, bein' Blood Brother to me. It was another time when it was either an outlaw or me. Seems I had a few 'a those over the years. I thanked him every year when I remembered it for choosin' me.

It come to my thinkin' that for the last good while many Choestoe folks was bein' put in a bad way by some 'a the strangers wanderin' the valley lookin' for profit. Few of 'em actin' full on like proper visitors. The bunch chasin' us weren't among the friendly. Many, like them, come to the valley lookin' for gold or what not, but for the way they'd act, never made it back home. It was a bad, bad spell for those who'd chose to settle in the mountains full time. It changed the way we all lived when that slave owner told folks he'd found gold across the ridge toward Yonah. If he'd kept his mouth shut, the evil might never 'a crossed the mountains till later. The way Wolf and me saw it, most of the blood what got shed durin' the gold rush was 'cause 'a him or his lettin' out word 'a their find. We'd all found gold. Settler and Indian. We just didn't make it known to outside folks for fear 'a what might happen, like the very things folks was havin' to deal with throughout the Southern Appalachia in 1829. All kinds 'a greedy fools rushin' to the prize bringin' ways we weren't accustomed to. Some good--some bad. Most bad to me. Change didn't happen in a short while, neither. It worked on for years 'fore the U.S. Government decided to go ahead and forcibly take the mountains. The Cherokee ended up gettin' the bloody end 'a that butcher's knife. The bunch after us was just a small part 'a that whole big problem. God had His way 'a doin' things. He knows all. He'd see to it all would come square. In faith, I followed Him all my life. Smartest thing I ever did.

Not all the gold hunters was bad. We'd made a friend in a younger man named Sean. He lived in a small one room cabin he'd built just east of the river Notla. He'd found us at Wolf's place near two years back of our present trouble. Said he know'd our dads but never told how. We never asked. Figured if he'd 'a wanted us to know he'd 'a told us. He was a good hunter. We spent many hours with him and my brother, Cain. Huntin' . . . campin' . . . raidin' . . . After gettin' to know his heart, we helped him find a little color to trade for coin. We did it even though we didn't like folks takin' the mountain's gold. We did it 'cause his heart was pure. He walked in truth. Believed in Jesus. Worried over his fellow man, at least the good ones anyway. I'd seen him fight. Cain was learnin' him warrior style, and Sean had took to it. My brother had experience. It was wise for Sean to listen to him. He was a battle tested Cherokee warrior of the purest kind. One of the bravest of all the warriors in the mountains, even though he was the grandson of settlers. Respected by his brethren. Honored by his foes. He weren't afraid 'a nothin' I ever know'd of. I could only hope to be near the man he'd become. He was plumb savvy in the mule tradin' business, too. Doubled Dad's rake in the couple years he'd been a husband . . . father.

The other folks we'd come to know durin' the gold doin's was why we was tradin' shots with them outlaws 'fore headin' to Panther Cave. Young couple come to Choestoe with the wife's widowed Father in company to homestead. They was folks of the Weaver family what lived on, and farmed, a big place in the southern end of the valley east of the River Notla. Not far from Sean's. They grow'd the best tobacco in the mountains. Folks called it Weaver Tobacco for the quality and uniqueness of its smoke. A favorite of the Cherokee. Wolf and me, too. They had a bait 'a kids. Grow'd a storehouse full 'a crops every year. Shared with anybody what needed it. Good folks they was, for sure.

We liked them new folks a sight. Made friends with the old man. He was wise. Taught me and Wolf how to use our knives different from normal Cherokee, weren't no better, just different, and how to think our way through a fight. How to hobble folks without killin' 'em. That was real interestin' to me and Wolf. He'd been a soldier somewhere I'd never heard of. Had a strong accent I only come across the once in my life. Sounded different from any other types of accents you'd ever hear common in the mountains. Bandits stabbed him dead for a small pouch 'a gold nuggets he was so proud 'a findin'. The old man thought them outlaws was good folks, but they weren't. Took his possibles, too, and a mule he'd got from Dad. Well, Old Man Weaver weren't gonna stand for the murder of one 'a his own, and neither was anybody else in Choestoe that know'd about it. That's how we'd come to be mixed up in the mess we was gettin' away from quick as could be. Dancing Bear, Black Oak and Dad went with Mr. Weaver to see justice done. Told us to stay put at the house for not wantin' us to witness such as they was headed to do. We should 'a done what we was told. No, Wolf bein' Wolf, he just had to follow. Of course, I chose to go with him. He never meant for me to go no place I didn't want to. We'd near got ourselves kilt for disobeyin'. Still, nobody but us ever know'd we slipped in on that fight. Nobody but us ever know'd what I'd had to do. As Wolf and I sat the rocks outside Panther Cave, we said a prayer of thanks to the Great Spirit for helpin' us get out from the fix we never should 'a been in. Watchin' the woods close, enjoyin' a pipe of some good dried burley, we know'd they weren't nobody gonna come. Dad, Black Oak and Dancing Bear would 'a made sure Mr. Weaver got justice. Me and Wolf helped some, in our own secret way. I wondered if the two Cherokee got away. They should 'a never left from their families to follow the trash they was with.

We stayed two more nights in Panther Cave after the shootin'. We'd 'a lit out after the first night but it come a "frog strangler" rain that next morning, forcin' us to keep to the dry. Them's heavy rains you can't see thru what come off and on for a day or two. Hard to travel in. Them kinda rains was good at the first 'a Spring. Helped get the fields ready to plant. Made the wild onions and ramps sprout their tops nice and green so we could find 'em late in the season. We'd be goin' for ramps soon. I looked forward to that trail.

Chapter 2- The Most Perfect Creature Ever Made

The time of falling leaves was a welcomed season for me and Wolf that year. He'd come to live with us at the start 'a plantin' season, which weren't long after our outlaw trouble earlier that spring. He'd stay 'til harvest was done. Reason was, the Cherokee crops was gettin' stole out in the mountains. Hungry gold miners what didn't pack enough provisions to last as long as they'd ended up stayin', got to starvin'. Most too lazy or too ignorant to hunt their own meat. No thought to plantin' crops for their providin'. The growin' season of 1828 give plenty 'a food-stores for the ones what grow'd it, but the miners come in durin' the night slick as coons stealin' stock oats. Took it all without nobody knowin'. Left several Cherokee families to go hungry while havin' to face the coming cold time without proper stores of food. The Cherokee Guard could do very little against common, random, nighttime thievery. Still, they caught a few. Just not enough to scare the other hungry gold lookers. Keep 'em from raidin' more Cherokee gardens and cellars. They didn't bother the settlers much.

Dancing Bear wanted to make sure his clan didn't suffer the hunger again because of the evil from the gold lookers. He felt our place would be less likely to get stole from so he come and talked with Dad about it. Dancing Bear reasoned that closer to where settler folk lived might be less likely to get hit by thieves. Settlers what looked out for one another. Settlers who owned weapons. Dancing Bear asked Dad to start growin' all the extra he could for the Choestoe clan what would end up gettin' took from that fall. Dad was happy to oblige. Mr. Weaver, too. That's how Wolf come to stay with us all summer to help work. Other clan members did as well, but they all made camp out in the woods. Most 'a them was women.

Me and Wolf didn't have no big adventures much durin' the hot months. We was workin' the farm near all the daylight hours gettin' it ready for the fall harvest. We know'd our lives depended on the food that harvest would provide each year. Kept us and our stock fed through the cold time. We were tired at night from the hard work 'a farmin', so we slept. That give us energy to work all the next day. That was some good sleep, too. We rested on Sundays, so we never had much time away from the farm durin' the summer or early fall. Our fourteenth summer was no different, even with all the gold miner trouble. A calm time was just fine with me 'cause gettin' mixed up in that fight 'a Mr. Weaver's was enough adventure to keep me a while. He never said it, but I believe Wolf felt the same. Yep, work and harvest was most definitely welcomed that season.

Unfortunately, or fortunately, Wolf and me learned shortly after Dad returned home from seein' Mr. Weaver get justice that the man I'd shot at was dead. Had a hole shot through his person. Dead center his chest. They found him layin' beside a big white oak. His back flat to the ground, but not near where their fight had been with the other outlaws. Like he'd turned scared and run off leavin' his mates to fight it out, then met somebody what shot him as he was leavin'. *That must 'a been how we run in to him.* Dad said he and Dancing Bear and Black Oak all found it curious how the killer was dead when none 'a them know'd where he was to shoot at. His look to me when he said that was one of curious intentions. They thought he'd got free 'til they found his body. Me and Wolf know'd how he got dead . . . I'd shot him. They weren't much doubt after hearin' Dad's words that I'd become a killer. The punch to my gut was not as fierce as the original by the fire in Panther Cave, but it was bad a plenty. I wondered if that sickness would ever go away. Strong and sickinin' as it felt, I doubted it.

It was corn-pullin' time at our farm early that fall. Not corn for eaten so much, but ears of corn what air dried hard on the stalk in the field. It's the corn we had ground-up at the mill to feed our stock when the cold time come makin' the grasses in our pastures die. The same stuff we fed the hogs and beef we put up every year for meat. We'd stock a right smart of it, too. Our corn crib was big enough for several acres, and what Dad grow'd would pack it full every year we had proper harvest. Most all would be ground whole for the animals. Some kernelled from the cob for corn meal mixin's. Dad would store that in the cellar for Momma to use if we run out 'a good flour or meal at the house. The corn we was pullin' is what we let dry standin' in the field. It was of a kind that worked well for the stock.

Most of our eatin' food come from our Three Sisters and Four Sisters gardens up by the house. Granddad learned that growin' style from the Cherokee. Taught it to Dad. Growin' a garden the Three Sisters' way kept the weeds down. If you added in sunflower, it was good for replenishing the soil from the year before. It was so called 'cause you planted corn, vine beans and squash close together in the same rows. It was a mix learned by the Cherokee ancestors from the north many generations before me and Wolf ever run in Choestoe. Roast'n ears, vegetables, berries and white flour corn come from the house gardens. Corn for hominy come from the field. I never liked hominy, but my granddad did, so Momma would cook it up for him. One of my most favorite meals of all Momma ever cooked was Cherokee White Flour cornbread and buttermilk sidin' with a mess 'a beans, corn, onions, potatoes, wild mushrooms, sweet pepper and apples what'd been boiled in with a ham bone all seasoned with salt and dried red pepper. Momma always left a right smart 'a ham on the bone for cookin'. Partner all that with a big ol' fire baked sweet potato covered in a thick layin' 'a butter, then finish the sittin' off with a generous helpin' 'a grape dumplings washed down with a gigger 'a warm apple brandy. Mmh! Mmh! Makes a body hungry just thinkin' on it. I don't reckon food got any better than what I was raised on. A gift from God you might say.

Dad made it a purpose to always grow more than we could ever use anyhow. He know'd folks might need it along if the cold time held late in the spring or if some other happenin' come on 'em, then there they'd be, without. That didn't sit well with him when it weren't no trouble growin' more as less. It's just what neighbors did. We had a means to grow plenty, other folks not so much, so we did. Dancing Bear was smart enough to recognize that Dad overproduced when he felt concern for his clan. Called on him for help. Folks around the valley come to depend on Dad for growin' extra, and he obliged 'em. Discussed it with a few 'fore gettin' the ground ready in the spring. Figured for others when he did the plowin' and plantin'. He know'd they'd be some come to our place in the late 'a winter lookin' for provisions when their cupboards and barns got to runnin' empty for whatever reason. Some would try and give Dad gold coin for providin' fer 'em, but he'd not take it. He'd not let 'em pay. Never charged a single soul for any food makin's they took home with 'em that I ever saw. Give folks whatever they needed no matter if it was for stock or families. He didn't feel right makin' profit off another's bad fortune. That was just the way. He didn't help for this reason, but he know'd most 'a them folks would do for him if they ever come a time when he needed 'em. They know'd it, too. It's how God made us to live -- in peace . . . with balance. I've heard Cherokee call the Baby Jesus, "Peace Child." Now ain't that somethin'?

Any leftover corn in the crib when the grasses got to growin' in the spring was loaded in the harvest wagon, then toted out to a certain place in the woods. We'd leave it in small piles for the critters. Hunger could hit them in late winter just like it did regular folk. It weren't uncommon to see several ol' skinny bears around the piles come spring. They was hungry when they woke from their winter rest. My totem, Brother Bear, would come every year. We know'd it was him by the Cross Star on his chest. I saw him there for many seasons, then one season he was not there. By fate, that was the same year I'd set my mind for leavin' the valley. The mountains had just got too crowded for me. I guess me and him both felt the need to get away from all the folks comin' south fillin' up the hollers and river bottoms. Unfortunately for the mountain folk, the Confederacy lost the War of Northern Aggression. That opened the door for northern folk, whose money still held value, to go south for business opportunity. Many figured the down and out south a recovering land where huge profits could be made. That bein' so, the ones with money commenced to takin' over commerce for that profit. They weren't all bad. Most had an interest in seein' the south restored to its once grand status, but some did a lot 'a terrible things to folks what trusted 'em. It would 'a been a heap better for mountain folk if the U.S. Government hadn't won that war. Kept greedy business folk from comin' south to take advantage 'a whooped folks. At least the slaves got their freedom. Most Southerners never liked slave holdin'. It was the rich families what profited from it, not common folk like me. Most I ever met in Choestoe allowed ownin' a body just weren't right. It seems, when you think on it, the whole mess could 'a been handled better, especially from those runnin' our representation. Maybe not. It was a bitter tea what'd been brewin' for a while.

You could say the control over mountain folks started actual back in the day with the Indian Removal Act President Andrew Jackson fought so hard for and won in 1830. It only passed by a few votes in the whole 'a Congress. It was told Davy Crocket went back to Tennessee after politics in Georgia. Later movin' to Texas sayin' he'd never come back after what was bein' done to the Indians. He didn't. Dyin' out there in 1835 fightin' for freedom. The way those like me, who opposed the removal believed it, the Indian was a part of the land just like the mountains and the trees, the rivers and the creeks, and the air. Their ancestors was there long before any settlers or government folk come lookin' around. The only true native folk if you study on it. Should 'a been treated like Americans when our nation come into bein', at least those loyal to General Washington should 'a been. Many deserved respect like Water Runs Deep, Dancing Bear's father. He was one 'a Washington's favored secret scouts durin' the Revolution. Saved many American lives with his scoutin' and spyin'. Those Cherokee friendly to America did nothin' wrong 'til it was forced on 'em. Creeks and other Indians, neither. Mountain folk know'd the Indians accepted their European ancestors when they come lookin' to settle. Taught 'em things that helped 'em survive in the cold mountain wilderness. I don't believe I met many settlers in my day that wouldn't 'a done the same thing a lot 'a Cherokee did when the removal was forced on 'em . . . fight for what was theirs . . . a way of life.

I've said it before, but just to be clear, families in the mountains like a good "comin' together." Visiting for means of purpose. Many times a year it would happen. Killin' Time after the first hard frost was one 'a them times. Weddings and deaths for sure demanded a big "comin' together." Spring plantin' and soap makin' time was a couple more. There were others. Of course, we all went to Revival when the preacher come each change 'a season. Women and girls would stay at the church house a few days after Revival ended to gather and make quilts for those who needed the comfort, kinda holdin' their own little "comin' together" in a way. They had a big time when they did that. Looked forward to it all through the seasons. Momma talked woman speak to me and Dad about patterns and materials and types 'a thread and certain needles almost constant as Revival draw'd near, but we know'd little about those things. Couldn't answer back a bit except for maybe a "yes ma'am" or a "no ma'am" or a "I figure you're right, Momma." I had used one 'a her needles with thread to sew up a cut on Wolf's leg made by an arrow what'd spun too close, but that was all the needle and thread sewin' I'd ever done. I could lace leather string through pouch edges with a fine sharp tipped carved bone what had a hole through one end. Sewed on handles with heavy hemp string usin' that same bone "needle." Me and Momma would go with Dad when he went south to market at Gaines Town in the spring. She'd buy up all the makin's needed to build great feelin' quilts. A couple every year; warm. Some heavy-some light dependin' on what was needed. She was sewin' at home on the final quilt of a set for her new granddaughter, Isabelle. Momma was makin' the set as a gift for Christmas. Isabelle was the daughter of Cain and Rose. She was my niece. I was her favorite all her life . . . outside the women folk, of course . . . and Cain and Dad and Wolf and Dancing Bear and George. Ah, we all claimed her. Loved on her. Spoiled her as much as her momma would let us. She lived a different growin' up life than we all did. The mountains changed not long after she was born.

Them Choestoe women could cut and sew them covers perfect. Problem was, they tended to get in to the church's store 'a medicinal brandy durin' their post Revival "comin' together." Dad and the deacons learned after a few revivals what was happenin', so they took to makin' sure they was plenty left about for the ladies quiltin' time.

Babies bein' born or folks gettin' over a serious illness also demanded a comin' together or when a body died. Anything special was a good time. Give folks a chance to comfort one another from the loneliness of frontier life. Be with each other for a while outside 'a family to fellowship and catch up. These times together as a community was comforting, needed by folks.

Corn Pullin' was one 'a them times when the men folk would gather at certain farms to pluck the dried ears from their respective stalks, brought their families to help. It was a big comin' together 'cause gettin' all the fields collected took a lot 'a hands. Not every farm had enough cleared land to grow stock corn so just a few of the farms grow'd enough for all the stock in Choestoe. Helped smaller farms out a sight. When the corn got just dry enough to pull, word was sent out by the growin' farmer to hurry on with wagons to whatever farm they was needed. All the men in the valley, Cherokee included, expected the call for corn pullin' help. Know'd when it might come. Watched for it, or sometimes just come on 'cause they figured word was on the way anyhow. Mountain folk had smarts that 'a way.

It usually took about four days to get all our corn in our crib, providin' the weather stayed dry. It was strange to watch it all happen. The settlers always pulled and loaded the corn into the wagons while the Cherokee stood around at the corn crib waitin', prayin', playin' games or gamblin', tellin' stories or what not. Then, when the wagons in the field was full, the dried ears of corn would be brought in to be unloaded. The settlers would drive the wagons up close to the crib door, lock the wagon binders, and back away to stand around watchin' or gamblin' or tellin' stories or what not, lettin' the Indians have at packin' it all into the crib proper. They stacked it gentle like, usin' only their hands. One or two ears at a time. Corn was important to them. Sacred even. It had to be handled respectfully. Them Indians packin' that crib was amazin' to watch. Weren't nobody shoutin' orders or nothin', it just happened. Worked smooth as soft cheese renderin'. They liked eatin' that stock corn, too. That's one reason they come to help. Dad give 'em all they wanted for helpin' with the corn pullin' when it come time for 'em to go back to their homes.

Camps spread all around our place for over a week durin' our farm's time for corn pullin'. It was hard work for those fillin' the wagons. Dried corn weren't as easy to get off the stalk as green. Had to be dry, though, so it would grind smooth and not rot in the crib. Most of the shuck come off when you give the ear a kinda pullin' twist with your hand. That kinda jerk would snap it loose from its stalk most times, but a lot 'a ears hung on tight, had to be twisted a few times. That was the work that made the job tiring. Your shoulder, arm, hand, wrist, back and fingers got sore after a while from not bein' accustomed to the motion it took to pluck the ears from their beds. Men had to take turns pullin' and loadin' the wagons, that's one 'a the reasons why so many hands was needed. It was all worth it to everybody. Dad sent every wagon home with what field corn they needed, and as a way of sayin' thanks for the help, a few bushels of white flour corn. They was proud to get that 'cause 'a how good the cornbread and such was a body could make from it. Wolf's family come to our place 'fore any other folks. They stayed in the house since they was family and all. I liked 'em stayin' in the house. Dancing Bear would tell stories late into the night. It was some of my favorite memories. Rockin' by the fire while listenin' to the Indian tales he'd tell. He was a great story teller.

The best part about corn pullin' at our place was gettin' to see all the neighbors you'd not seen since probably Revival back in the summer. The number 'a folks settling in the valley was growin', farmers mostly. Good people what feared the wrath of God, but humbled themselves for His love, buildin' new homesteads up and down the river ever few moons. Dad and Cain's mule business was bringin' in a lot 'a gold coin. Dad never spent much of it. If he did, it was on Momma most every time. He loved my momma more than words can say. You could see it when they was around each other. Made me feel good.

The England folks come to help with the corn pullin'. Elizabeth was with 'em. I hadn't seen her since me and Dad went to help pick and string their beans and shell their peas a couple months back. Mrs. England needed the help, so we stayed on a few days makin' sure all was took care of proper. Her recent husband spent all his time in the woods. Didn't pay much mind to his home duties. He lived Indian more than he should 'a. Dad whooped him over it once. Beat him good for not takin' proper care of Mrs. England and her brood. Dad favored Mr. England what got killed by the she bear over her new husband. They'd had a bait 'a kids 'fore he died.

I was sure proud we did that 'cause I got to spend time with Elizabeth durin' them days . . . I fell in love with Elizabeth durin' them days . . . couldn't help it. I tried hard not to, but I learned while bein' around her that love weren't something you had much control over. She took me. I really didn't understand what this love was, but I could feel for sure I'd got mixed up in something powerful. Didn't care to be away from it. It's hard for me to explain how it felt to be near her, to see her, to catch even a tiny pull of her scent. When I looked at her, I could feel her heart beatin' inside my chest keepin' time to mine. It felt like the steady cadence of a Cherokee drum off the top 'a Big Bald mountain; spiritual. It seemed I felt her breath go in and out from her chest as I watched her breathe. I felt her eyes as they moved in rhythm to the silence of her thoughts. Her voice made me almost fall to my knees in weakness when she spoke. I come to realize, love was just awful. I worked to avoid it hard as I could by not lettin' myself think on her while we was apart, but that didn't work. I couldn't stop myself. I would think on her constant, without even knowin' it sometimes. The softness of her skin. The warmth of sittin' close to her. The quivers I felt when I first held her hand durin' that bean pickin' spell. It was up on the ridge above their home as we sat watchin' Old Man Sun go home for the night. After we left from their place helpin' with the beans, I did alright forgettin' what I could about her for a time, but when she show'd up at corn pullin' my heart stopped. I was near to blackin' out from not breathin' 'fore I come to my senses. I had to go talk to her, so I could start takin' air proper. I know'd I'd done got in sad shape. She'd draw'd me in like a fly caught in a spider's web, wrapped up and way too tight. I felt danger was lurkin' for me. My spirit was screamin' to stay away. Weren't gonna happen, her blue eyes stopped me in my tracks whenever we looked at one another. I'd give in full. She'd sprung her trap. I was hangin' upside down caught in her snare. It was a gift from God the way I saw it. I wanted to waller in the feelin' of it like a fat hog in a cool spring. She was perfect.

They come to our place the day before we planned to start the pullin'. Mrs. England was drivin' the wagon. Some 'a her kids was ridin' in the back, others walkin'. She had a whole litter. Looked like baby chicks followin' along behind whenever she took 'em somewhere. She was a great woman. Every-last child 'a her's minded what she said. Most times any trouble was ended with a simple look. They know'd when that look come it was time to commence behavin'. Dad and Dancing Bear never liked her travelin' alone with all them kids, although Mrs. England was a tough mountain woman, so he sent George Black Oak, Wolf's blood uncle, and a new member to our family, Wind Is Strong, a Cherokee woman we helped rescue from bein' a slave, to escort 'em.

I loved George. He was family to me now. Dancing Bear had adopted my whole bunch into his clan. That meant we was folks. Cain was a full-on Cherokee warrior 'cause 'a Dancing Bear. Cain turned out to be his son-in-law. Married his daughter, Rose. Some Indians didn't feel Cain was right to be seen as full warrior 'cause he looked different than the rest of our blood family. He had light colored hair and the bluest eyes you'd ever see. He weren't as tall as Dad and his kind but was tall enough. Nobody wanted to fight him. Only the toughest of warriors ever fought him as an equal. He'd never been whooped by a single man except my dad. Dad could whoop everybody 'cept Black Oak. That was a fact that nobody argued with, but Dad had the softest heart of all in our clan. Momma always said she had to marry him, 'cause if she didn't, his heart would 'a busted 'causin' him to die. She allowed she didn't want to be held on account for his death, so she took to him. I know'd that weren't true. My momma loved my dad. He was most Christ-like to us all through our growin' up years. We'd a not made it without him. I look forward to bein' with him across the Great River. He is missed.

"Elizabeth, how have you been?" I asked as I helped her down from the wagon seat she was sharin' with her momma. "That is a most beautiful blue dress you have on." I watched for her eyes to speak to me. They didn't need to. She spoke just fine.

"I am well, Mr. Jeb Collins! No thanks to you," she said back as she folded her arms across her chest while pinchin' her lips together leanin' in close to my face. She looked me straight in the eye like she was waitin' on me to say words. I didn't have any words to say. *What? . . . was she mad? Had I done something wrong? Not done something right?* Oh, I was not likin' love much right then. It was a most confusin' circumstance. All I could do was look at her. Try and cipher what it was she was heatin' over. I would just have to ask. God help me!

"Well, now, Elizabeth, I don't think I know what it is that I would be needin' a thanks for," I said as I removed my hat tryin' to be respectful. "Could you tell me what it is I missed doin' for you? I sure don't ever want to not do it again if you're this upset about it!"

"I shouldn't have to tell you what it is that you should've done. I thought we were courting? I let you hold my hand that evening when we watched Old Man Moon above our farm. Ain't we courting, Jebediah? If we are, why didn't you come check on me a time or two these last few moons?"

Oh, my. There it was then. I should 'a gone to check on her sometime between seein' her at Revival and corn pullin'. I won't forget to do that again. *How could I 'a know'd?* Nope . . . won't forget . . . *Courtin'?*

"Courtin', Elizabeth? You reckon we're courtin', now? I mean, is that how you see it? Is that what this is? If it is, it makes me feel plumb perfect. I am so glad you are here. I should 'a made a trail to check on you these last few moons. I will remember in the future now that we are . . . courtin'?"

"Oh, Jeb Collins! Why are you so blind?" she said kinda flustered suddenly snatchin' my hand pullin' me toward the mule barn as everybody else turned to go in the house. Once inside the main door, she grabbed me face on by the shoulders, leaned in close starin' me eye-to-eye, then commenced to givin' me the longest, most wonderful kiss. Not sure she ever give me one any better. I believe it was her way 'a answerin' whether or not we was courtin'. I figured she'd just made it for sure. At least for me she had.

My world went black as I was overcome by my first ever kiss . . . from the girl I loved. The next thing I remember was wakin' up on the barn floor with my head cuddled against her chest realizin' I never wanted to be apart from her again. She was wipin' the sweat off my face with her dress bottom. Soft homespun she'd done herself. I could feel her heart beatin' against the side of my head. Hear it in my left ear. Her scent made me weak. I wanted to rise-up and squeeze her in my arms as hard as I could. Melt our two bodies together as one. God made her in a way that draw'd me like a bee to flowers. I know'd then I was a lucky young man to have met such a creature of the woods. Far as I was concerned, she was the most perfect creature ever made . . . 'cept for Jesus . . . or Momma.

Chapter 3 - "a sight few folks ever witness"

I looked forward to those times durin' the year when the whole of the valley made trail south on the Keowee Path to market in Gaines Town. Near all settlers went, 'cept those what was needed to look after things at home. It was a big to do with all the wagons and all, everybody comin' together once in the spring and again in the time of falling leaves. The spring trip is when Momma went to fetch her sewing needs. We'd go as a whole family for that trip. Momma, Rose and Anne didn't always go in the fall, but often times one of 'em would. It was planned goin's, so families could travel together for fellowship and safety. That was important 'cause the wagons was loaded with homemade or homegrown bounty to be sold for gold coin or traded for necessities that families needed to help them survive. Easy for the takin' if not guarded. Everybody in the valley that wanted, or needed to go, went. Many Cherokee, too. Wolf and all his family for sure. Me and him would go in the spring and the time of falling leaves. Dad went three times a year. The other with Cain and Black Oak to take mules in the late part of cold time when Old Man Winter likes to play. Me and Wolf went with 'em after we got old enough. I never made that trip as a young 'un. Dad didn't want me goin' till I got older. Dancing Bear and several Cherokee warriors followed along hid close when Dad made his mule tradin' trips come winter. It was good they was there a few times, that's all I heard Dad ever say about 'em bein' there.

Took us two days to make the trip south up Lord 'a Mercy Holler then on out south 'a Hog Pen Gap followin' the Keowee Path. Hog Pen Gap is where a lot 'a folks built make-shift three sided holdin' pens formed from chestnut or locust rails. Used 'em for keepin' their farm critters in after they was caught back up to bring home in the fall. They's quite a bit 'a flat around that top for gatherin' in stock, and the main trail laid close by. That was handy for goin' to market if your stock was headed that way after bein' gathered. The reason their stock needed catchin' back up was, the farmers turned 'em out from the pastures to the woods come late spring to early summer. Hogs mostly, some cattle. Let 'em out to run wild in the mountains feedin' on chestnuts and acorns and fresh growth. Left 'em there till on up in the fall. Them runnin' open like that allowed 'em to fatten up good from a rich food source like chestnuts, acorns and fresh greens. Them eats got them critters to holdin' fat. Dad said lettin' 'em to the woods like they did then catchin' back up made the meat softer. Less tough like ol' wild mountain hogs what lived in the woods year 'round. Said it made the meat taste better, too. Sweeter. I couldn't argue that. I favored the taste 'a that meat.

When the leaves was near all off, the chestnuts and acorns would be 'bout eat up. The farmers would then have to go and fetch their critters back for meat makin' time. A few didn't want 'a come back. I couldn't blame 'em for not wantin' to find their way home after bein' set free for a spell. Weren't hard to find 'em, though, when the time come. They liked bein' on them big tops. Seems like they fed up that way every season. Dad allowed it was 'cause their front end was closer to the ground than their back end. Sometimes you had to watch what Dad tried to make you swaller. He had a keen sense of enjoyment when he set his mind to worryin' a body. I figured them hogs headed high 'cause that's where their needed food was. Dad know'd that too, he was just funnin' on me. I liked it when he did that. Made trail enjoyable.

Catchin' them hogs back weren't no easy chore on occasion, for sure them what liked bein' free to roam. They didn't care to be caught up and hauled back to the farm they'd done escaped from. One such hog was a huge old boar we named Junior. He'd got mean livin' out in the mountains. His tusk was showin' strong from growin' more wild. Old man Pickens from the north end 'a the valley owned him. Dad helped catch Junior the last he'd ever been caught. Took me along for bait I reckon, 'cause that's about what I become. Mr. Pickens come to us in the fall recent askin' us to help him again. Dad said he was sorry, but us catchin' that pig weren't gonna happen. We know'd that 'cause a what'n all happened that last time we tangled with it. He'd got way too big and cantankerous for common folk like us to bring back after livin' another season in the wild. Could be a near death chore for me if I turned up bait again.

Mr. Pickens understood it clear after discussin' it with my dad over a smoke fire at our place. He was gonna need some more skilled fetchers to hog tie ol' Junior. Dad sent for a couple young Cherokee warriors in trainin' Wolf know'd. That was all it took. They had the smarts to think like an old hog and we didn't. You'd not believe what they did to catch that heathen. It's a story that'll be told for generations around more smoke fires than a body could count. It really was proof of just how smart them two Cherokee brothers was. I'll never forget seein' it. I still laugh when I think on it. God bless 'em for their courage.

Ol' Junior was a breedin' hog, and he was big. Made good shoats. I don't mean your normal kinda big. I'm talkin' the George Black Oak of the mountain hog world big. Dad allowed three grow'd folks could ride on his back if he'd have it. He'd not, but they could. He had thick, nasty, near full curled tusks stickin' out from his big ol' fat, hairless snout. He know'd how to work 'em on you, too. Done cut Mr. Pickens good on back 'a the leg the year before near sendin' him across the River. Got after Dad rippin' the pants on his heavy deer hide leggings but drawin' no blood. Worst part was, ol' Junior was a dog killer. He'd killed a half-dozen good hog dogs over the years, so nobody what used dogs would help Mr. Pickens fetch him home anymore. Feared loosin' a trained dog. It seemed near hopeless, till Wolf remembered the Cherokee he know'd. They'd caught hard-to-catch hogs for folks before. Wolf said they know'd what they was doin'. I allowed they may know what they was doin', but I know'd it would take all their skill to snag ol' Junior without comin' to harm. That hog just weren't gonna have bein' fetched up again. Dad figured to just shoot him. Leave him lay and be done with it. Let the scavenging critters have him as part of their nighttime hunts. But, he'd bring good coin 'cause 'a him bein' a dominant stud hog, and Mr. Pickens needed the money from sellin' when he got done usin' him as a breeder. Junior had to be replaced. Dad said later he wished he'd a bought Junior then shot him his self. Dad hated that pig, but admitted Pickens was right about him bein' a good breeder with his size and all. Sides, he'd calm down some after gettin' penned up all winter. Be easier to handle if a body wanted to buy him.

Mr. Pickens decided he weren't gonna fool with the small hog pens in the woods. Didn't figure 'em to hold Junior no how if by chance they was able to get him in one. He paid them Indians to work that pig all the way back to his farm down on the River Notla. They obliged him. Me and Wolf followed, stayin' back a ways so's not to be a bother. We just wanted to watch them boys work their fetchin' chore. Maybe learn something. It's a happenin' I'll never forget. I still laugh out loud even now when I think on how them Indians did ol' Junior. I almost felt for him.

Didn't take them young warriors long to find the mean ol' hog. Most any Cherokee could have. He'd made it too easy to be found. Me thinkin' like a nasty ol' hog, I guess I'd figure nobody bull enough to come tryin' to fetch me up for home considerin' how hateful and mean I was. Well, if that pig was figurin' anything near them thoughts, he'd not figured on the likes 'a them two Cherokee gettin' after him. They come as cunning and brave as any I ever met. It was a time I will never forget. I learned much that day.

It was fetchin' to see how they worked that pig when they finally caught up to him. He was feedin' off the north end 'a White Oak mountain one morning just after Old Man Sun had woke good. Each carried an oiled leather scent pouch what had another smaller Copper Back Snake skin scent pouch inside. That pouch held the mixin's. They never said how they done it, but them mixin's was stout. Brought the fear 'a death out in that hog. It was plumb mindful seein' 'em work Junior back toward Mr. Pickins' farm with them little pouches. Weren't but a mile or more as the crow flies from where they started catchin' his attention with the foul scent. It was smart how they done it.

Workin' their way upwind of the direction they wanted Junior to go, they'd raise them little skin pouches up to near shoulder high on a standin' man, then give 'em a little shake. The scent comin' from them smaller pouches was something that pig did not want to be near, for fear or otherwise, he felt he needed to get clear from what them boys was sendin' his way. That need would head him downwind from the scent pouches straight in the direction they needed him to go. It was amazing how good it worked. Me and Wolf learned much by layin' back watchin' the young warriors workin' their scent pouches. We would need to learn what was in the mix.

Eventually, if all worked proper, they'd end up somewhere near where they hoped to bring their catch back to. But, it was plain as rain fallin' to us, them workin's they was usin' on Junior weren't gonna put that ornery ol' hog through the gate of a small confine like a hog lot, or even the wider openin' of the barn door. I figured at some point in time they'd have to change their herdin' ways and commence to puttin' a rope or some other guidin' truck on Junior. Then they could make him go wherever it was Mr. Pickens wanted his hog back to. I was not wrong in my thinkin' as we followed watchin'. 'Bout a quarter mile from the Pickens farm, the two young warriors were met by another warrior of their same age and a Cherokee maiden 'bout mine and Wolf's age. The warrior had a looped up braided hemp rope slung over his head layin' a' top his left shoulder hangin' down under his right arm. We know'd then it weren't gonna be long till they'd be movin' in on a huge, very angry, spiteful hog. God help 'em.

We was right. It weren't long. They hardly even hesitated when meetin' the other Cherokee, but went face on right at ol' Junior. I almost felt sorry for him, but I didn't. He was a mean ol' cuss. Killed a bait 'a good hog dogs. Near killed a few folks, me included. It was dangerous to mess with him, but this bunch know'd what they was doin'. Even though what they was doin' might 'a got one of 'em hurt or kilt. I still ain't never laughed so hard as me and Wolf did watchin' them Indians steer Junior in the direction they needed him to go. Ol' Junior just had a terrible time with it bein' that hogs don't see real well afar off. It worried on him like a bee that won't leave you alone or an itch you can't get to. I still laugh when I think on it or hear it told around a story fire. It's one 'a them things you can't hardly believe till you see it. Me and Wolf seen it. It was legendary in the story tellin' world for them Indians doin' the catchin'.

First, they used whatever was in those small pouches to move him as far as they felt they could without him goin' on by where they needed him to go. Then they eased around and circled ol' Junior, without even bein' able to see him full on good, they took off on a dead run straight at him hollerin' near loud as they could. That way the old pig could know they was comin'. That got him terrible confused when he heard 'em chargin', not knowin' which way to go with four different dangers movin' on him at once. He was spinnin' around like a string top tryin' to catch a whiff of what it was comin' on him. Closer and closer they got. Still, he never run. Just kept standin' there spinnin', waitin' on a fight. Nose makin's flyin' out as he snorted hard tryin' to pick up a clear scent. We could see it all from where we watched up in a white pine not fifty 'a Dad's paces away from where Junior stood spinnin' like a dog chasin' its tail. His feet diggin' deeper and deeper into the forest floor with every circlin' of his body. He didn't know what to do or where to go. Them Indians used his confusion to make their way in close 'fore stoppin' dead still in their tracks some ten paces away. The young warrior, who'd met them on the trail with the maiden, slowly and quietly slid the braided hemp rope from off his shoulder. He know'd hogs could hear a sight better than they could see. Laid it back over his head bein' very careful to not make any noise, then findin' the end with his fingers while keepin' an eye on Junior, he commenced to tyin' a slip knot. Give the knot end to the girl when he'd finished. She took it, then hunkered down like she was fixin' to run.

Junior had stopped his spinnin'. His head was near straight up scentin'. His tail swishin' like a lamb's when it's feedin'. An unseen gesture from one of the brothers sent the maiden streakin' at Junior quick as lightening strikin' while carryin' the slip knot in her left hand. Her strides were long and determined. She never side stepped or tried to stop but run like her life depended on it straight at Junior. I figured it might if she kept chargin' a full grow'd boar like she was. What was she thinkin'? I couldn't believe what I was seein'. A young Cherokee maiden, near our age, runnin' full out toward a rogue boar mad enough to be lookin' for something to kill. I was pullin' for the girl. I hoped she know'd what she was doin'. It looked as though she did. We kept watchin'. Never breakin' stride, she lept onto the pig's back landin' solid with her left foot square his center, her right landin' next to the left a second later. She was standin' on Junior! What? That don't happen! I almost forgot to breathe. I looked at Wolf. His mouth had dropped open. His eyes frozen on the happenin's in front of us. As unbelievable as it was, I was still seein' it.

She stood that hog while the other warriors quickly moved in closer. All at once they screamed their best untrained battle cry that still curled the hair back 'a my neck. Junior froze where he stood. One of the original warriors of the chase moved in beside the new warrior takin' hold 'a the rope with him. As soon as the pig stopped, the maiden jumped down on its left side droppin' the slip knot on the ground beside Junior's left front hoof. For spite, she grabbed his ear givin' it a twist as she turned to run back to the warriors. Junior seen her move bein' close up like she was, so he turned hard left commencin' his chase after the varmint what'd been pesterin' him. We seen it clear. Soon as ol' Junior made that move to go hard left, them warriors jerked the rope up quick, slippin' the knot over the front hoof pullin' it tight so the hemp would lock in and not back off. Oh, that made Junior mad. He started up a hard turn back to the right tryin' to get at something, anything a tusk would rip. He was plumb crazed with mad. Slobberin' a sight. That turn to the right was just what them Indians was hopin' for. As Junior turned, they run the opposite way lacin' him up in the rope long ways. Got half a dozen good wraps around him 'fore he hit the ground. Ol' Junior had met his match. He was caught.

Catchin' that big of a pig was one thing, but fetchin' him home was gonna be another. Me and Wolf reasoned on how they'd get Junior back to the barn. Wolf figured they'd mix a potion what put him to sleep then sled him over. I couldn't see how they'd do that. Too many thick places for a sled to run, creeks, branches, rocks and steep. No, I figured they'd leave him bound, then drag him with a mule. I'd let 'em use my mule, Peter, if they wanted. He'd drag that ol' stinky hog. He could do anything a mule could do. Plow, harrow, log, sled, wagon, ride and even fetch in the stove wood if I asked him to, if he could 'a, him bein' a mule and all. Nobody in the valley had a cart what would hold a monster like Junior. Couldn't haul him through the woods without gettin' folks hurt if they did. He was all muscle, and as mean as they come. Don't let nobody fool ya, that hog liked to kill. He had evil in his spirit. Dad found a bobcat with his head bit clean off trailin' Junior from the year before. None 'a that cat was eat, just kilt. This weren't your ever day bacon and sausage makin' hog. He'd kill you without waitin'. Shootin' at him hadn't done much good. He'd been shot a few times in the gristle layin' around his shoulders. Lookin' close I could see one such wound festered up what must 'a happened not too far back as we come up close to him layin' on the ground breathin' hard. I show'd it to Wolf. He stuck his finger in as far as it would go then rolled out the finest lookin' .54 caliber lead ball you'd ever see. Most likely shot from the same kinda gun me and Wolf had. Wolf know'd that ball once he studied it, or rather he know'd the Indian what made it. Had his mark cut in it. That way if he killed another warrior in battle, the dead's family would know it was Dancing Bear what done the duty. Come callin' on the correct one for revenge after the time of mourning ended, if they felt the need. That would be very dangerous for whoever that might be. Dancing Bear had got to where he weren't as tolerable with folks as he once was. The strangers in the valley was havin' that turn on a lot 'a Indians. I was glad I was part 'a him and his. I loved Dancing Bear. We was folks. I took mind to ask him about this ball when I saw him next. It was over a smoke fire at Killin' Time a couple moons after the hog catchin' chore.

"Dancing Bear. Father," I said with respect after sittin' with him and Wolf for a while. "Wolf found this in the left shoulder of a hog a couple moons ago. He said he believed it might be yours. Would you like it back?" I asked as I took the ball from my possibles pouch then held it up for him to see. He grunted as he took and pinched it between his thumb and forefinger holdin' it up to catch the light from our fire.

"My son, Jebediah Collins, of the Choestoe Clan, you know this ball came from my mold. My son has said. It has my mark. What did this pig look like where Wolf found my shot?"

"He is a nasty lookin' hog, Dancing Bear. Dark. Very big. Has near on a full curl set 'a tusk that are wicked and sharp. Thick hair all over except around his head and neck. Wolf will tell the story later about the girl who stood this boar. You will not believe what we saw. This hog is bad. Dad says it needs killin'."

"Needs killing?" Dancing Bear asked. "This hog is still among the living? How can this be? Yes, this is my ball, but I do not want it. It is a bad ball. Refuses to kill. Must hold a bad spirit. We will feed it to the fire. Let it lay and burn until it melts. Leave it there. This will remove the evil that lives inside it. Once this is done, it will be safe to use. Thank you, young warriors, for returning it to me." With that said he lifted his arm and tossed the used lead ball into the heart of the hottest pile 'a coals in the whole fire. That was the end of our talk. He left. I looked over at Wolf. His eyes was closed. Smilin' as he sat listenin' to us. *I thought he'd want it back.*

Watchin' them warriors lead ol' Junior to his barn was a sight few folks would ever witness. Me and Wolf was fortunate enough to be there when they commenced to gettin' it done. First thing they did was the last thing I figured 'em to do. They unwound Junior. Set him to his feet again. I couldn't figure that till one 'a the warriors run up and slapped him right upside the head with his little Copper Back Snake pouch. Junior looked shocked. He shook his head and let out a squeal you could 'a heard on top 'a Blood Mountain. The warrior stood for just a second makin' sure Junior seen who it was slappin' him 'fore takin' off runnin' for the Pickens farm. Well, Junior got so mad 'bout gettin' slapped that the fear 'a whatever it was in the pouch got replaced with pure mad and want to kill. He took off after the slappin' warrior like he was possessed. The other two Cherokee in tow runnin' for all they was worth. One still holdin' on to the end of the rope what was around Junior's left front foot. It's obvious to a body watchin' a full grow'd boar hog chasin' a young, skinny Cherokee through the woods wide open that the Indian will get caught up to after a bit. No different here. Junior was gainin' on the warrior in training. You could see the Cherokee lookin' back over his shoulder as he ran north. Worry on his face. He seen Junior was movin' closer every time he made a mad lunge, so he started cuttin' quick left and right jags to try and slow ol' Junior up. The look on that Indian's face as Junior gained on him was of concern. That old pig could run a little better than they'd allowed he could. The deadly tusk was comin' way too close to the warrior's backside for his comfort. Suddenly, he raised his arm sendin' some type 'a signal to the rope holders. Immediately, they sunk their heels into Mother Earth as hard as they could, jerkin' the rope tight after a few more steps. The old hog didn't fare well when they did that. His front half went down quick with his rump rollin' over the top of his head. His snout sinkin' hard into the forest floor. Ol' Junior jumped up from his fall like it never happened, lookin' left then right, mad as he could be. His breathin' hard makin' his chest swell and sink kinda mean like. Rottin' leaves and dirt coverin' his face. Ooh, he was mad.

'Fore Junior could get back right and start after the Cherokee what'd slapped him the first time, the Indians changed places fast. Junior never noticed 'cause 'a his bad eyesight. One of the other original warriors run up and slapped ol' Junior upside the face again. Another squeal and the next chase was on. The warrior took off runnin' due north toward the Pickens farm while lookin' 'back watchin'. Again Junior put the fear 'a God in the one runnin' 'cause he got close quicker than the Indian bein' chased allowed he would. He threw up his arm signalin' his friends. The two runnin' with the pullin' end of the rope sunk in hard sendin' Junior face first into the rotting mast of the forest floor. Up he come. Mad all over his bein'. By then the Indians had changed places again and another warrior went up and slapped ol' Junior with his little pouch 'a mixin's makin' him even more mad. Junior's whole body shook that time when he squealed. I promise you, it went on like that the rest of the day. Almost takin' till dark, but not quite. When they finally got Junior back to the barn, they simply had to tie the rope around his dirt covered head and lead him inside. He was whooped. I figured his leg was startin' to hurt some, too, as it'd been jerked back hard many times on the trail home.

The hog catchin' chore was complete. Mr. Pickens had Junior home. The warriors and maiden left. Wolf watched 'em go with a strange look in his eye. I know'd that look. All the trouble turned out for naught, though. Three moons later Junior passed on. Anne allowed one of them lead balls had finally done its job. It was almost sad, but it weren't.

Chapter 4 - Me and Wolf Learn Tooth Cleanin'

Gaines Town was a growin' place. It raised up from a make shift tradin' house where Indians and Settlers met to trade for many years called Mule Camp Springs. Laid near perfect bein' that it was built at the comin' together of two main Indian trade routes. Give good connection to most everybody travelin' or livin' in the mountains to them what lived south or outside the Appalachian wantin' to trade. It was the closest market to where we lived in Choestoe.

Market meant trade goods. You could find almost anything you needed at market, and, of course, things not needed. Dad didn't need to buy Momma a new cookstove, but he did. Hers was workin' just fine for the time. Fact was, they give it to Rose when her and Cain got married. They cooked on it like it was a new 'un for years on after. Dad didn't figure we needed a new stove, he just wanted Momma to have it. He loved my momma. He'd seen it sittin' in one 'a the new storefronts bein' built around Gaines Town. It hooked him at first sight. Market was a great place. Folks come from all over to sell and trade. Cherokee was welcome, too, 'cause their trade goods fetched gold coin outside the mountains. City folks required their makin's for culture. I could understand that. Most I ever met had a fine hand.

Goin' to market was always a special time for me and Wolf. We'd ride Peter, my mule. Momma and my sister Anne would ride what wagon we took. Dad would lead ridin' Brutus, his stallion. Dad had a team 'a matched mules what pulled our wagon; them two mules never worked apart. Did all their work as a pair. Cain got to ride Big Jim, our lead mule. He was too strong to put in a team. No other mules could pull with him. He was something else when it come to mules. Near human in his thinkin'.

The trail south to market was not only special for me and Wolf, it was a big time for all who went. For some, it would be their only trip for the year. Most times in the spring they'd be up to thirty or more in our bunch crossin' through the gap under Hog Pen, makin' trail to market. We'd camp the first night by the headwaters of the Cha-ta-hooch-ee River when we hit flatter ground a few miles south 'a the mountains. A good, hard days travel from home for the mules pullin' the loads. You had to post a watch when you made camp in them flats. Bad folks know'd where it was. Watched it on occasion for possible thievin'. Had some goin' on's there a while back when me and Wolf was on watch late in the dark one night. It was our spring trip, and the first time Dad and Dancing Bear ever trusted us to protect the families in camp by standin' watch. We was posted watchin' the south side 'a camp that night while Cain and Cooper was posted watchin' the north. They'd become good friends. We all loved Cooper -- trusted him. Our Dads had give us the order to stay hid. Watch for folks tryin' to slip in quiet durin' the night lookin' to take whatever they could find handy. If we did see sneakers, I was to stay there watchin'. Wolf was to go get our Dads. Let them handle whoever it turned out to be. Those was basically our only rules other than not to go to sleep. Seemed simple enough to skirt around for Wolf and me. The only weapons we had was our knives, but when slippin' around in the dark, they'd do fine. I'd never stabbed nobody to death. I did have to cut a body once for threatenin' my intended. He lived, but I did not like havin' his blood on my knife. Made it feel dirty.

Old Man Moon was on the rise when we went to our post to watch not long after most everybody had gone to their bed rolls for sleepin'. He'd rise on full as the night aged, addin' light to the woods as the night went on. We set up our main watch point among some fell logs no more than a hundred paces away from the center 'a camp. I say main 'cause Wolf ended up with more as the night went on. We had a time on watch that night. We was supposed to wake Dad after a few hours but we didn't. Couldn't sleep anyway what with goin' to market and all. We loved market time. All the workin's goin' on there was a paradise for young 'uns like us what held a need for adventure. We'd see all kinds 'a interestin' stuff there. Learn about things we didn't even figure existed. Like this little, small brush with a bone handle and hog hair for bristles Momma found at one little place run by what Dad called Chi-na men. Changed my life. Wolf's, too. I gotta tell you about them little brushes. Me and Wolf hated 'em.

The man what sold 'em to Momma was from across the great water, Chi-na. She got to know him after she learned what them brushes was for . . . tooth cleaners . . . we couldn't believe it. His family made 'em. Sent 'em to him from their home in Chi-na. Momma bought or traded with him or his every year. He made a salve lookin' mess you put on it to clean with, too. Burned your mouth skin like hell's fire. He made that to partner the brushes from his family. Helped with the cleanin'. Made your mouth taste hot for a time after you cleaned with it. You'd use them little brushes, with the salve laid thick on the hog hair, on your teeth. Kinda like you was scourin' dishes clean. You kept at it with the salve till your teeth felt smooth, clean. Then, you'd take a big mouthful 'a good clean well water and swish it all out on the ground. You for sure didn't wanna swaller it. I seen Wolf swaller a mouthful once. Turned him kinda green after he'd gagged near on a half hour or more. I made sure I got it all out on the ground when I did my tooth cleanin'. Weren't hard for us to get the well water 'cause that's where Momma made us do our cleanin' chore. Out by the well. No choice, really. We made such a mess when we went to washin' out and spittin' she weren't gonna let us teeth clean in the house. She did, though. Anne and Rose and Wind is Strong, too, but me and Wolf and Dad and Cain and George had to do our cleanin' outside. Yep, she got him a tooth cleaner at market as well. We all had to work our teeth washin' out by the well, even in the cold. She made us use homemade soap when the salve run out. Couldn't get no more till we went to market again. I just thought I didn't like that salve. Puttin' her cleanin' soap on your teeth was plumb awful, but she'd not have it no other way once she seen to it we had the habit 'a teeth cleanin'. Momma got a brush for each in our family every spring at market, and a whole pound 'a slave what burned your mouth skin. She talked to A-Ga-Li-Ha about how much stock she put in teeth cleanin' for health purposes and A-Ga-Li-Ha then made Dancing Bear and his family get 'em, too. Him and Dad know'd better than to talk back at Momma or not do what she said do. She'd get a certain look about her when makin' sure she got what she had on her mind. They both know'd that look. We was all gonna have clean teeth from the time she found them little brushes on. She saw to it. No cleaner teeth in the mountains once she got us all taught the chore.

No, Momma weren't gonna let us pass on the mouth and teeth cleanin'. Nope. She'd always been that way ever since I could remember. Worried over our teeth like they was gonna run off if we didn't pay mind. Most mountain folk used a small piece 'a Blackgum limb to clean their teeth with. My family included. Weren't no bigger 'round than your little finger, near long as your hand. We called 'em "chew sticks" 'cause 'a how you got the end where it would clean. We never used chew sticks again after that market trip. She'd found them little brush tooth cleaners and put us to usin' 'em straight away when we camped that first night goin' back home. Had to use river water then. It was a sight seein' five grow'd men and two half grow'ds standin' in the river washin' their teeth. We never used Black Gum again. Changed us over from chew sticks. Momma always said a clean mouth kept sickness away. I loved my momma. I did what she said. Least none of us ever got that black rot around the edges what'd eat your teeth up if you didn't watch. I loved my tooth brush . . . after I realized that fact a few years later. I didn't really mind the brushin' part, it was the salve I hated. Burned if you left it on too long. Made your eyes leak like you was cryin'. Your mouth taste funny. But, Momma wouldn't have it no other way, so neither would we. I still have all my teeth to this day when a lot 'a folks I know'd growin' up don't, or didn't, rather. The very ones what thought it funny us rubbin' salve on our teeth with little hog hair and bone brushes. God Bless you, Momma.

Our lookout among the little patch 'a fell logs we'd found scoutin' 'fore dark was our main watch post. We could see most all the side 'a camp we was responsible for 'cause the ground around us was mostly flat. There was a small rise off to the north a ways. Wolf had gone to set up another lookout near it. I was by myself sittin' on a small log watchin' for anything to move out in the dark. I could see fairly well with what moonlight they was. Wolf figured we ought 'a have more'n one spot where we could see without bein' seen. Come in handy if we had to move while watchin' bandits or the such. Wolf was smart that way.

It's a weird feelin' watchin' in the night as Old Man Moon rises addin' light to the dark. Makes your surroundings more visible the closer toward morning it gets. It has an effect on a body bein' out in it. Walkin' through it. A kinda pullin' like feelin'. Makes time seem to slow way down as the light keeps growin' then blends with the first light of day. You feel like your spirit's out walkin' beside you down the trail instead of within' you. It gets spooky amongst the trees. Their shadows seem backwards. Like they are on the wrong side from where the light is, and, they move. Trees seem to slowly change shadows with other trees. The air is cool. Feels like haints is wanderin' around you. Some trees have no shadows. It all put together can make a body jumpy if they ain't used to it, sometimes if they are. Gets critters confused, too. Daytime critters get to stirrin' thinkin' its morning come. I've been in that kinda night many times, and I've seen deer and hogs get out to feed it was so bright. I've hunted 'em when it was like that, 'cause some nights you can see near like it was day. I like to go on walks when the moon is lightin' the woods up good. Romantic if you've found love. I went walkin' in the moonlight with my sweetie many, many times durin' our life together. Everybody ought 'a do it with their chosen. It's a special time, let me tell ya. Don't seem right, though, when you're out in it, bein' able to see better as the night wears on. Seems like day, but it ain't.

The soft owl call I was hearin' meant Wolf was on his way back to our main watch post from the east. He'd left goin' west. Been gone an hour or more. I'd watched close while he'd been gone not spottin' nothin' more than a couple coons chasin' each other around a big chestnut log what laid close by. They was big stud coons workin' out spring matin' rights. Don't think either one whooped the other. They both just kinda went their own way after a good half hour 'a some serious growlin', bitin' and clawin'. I told Wolf about it. We looked next morning where they'd been fightin'. Found a right smart 'a blood and hair on the ground around the log. Very little blood leadin' away on their escape trails. They was both hurt some, but both would most likely live to fight again when the matin' urge returned to 'em. Racoons was tough critters. You should never tangle with a full grow'd adult, male or female. They could be some kinda mean when they got their back up. But, I'd seen Indains what kept 'em as pets. Them coons was friendly as could be after they'd been tamed down from livin' wild. Very curious around folks. I never cared for havin' one. Don't trust the thievin' varmints. Wolf's grandmother, Owl the Wise One, the old medicine woman what taught my sister Anne the Cherokee healin' ways, had one what stayed with her some. She didn't own it. Nobody owns a wild critter. They may cage 'em, but they don't own 'em. The Great Creator owns 'em. That coon just chose to walk its path with her on occasion. She could talk to it. The critter would listen to her, too. I'd seen it. I ain't kiddin'. Saw it a time or two when stayin' at Wolf's place on Slaughter Mountain. She'd tell it to do some thing or another and there it'd go straight off to do what she told it. Don't think she ever figured nothin' unusual about it. She expected it to do just what she asked it to do, and it did. She had the gift for sure.

"Jeb, my brother," Wolf said as he slipped quietly into place next to me in our main lookout. "I have made two more posts for which I believe we can use to watch from as the night slips on. I moved to the north for a short time. Saw where our brother Cain, with his friend Cooper, are hid. It is a good spot. I was lucky in seeing them. Looking very close, I just happened to catch a small movement as they eased into their blind. None but a true Cherokee warrior would have known what they saw. Both had guns."

Wolf was proud to be Cherokee. He was right in his thinkin', too. I do not doubt that only trained woodsmen like the Cherokee would 'a seen Cain and Cooper slippin' into their hidin' place, but, Wolf had an advantage in his efforts, he know'd they was there, somewhere. Knowin' that what you're lookin' for is for sure where you're lookin' really helps about seein' it. If he hadn't had that knowledge, I doubt he'd a seen 'em. Cain was good about stayin' hid. Wolf sayin' only Cherokee would know what they saw didn't bother me none. See, to him and his family, his clan, the tribe, me and my whole family was Cherokee. Adopted by Dancing Bear. That brought us under the care of the whole Cherokee put together. Made us a part of their nation. No question to them what we was. My whole family was know'd as Cherokee. We was proud to be, too. I considered it an honor. To Cain, it was a way 'a life. He was a full on Cherokee warrior tried and true. Had the scars to prove it.

Old Man Moon was on his way home for a day's rest. He'd passed his highest point for the night when I first caught sight 'a somethin' movin' along in the dim light. Slippin' along from tree-to-tree crouched low so as not to be too visible. I seen 'em clear once I spotted their movement. Weren't a tall person. Could move near un-seeable. As I watched, two more followed just as crafty, but I had their effort spotted, too. No doubt their mind. They was comin' in close for takin' purposes. Crouched low last I seen 'em trailin' west toward camp. Wolf had left to go watch from another post leavin' me alone to watch from the first, not too long 'fore I seen our visitors tryin' to slip in. I lifted up a soft owl call and waited hopin' he'd call back then move my way. *Nothin'*. There should 'a been an answer, but they weren't. Where was Wolf? I lifted up another soft call. *Nothin'. Why was Wolf not owlin' back? Had he gone to check with Cain? No tellin'.* I was alone -- watchin' everything. Listenin' so hard my ears was wigglin'. Scentin' the air. Lookin' for any clue that would tell me what might be movin' around me. Stayin' calm, thinking. Not knowin' what to expect or from which direction. For sure never expectin' the huge hand what closed over my whole face blockin' off my air while leavin' only my eyes a place to see out. Nor the second huge hand laid center 'a my back joinin' the one over my face. I know'd those hands. They was the same ones what lifted me up and sent me flyin' into Wolf Creek on my first ever trail with Dad. Together they lifted me clean, and most importantly since they was friendly hands, quietly from my watch. Where had he come from? It always amazed me how quiet Black Oak was in the woods. He was a mountain of a man but could move like a mouse across the forest floor. He'd even caught Wolf by surprise a few times. Did the same thing to him as he'd done to me that night. Near scared me to my death. He was very strong. Lifted me clean out from the logs I was hid in settin' me quiet as soft wind on the forest floor next to him. Someone else, too. Oh, that scent. Wind Is Strong. I'd grow'd to just love her. She'd become like a mother crossed with a sister to me. Wolf, too. We liked bein' around her.

"Be very quiet, Jeb," she said in a low whisper. "There are traitors about. Dancing Bear and Thompie are here as well. You stay where Black Oak has set you. Watch our backs as we find these evil Cherokee. They are careless, but they are warriors. Wolf is here. Stay where you are." With that said, they left as quiet as they'd come.

Danger was near. Lookin' at Wolf it was clear we was gonna do exactly what Black Oak wanted. Wind Is Strong might 'a said the words, but we both know'd they come from George. It was in neither of our wills, more so out 'a respect than fear, to cross the biggest Cherokee to ever live. Strongest, too. I figured he might could whoop Cain, but that fight would never happen. Wrestlin' tangle for enjoyment maybe, but never a fight 'cause 'a anger. They'd been through much together. Bonds no life trouble could break.

"It is an awakening when Cherokee warriors slip up on you in the dark the way Black Oak does," Wolf said as he sat actin' stunned from what'd just happened to us both. "How is it that they can move so quietly? I have not learned their way. It is something I must come to understand. My father does this as well. It is almost as though they change into spirit. Float to where they need to be. I do not like being taken so easily. I will worry on this matter later. For now, we must watch. What say ye, Jeb Collins. Slow Like the Turtle."

I looked over at Wolf when he called me that. He know'd I didn't like that name. He was funnin' on me. A smile raisin' both corners of his mouth as he kept lookin' out south watchin' for trouble. He was funnin' with most all he'd said. Wolf could do slippin', just not near like savvy warriors. Still, he was a quiet one. I'd been the victim many times. I was learnin' to move like they did, just didn't have the feel yet. It took time to learn how to move softly in your walk. Not make noise. Be able to step but not break sticks or crunch leaves. That was a challenge when the woods was dry. Nobody could move quiet then unless they was spirit, not even critters. It just weren't possible.

Kinda like the woods was at our camp that season. Hadn't had much rain through the winter and early spring. It was dry. We watched where we built camp fires and such on trips when it was dry like it was. The crunch, crunch, crunch of a body movin' quick toward us laid proof to just how dry it was then. We sat a ways back of our post listenin' to 'em get closer, louder. Constant in their direction. Not stoppin' to listen out for danger told me they know'd where they was headed. The trail they was on familiar. That meant it was somebody what know'd the area. I looked over at Wolf when I first realized who we might be hearin'. He nodded slightly with a near grin on his face. He'd figured it, too. That little smirk 'a his said to me he was lookin' forward to meetin' the warrior what was movin' our way. I remember hopin' them was friendly steps comin' on us but I know'd they weren't. We'd find out soon enough 'cause it didn't sound like they was stoppin'. Wolf stood drawin' his long knife with his right hand, sharp edge up. I did likewise. It was a habit I'd become more comfortable with of late. Too many strangers about.

Chapter 5 - Our First Night of Watch

It was an Indian comin' toward us. We seen him as he passed through a moonlit spot on the trail he was followin'. The very trail me and Wolf come to notice we was standin' in the middle of. Not good for us with him movin' on it. We both seen his form whole -- warrior. We had to be smart. He was runnin' from something like he needed to get clear from it. Would be on us within the next minute or less. Wolf looked around real quick spottin' just what he needed but a few feet away. A young poplar tree about the size of a man's wrist at the base and maybe ten-foot-tall stood to the edge of the trail. They was common. Wolf grabbed it high as he could bendin' it down to his left. With his right hand, he whipped out his long knife quick as a Rattle Maker strikes, sling cuttin' it 'bout quarter way up from the gound. That separated the top from the bottom which stayed rooted. The top didn't have no limbs of its own hardly. Just fingerlings. With his left hand, he flipped the cut top across the path then motioned me over. I'd made it across when he grabbed 'a hold of the end he'd cut with both hands and bent over to hide. I did the same on mine. I'd barely caught it square 'fore the runnin' warrior was on us. Out 'a instinct we both raised our ends catchin' him mid-stride just below the knee. That was good and bad for all of us. Mostly bad for him, 'cause me and Wolf weren't sisters. We had a fair amount 'a strength between us when it come to holdin' the small poplar tree top solid on both ends. Mostly good for us other than the fact that the comin' together of Indian shin bone and fixed wood was as hard a blow as I've withstood to date. Him bein' a full grow'd adult warrior in his prime meant he was very strong. He must not 'a seen us 'cause his pace never let off as he rounded a short curve in the trail just shy 'a where we'd set up. He come on that stick not havin' a clue it could be there. Not until we felt the blow and heard two hollow pops, what sounded like bones breakin', did we understand exactly what we'd got in to. Didn't have time to think much 'fore it all come together. We just did it. Wolf said later it was spiritual, guided. I believe it was. I hardly remember movin' till my teeth got rattled.

The comin' together of me and Wolf and that Indian runnin' full on into the little poplar top we was holdin' across the trail had to be like gettin' punched in the middle by an angry George Black Oak. My whole body got slammed in front, then again as it hit flat against the ground on my back. That lick between me and the ground turned everything black. The air went from my lungs with a hard grunt. I couldn't hear. Every joint in my bone structure rattled like a loose mule shoe. My tongue slammed against the back of my throat. Stayed there until I realized I couldn't breathe and rolled over. Had to use my finger to pull it back in place. Near choked with that happenin'. My world was black. I couldn't hear, so I had no idea how Wolf'd made out. Had he been hit as hard as me? Where was the one we'd ambushed? Was he hurt bad? Did he lay nearby? Did we kill him? I had questions, but I had no senses. All I could do was wait for my body to fire back up. I had no control over what parts of my person I could move for a few minutes time. That was dangerous when fightin' rogue folk.

"Jeb! Jeb!" I could hear Wolf screamin' as my senses come back a little. Kinda felt like wakin' up from an uncomfortable bed what hurt your body from sleepin' on it all night. I could feel layin' flat 'a my back in what was most likely center 'a the trail we'd found ourselves on earlier. My eyes draw'd light just as a dark arm raised up over where I lay. I couldn't miss the shiny edge of cold steel as it was bein' raised overhead. I felt like Abraham's second born layin' there near helpless . . . but I weren't helpless. Weren't no bonds holdin' me down on Mother Earth. I'd come awake with Wolf hollerin' enough to know I could move so move I did. Death comin' on you gets your attention no matter what your mind is feelin'. Makes you fight back all a body can.

He was on me close. My arms flew free from the ground as the future warrior in me took hold of my being. It was power from Holy Spirit and I recognized it as such. That gave me courage I'd not normally know. I could feel the evil over me, so I drove up defending my life with the base of my right palm hard as I could. Prayin' the whole time he'd not stab me 'fore I could strike out. It landed solid under the killer's chin with more power than I ever remember havin'. I heard bones crackin' as I felt my arm straighten out through his face. Could 'a been teeth or jaw or a mix 'a both. I cared none. Him sufferin' damage to his person was his own fault. I just weren't aimin' to die that day.

Rollin' to my side I brought my left arm up blockin' the droppin' of his right arm. His knife fallin' to the ground like a shot squirrel from the side of a tree. There weren't no punch left. He was out. His arms limp. Mine went limp no different as my world spun black again with the ending of his threat. My fear had turned to strength when I realized that the Indian movin' on us through the woods meant to end my life. Wolf's, too. Thank God Wolf hollered at me. I thanked him later.

"Jeb, wake up. Jeb? Can you hear us, Jeb?" I know'd that voice what was whisperin' in my ear. Her scent. I'd been listenin' to it near every day since she moved in with us a few moons back. Wind Is Strong! "Answer me, Jeb, if you can hear me. Jeb? Jeb?" she whispered a little louder as she shook me some.

"I hear something," I kinda mumbled in response. "Sounds like the wind. Is that you? Are you here?"

"It is me, little brother. I am here. I left Black Oak for this one when I saw him turn down the trail you and Wolf were watching. I could not stop him or signal because his friends were around us. I believe them to be gone now. Only this one do we have for our efforts. Black Oak also captured one, but he is no longer with us. We will speak with this one. Know soon where they are from. Why they are here. We saw no effort from them to steal. No, there is more to their being here than taking. It is a curious thing. I would like to know the reason for their spying on this group of wagons. Do you know this Cherokee, Wolf? Jeb? I do not."

I stood on wobbly legs then moved over closer to the bound Indian layin' hog tied on the ground. I noticed Wolf weren't movin' too good, neither. Kinda slow for him. Looked like we both took a hard hit stoppin' that runnin' Indian.

The face was swelled up from me knockin' him cold. Breakin' his bottom jaw. That was what I felt break, but when I thought on it a minute, I didn't remember feelin' that strong. Blood trickled from the edges of his busted mouth. I didn't know him. He was younger than I thought he would be. Not much older than me and Wolf. It felt like the one we tripped was heavier than this Indian I was lookin' at. Provided more knock down power than the body I was seein' tied in the trail. I checked his right leg. No, it weren't bent funny. Straight from the knee down, normal lookin', not broken. This was not the warrior me and Wolf tangled with 'fore gettin' knocked out. Fact was, this weren't no warrior. He looked to be no more trouble than a common thief. I dropped to my knee fast when I seen that Indian weren't the one we'd hurt. Wolf and Wind squatted quick beside me. A look of question on their faces.

"To answer you, Wind Is Strong, no. I do not think I know this Cherokee. It's hard to tell for sure since his face is hurt, but I don't remember ever seein' him before now. Yet, and I don't understand it, this is not the Cherokee warrior me and Wolf fell. His legs are whole. Not broken. The Indian we tripped will have a terrible broken right leg. If I heard correctly, both bones in his right leg below the knee will be broken. We must find this warrior before he finds us. He can't be far away. Did you not see him when you came to us, Wind?"

"No, Jeb. This one lying here is the only Indian I saw when I found you two. Both of you were out cold. Wolf woke after you. He did not see anything. If this is not who it should be, we are in danger. If it is indeed a warrior we are missing, we must be very cunning. He will be close. Come, we will sit the trail with our backs together. Stay quiet. Listen until Old Man Sun brings us light. Then we will track this Cherokee. Soon he will be in more pain than he will be able to stand from his broken leg. I do not think it will be difficult to find him then. We just need to make sure he doesn't find us before there is enough light to see him."

The night had gone. We couldn't see as good as we could before Old Man Moon left. I don't remember him leavin', but he was done with his lightin' chore for the night. Old Man Sun commenced to risin' as we sat the trail in a triangle. Our backs touchin'. Our ears strainin'. No one sayin' anything for fear 'a missin' the single sound that would give our visitor away. It was just a low moan when it come, but it told us right where to find him. Wind made us wait till first light was showin' good 'fore we could go look for him. He weren't twenty 'a Dad's paces away. Layin' still under a Hemlock tree with low hangin' limbs coverin' its base. Wind went straight to him. We followed. She wanted information. I allowed she'd get it.

We all stood studyin' the warrior as he laid still under the limbs of the hemlock. His eyes closed. He toted very little battle truck, which meant he was travelin' light, so he could move faster. Most likely weren't lookin' for no trouble. His right leg had swoll near twice the size of his left. The moanin' we'd heard was him speakin' his death song what little he could bein' rattled like he'd been. His mind seemed whole. He could talk, and understood talk, plain enough. Still, he was in bad shape from our comin' together on the trail. Weren't lookin' too good. I hoped he'd live, but it did not look like he would. That was mindful to me 'cause I didn't think we'd done anything that bad to him. He could 'a broke his neck in the fall, yes, but that was about all the chance they was 'a him dyin'. Broke legs don't tend to take life most times. I finally realized he was hurt more'n we'd done to him. He had a good-sized knot on the right side of his forehead where there was a cut leakin' blood. Another cut above his right eye which was leakin' some, too. A right shoulder that laid lower than the left lookin' out 'a place. The right arm locked straight. Most likely from where we'd piled him up in the trail after he'd tripped. It would stand to reason since he'd 'a landed on his right side.

Wind was not gentle as she grabbed his good leg draggin' him out from the limbs of the hemlock he'd been able to crawl to; hide under. We seen his crawl trail once Old Man Sun was up enough. It was the best spot for him to 'a made it to considerin' him injured like he was, but he was a full-on Cherokee warrior, anything them Indians did never surprised me. I kinda felt for him, though. He was hurt. You could see it in his face as she dropped her hold on his leg lettin' it fall to the ground from about waist high. Left him exposed to the light 'a day for us to see. Me and Wolf didn't know him. Who was these rogues what'd come into the valley lookin' for who know'd what? We needed answers.

Their conversation was in Cherokee, but I understood most 'a what Wind and Wolf was askin' him. At first the wounded Indian was not gonna say anything, but then Wind Is Strong put her foot square on to where the bones was broke in his leg, changin' his thinkin' quick. He didn't mind talkin' to 'em after that.

"What is your name, warrior?" Wolf asked soon as Wind removed her foot from his leg. "And why is it that you and your kind are spying on our people? What is it that you want to know?"

"My name . . . not important, young warrior," he struggled to speak good. His lungs was wrong. You could hear it when he spoke. "We are here . . . because . . . we hate the light skinned one . . . who . . . is coming to our home . . . not welcome . . . hurting our women . . . steal . . . taking color from the waters . . . destroy farms . . . burn food . . . our hope is . . . to take his things . . . maybe he will see . . . not want to be here . . . anymore . . . We were paid gold . . . take his mules . . . here. Leave him . . . in the river flats . . . others come . . . take his wagons. I do not know . . . . man who paid us . . . a soldier. . . blue coats . . . one of their own. Traitor to his people . . . to A-me-ri-ca. So, . . . young warrior . . . see how . . . light skins can be. Two faces . . . one mouth . . . They pay to steal . . . from their own . . . I do not understand this tribe . . . evil is its way . . . I take their gold . . . do their work . . . not hurt people . . . That is all I will say of the evil ones . . . I want them to leave . . . my mountains . . . Our home." He waved his arm like he was swattin' away a nat.

"Warrior," Wind asked in a softer, kinder voice. "Where is this gold you were paid to take the settler's mules? Do you have it with you, and if you do, may I hold it? Look it over? I will give it back."

"Here, woman," he said with more life as he reached his left hand into his possibles pouch. His right not movin'. "Take this evil from me. Keep it . . . I do not want it back . . . I know . . . it is cursed by . . . Dark Fallen One . . . most evil of all . . . Throw it . . . hottest coals of holy fire," he near screamed at her. "Rid us of its evil . . . Only fire . . . make it pure . . . Burn it . . . seven days. Take to Big Bald . . . give to the ancestors . . . they watch over . . . decide if it should . . . ever be touched . . . by Cherokee . . . again . . . Brought me . . . nothing but sadness . . . much pain . . . from the first time I felt it . . . I pray. . . family . . . not going to suffer . . . from my ignorance of . . . new evil . . . here . . . our home . . . Great Spirit . . . forgive me."

"Yes. You are right, warrior. This gold is evil, but we will use it for good. We will find this soldier who gave you this. We will give it back to him. He can hold it in his cold, dead hand after I rid him of his worthless life. My knife will be your justice, warrior. Now go, be with your ancestors," Wind said as she covered his eyes with her left hand slidin' the edge of her very sharp long knife across his throat with her right. A red bead of blood followin' the tip as she cut deeper into his blood lines. He smiled as his eyes faded into death. He accepted his mercy. He was now free.

She looked over at me after doin' her mercy killin' deed. I was hopin' my face would not give away what I was thinkin'. It did. She read my thoughts. Reachin' down she lifted the warrior up to his left side. Raisin' the side with the shoulder and arm what curiously didn't seem to work right. Looked noticeably different than the left when he was layin' under the hemlock limbs. There was a sight 'a blood stainin' the warrior's skins at the top right of his back. Centered over a near perfectly round hole. A hole made by a lead ball. *How did she know he'd been shot?* After thinkin' on it, I decided not to ask. Might be I didn't need to know. That was just fine with me. A lot 'a the time not havin' information was safer than havin' knowledge of it when you lived in the mountains. This might be one 'a them times.

The other Indian I'd fought was bein' helped to stand when we went back to talk to him. Dancing Bear and Black Oak was standin' with him while Dad had a hold of him. He couldn't say nothin' 'cause his lower jaw was broke. Some of his teeth was layin' on the ground. Wind told Dancing Bear what'd happened that caused him his injury. The way Dancing Bear and Dad figured it, the Indian was meanin' to kill me. I certainly thought he was. I had his knife to show for it. The justice was quick. We would have no more trouble from either of the two Indians we encountered on that night.

It was good we got information from the warrior 'cause the bunch what paid him was layin' a trail we'd get caught up in soon. It weren't a good time when it come, but the knowledge give to us from the warrior helped save many lives. It's strange how the Great Creator makes things work sometimes. It is important to listen for His voice when troubled times come. Spared me heartache many times in my life.

"Wolf," I said to him later as we sat by the fire to smoke. Pray thanks. "I want 'a thank you for hollerin' out. Savin' my life . . . again. Thank you, my brother. I appreciate you watchin' out for me when things get nasty."

"You are welcome," Wolf replied. "I am glad I did this. But, Jeb, when did I do this thing? That I hollered, saved your life? I do not remember a time recent. Only several moons ago when the soldiers were camped on Wolf Creek, wait, no, it was before that even. I do not remember this time. You must say when this time was, Jebediah."

"What do you mean, Wolf? Don't you remember hollerin' at me when that Indian was raisin' his knife to kill me this morning? You don't remember that?"

"No. I am sorry. You woke before me. I do not remember hollering at you. I believe that I did not do this. We should smoke on this account. Maybe the answer will come. If it does, I believe it will be spiritual. That is all I have to say on this."

Huh? He says he didn't holler. Well, I wonder who it was then 'cause it sounded just like his voice. Maybe it was spiritual, or maybe Wolf took a harder lick than he allowed he had. Either way, it was over. We made it out alive. Thanks be to God – again.

Chapter 6 - A Foul Sound on the Breeze

When a wagon train like ours rolled into Gaines Town, folks took notice. Mostly business folk lookin' to buy whatever it was the wagons were haulin'. Turn it for gold in their stores or storefronts with tents in behind. Worked good for the settlers. Worked good for the business folk. Dad called the way you traded at market . . . Cap-til-ism. He preferred that style 'a tradin' over any other 'cept bartering. Simple doin's, really. Only government folks was fool enough to mess up such a natural form 'a trade over the years. Works great for all involved. If folks need it, somebody makes it and sells it to 'em. What could work any better?

"Supply and demand, Jeb," he'd say. "Somebody demands a thing, you supply it for trade or coin. Best way to trade if you ask me. Fair to all unless the buyin' man charges folks too much when he goes to sell it, then it ain't fair. Figure our mule tradin'. We raise 'em up to do a certain chore or work a certain way, right? Then a body comes along lookin' for a mule to do just what we trained 'em for. He lays a gold coin on the barrelhead, we shake hands and they take our mule. That's how it works when folks are in charge of their own tradin'."

You had to respect Dad when tradin' with him. He was savvy when it come to talkin' agreements. Been doin' it ever since he was a boy. Learned it from my granddad tradin' mules for many years growin' up. He'd get more out 'a them store owners than they'd usually want to part with. Most all the folks what come in on the wagon train let him make their tradin' deals for 'em. He'd see to it none got took for. Business folk liked dealin' with him 'cause he was fair, honest. They liked what come from Choestoe, too. Said it was quality. Made to last. We appreciated that. Tried to do better every time we went.

One 'a the things I hated about the market at Gaines Towns was the slave tradin' barn. That's where they kept the negro folk, Indians and others when time for sellin' come. Dad never went near that place, if he could help it. Told us to keep clear of it. Town folk built it at the most distant south end of the town as they could. Folks comin' to market from the mountains didn't have to get near it 'less they wanted, but you could still see the whole put together, 'cept for the sellin' blocks out back. You'd not miss the smell from it, neither. That scent had a sickness to it. Took me a couple days to get the stink out from my nose if I ever caught wind of the place. I hated it, too. Weren't a bad lookin' place on the outside, but knowin' what went on inside and out back made it a dark, dark place for me and Wolf, for sure Cain. He looked on it with a serious hate 'cause he believed all are free to live in peace on this rock the Great Creator provided. Cain figured only outlaws and them what kill ought 'a be penned like animals or treated as such. He wanted to burn it down. We near did one night when Cain's temper sparked. It was when me and Wolf was younger. Several moons after me gettin' tore up by Old Man Bobcat while on the trail back from workin' down on the river Notla with Dad. Fact bein', I was still healin' a right smart at the time. Momma had told me to take it easy. Not do no liftin' or carryin' heavy things or runnin'. As for me, I was still stiff when tryin' to move. Couldn't do like I wanted for fear 'a tearin' open the deeper wounds still leakin' some on my head and back. Them cuts was 'causin' me to suffer a right smart 'a pain. I never regretted it, though, helpin' Cain that night. Nope, not to this day do I regret it. Ownin' other folks was a terrible thing. My clan didn't agree with it. We did our own work.

Cain got all the slippin around goin' not long after supper. We'd parked our wagons near the river for camp. Momma put a new piece 'a clean homespun on my cuts soaked in salve after she'd cleaned up from our eatin'. Them healin' fixin's struck me to feelin' just fine once they draw'd down in my wounds good. Took away the pain. Eased my soul.

The soft movement of the night air was travelin' strangely upriver that night. Meant bad weather was movin' north. The sounds comin' from the barn could be heard clear, lettin' all in camp know tradin' was goin' on. A body couldn't help but smell the stink layin' thick as it eased up the valley . . . weren't critter stink, neither. You could taste it through your pipe as you draw'd air over the tobacco. The auctioneer had a very strong voice. Every time his hammer fell on a sale, Cain would drop his head. Mumble somethin' I probably didn't need to hear. I know how he felt. My stomach was sick listenin' -- smellin'.

Cain never said much, so when he did speak you should take it to heart. This night weren't no different. You gotta remember, Cain ain't your normal, common settler. He had a way 'a thinkin' most folks was too cowardly to consider, even some you'd figure had good courage. Cain weren't scared 'a nothin' I ever know'd of. He made a habit 'a makin' things right for folks he loved, family for sure, but this night his compassion fell on the folks bein' bought and sold he didn't even know. I truly believe he'd a burnt the whole thing to the ground if me and Wolf hadn't been with him. I was hurt, so it fell to him to look after me. Not sure Cain ever settled with us goin' with him that night. I'm glad we did. His rage went beyond common for a young 'un of his age.

"I'm goin' down to the river, Jeb. You and Wolf stay with the wagons. Hear?"

Cain weren't talkin' right. Like he was distracted. Made me nervous.

"How long will you speak to the river, my brother?" Wolf asked kinda more than curious. "It is late, and dark, for fishing."

"Yeah, I ain't goin' fishin', Wolf. Just gonna take a little walk. Clear my head. Not comfortable just sittin' around not doin' much I guess. Restless, you know. Ready to go to market tomorrow."

"Can't we go with you, Cain? We ain't needed around here and . . . and you ain't goin' to the river. We know where you're aimin' to trail to. You might need us to help. Reckon?" I asked with much hope in my voice.

"Now, little brother, where in the put together do you think I'm goin'? I just wanna go sit by the river. Listen to the water. What's wrong with that, huh?"

"You are going to the slave barn. Look for yourself on what it is that you hate. I know you, uncle." Wolf said as he stood to speak direct to Cain.

"Y'all got that figured, have ye? Well, if you're comin', come on. I need to fetch some possibles from the wagon then we'll head out," he said as he turned to leave the warmth and light of the fire.

We followed. I weren't movin' as good as usual. They both took notice. Slowed their walk to mine bein' respectful since I was still healin' across my back. Bein' wounded made me have to be more careful which slowed us all down. Them cuts I'd took was bad. Near brought me to death. That cat tore me up from the back of my head clear down to the middle of my back. Got Big Jim, too. Locked its claws in his rump tryin' to get to me. He was much more healed up than I was. Made me figure mule meat healed faster than folk meat.

Once we left from the wagon fetchin' Cain's possibles, we stayed to the shadows of the forest movin' back down toward the town. It weren't a dark night, but we couldn't see too good from what little light they was. Town was lit up. You could hear the noise from the restaurants, saloons and gamblin' houses. We weren't allowed to go near them, neither. Fact was, if Dad found us gone we'd most likely be in for the strap. Bein' gone with Cain could go either way with Dad, but the orders from our folks was to stay put with the wagons. Most everybody did. As mountain folk, we weren't used to the life you could hear comin' from the center 'a town. Seemed like it was near as busy of a night as durin' the day. I wished we'd 'a camped farther upstream so we'd 'a not heard none 'a the town noise; smell. Usually you'd not hear anything from where we was camped. It was just that peculiar wind what was movin' that had things stirred up. Felt unnatural when walkin' into it against your face when on a normal night it would 'a been at your back. Weren't a strong wind. Just a movement. No struggle for a woodsman to feel. I doubted town folk would 'a even noticed it. Critters do.

We steered clear of all the lights as we moved through town. Cain led us down near the river where it was dark, quiet. We followed downriver till we come to the grounds where the slave barn stood, stinkin'. Felt like bein' in a burial ground or cemetery on a dark night in winter when haints is known to prowl. I was near spooked. I think we all might 'a been. What we was slippin' up on was dangerous. Guards would surely be watchin' to protect such valuable property as slave folk. Not sure what Cain was thinkin'. What it was he needed by comin' to see the evil we know'd lived in the barn. He weren't stoppin' as we turned up from the river, so I figured I'd be findin' out soon enough.

We turned left movin' toward the back of the barn then toppin' a little rise where we could see what was happenin'. There was three sets 'a double doors separated by several feet 'a solid barn wall. All lay open with the middle door bein' the auction door. The light comin' through them doors near blindin' compared to the dark we was standin' in. They had corrals on the sides of the barn which held stock for the days when they sold stock. I didn't care to know what held folks on slave sellin' day, which usually only happened once a year in the early spring. We never did find out why they was havin 'a slave sale that fall. Typically, we'd not encounter such evil 'cause our goin' to market time was different than the slave sellin' time, but on that trip, it all paired up.

I never forgot the sight I seen when we crested that small rise not fifty 'a Dad's paces away from the auction tables. More than five dozen slave buyers standin' on a covered platform just outside the barn doors with all the slave traders standin' around next to it. They was there to make sure their slaves was sold proper. Buyers was mixed in what bought for their bosses on the platform. They was a lot 'a them. The crowd stood nearly shoulder to shoulder extendin' up next to the barn. The buyer's platform stood on locust poles just higher than a man was tall. That way they needn't have to cover their noses with their little smell rags. Scented with costly European smellin' salts I was sure. They was all dressed in their fine Sunday go to meetin' suits, fancy hats and store bought leather shoes.

Funny lookin' shoes without no uppers on 'em. Had to be uncomfortable. I never did figure why them rich folk wore such out to the barn, and I doubted they'd been to church service even though they was dressed like it. The slave sellin' blocks was in the center of the middle doors a few paces inside the barn. That way all on the platform could see the property to be sold good without havin' to come in the barn actual. Their buyers did that chore for 'em. It was lit like daytime inside from several different huge oil lamps hangin' from the rafters. The light bein' a kinda red what must 'a been straight out 'a hell. I never wanted to see again what I saw that night. Praise God, Jesus and Holy Spirit, I didn't. I don't want to tell it . . . but I need to. Sorry.

I doubt many folks ever seen what happens at a slave sale. It is not in my understandin' how one body can do to another body what them slave traders did to those bein' sold. I'd seen animals treated more decent. They was stripped naked and washed by men with long handled brushes what most folks used for mules and horses. Rinsed clean by throwin' buckets of cold water on 'em 'fore bein' led into the light. It was cold for that kinda washin'. I could see 'em shiverin' as they was made to step up onto the blocks where they was to be sold. But, it made 'em more visible for all to see how healthy their possible property might be. Some had chains on their hands and ankles. After bein' made to stand up on the sellin' blocks, they was turned and looked over like judgin' horse or mule flesh for workin'. Tiny cuts was made on some of 'em's upper arm or leg to show their blood was red not black or yellow. Women, stripped of any dignity, was poked, felt, spun around and squeezed to see which will be chosen for breeding or work in the fields or service at the main house. Young strong women with long legs, wide backsides, some fat and a big bosom was considered perfect for birthin' and raisin' new young 'uns what could be worked or sold. The men and boys was made to stand naked on the sellin' blocks while buyers for the rich folk looked 'em over for any brands or beatin' scars. Those things would tell if they was hard to work or keep. It was all disgustin' to me. Wolf, not so much. He'd seen slavers and slaves all his life livin' with the Cherokee. Indians kept slaves for the most part. Wolf and his clan never held any. They didn't take to it like most Indians did. I was proud 'a that.

It was the auctioneer. I know'd it soon as I seen Cain studyin' him after he'd led us to the doors north of where the sellin' was goin' on. That was hard to do with all the folks we had to move through. I reasoned he thought if he could shut that evil one's mouth then the sellin' would stop, not forever of course, but at least for the night. I was near positive that's how he figured it. Simple to him. The question was how? How was he gonna stop him? I had to figure that out, so we could hopefully keep Cain from gettin' himself into some real bad trouble. Maybe even his killin'. I needed to converse with Wolf away from Cain. I motioned him to come to me like my cuts was in need. We had to talk. Figure this out 'fore anything happened we'd all regret.

"Wolf, have you seen the look on Cain's face? He's got me worryin'. It's one 'a the ones you don't ever want 'a see on him. Determined mixed with notion mixed with mad. I seen it tonight. They's something he wants done here. I believe he aims to silence the feller what's callin' the prices. The auctioneer. I figure he's thinkin' if he could quiet him then the sellin' would be over. We could then go back to a quiet camp. He may be right, but we gotta figure how he's studyin' on doin' it. We gotta stop him, Wolf. Figure me at half able. I might be best as a watcher."

"He needs to talk to us. I will go to him. Speak to him. Try and understand his mind. Then we will come together again and talk. Maybe he will share his thinking without knowing he is doing so. I will signal you when I am ready to meet. What say you, Jeb?"

"Be very careful, Wolf. Cain has a gift. He reads folks like a book. You know this. Do not let him see your thoughts, or he will give you knowledge of little value or worse, confusin'. Good luck in your efforts, my brother. I wish you well."

It was a while 'fore Wolf come back over to me. He'd been with Cain no different than if we was just standin' around lookin'. I don't think Cain had any idea we was concerned for his future, or other folks' future, but he told us little. Wolf learned nothin' from Cain.

"I am sorry, Jebediah. I have failed to learn much at all. Cain only said he didn't like it in here. That we should leave soon. I did not get the feeling he wanted to stay much longer. Maybe it would be good if you were to speak with him. He might be willing to share his thoughts with family closer than me. You should try."

"I will. That's a good idea, but let's just watch a while. See if he makes any moves toward easin' his unhappiness. I believe he will. If we see him gettin' set to move, I will call to him."

"I trust your feelings on this, my friend. I hope you know him as well as you think you do. Brothers can be a problem when they are headed for trouble. I know. I have two."

We stood watchin' Cain from no farther away than a few feet. It was hard watchin' him 'cause 'a the unfamiliar things goin' on around us. It was really noisy. Folks was packed tight. Seemed like everybody needed bathin'. I was thinkin' that all those around me could be the source 'a the foul odor we could hardly stomach back at camp, but then they turned up the lights toward the back of the barn so the buyers could look over the human stock they aimed to bid on. They was holdin' pens inside the barn, too. They held the slave folk. I realized quick it weren't the bunch I was standin' with makin' the air stink, it was the rot what come from inside the holdin' pens where those to be sold was bein' held. Weren't no privies for them.

I could not believe what I was seein'. People penned like stock animals so tight many looked like they was asleep standin' up. Could 'a been dead. No different than if they was cattle or hogs or oxen bein' penned for sale. My knees got weak from all the stench and foul things I was lookin' at. I looked over at Cain, wonderin' how he felt about seein' all them folks ganged up the way they was. I'd not know how he felt from the look on his face 'cause him, his face and his looks was gone. I reasoned he'd seen me and Wolf get distracted as they uped them God forsaken lights. Used that few seconds we was lookin' the other way to make his move. He was on to us. Now we had to find him. That was not easy when it was Cain what didn't want to be found.

"Wolf," I near hollered as I grabbed his arm pointin' to where Cain had been standin'. "Look."

"He is gone, Jeb. When did he move? I was watching him very close. He is a warrior true. Come on. We must find him," Wolf said as he started to leave.

"Wait, Wolf. Remember, I'm boogered up. I can't move as fast as you. I will slow you down. It is best for me to stay here. Watch for Cain. I will move over closer to the wall. Find a place to stand where I can see all inside. Cain is lookin' to quiet the one callin'. Go to the auction tables where the money is bein' taken. I believe he will be there."

I know'd Cain would be at them auction tables. That's where the callin' man was sittin' just inside the barn not far from the blocks where they stood the one bein' sold. They was steel rings strapped to them blocks. I worked my way around to the east wall of the barn next to the back doors easin' into the shadows toward the very back tryin' to stay hid. Searchin' for a place to stand where I could look out but not be seen 'cause 'a the dark. The lamp light kinda played out toward the back where I'd went to watch, hide. A weird feelin' come on me soon as I got somewhat settled near the back, but I couldn't see much since I'd just come from the light. Felt like bein' watched by haints. I heard mumblin', so I kinda peeked around back 'a where I found myself standin'. What I saw when my eyes got used to the dark chilled my soul. Without realizin' I'd done it, the shadows I was standin' in laid up next to the rear holdin' pens where the slaves was. I realized they was more penned in the dark outside the lamp light. I did not want to be where I was. I quit breathin' for a second till my warrior side come out calmin' me down. Slowly, I turned to my left. I know'd what I was fixin' to see. It was somethin' I hoped not to get close to, but I had. What I seen was a thing that shouldn't be. The sight brought me to my knees. It's hard to describe the scared stares of the captive negroes what the evil ones was sellin' for trade. Adults -- men and women -- half grow'ds and little ones, all bein' held like critters for a stock sale. Men with long knives and whips walkin' outside the front of the pens to keep the others back when one was chosen to go be sold. My insides went foul. My heart sank. How could this be?

It took all I had to rise back up on my feet. The cuts on my back stingin' from me leanin' against the end of the barn tryin' to give my weak knees a chance to firm back up. I looked close at the ones bein' held captive. I wanted to open the pen gates and set 'em all free but I know'd them men what was lookin' out for 'em would not allow that. They got paid to see to it none escaped. A body could see clear they was good at what they did. Used the whips like they'd used 'em before. Made me want to kill 'em all. That was a lot 'a anger for my young body to hold. It near eat me up 'fore we finally got out from that awful place. Feels like the stomachache every time I think on it still. I hoped the ones what got free that night stayed free. It would be a hard chore, but if they kept their smarts about 'em, moved at night and hid of a day, freedom could be had. I'd heard of a trail what run underground that those tryin' to get free could follow. I couldn't imagine it. A trail what run underground. Who'd 'a ever thought it? Never seen it. Never walked it. Figured it for spiritual, but I hoped they all took that trail if such a thing existed. Maybe it would take 'em some place nice.

Chapter 7 - Cain and the Auctioneer

Wind Is Strong come to live with us in our home at the base of Ben's Knob mountain what lay to the west side 'a the Choestoe Valley. Me and Wolf found her near death up on small "ridge-a-hidin'" near Blood Mountain. Ended up in Panther Cave tendin' to her. She'd been a slave held by a clan west 'a the ridge boundary for Choestoe. Her escape across the big ridges had brought her to us wounded, bein' chased by the brother of a man she'd had to kill to get free. I've never held that against her, after meetin' the ones what'd owned her previous. I'd come to love her as a sister. She'd become family. Near like a mother at times. She was strong. A hard worker. Honest. Dad trusted her. Told her she could be a part of our family if she so chose, after she'd healed enough to think a decision like that through. Could stay in our home as long as she wanted. She accepted his offerin' after her healin' grow'd complete. That's how she come to live with us. It was good for our clan, too, 'cause her and Anne spent many hours together with Anne teachin' her the healin' ways she'd learned from Wolf's grandmother, Owl the Wise One. George Black Oak had become a very special friend to Wind, and her to him. No one doubted they'd already be hitched if Wind's family were whole. They was together a right smart durin' her healin'. Got to know each other close. Spent a lot 'a time in our big hemlock tub sittin' in hot water, too. Said it aided with the healin'. All that didn't seem right. Hard to swaller bein' that it was Black Oak what'd been caught by the love demon. I couldn't say nothin', it had me, too. Wolf'd be next. I'd done seen that look in his eye with the hog jumper maiden. I figured he liked her spirit. She was mountain tough like us, but softer.

I felt for Wind Is Strong. Prayed for her often. The path she'd ended up on in life was not of her choosin'. Her body might be livin' with us, but her mind was elsewhere most times. She'd been stole by a bad clan, The Lost, on a spring raid over to Yonah what got her husband kilt'. Her son took. The Lost sold the boy to rogue Indians movin' north. The women of The Lost what kept her as a slave made sure she know'd that for meanness sake. A little extra torture to Wind in their mind. The child was only a year old when he was sold away. That sale determined her need in life -- find her son -- then do what it took to get him free. Bring him home to wherever she determined that to be when the time come. I allowed it would be with Black Oak. He'd make a great father to a full blood Cherokee boy. I reasoned he'd be going with her to fetch him when she felt ready. That would be a long trail for them. Findin' the boy would be a chore, but buyin' him back or stealin' him might be a heavier chore. Still, Black Oak will have the boy when found. I had no question over that.

***

Wolf signaled at me. Got my attention. He'd found Cain. Pointed toward him to show me. I was wrong in my tryin' to figure him. He weren't goin' for the caller direct. He was goin' for the lamps. The hangin' lamps what lit the barn like day. The big single bowl oil lamps what held a right smart 'a wick oil to feed six separate light-givin' flames per lamp. Soon as I seen Wolf pointin' toward Cain off in a dark corner, I could see his thinkin'. He was tryin' to stay still but his head was bouncin' just enough to give away what he was doin'. It was clear as lookin' through clean glass to me. He was usin' his sling. His short sling, and it looked to be loaded full. He was whippin' it underhand to full whirl with his right arm. His left scratchin' his chin like he was cipherin' on what was for sale. That way folks wouldn't catch on to what was fixin' to happen or who might 'a been responsible. A rifle shot pouch showed hangin' from his braided leather belt slung loose under his possibles pouch off his left side. Easy for his left hand to slip into for grabbin' more shot. That told me his sling was loaded with .32 caliber shot. Oh my, Cain was gonna bust the lamps. Hell was on its way.

Cain was the best slinger of all of us. He hardly ever missed when he loosed his sling underhand. He'd come up with a way to spin the thing off to the side kinda behind his back. Kept the twirlin' action hid from whatever critter he was tryin' to kill. They couldn't see him windin' up till they'd waited too long to get free. I'd never seen him miss if it was an easy shot. The way he done it allowed him to throw several shot at a time. More shot to the throw meant a better chance at hittin' whatever it was he aimed to hit. Up'd his odds for a kill when slingin' at critters. He didn't miss that lamp, neither. King David would 'a been proud. Soon as Cain loosed his shot, the oil lamp hangin' some twenty feet above the auction table exploded into a fireball as half a dozen .32 caliber shot shattered the oil bowl and lamp all at the same time. Flames commenced to fallin' to the floor like hell's own breath coverin' the auction tables with a flamin' blanket of burnin' oil. All the paper records layin' about was of a sudden soaked in hot oil flames burnin' what weren't gonna be stopped. It was a slow burnin' oil, but when opened up real quick to air like it was, that fire spread like something wild. His second shot hit no different than the first as I looked over at him hopin' he was done. He weren't. His attack was just gettin' goin' good. I saw that in his eyes, the expression on his face. He was havin' fun. Revenge for the slave folks he said later. Lookin' over at me, I saw his eyes move slowly to his right. I followed his gaze until I saw the gate. Motionin' then with his head toward the holdin' pens, it was clear he wanted me to open that gate. Let the negroes behind it free. I had no question 'a that. The third lamp he took out was close to the pens where all the folks to be sold stood. They was now in the dark. Perfect for freein'. I did not hesitate.

Movin' fast as I could, bein' wounded and all, I headed for the nearest gate to where I stood. The lock had been sprung by the guards so they could get the negroes out for walkin' to the washin' place then on to the sellin' blocks. I reasoned Cain had waited for 'em to take them locks off 'fore he commenced to bustin' oil lamps. That was smart 'a him. He was always thinkin' like that. Wolf seen what I was doin'. He run for the other gates knowin' how I was hindered to move full out. He opened two more 'fore the boom of a flintlock musket filled the slave folk with terror sendin' 'em runnin' out their gates toward the back doors . . . and me, for I'd put myself in front of 'em when I moved to open the gates. Slaves was escapin' hard as they could. I heard another lamp explode makin' big flames start fillin' the barn. Another musket shot, then another. Things was gettin' out 'a hand. I had to find Cain. See that we got out without bein' trampled or shot. I never figured on all them goin' on's when we left our nice peaceful fire back at the wagon camp.

I was fightin' pain while workin' my way shoulder-to-shoulder with the ones escapin' when it come to me that I'd better keep my feet 'cause I was movin' slower than all the rest around me. Not get tangled up under all the folks what was movin' for their lives, when of course, it up and happened. I took a lick from behind makin' my feet go up and my head go down. I found myself under a thumpin' of escapin' bare feet - constant front-to-back, side-to-side. Weren't no place I could see they weren't feet runnin' for freedom. They was stompin' my head, my chest, legs, arms, hands, feet and back. Didn't feel a place on my body where feet hadn't stomped. I rolled to my front tryin' to keep 'em from steppin' on my face when I felt the tug of cuts bein' ripped open from a body fallin' on me. I soon realized they was more than one when I become smothered in 'em. Oh, the stench. That was near more'n I could stand. I hollered out for Cain best I could through the mass and madness surroundin' me. It was like a stampede from a herd 'a two-legged hogs. I had to stand. Try and get air. Move to the wall for protection if I could. *God help me I prayed! Please help me! I can't do this alone!* I swear to this day He heard me. Had to 'a. I'd no more'n got the need out to Him when a pair 'a strong hands slipped under my arms liftin' me clean up settin' my feet back flat on the barn floor, then those same hands helped me to the side wall. I think I would 'a died had someone not helped me. Answer to my prayin' for sure. I figured it for Cain, but it weren't. It was a boy, no older than me, but over a foot taller with strong arms. He had on no clothes other than his britches. No shirt. No shoes. Only pants, which was more'n some had on. His eyes was kind. I thanked him for helpin' me up. He could 'a run on like all the rest of 'em did, not seein' me, but he didn't. He stopped to help. *Thank you, God!*

"Thank you, my friend. I believe you saved my life. I am Jebediah Collins. What can I call you when next we ever meet?"

"My name is Opah. I am from the lands below. Thank you, Jebediah Collins, for freeing me. I will never forget you," he said with an accent I'd never heard before. It was nice to listen to.

With that said, he ran into the night. He was a very dark negro. More so than the others. I hoped to see him again someday. I would like to sit with him. Have a smoke of some good burley tobacco. I was thinkin' we could be friends.

Cain weren't done. He'd chose his lamp bustin' trail with caution in mind. None he broke was over folks other than them at the auction table. Some 'a them was screamin' burnt, though. They was at least a dozen big oil lamps what lit that stinky ol' barn. He'd blow'd four already. It was chaos all about. The guards was busy bustin' negroes over the heads with these short black sticks as they ran by where they stood. Knockin' 'em out cold so's they didn't get away. *They know'd hittin' 'em over the head like that damaged the property some, but at least those didn't get away*. I allowed God had a special place for them kinda folks with their little black sticks. I wanted to send 'em there myself.

I held tight to the side 'a the barn in behind one of the support posts what held the barn's roof up. I know'd more was comin'. BOOM! . . . BOOM! . . . BOOM! Three more lamps exploded. Fire fallin' like rain sheets, but no rifle fire in return. All the guards was most likely fightin' the fire or busy knockin' folks out. The flames inside that barn was reachin' unbearable for me. Some of my cuts was stingin' so bad I was near to fadin' out. Only thing burnin', really, was the oil, but it burned hot. Weren't much in that barn 'cept folks, and all them that could got out. Weren't no stock inside it bein' a folk sale that night and all them had got out. Most all the flames landed on the barn's dirt floor. Some did land in a pile 'a hay. It was goin' hard. Would 'a caught the main beams up if it could 'a been allowed to keep buildin', but it weren't. Fortunately for them town folk, their water supply for the local fire fightin' bunch was just outside the barn. It was bein' used to supply the water to wash the slaves. They managed the blaze inside after gettin' their wagon pump set up. Wet everything down good to let the oil burn away. Saved the barn to sell another day.

I seen Wolf headin' my way. Cain, too. The sling and shot pouch nowhere in sight. They was walkin' like they was gettin' out of a burnin' barn same as everybody else that weren't fightin' fire. Nobody seen him sparkin' them lamps so weren't nobody suspicious of us leavin'. We met at the back doors. Wandered on down to the river then turned for home. Never saw the first negro all the way through town nor up the trail to our camp. It was like they'd all just vanished. I would 'a too, if'n I'd been facin' what they was facin'. We heard stories for many moons 'bout negroes bein' seen all over the mountains. I was proud 'a that. Me and Wolf actually seen some 'a the ones we'd freed at Big Camp what married into a clan or two 'a Cherokee. The Cherokee made a habit of adoptin' escaped slave folk. They made good Indians. Strong. I'd met a bait of 'em. Most of 'em good folks. Some not so much. I could understand that. Life was hard for them.

We never told one soul what we did that night. What Cain did that night. Wolf patched up my leakin' cuts with fresh cloth and salve. Burnin' the wrappin's Momma put on after supper. If folks would 'a found out what we done, they'd a been trouble with the Gaines Town law for sure. Dad would 'a got fetched up in that, since we all kinda belonged to him. Families from the wagon train would 'a been blackballed. Nobody would 'a bought their stuff. As it was, nothin' come to that year's train no different than what was expected. On the good, we got to enjoy a laugh anytime we heard the story of the slave freein'. I never heard it as a story about the slave barn burnin'. I always heard it told as a bunch 'a slave property caught the place 'a fire and escaped. I don't think anybody ever figured it any different. Them negroes weren't guilty. Cain busted them lamps. Freed them slaves. I guess I learned what he had in mind for that barn; its goins' on. I believe he meant to burn the thing to the ground. He'd a not brought a whole pouch 'a shot otherwise. I don't believe things worked out just as he'd hoped they would. Them havin' that water so close saved the whole of the barn. Next time we went to market we slipped out to have a look at the inside. It was all back whole. The busted lamps replaced. By the smell, you could tell it'd been used recent. Cain settled with it all. He'd done more'n most would 'a. Still, I believe he was unsatisfied with simply settin' some folk free. He wanted that barn to burn like it'd fallen into hell.

***

Red Hawk had concern for the new wagons comin' into Choestoe. He'd watched 'em from the low gap all the way across the steep ridges of the Rattlesnake, then around the north side 'a Frozen Top. There they picked up the Keowee Path which took 'em on down to the river Notla. Once the wagons made the river, they all turned south to follow upstream reachin' the headwaters 'fore stoppin'. They set up a stayin' camp on a small branch layin' at the bottom of the holler to Wide Gap. Five wagons with eighteen men. No women. No children. A dozen mules all total givin' 'em a team for each wagon with a spare team bein' led behind. They all looked like farmers what was tryin' their hand at maybe pannin' some gold. Red Hawk wanted to talk to these men, but feared their treachery. He retreated to a small ridge just north of Lord 'a Mercy Holler makin' a small camp nobody would find. He decided it best to watch these parasites for a while.

Red Hawk had a pure hatred of the folks comin' to the mountains to make their way workin' the creeks for gold. He didn't understand the value of gold coin like settler folks did, or why they wanted it so badly they would do the things they was doin' to get it.

"Should a man give himself away for the feel of gold in his hand, Jebediah?" Red Hawk asked as we smoked by our outside fire pit one clear, dark winter's night. "Does he lose who he is for the little he finds at the bottom of his searching pan? How is it that a man who knows himself true, can deny who he is for a small bag of gold nuggets? He cannot eat it. Only if he had spent his time hunting or fishing could he eat his prize. That would be time better used for him. This gold does not speak real words. It cannot heal you. It will not comfort you. Why then, Jebediah, are these who come here so determined? Are these evil ones who come to my home so foolish as this? I do not want to live with their kind. They are dirty on the inside as well as the outside. I want to live among The People. Know that their heart is true. How is it, young one, that other settlers can stand among those who have lost their way as these taking our mountains? I would feel for them if they were not so ignorant of life."

"I am white, Uncle. I am a settler, Uncle. I am no different than they. Why is it then, that I can see the way and they cannot? Have their eyes been shut by greed so hard that their visions tell lies? I wish I could answer your questions, Red Hawk. I, too, would like to know these things."

Red Hawk watched 'em constant the first two days of their visit. Seen that the bunch 'a "farmers" know'd exactly what they was doin' when it come to settin' up a proper camp. Who they might be come to him as he studied on it late into the night the third day of their stay. The spot they chose for the camp was correct. Their fire pit laid good for catchin' draft. A privy was dug some one hundred paces east from the center 'a camp. Blankets hung on temporary poles until they could wall it up proper. Supplies stored in squared tents in order of their content. Mules quartered, scraped and tied off the exact same distance apart to a taught lead rope. The knots square. Oat bags slipped neatly over their heads with what looked like the exact same amount of oats for each mule. Every farmer had his own tent. Dirty white hemp canvas, every one exactly the same 'cept one, laid side-by-side in rows of six. Stobbed with eighteen inch locust stakes all the same distance apart drove in perfect lines. When one looked down 'em from the end, the stobs made perfectly spaced walkways in between the tents. But then the guns, they stood leanin' again' one another in stacks of six. Each positioned for easy grabbin' from any part 'a camp. Them doin' that mixed with all the rest Red Hawk had seen give the battle-hardened warrior a sick feelin' down deep in the pit of his gut. This bunch was gonna be trouble. They weren't farmers, at least not recent. These men was trained. One full look over the camp give it away. It now got very important to speak with one of these . . . blue coats.

The watcher what come was older. Red Hawk was hopin' for a younger lookout when he chose to wait in the place where he know'd military folk would come to for standin' guard. It was how they was trained. Near same as Cherokee. A small rise some one hundred or more paces to the north would be the chosen spot for one of the farmers. Not far from the base 'a the big ridges. Red Hawk did not have to wait long 'fore he come. He was tall. Stocky. Most likely a dangerous enemy if he ever saw Red Hawk. With ease and quiet that the seasoned warrior was know'd for, Red Hawk was able to slip his long knife under the man's chin from behind. Red Hawk held that the big one had just become a lot less dangerous.

"Soldier," Red Hawk growl-whispered into his ear. "Do not try to get loose from me. If you do, I will leave you here in your own blood. I mean you no harm, watcher. I just need to speak with you. Do you understand me? Farmer?"

All the man could do was nod his head some. If he tried to talk the edge of Red Hawk's knife would cut into his neck meat. He moved his head what he could.

"I will lower my blade only enough for you to speak. If your voice rises above a whisper, I will kill you. Cut out your heart. Feed it to my dogs with the other hearts I have hanging at my lodge. Believe me soldier. I will do this. You know I will." Red Hawk lowered his blade a bit. A smile raisin' at the corners of his mouth where his prisoner couldn't see. He had no plans of cuttin' the man's heart out. Nor did he have any hangin' back at his lodge. For that, he didn't even have a lodge. The watcher merely whispered understandin'.

"Why are you here, soldier? What land are you from? Is General Wash-Ting-Sun coming to your camp? I would like to speak with him. He holds much honor among my clan. What will be the length of your time here? Why are you hiding in regular settler clothes? Where are your blue coats? I should kill you now because I know you will lie like all other soldiers."

Red Hawk pressed his long knife hard against the man's throat, restrainin' enough so's not to kill him. Thinkin' about blue coat soldiers got Red Hawk's anger stirred. Unfortunately for the watcher, that thinkin' made the warrior press a little harder with the edge of his long knife than originally intended. Red Hawk needed information. The soldier could only speak if he was alive, but Red Hawk's soul wanted the evil to die after his thoughts turned to the things he know'd blue coats had done to his clan. He couldn't help wantin' to kill for revenge's sake. The knife fetched a small, stinging line of blood on the watcher's neck. Red Hawk could smell it.

"No!" The captive whispered all he could at Red Hawk. Cuttin' his neck meat a little deeper. "I will tell you. Please! Please don't kill me. I can tell you everything you want to know. Just don't kill me! Please, Mr. Indian, promise me."

Red Hawk had to fight laughin' as he spoke back, "Listen, foolish one. I have said I have no plans to harm you if you speak the answers I need. Answer straight and we will be done with this. You smell bad. I do not want any more of your scent on me than I can wash off in a day. Why do you trespassers not bathe? It is a simple thing, soap with water. There is water everywhere here. Clean yourself. We Cherokee despise your filth."

"Alright. I'm dirty. I understand you don't like it. Okay. I'll wash. Now, let me speak answers. We are here to prospect gold. We are no longer soldiers. Yes, we were, but our time of service has ended. We come to find fortune for our families. We are from the north. York Town is where. We have traveled far to find the gold all the papers are writing about back home. We need help. We can pay. Would you consider . . .?"

"NO! Never could I consider helping varmints like you. What is this you say? Papers? Writing about gold. What do you mean? I do not understand about folks reading in paper."

"Not in paper, on paper. Words printed on paper that are telling everyone that there is gold here in these mountains. That is why we are here. We look to find gold. Plain and simple. Do you believe me? Mr. Indian? Do you?"

"Listen, foul smelling one. I am Red Hawk. Senior warrior for the Cherokee Guard. I have marked you with my blade. If I ever see you again, I will make this mark much deeper. Send you across the Great River to be with the ancestors. You and your . . . pa-per. Agh, I will kill your pa-per, too. Tell your leader we are watching. We will let you stay for now, because killing white men is troublesome. It is like the yellow bee. Kill one, more come. I hate you being here, white man. My soul hates the change your coming brings to my home. Remember my name, soldier. I am Red Hawk – of the Choestoe Clan. If you find your courage, weak one, then send for me. I will come. We will fight. You will die. Then I will feed your heart to my dogs. Now, to answer your question. NO! . . . I do not believe a word you speak, white man. My spirit knows there is more to your coming than gold. I will wait. Watch to see your efforts. I may get to kill you yet, farmer. The rest of your bunch, too. That would make my spirit sing. My ancestors would dance."

With all that said, Red Hawk slipped his knife back from the man's throat bringin' even more blood as the blade's tip passed across under his ear, then he slipped off into the night. He stopped a few paces away to watch what the lookout did. Red Hawk smiled as the man slumped to his knees while dumpin' his supper out on the forest floor. It's what happens to some folks who've been scared near to death. I couldn't blame the soldier man for wretchin' out his guts. It was Red Hawk what held that knife to his throat. Maybe the most deadly Cherokee warrior in the whole put together of the mountains . . . and he was my uncle.

Chapter 8 - A Visit to Cain's

Isabelle looked like her mother. The features of her face matched Rose near to a twin. It was a good thing, too, 'cause you wouldn't want a girl child what looked like her father, Cain. She was just over a year old when me and Wolf stopped by that spring. Hadn't been long what she'd started walkin' good. Went all over explorin' if you turned her loose. Learnin' to talk a bit. But what you really noticed about her when first meetin' was her eyes. They weren't brown like Rose's. They was blue like Cain's. Noticeable blue, like the clear sky of winter at mid-day blue. Her hair was like Cain's, too, kinda yellow lookin', but those eyes. Her eyes looked right inside your soul when she locked 'em on you. They was spooky blue. Shone like stars on a dark night against her brown skin. Wolf allowed she'd been touched by the Great Spirit. Dad said she had angel eyes 'cause she was most likely kissed by one while the Great Creator was puttin' her together. He allowed she was gonna be some kinda special. Not sure he know'd how right he was. Maybe he'd had a vision? The elders figured she would have courage uncommon for woman folk. Prob'ly fear nothin', just like her dad. She'd already turned a lot like Cain. Climbed on everything she could reach, folks included. Could run up the side 'a Dad's leg like a squirrel to a tree. He loved that. Rose tried to make him stop carryin' her so much when he come to visit. Him and Momma went a right smart. She allowed "Izzy" would get spoiled if he carried her everywhere when he come. Her tellin' Dad didn't do much good, though. He held her all the time he could when vistin'. No matter to him. Said they weren't no spoilin' to it. He just wanted to tote her around all he could 'fore she got too big for him to hug carry.

It was late spring when we come to Cain's, not long after all the gold lookers started intrudin'. Word had got out that the mountains held gold. Folks was beginnin' to show up along the streams in Choestoe, dippin' their little pans in the cold mountain water lookin' for nuggets. Me and Wolf laughed at 'em. They was much easier ways to find gold than how they was goin' at it. The Cherokee had found a right smart 'a gold. Know'd how to find it. They just kept it hid. Know'd if folks found out, the mountains would get swarmed like a cornfield after tosslin' time. Still, the intruders took a right smart once they figured out they could find it by diggin' into the mountains instead of panning in the creeks. Unfortunately for some, they found more than the Cherokee was happy to part with which caused killin' to happen. I allowed folks figured it all worth the effort to invade Cherokee lands for the profit, but to me it weren't worth the risk. Every soul that crossed a ridge into Choestoe was watched constant. Not sure how many gold lookers made it back home from their searchin' once discovered by certain mountain natives. Not sure they all know'd just how close to death they was every single day they woke in Cherokee land. Many saved just by the good nature of what native folk discovered 'em. The Cherokee considered all the gold in their lands under their care same as the critters, the trees, and the waters. A gift from Mother Earth passed on by the ancestors, and just like everything else in their world, they were thankful to the Great Creator for it. Know'd he called on 'em to be good stewards. All it took was some form 'a disrespect to that thinkin' toward a clan what used a certain area bein' looked in by strangers, and the lookers was in trouble. Indians treated each other with common respect. They expected it out 'a their visitors as well.

"Jeb! Wolf!" Rose near hollered as we rode in to the back 'a her and Cain's place on our mules. Two woven sacks full 'a ramps strung across each one's rump. Well, Wolf couldn't call the one he was ridin' his 'cause Dad hadn't gifted it to him yet. I know'd he would 'fore too long, though.

Rose was workin' the herb garden in back 'a their log home when we come in from the south -- down the creek. We'd been up on the big ridge tops harvestin' ramps most 'a the last week prior. Thought we'd come down by their place for a visit. Wolf wanted to see his new, first ever niece, Isabelle. He'd got to meet her only once not too long back so he was anxious to pay a call while we could. I wanted to see her, too. Plantin' time was comin' soon and we'd all be busy for a while then. Wouldn't be doin' much visitin'. I always loved goin' to Cain's. Me and him was close all our lives. I know'd they'd favor some fresh greens, too. It'd been a long winter.

"Welcome, Brother Wolf," Rose said welcoming her blood kin. "I am so glad you are here. Come and see how your niece has grown. She is walking now. Are you alone? Is Father or Mother with you? I would like to see Momma. Talk to her as a daughter. How is Father? Has Dancing Bear quit speaking of his granddaughter to everyone he sees? I have had to scold Thompie as well, Jeb," she said, lookin' over at me. "He will not put Isabelle down to walk all the time he visits. I do not know what I am going to do with two spoiled grandfathers! Now, both of you, come give your sister a hug."

Wolf grabbed Izzy up meetin' chest on with Rose and me at the same time. We all stood huggin' around our newest family member. Wolf finished the huggin,' settin' Izzy down to the ground. We both dropped to a knee puttin' our faces at eye level with hers, starin' straight into those haunting blue stars she was blessed with.

"My little sister," Wolf near sang. "How you have grown since our last visit. You are as beautiful as your momma. One day you will confuse the heart of a great warrior just as she did my brother, Cain. I fear this. Her cunning is known. She will teach you."

Wolf said all that as he grinned real big in her face. Rose slappin' him on top of his head for funnin' on her while watchin' me try not to laugh out loud. Izzy grinned back. Near laughed when Wolf got popped on top of the head by her mother. Later on, after supper, we got our little niece to laughin' so hard tears was comin' out from her eyes. I mean layin' down on the floor belly laughin', laughin'. She was so much fun. I loved her. Wolf picked her up again handin' her to me. She sat with her bottom on my forearm. Her hand on my shoulder. My heart got hot when she looked me straight in the eyes. That's the only way I can explain it. My soul felt her stare as our faces come together.

"Izzy," I said, lookin' her eye-to-eye real close. "Don't listen to your ol' Uncle Wolf. He can be a might troublesome at times. Your momma ain't nothin' but the best. I don't blame Cain at all for gettin' confused over the likes 'a her." That earned me a slap on top 'a the head as well. Izzy laughed at that one, too.

"My sister?" Wolf kinda asked. "Are you here alone? Where is Cain? We have brought ramps. They are very strong, too strong to eat raw. They must be cooked. The heads are big this season. Many are as thick as our father's thumbs. We will boil them for supper if you would like us to, but I think we should do it in the outside kettle. The smell will be too hard for inside the house. I know this from when we took them from Mother Earth. We have many for all who would like some. You and Cain are welcome to take what you need to dry for later. Please, take what you will eat."

"Thank you, Brother. We would love some fresh greens no matter how strong. Our spring gardens will be ready soon, but it will still be a while yet. Our winter turnips lasted but half the season. Cain and Father fattened two extra hogs last year. Thompie did an extra steer, so thank the Great Creator all our families have had plenty of meat to last this cold time. These ramps will make the bear cuts we are having tonight even that much more special."

"Bear?" I asked kinda quick. Wolf looked at me.

"Yes, Jeb. Cooper Whint is here staying with us for a while. He and Cain are working on some chores together around the fields. He killed it this morning hunting with Cain. It is a young bear. The meat will be very tender."

Wolf looked at me hard while she was tellin' what bear Cooper had shot. It was a young bear, so it was not my Brother Bear. The bear I'd met on my first ever trail with Dad. My bear was a big bear. Had a star on his chest what looked like the pictures I'd seen in the Bible of the Cross of Christ. That bear was special to me. I'd seen him many times at particular moments. Not sure I could eat him, although fresh young bear cuts did make my mouth shoot water out on the inside of my jaw. I favored bear meat sometimes when Momma cooked it. That was a problem for me when out huntin' for meat. I didn't wanna kill my totem bear. I hoped I would not.

"Go on and put the mules in the barn," Rose said as she moved to take Izzy from me. I didn't want her to take the little sweetness. I understood how Dad felt as she left my arms to go with her mother. I just wanted to keep hold for a while. Carry her around some. "Provide for them all you need. Loose them in the corral if you'd like. Cain has our mules with him and Cooper. I will take Izzy in and get some hot coffee ready. You two look like you could do with some. Not slept much the last couple days? Been busy? Are ramps the only reason y'all went up to the big tops? Hmm?" she asked lookin' us in the eye good. Neither one of us answered her.

Cooper Whint was there. Maybe that had Rose curious. Weren't nothin' fetchin' in her question from us, but for some reason we didn't answer. We'd only gone high for the greens. Her bein' curious about what we was doin' made us wonder what "chores" Cain and Cooper was really out doin'. Huntin' bear? No. That weren't a chore what was soundin' right to my thinkin'. I didn't believe that was what was happenin'. We didn't kill bears in the spring. We waited 'til fall when their hides was thick and they'd put on plenty 'a meat. I'd heard enough from Rose to know Cain was into somethin' serious enough to make him lie to his wife about what he was doin'. Cooper bein' there was only more proof to the possibility. He weren't no warrior like Cain, but he was Indian all the same when he wanted to be. Could move through the woods like a mist. Me and Wolf liked him a sight. If ever there was a soul as risky and troublesome as Wolf, it was Cooper Whint. He was curious about everything. Felt at home in the woods. Had a look to him where you couldn't figure what he was thinkin' unless he wanted you to. Him and Cain had got close ever since the trouble over at Yonah a few years back. Cooper worked with his family on their farm just like all the rest of us, but he was good about comin' to help others when he had time. He liked bein' around Cain and livin' Indian. That's kinda how they'd got so close. Yep, if Cooper was there, Cain was busy with somethin'. We didn't figure it for land workin' 'cause his growin' fields was huge. They had to be tended to early in the year. That'd been seen to by Dancing Bear and the Cherokee. We know'd them was ready to plant.

Both had battle truck on 'em when they come to the barn. Heavy skin britches under knee high leather foot skins. A thick homespun shirt with braided leather cord holdin' the sleeves tight just above their elbows. Their possibles pouches laid over their heads hangin' under their left arms. Looked to be near full. We was seein' to the mules out front 'a the barn when we heard 'em cross the creek from the east. Wolf Creek Branch was close to Cain's barn that way. They was slippin' in. Weren't no path or trail where they crossed the branch. Cain had one of our Harpers Ferry .54 caliber flintlocks we'd give him slung over his right shoulder. Shot pouch and powder horn tied to his belt hangin' off his left side under the possibles pouch. Stayed hid that 'a way. Cooper with his bow and full quiver 'a huntin' arrows as was normal. Both had two knives what was visible.

Cooper always hunted with a bow. Carried it in a special sleeve what slung across his back. Kept it unstrung most times. Never saw him hunt or go on trail with a gun, and if you ever hunted with him, you'd see why he didn't need one. He was bow strong. Been shootin' since he was small. I couldn't near bend the one he used common. He was unusual good with it, too. The Indians allowed he was touched by the Holy One when tellin' stories about what they'd seen him do. He never lost shootin' against folks at Big Camp. He could put the flame out on a lit candle from over thirty paces away. I'd seen him do it many times just for fun. He even shot quail with his bow, fish too, and of course all the other critters we liked to eat. He made his own bow out 'a locust. His arrows out 'a different kinds 'a wood dependin' on what he wanted 'em to kill. Cedar and poplar for birds and squirrels. Hickory and oak for heavier game. Dried just so with the proper amount 'a sunlight, smoke and air. Me and Wolf seen many bows he'd made over the years. Weren't uncommon to meet folks what'd been gifted one 'a his builds. Not all mountain folk had guns, and even if they did, lead and shot could be hard to get without gold coin or trade goods. Him giftin' folks a good bow with a quiver of arrows helped 'em feed their families. Kept' 'em safe. He kinda made a name for himself makin' quality bows what held up for folks when they needed 'em to. You couldn't buy his bows, though. He never sold one that I know'd about. He just didn't feel right makin' profit off somethin' gifted to him by the Great Creator.

Cooper claimed an old Indian warrior taught him how to shoot when he was real small. Said he come to him in a vision 'fore he ever come to him in the person. I understood that. He believed in his heart from then on that his talent with the bow was purely spiritual. Claimed the old Indian told him to fetch his huntin' points from a medicine woman what lived somewhere on the Big Bald. I never went there. He'd not take you. I'd seen him makin' points, so I know'd he could flake his own. Still, the points he used for huntin' was different lookin'. Same kinda flint as most, just worked different. Wolf seen that when huntin' with him. They was deadly when he used 'em. The power in his pull would break bone on a bear if the point didn't shatter.

"Jeb, you are here. It is good to see you. How is it that you have come here, little brother?", Cain asked as he grabbed my forearm while starin' me eye-to-eye. He then moved over to Wolf. "Wolf. Welcome. It is good to see you as well. Cooper is here. It is good y'all have come to visit."

"Jeb," Cooper said kinda loud. He had one of them voices you could hear from a long way away. "How you been, young 'un? You and Wolf been behavin' like your folks tell you? It is good to see you again. Peter is lookin' fine. How is Thompie and Celia and, oh yes, Miss Anne, of course?"

He said that last part about Anne with more of an interest in his voice than when he asked about Mom and Dad. I'd never noticed nothin' with them two whenever he come by to visit. He come with his dad a right smart through the years to trade with my dad. We'd go to their place some, too. They grow'd the best corn what popped over a fire. Cooper never told us his dad's secret for making it grow so special. He was the only one who could grow it to such a fine quality taste. Nobody else ever had any luck with it. I had a taste for Mr. Whint's popping corn. Momma would do it on the stove in a big, covered cast iron roastin' pan. She'd sprinkle salt on it once it was done poppin'. Oh, that stuff was good.

"Are you plannin' on stayin' over a day or two, Jeb?, Cain asked with a strangeness about him. "Or will you be headin' out soon? I hate I weren't here to greet your comin', but had I know'd I still couldn't 'a been here. Me and Cooper been workin' a right smart. You know, gettin' the fields ready to plant since spring is comin' on us. How 'bout Dad, is he ready to plant? I figure he is."

"Uncle," Wolf said softly. "You are not dressed for work. You carry battle truck. Your pouches are laid for travel. I know your fields are ready for the planting, for that time will be soon. With respect, I believe you are on a chosen path. A trail that takes you deep into the mountains. Possible that it is a dangerous trail. Am I right, Uncle, or are you not deceiving us?"

"You're growin' smart with age, Wolf, my brother," Cain said as he pulled me and Wolf and the mules on in the barn. "Dancing Bear has taught you well. You will make a fine warrior when the Great Creator sees to it. Now, listen to me full, both y'all, and take heed. Wolf, what you sense is for sure. Danger has come to Choestoe. A warrior. A soulless warrior who kills for profit or pleasure. Red Hawk has fought this evil one. He and Moon Shadow were able to kill his two fellow murderers travelin' with him moons ago. Red Hawk tracked him for many suns never findin' the outlaw's principal trail. This warrior was not forgotten. Guards have been watchin' for him on Red Hawk's word. That's how come 'em to see him slippin' through the low gap with three friends at first light several days ago. They was makin' their way into the valley. No one has seen 'em since. He is not welcome here. His sign moves like the night. His cunning like the coyote. We have been helpin' look for this heathen. It is bad he has come here. You must watch to take care when you leave."

I'd heard stories 'round the smoke fires told of this slave tradin' warrior and his run-in with Red Hawk. He was bad blood. Talked to dark spirits some said. Likes to cut out his enemy's heart. Roast it over a fire for eatin'. Them type believed eatin' the heart give 'em power over death. I allowed that behavior was straight from hell. Fortunately, that heart eatin' weren't an all-around Indian thing. Only warriors who'd allowed bad spirits into their souls eat folk meat. Them kind even smelled bad. The stories told of Moon Shadow savin' Red Hawk's life by killin' one of the evil ones just as he loosed an arrow at Red Hawk. Then

Red Hawk returned the favor killin' the other, but not before Moon Shadow got stuck with a huntin' arrow under his arm. Fortunately, the point didn't kill. This was the warrior Red Hawk killed. The third of the warriors with the bad spirits escaped, but not before threatenin' Red Hawk with revenge for messin' up one of his slave trades of a girl he'd took. Challenging him for a future fight. Red Hawk hunted him, but did no good. Now this heathen was back in Choestoe, and we all know'd why. His black soul was set on revenge against Red Hawk.

"I have heard of this evil warrior who kills because his soul has turned," said Wolf 'fore I could answer Cain. "My father, Dancing Bear, knows of him. Has warned me about him because Red Hawk saw him murder Ruby Smith from up on the river Notla. They say this warrior has a black heart. This one they call Laughing Beaver. I believe he must be on his Death Trail coming back to this valley. Jeb and I will watch as we make our way to my home on Slaughter Mountain with the ramps. My family needs them. From there, we will go to Jeb's home. We will take care to look for his sign. We will come to you if we find his trail."

Me and Wolf was considered not quite grow'd by the elders of our families. They figured us able to do simple watchin' or trailin' or fetchin' and totin', but no more than that. For sure we weren't allowed near killin', and that was what Laughing Beaver was bringin' to our home. It really didn't matter to us what they allowed us to do or what they didn't allow us to do, me and Wolf did most all we ever wanted to do when on trail out in the mountains. Folks never even none the wiser. I could see it in my Blood Brother's face. This was a trail he weren't gonna miss, and I had no notion 'a missin' it, neither. We always watched each other's back. Never figured it no different all my years runnin' with Wolf. Like Red Hawk, we'd see Laughing Beaver had for killin' Ruby Smith. I believed that. She was our friend.

Chapter 9 - Laughing Beaver Returns

Wolf and me dropped the ramps off with Dancing Bear on Slaughter, then hurried on over to my home at the base ‘a Ben’s Knob Mountain. We finished our ramp unloadin’ and storin’ chore just as Old Man Sun was breakin’ day over the Horse Trough to the east. I could tell Wolf was eager to get to the hunt for Laughing Beaver by the way he was doin’. I seen it clear -- his mind had done gone to trail. We talked it over while puttin’ away our mules.

“Jebediah, I do not like it that our families must fear for their lives from this heathen that has come to our home. Isabelle would be a prize for a trader such as he and his. I will hunt this evil one. Help my people put an end to his murdering, slave trading life. I may not be able to kill this warrior, but I know plenty who can. Let us help in the hunt Jeb. What say you, my brother?”

Flirtin’ with death weren’t as excitin’ to me as it was to Cherokee warriors, young or old, but I was full on ready to take this huntin’ trail. I know’d Ruby Smith. She was close to my beloved, Elizabeth. Her killin’ hurt Elizabeth, and it brought a bother to the whole of everybody on upper Wolf Creek where Elizabeth lived. Ruby was stole less than a half mile from upper Wolf Creek on East Wolf Creek Branch. That put fear in their lives that weren’t necessary. It made me mule kickin’ mad knowin’ that Ruby’s killin’ hurt the one I never wanted to see hurt.

Through gritted teeth I realized I'd grabbed the handle of my long knife just thinkin' about Laughing Beaver's doin's. The knowledge it could 'a been Elizabeth that Laughing Beaver took turned me cold – cold like death. Not sure I could 'a handled her bein' killed. I said a little prayer for Ruby and her family. She took the place of all the other girls what lived in Choestoe the night she got took, whether she meant to or not. I appreciated her doin' that. Thanked Holy Spirit for her. I grinned knowin' how cantankerous she could be. Prob'ly made their trip to the tradin' grounds on the Blood 'bout as miserable as she could 'a, but my heart still hurt.

"Wolf, I will hunt this evil bunch same as you. Help our kind find him, but first I need to go to the England farm. I wanna check on Elizabeth and her bunch 'fore we strike out on trail for serious after Laughing Beaver. Make sure no trouble has come their way. Remember, East Wolf is where Laughing Beaver stole Ruby. I'm just thinkin' he might feel comfortable settin' up camp near there. I'd have a clearer mind lookin' for sign if I know'd she and her's was safe. Help me trail better. What say ye, brother?"

"I believe you are true in your thoughts on this evil one, Jeb. I, too, worry for Miss Elizabeth. All those who live on East Wolf could be in danger as well. We should go there. Ease our concerns . . . then make trail to the rock ridge. I believe this is where we will find Laughing Beaver. His traitor friends."

Well, there it was again. That knowin' of a thing 'fore ever really knowin' of the thing. It always amazed me how some Indians just know'd the what-for of a matter 'fore it ever happened. No, Wolf didn't know for sure that them rogues was there, but his figurin' for 'em made him most positive they would be. I'd hung my hat on less than what confidence I had in his "feelings" for a matter. It was unsettling him bein' able to do that. If they was holed up at the rock ridge when we got there, it would not surprise me at all. I think I'd be more surprised if they weren't there, really.

"We need sleep first, Wolf. I think we should finish tendin' to our mules, then re-pack our truck for stayin' gone a while. Momma will have a good supper soon. We can take the leftovers for our keep the next couple days." I draw'd in close, not wantin' any other folk that might be near to hear. Kinda whispered to him. "You're gonna need to tell her where we're goin' and when we'll be back durin' supper. You need to come up with a story she'll swaller without question. She's sly as Old Man Fox. If she doubts a word, she'll know." I leaned back away. "We can sleep the night here, headin' out at first light. Elizabeth will want us to stay the night there. Share supper with Mrs. England and all the kids. We can get on our way next morning, after breakfast of course. Does this sound proper to you, Wolf? It feels right."

"Yes, I like your thoughts, Jeb. I need sleep same as you. And, there is no way I'm gonna miss supper cooked by our mother. Spending days on the big ridges looking for greens has made us too long without good eats. Mother Celia has a special hand for making things taste so good. Besides, it would be disrespectful not to share. I would not want her to be mad at us for not staying supper. Sleep will be a welcomed time when we finally finish our day. I believe we should do just as you say, my brother. Eat, rest, then leave out at Old Man Sun's first light. Maybe our fathers will have found the evil one by morning, save us this trail, but I doubt that will be true. This evil warrior does not want to be found. Now that he is in the valley, he can stay hid same as us."

Sometimes it sounded strange hearin' Wolf call Momma "Mother." Speakin' of her like she was his momma. I never thought much of it. We was all family 'cause Dancing Bear had adopted us. To Wolf, callin' her Mother was proper. A common show of respect. He loved my momma. I loved his momma. Called her mother when she was near. I treated 'em both like my momma, but I know'd I only had the one birthin' mother. Same with him. So, it did sound strange sometimes. That kinda bond made livin' in the mountains safer for all of us. For sure since trouble had come to roost in the valley. Laughing Beaver, gold lookers, government men and blue coats. All carried their evil with 'em when they come, too. I hated all the strangers was movin' in on the mountains – movin' in on us. Their comin' brought terror and destruction to the Indians. It was an insult to the rest of us who had ancestors what fought for freedom as Americans.

***

Wind Is Strong was alone with her thoughts as she sat the rock seats Granddad had carved out years earlier on a small top just south of our home. She wished she'd brought a quilt, but her mind was distracted when she left out that late spring morning. All she wore was a homespun top with skin leggings. Fortunately for her, she'd thought to wear her cold time foot skins what come up near to her knee. She was warm for the most part, while sittin' the rise waitin' for first light, if she kept her arms crossed close in front of her chest. The light was wanted. The light would bring warmth. She would soon see Old Man Sun ease up over the Horse Trough Mountain to wake the valley for a new day. She could scent the morning dampness of the forest as she breathed in deep to calm herself. Could hear the singing of the birds calling. The rustlin' of squirrels startin' their morning by lookin' for acorns they'd buried back in the time of falling leaves. Somewhere a hawk screamed tryin' to get some poor critter to jump scared so it could spot it, then the hawk could eat. She prayed as she sat, listenin' close to her heart for the voice of Holy Spirit. Her prayers were bein' lifted through the sweet taste of some barn cured Burley tobacco mixed with a touch 'a medicine herb she'd got from Anne. It was a blend Owl made for the women of young warriors who was goin' into battle for the first time. The wives, mothers, sisters, and aunts would smoke the special tobacco. The herb mix settled their fears for the loved one who might not come back. Wind Is Strong prayed for her son. Prayed Holy Spirit would show her the way. To this day, I believe God got pulled listenin' to her heart. Spoke guidance to her spirit from concern. The Bible says He has a special place in His heart for widows and orphans. Her prayer was simple.

"Holy One. Great Spirit. It is I, Wind Is Strong. I must speak with you about my son. I want him back. I know that only through You will I ever see him again. Take up my burden, Father. Hear my sorrow. Know that I trust in You. I ask for You to show me where to start my search. Guide me as my friend Black Oak and I begin our trail. Send messengers to show us the way. I pray that my emptiness will be filled with the love of my son . . . soon. Please . . . Great Spirit . . . hear my heart. Give my soul Your words. My spirit will listen for Your voice."

She sat prayin' for several hours after Old Man Sun woke. Speakin' some -- listenin' more. Her body was weak. The fast had taken its toll on her mind. She'd not eaten for three days taking only water when the tightness come on her. She removed herself from the stone seats to a place where she could stretch out flat on the ground. Her head uphill from her feet. She was tired. Her body was tired;

muscles cramping. Her hands had been knotted in tight fist 'til the calmness of the herb soothed her. She felt cold. Her person needed sleep. The back of her head barely had come to rest on the soft mast of the forest floor before her eyes closed in deep sleep. That's when the vision what would change her life commenced. The medicine herb helped her body rest, but her spirit connected to the Holy One as she drifted off into the dream world from where that vision was sent.

I'd been around the Old Timers enough to recognize the signs of real visions. You could know by the way a body told what they saw if they'd seen it all actual or not. I never doubted a word she said 'cause I'd been to that world myself. That's where I met my totem, Brother Bear, in a dream vision, long 'fore I ever met him for real on Wolf Creek. Holy Spirit spoke to me through this huge bear what had a white star cross on its chest. I tell you true, that bear spoke to me in a vision when I visited the dream world. It come to me after bein' jumped and near kilt by a mountain cat. Bein' near death can take you to the spirit world as well, when it's natural. I know'd her words was true when I heard her speak about it after comin' back to our home – her home.

"I woke where I lay, on the small rise south of this place," Wind Is Strong said as she told me and Wolf about her vision. It was a powerful vision. "There was a breeze blowing that felt like it was coming from all four directions. North felt cold. South felt warm and wet. West was dry, stinging like when the sun burns your skin. East was pleasant. Inviting to the soul, but I knew not to go that way. My spirit told me I was to go north, so I began walking north. All day I walked, then night came. I could not see to go on, but I did not want to stop. I needed to keep moving north. No stopping for any reason. I prayed to the Great Creator for help. He heard my need. Gave me sight. I could suddenly see in the dark like Owl, so I became Owl. Kept flying north. I could not stop. Daylight rose as I flew from the dark. I chose to remain Owl even though Old Man Sun was shining hot over my head. Flying over Mother Earth for the whole of the next day and night. North, always north. High over the mountains. Finally, on the morning of the third day, I landed in some strange woods way up north turning back into my human body. I could see my feet. They were covered in leather knee high foot skins. My body was covered in cold time skins. My head wrapped in a rabbit fur hat. My hands covered with cold weather skins same as my feet. I could not feel the cold, but I could see it. That was very strange."

"Snow began to fall. Huge flakes with some bigger than my hand. It got so deep I had trouble walking, so I changed back into Owl. Flew through the snow for the rest of that day landing in an oak tree not far from a small camp of not more than three dozen Indians. Mostly men with a few older women that reminded me of those who had held me slave. That was bad for them. I flew into their camp. They tried to hit me, but I fought them off with my claws. Sharp claws that tore meat from bone. The women begged for their lives, but Owl had no mercy. It killed them, I, Wind Is Strong, killed the evil women, with great power. I could taste their blood as it dripped off my beak. I liked it.

"Children! What? All around me. Young boys and girls with smaller ones following started coming from the woods or a building of some sort. It was hard to know exactly. They were everywhere. Scattering in all directions. An older girl. Black hair with black eyes dressed in a black robe came to me. She wore no shoes as she walked through the snow. She was not scared of what I'd done.

She thanked me. With her was a little boy no older than two years. He had the black eyes as well. It felt like my son. I knew him. Could scent my blood in his veins. My heart swelled as my wings unfolded. I saw my claws reach for my child as I lifted off from the ground. Grabbing him up I left that evil place with my son in my claws and a huge Indian riding on my back. That is the first I remember Black Oak. I don't remember killing any but the women, then seeing that two men lay dead as I climbed told me he had been there with me.

"For many days I flew, landing back on the small rise from where I'd left. Black Oak was with me. His skins stained in blood. My son, nowhere in sight. He was in my claws as I started to land on the rise, but when I got on the ground, he was not there. I jumped back into the sky flying over all the trail from where we'd come, but there was nothing. No boy anywhere. I never found what happened to him in the vision before I woke the next morning still lying flat on the forest floor. Someone had come in the night. Sat with me. I could tell because there was a small fire built close to where I lay. Footprints marking the ground around it let me know someone had been there for a time. They'd made no effort to clean up their sign, so I figured whoever it was trusted me. It was not Black Oak. The tracks were too small for his foot. I understood who it was later. Once I did, I couldn't tell a soul."

Her vision was strong. It would need to be smoked over by the wise men of the clan. They would tell her exactly what it meant. How she should do. I had my thoughts, but I weren't savvy to all I needed to know on spirit doin's to figure it proper. This was a powerful sign her havin' that vision. It meant she was touched by the spirits. Once they found out, the old ones would look her over for signs she'd been travelin' in the spirit world just like they'd done me plenty 'a times. They'd squeeze her hands and arms till it hurt, same as they did me. Pinchin' here and there on her person what left little bruises wherever they did it. They'd rub her face, ears, nose, mouth and teeth real slow like with their fingertips. Then get close so they could look deep into her eyes. Wolf said they was hopin' to find sight 'a the spirit what carried her to and from the dream world.

It all told 'em somethin'. I never know'd what 'cause they'd not say a word when seein' to you. Just grunt on occasion while they looked your person over real close. She weren't gonna like none 'a what they'd do. It was awful how they did from bein' so curious. But, it was their way. I know'd all that trouble give 'em some idea 'bout how things was, but none but them could explain their thinkin'. It was sad when I thought it over later, smokin' and talkin' with Wolf. Their gift for spirit sign readin' never made it to the next generation. Them what was left durin' my growin' up time in Choestoe was the only ones that could read all that strange sign. None younger than them ever got the true gift. The old voice was dyin' out. It'd be gone with the old ones of my youth. That was a shame.

***

Sean know'd he was bein' watched. Felt the eyes for a couple days 'fore he found sign tellin' him for sure somebody'd been spyin' on him. Had been off and on for a few days accordin' to what the sign said. Indian, by the look of it. Full grow'd. Most likely a warrior. Common folk wouldn't watch from where his visitor had been hid. It weren't easy findin' the watcher's sign, but Sean had become very woods savvy livin' life in the mountains on his own. He liked it that way. No folks dependin' on him for nothin'. Pannin' gold without nobody knowin' he was there. He'd made friends with a lot 'a the Cherokee. Honored them by givin' 'em some 'a the gold he'd find in the creeks. Often brought Dancing Bear cuts 'a fresh meat from game he hunted in the valley. His way 'a sayin' thank you for allowin' him to live in the mountains with 'em. The Indians respected that. Treated him as such. He'd become their friend. They trusted him. Me and Wolf visited his place from time-to-time. He'd homesteaded himself a one room log cabin with a small barn, a well, corral, smokehouse and privy, not far from the Keowee trail. South 'a the Frozen Top. A little way back from the river Notla. He liked goin' on trail with us when there was somethin' stirrin'. We was gonna pay him a call when we left our visit to the England Farm . . . Elizabeth.

Bein' watched at home in the secret don't sit well with most folks. Means somebody is lookin' for somethin'. Knowledge usually. Who lives there? How many are there? And most times the question is, what around the place can be took, then sold for gold? Or, is their gold hid nearby? Bein' watched weren't sittin' good with Sean neither. He took to watchin' back.

Sean was careful when he scouted around his home lookin' for anything that would tell him more about the watcher what had been there. Paid mind to leavin' no sign. Didn't want the bad folk to know he'd been slippin' around watchin' out for them. He was always careful even when folks weren't watchin' him. Never left his house or come home the same way day-after-day for fear 'a makin' a trail straight to his front door. Bein' close to the river like he was, folks followin' upstream could see his place durin' the cold time. You had to look close, but you could see it if the leaves was off. Bein' careful like he was give Sean the confidence to know the watcher would not know he'd been found out. It was time for Sean to see who this shadow was. He hoped he was friendly.

It's the simple woods snare that typically brings home meat for supper. That's how Sean was gonna get to know this stranger who'd been watchin' him. It was a simple task to make his place look like he'd left it for a few days. Gone out on trail. At first light from Old Man Sun the next day after decidin' his defense, Sean set his counter watchin' plan in motion. He put all his common use day truck on the inside of his log home like his sittin' chairs, pole axe, boilin' kettle, water buckets, bow and quiver what hung to the left of the front door on the outside for easy grabbin'. Turned the chickens out to feed wild while throwin' out enough dried kernel corn to keep 'em a few days. They'd find food close when the corn ran out. Cleaned up around his small log barn and makeshift corral. Then, to make it all look real in case the watcher was already on post, he loaded up his camping truck on a mule he'd traded Dad for. Fetched his possibles pouch, rifle, powder and shot, his only two quilts, and a sack 'a dried fruit with bear jerky laid in it. He was makin' it look like he was gonna be out in the woods for maybe a couple days or more. His aim was to set up across the way from where the watcher sat. Look for him to come. See if he wandered down to the log home for a closer look after most likely figurin' the owner to be gone. Then Sean could get eyes on this intruder. Call him out for sneakin' looks at his home. Shoot him if the call come. He was gettin' tired of all the hateful folk what was comin' to the mountains actin' like they owned the whole of it all. Show'd little respect for where they was.

Sean seen from the sign in his scoutin' that the unknown watcher made it to his stand usin' the same small game trail east 'a where he watched from every time. Weren't no other way in or out. Sean figured to set up his watch from the straight on opposite direction of that trail. He know'd of a blow'd down white pine not a hundred paces north downstream. It was an old tree when the lightning had struck it blowin' the top two thirds some fifty paces south of where the huge trunk stayed in the ground. Its splintered top a witness to the power of nature. It was a huge tree. Tallest one around when it was kilt. Had a lot 'a big limbs in its top. One main fork, side up from the ground, ran upwards some twenty feet or more. This is where Sean figured to begin his counter watchin'. It weren't gonna be the most comfortable seat for sittin', so he hoped his prey would get curious soon.

Sean had found a good place to sit. He could see the watcher's hidin' spot full on. The limb he aimed to sit on was dead but strong. Another limb just up from his right side was broke in a way that allowed him to lay his flintlock long ways pointed straight at the back of his home. A simple lean to his right put the stock square solid to his shoulder. He figured that sittin' place a gift from God it laid so perfect for what he was needin'. The rifle was loaded with a fresh packed .54 caliber lead ball over an extra strong load giving more length to his range. We'd traded him one of our Harpers Ferry flintlocks we got in our first ever raid on a soldier's camp up West Wolf Creek several moons back. We didn't know it that night, but he was there. Watched out for us as we took a whole crate 'a them rifles from the blue coats. Killin' weren't in his plan for the watcher, but nobody was gonna move on his home if he could help it. Sean had some backbone about him. He didn't fear much.

It was a full day 'fore Sean's efforts brought him answers. A short glimpse of a shadow movin' just as light was fadin' to dark. There may 'a been only one watcher before, but they was three of 'em now. Crouched low. Slippin' up on the back door of his log home. All had long guns. He never seen 'em come to their hidin' place. No tellin' what happened. They probably decided to slip in from another direction. Bein' three now told Sean they was there for no good. Sean allowed the one warrior must 'a found his home then took what knowledge he'd got of any valuables back to the other two. Now all three had come to rob him, of that he had no doubt. Probably wantin' his mule. That weren't gonna happen. He had his mule with him. His rifle and his knives as well. The only other thing left home 'a value was what little gold he had hid and a short list 'a provisions. That weren't worth killin' a body over, most times.

Sean waited to see what the lookers had in mind to do. Kinda angry watchin' stangers invade his home ground. Lookin' in his windows. Tryin' to get in the front door. Slippin' around his barn. He wanted to shoot all three of 'em for what he know'd they wanted. Save some other poor soul the trouble. But these was warriors. A mistake would cost him his life. He know'd it best to just bide his time. Stay calm. Maybe they'd not cause him to do somethin' he might feel bad over later, or not.

Chapter 10 - A Hunt on Yellow Mountain

Elizabeth lived with the England family toward the south end of the Choestoe Valley not far from Wolf Creek. She was not born of Mrs. England, but always seen her as Mother. She loved Mrs. England. Mr. England, too. I met her for the first time just after Mr. England was killed one evening by a mean black bear sow what come with her pack lookin' for food. Black Oak was camped close by at the time, but he heard the fight too late. Got to Mr. England just as the bear broke his neck with a slap of its front paw. Black Oak dove on its back as it tried to make its escape. He killed it with his long knife by finally stabbin' it in the heart. Suffered a mean claw slash across his chest 'fore it was all over. Left him a long scar for the effort. I seen that scar fresh the day after it was made. The day I met George Black Oak for the first time in my life. He was roastin' rabbit for breakfast while we was camped on Wolf Creek. The biggest Cherokee I ever saw. None come close in my whole put together.

The England farm was a proper farm. They had a bait 'a kids dependin' on it. She grow'd all kinds 'a stuff from food eats to herbs for cookin' and healin', to nuts and fruit, to tobacco. Grow'd a small cornfield for her jug whiskey on top 'a short ridge runnin' west from Yellow Mountain. Me and Wolf like to hunt that field for deer and hogs in the late fall. It was higher up in the mountains than most cornfields, that made her harvest late. Draw'd game food there later in the cold time than farther down in the valley. Wolf killed the biggest buck whitetail I ever saw on the edge 'a that field late one evening. I'll never forget it. Wolf allowed it was spiritual. I allowed it was near unbelievable, but then many things I saw Wolf do seemed that way.

We was camped for that hunt in a big flat place at the head of a good set 'a falls near a small creek what head watered on a farm owned by the Helton family. It laid near the north end of the Blood. Kinda southeast 'a Yellow Mountain. Great place for settin' up camp in late winter. Them flats laid low off the big tops. That kept the cold winds what could blow that time 'a year more over your head than down low on camp. I'd listened to wind blow over my head in that holler so hard it sounded like thunder rollin' through the big tree tops above ye, but still be able to sit comfortable and light my pipe with no trouble. You could get night spook when that happened. Made what was around you not feel right. I was always thankful we camped where we did when I heard that sound durin' the night while bedded down. Bein' in hard winds in the woods is spooky night or day.

The ground between Yellow Mountain and Blood Mountain ain't nothin' but a big ol' gap, really, they lay so close. Huge. Both sides of the gap is steep with hollers runnin' in three different directions. It was fun to hunt. You could slip up on critters in them hollers from three different ways. Near always able to hunt with the wind in your face if you worked it right. Wolf and me know'd how. We took a lot 'a meat in them hollers over the years. For sure after we got our new flintlocks. Them huntin' places laid above where we'd camped to the southwest near the head of the falls. From where we was camped, it was an easy walk to good huntin' on either side of the big gap.

But, easy as it was with game a plenty, that ain't where Wolf was aimin' to hunt that year. He had a pull for a certain big ol' buck what lived on top 'a Yellow Mountain, just above the England's special cornfield. Been there for the last two seasons that we know'd of. Wolf missed him already once the first season he found him. He was big then.

The first time he shot at it was durin' matin' time for the deer. Wolf was sittin' a limb watchin' the buck's back trail just off the top. Caught it after leavin' a scent tree it'd rubbed and pawed around. It was a hard shot to make with a bow. He missed it clean. Never found his arrow. He wanted another go at matchin' wits with that wily old buck. This time with his Harpers Ferry .54 caliber flintlock musket. Wolf could hit with that thing, too. We practiced a right smart with 'em. To Wolf, huntin' that deer was a smoke fire story what hadn't ended yet.

"Jeb," Wolf said as we sat enjoyin' our pipes the first night before we started our hunt. "I would like to go back to the big top. Hunt for the one I call Slew of Foot. I've heard no word that any warrior has taken this deer, so I believe him to be there still. Only a true warrior could find him, so if no warrior has taken him, Slew Foot will still be there. I would like to lay trail to the top of Yellow Mountain. Move west toward the cornfield to start our hunt. We must leave long before Old Man Sun strikes light to the big tops. Stay there until we find him. Bring home fresh meat to hang in our smoke shed. What say you, Jebediah Collins, my brother?"

He called me by my full name from time to time. I reasoned it was his way 'a makin' sure the ancestors know'd it was okay for me to trail with him, bein' white and all. I never cottoned to that way 'a thinkin'. I cared none to be talkin' to the voices 'a dead folk. Not sure he ever heard real voices. He never said he did, but he'd talk to 'em. I only ever talked to God, Jesus or Holy Spirit in my definin'. The Three-In-One. I know'd They listen.

"I'll go with ye, Wolf," I said kinda slow like, enjoyin' the warmth from the fire. "I ain't holdin' no notion I want 'a climb ol' big Yellow, I don't, but I'll go with ye. I don't want you to be feared 'a such bein' you'd have to go alone if'n I didn't make the climb. So, yeah, I'll make that trail with ye. I wanna see ol' Slew Foot took myself. I look forward to it. I'll be ready to leave when you say. It is a good trail you have set. I pray the Great Spirit shines on our hunt as He walks it with us."

"You are being so funny, my friend, that if I laugh it will hurt my middle. You know I have no fear of this deer. I look forward to being alone in the woods with him. That thinking gets my blood hot. Makes my feet want to run to the top 'a Yellow. It is you, my Blood Brother, that I will fear for if ol' mean Slew Foot comes for us. He may not walk with his ancestors, but he can play tricks on your eyes. Do not worry, my fair-haired friend, I will take care of you if he comes. You do not have to fear." We both laughed as we made ready to bed down.

Our walk started way 'fore daylight. We wore our cold time skins packin' our possibles pouch, rifle, and five loads 'a powder and shot. These loads was already packed in tight, little meal sack fingerlings of cloth. Looked like about half your pointer finger cut off with a lead ball stuck in the end of it. Made loadin' a lot quieter, faster. You just had to worry over keepin' 'em dry. Dad come up with the figurin' on them little fingerlings of load. Built 'em for huntin'. That way you didn't have to carry a noisy ol' powder horn what tended to bang off your knife or gun barrel while stalkin'. With Dad's little handy pouches, powder, wadin' and ball was all in the load. You just untied two small strings on the powder end 'a the sack, then stuck it powder first in the end of your gun barrel. The primin' powder was in below the ball, so all you had do was pinch that little bit of powder between the finger and thumb of your right hand while pourin' the front contents down the barrel kinda guidin' it and rollin' it with the fingers of your left hand. That action put the powder in real smooth like. Made it slide even down to the bottom of the gun barrel without catchin' up. Worked like lickin' syrup off a fresh cut apple slice. Momma made sure we always fetched them little sacks back to her. They bothered her sewin' 'em.

The climb up the south side 'a Yellow Mountain, at a steady pace durin' the day when a body could see, took near two hours from where we was camped. In the dark, I figured three to make the top sure. We could see enough to walk by what light Old Man Moon could afford. If it were a dark night, we'd not be able to move at all without lanterns or a pine torch. I know'd what we'd do. Wolf would call halt near daybreak. We'd make ready our rifles for firing. Commence the hunt for ol' Slew Foot from wherever it was that we stopped when light got to breakin'. Stalk our way up lookin' for sign as we went. The top on Yellow ain't real big. Kinda long; skinny side-to-side. I never killed nothin' up there. Near did one time, but the cornfield off to the west was a good place to hunt.

Once you're within a half mile 'a the top, the main ridge leadin' up from the south starts to seem like big ol' steps the Great Creator would walk on His Self. Three all total. The last being sharp and steep like a mule's face when it's sleepin'. I liked huntin' off that steep, but I never liked climbin' it.

It was a while after Old Man Sun had made his self-full know'd that Wolf found our first sign 'a Slew Foot.

An old rub on a good-sized oak sapling just at the break of the last flat 'fore makin' the top. It meant the deer was still there when matin' season come a moon back. They made little sign after they got to runnin' females good. For sure, when they got done. The main way to find 'em late in the season was to find where they was feedin'. To find that, you gotta find what they are eatin'. Bucks that run the tops eat what they can find. Unfortunately for the squirrels a lot 'a times, that means buried acorns. The very ones the squirrels had worked so hard to bury back durin' the time of falling leaves. We walked the flat real careful like. Lookin' for the least little leavin' that would tell us anything about where the deer might be. You had to go slow, look close. Wolf know'd bucks used where they was comfortable. Only did different when they was fightin' for does prior to breedin' season.

The next sign we found was feed sign. Deer had been scourin' in amongst turkey scratchin's lookin' for acorns. The turkeys would scratch back the leaves while feedin', then the deer would move in to eat the acorns the turkeys missed while lookin' for grubs and bugs. Worked out perfect for all involved 'cept the squirrels. But, thinkin' on it, I don't recall ever seein' no hungry squirrel what weren't dispositioned in some way, sick or aged. I'd seen deer mixed in among turkeys many times late in the cold time sharin' the effort to find food. Nature's way 'a providin' for both hungry critters. God's creation never ceased to amaze me the whole time I lived in the woods. Near miraculous when you thought on it. Findin' that sign stopped Wolf dead in his tracks. It was fresh. That morning fresh. Slew Foot's track was clear. No question. He'd been in there feedin' recent. Wolf eased down to one knee lookin' toward the top. I did the same.

"Jeb, we have found him. He is close. Stay put right here. I want to slip around. Check his sign. I will be back."

Yellow Mountain is a big mountain. Covers a lot 'a ground. Has several ridges what meet up toward the main top. We was on the south side 'a the big top. Not far above where the Mrs. England grow'd her jug corn. It was steep all around where we was, but down near the field it was mostly flat with steep all around on the sides. Off to the west was an ivy thicket you wanted to stay out of. 'Course, that's where Wolf would have to go. He know'd the big buck would be beddin' in them ivies 'cause that growth held the heaviest cover of any place around the main top. He allowed if he could find where the buck slept, he'd stand a good chance 'a catchin' him comin' back to bed down. It was a chance I figured he was gonna take. I sat fast. Watchin' for any movement in the holler below me or the shallow gap behind me. I saw no game. Wolf come back.

"I have found his home, Jeb. We must move to the edge of the cornfield. He is gone from there now, but he will come back soon. His trail cuts through the north corner of the field. We will wait in a big white pine just east of where he will pass. His trail will take him west. My shot will be long, but it is a shot I will make. I fear any closer will spook this one. I will make sure of my rest. Help steady my aim. This one is big. He must be wise. I've left no scent to warn him. He will come when he is tired to find rest where he feels he will not be found. I will shoot him as he comes to the east edge of the field. There he will stop before stepping out into the open. I know he will come. He is tired from mating season. He will come to sleep before light is gone. We will be ready."

Wolf weren't stretchin' it. I seen that right off after we'd climbed the big white pine. It would be a long shot if the old buck show'd himself. Wolf was mighty confident we was gonna see this deer 'fore dark. I never doubted him with anything he ever said, but I remember thinkin' while we sat that big white pine, this might be the time he missed something. Some tidbit 'a sign he'd seen wrong or figured different than what it really was. Deer just don't settle in on doin' things the same way all the time. They're jittery critters. I've seen 'em run right by me plumb out 'a sight, then turn around and run right back by headin' to the exact same place they'd come from to start with. I never figured 'em too good. I'd watched too many do things what made no sense that I could figure. Still, if the thing show'd up, I'd not be surprised, neither. Wolf was a full blood Cherokee from a family what believed heavy in the spirit world. They was Christian, but their worship was mighty spiritual. I seen it firsthand so to speak.

It was movin' on toward dark. Wolf had kinda scooted himself into a way 'a sittin' that let him move the butt of his gun to aim toward the place he figured ol' Slew Foot to pass. If he come, Wolf would have a clear shot, just longer than you wanted when shootin' at deer. Had to be seventy or eighty 'a Dad's paces. Wolf was gonna need a little luck to kill this deer. Sittin' half way up a big ol' pine tree with a limb for a rest and the deer walkin', that would be a challenge if it come to be.

"They come," Wolf whispered a while after we'd got set. "Do not move, Jeb. Make no sound. Breathe very softly. I must be patient. Wait for the shot to open. The wind is right. He will never know we are here. Watch now. Make sure I hit where I aim."

I didn't see no deer. Nobody could 'a seen any deer 'cause they weren't none there. Least ways a body couldn't see 'em. Wolf know'd, though, somehow. I don't know how, but he did. 'Cause I seen 'em just a bit after he'd whispered they was comin'. Level back lines spread several paces apart movin' through the dusky dark. Steady. Not stoppin'. Not searchin' the air for trouble. Just walkin'. The first one eased up on the edge of the field stoppin' right where Wolf said Slew Foot would stop. He was a young buck. Healthy. Looked good for eatin'. His forks was showin' good. The second was some older but still not a big, nasty mountain buck like we was waitin' on. The third one I figured was gonna get shot when I seen him ease up to the spot where I know'd Wolf would pull his trigger, but he didn't. I near draw'd on that deer as he eased out 'a sight on the other side of the field. He was a good one. Several pounds of meat just walkin' away. We just let it walk off. Had I lost my mind? That meat was some good lookin' eats. I turned to look at Wolf. He was starin' hard at where the openin' was, but it was empty of deer. I could not figure why he let that last buck go. That buck had to be ol' Slew Foot. I was gettin' a little frustrated that we didn't shoot at least one 'a them bucks after all we'd done to get there when I caught sight of a dark brown form movin' like a haint down the same trail the other bucks had come on, and it was a big haint, too. I could see that from how it moved – steady. Different than the younger bucks. More majestic. Like royalty on show. I'd never seen a deer that big. His antlers looked like one 'a Dad's rockin' chairs what sat out on our porch for folks to rock in. Not Black Oak's rocker, but one of normal size. I started shakin' just like I know'd Wolf was. No true hunter ever pulled a trigger on game meat that weren't shakin' just a little. Wolf always said it was a spiritual thing to kill meat. I believed that. I considered it a gift from the Great Creator.

The deer weren't stoppin'. I watched as it moved ever so steady right into the spot Wolf wanted him to be. BOOM! Wolf's flintlock exploded sooner than I figured it would. Near jumped me from the tree it spooked me so. I settled myself. Dropped down a couple limbs right quick to see if I could catch a glimpse from under the cloud 'a smoke what blow'd out the end 'a Wolf's rifle. The buck's front half never made it through the openin' 'fore Wolf dropped flint on the big buck. I've never seen such in my life after I got clear 'a the powder smoke. The rocking chair antlers was layin' still as a stump. That deer was graveyard dead right where it stood when Wolf let go. He'd made a perfect kill shot from near eighty paces. I'm not sure anybody would 'a believed how good that shot was if I'd not been there as witness. It made me mighty proud to be his friend.

***

I could see Elizabeth as me and Wolf stood a top our mule's backs in a small gap what cut through the last ridge 'fore comin' on the England place. Our trail to help find Laughing Beaver had begun. Our mules didn't mind us standin' on their backs. I did it all the time with Peter when out on trail. Standin' on him that way give me a better view bein' higher up. Helped me see game or trouble comin' sooner, if it was there. Wolf hadn't named his mule yet. It took Indians a while to name things they'd get, if it needed a name. Names was sacred to 'em. Important. Let folks know what kinda thing it was what got named. Dad finally give Wolf the mule he'd been ridin' for his fourteenth birthday several moons back. He figured the time was right for Wolf, and me. I was so proud he'd got his own mule 'cause that gift give us a lot more freedom in the woods when huntin' or scoutin'. Didn't have to stay as close all the time when each person had their own mule to ride. One could look high on a ridge with the other low in half the amount 'a time as havin' to walk. Covered more ground that way. We'd made up signals we could use to let the other know what we'd found whenever we split up to search for whatever it was we needed to find at the time. Another thing was, it give Wolf his own way 'a gettin' around so he didn't have to ride double with me on Peter when travelin' a long trail. Just that helped a sight in our adventurin'. I think Peter was proud Wolf got a mule. Give another one like his self to trail with.

"Why ain't you named that mule 'a yours yet, Wolf? I ain't heard you call him nothin' in particular," I asked kinda pesterin' like as we sat back down to ride on to the England's place. Me leadin'. "I've done give you a bait 'a good names. You should pick one, so I know what to call him when I'm talkin' to him," I said with a big grin Wolf couldn't see.

"It does not matter what you say to him, Jeb. I have taught him not to listen to any words but mine. He is smart. I must choose his name wisely. The Great Spirit will speak to me on this. When that time comes, I will give him his name. Then you will know. Now, I am curious. Why would you talk to my mule? Has he ever spoken to you? If he has, we must go to see Old Mother. Get you something to clean out your ears."

I didn't need to go see no medicine woman. I would tell him he was actin' like a sister but then we'd be off our mules wrestlin' on the ground. He could have his worry over namin' a common ol' mule. But, I know'd how he felt. Peter's name come to me with no doubt attached. Fit him, too. I'd pick on Wolf more later 'bout namin' his mule. Right then, I was more interested in seein' Elizabeth, so I give it some time 'fore I said anything else.

"You name your mule when you feel it right, my friend. He is a good mule. Peter trusts him from what I've seen on trail. You are right. He must have the proper name. I will wait for your hearin' from Holy Spirit. I am curious, though, as to what his name will be."

The farm was mostly cleared with a few stands 'a oaks scattered about. Bein' late spring like it was, Mrs. England had all her kids out workin' the growin' spots gettin' 'em ready for plantin'. Might 'a planted some already. We'd know soon 'cause we weren't long from bein' to their place. We was still too far away to see which child was which, but I know'd Elizabeth was there. Know'd she'd be in the bunch 'cause all the kids was expected to work for the harvest. Their new Dad weren't much. He was a woodsman of sort. Fooled everybody into thinkin' he was good to start. Turned out to be a nasty one. Got caught lyin' to folks for profit. He stayed gone most all the time that I know'd of. Elizabeth never carried on like she missed him. The Cherokee didn't like him. That could turn out bad for him. Dad wouldn't speak about him. Wolf didn't like him. I didn't like the way he treated Elizabeth. Could be he'd been asked to leave. If not by Mrs. England, then by some concerned folk what know'd the trouble he caused the family. I hated it for Elizabeth, Mrs. England. Not havin' a man around the farm was bad in a way. Give other menfolk a reason to stop by, good or bad dependin'. That worried Elizabeth. I could tell when she spoke of it. Well, the way I figured it, she'd not be havin' to worry over such as that much longer. Holy Spirit done give me the plan. I loved Elizabeth. Needed to be with her. Wanted to protect her from such as Laughing Beaver slippin' around the valley lookin' to take or harm. Provide for her. See to her. Hold her. Soak of a night in the hemlock tub full 'a hot water with her. The full moon shinin' whole on her beauty. Them kinda thoughts was new to me. Thinkin' on it was more than I could stand without her bein' beside me to talk to. I wondered what Momma was gonna say.

Chapter 11 - I Declare for Elizabeth

Elizabeth had grow'd some. I'd not seen her since late fall before. We'd kept a few pounds 'a ramps out for Mrs. England and her brood. She had a lot 'a kids about the place, but like Elizabeth, they weren't all hers through birth. She'd got a few through family bein' kilt. Others abandoned on her doorstep. Settler kids what couldn't be cared for by their folks. Mrs. England was a faithful Christ follower. She loved 'em all. They was one there for a while what looked different in the face than most folk. Walked a little different. Couldn't talk good. Nobody wanted him. Mrs. England did. She took him in. Loved on him. He always wanted to ride Peter when we come. I'd throw him up on his back. Lead him around for near an hour sometimes. He never wanted to go away from the house, though, so we walked in a big ol' circle all around the place. He'd just smile and sing. Wavin' at the other kids. He loved to sing. I don't know why, but Peter would dip his head up and down when that kid sang. It was the strangest thing for him to act that 'a way. I never figured that. I studied on it a right smart, too. Wolf allowed it was spiritual. It was just a big ol' time for that little boy bein' up on Peter. He was a sweet kid. Died early the year before we come that spring. Consumption got him. He weren't never a healthy kid. I missed seein' him when we rode up.

A couple others was slave kids she'd bought to give freedom. Dad helped her in that. I remember when they come. Some strange kinda folks brought 'em late one night durin' a hard rain what'd been fallin' for a couple days. Jip-cees, Dad called 'em. Them young 'uns was scared near to death judgin' from what Elizabeth told me later. Couldn't speak a word 'a English. Them Jip-cees never said how they come by 'em. Just dropped 'em there for mercy. A runner was sent next morning to fetch Dad. I went along with him. They was from A-Free-Ka as the Indians said it. We all know'd where it was. Momma show'd us places what was talked about in the Bible. Our big ol' Bible had maps on the inside pages it was such a big book. Good for bustin' "Bible Knots" when you got 'em on your hand down under your skin. That smarted like hell's fire when you grow'd one what had to be busted. I had one between my pointer finger and my middle finger on my right hand once. Dad had Anne hold my arm steady while he slammed that Bible down so hard I heard the knot pop at the same time I felt it pop. When I could see clear again from the pain leavin', the bump was gone. Black around where it was from the bustin', but gone. He busted one for Dancing Bear one time. He never flinched as the Bible did its chore. On another man I saw him do, that slammin' down made blood shoot plumb out from under the Bible after the knot popped so hard it made the blood tear through his skin. That man went out cold from the pain. But it hurt like the devil havin' 'em, so folks had no choice, really. Them things was awful. Anne never slammed 'em with the Good Book. She'd poke 'em. That must 'a hurt just as bad 'cause full grow'd men would come runnin' out 'a the house screamin' like a wildcat after they'd got loose from her. She'd tie folks down if she needed. You never wanted to have something so bad as to have her tie you down. I remember a man who come to her for a broke tooth. The pain was more'n he could stand so he come to her for some relief. That poor soul.

Me and Dad was inside the barn workin' on a mule when he come. Had two of his boys with him. They rode a couple 'a Dad's trade mules. We know'd 'em so we went out the barn to say howdy. Dad figured right away we might be needed foretold by the homespun rag what was tied across the top of the man's head holdin' tight his bottom jaw. We know'd what was comin'. There was times when doctorin' was almighty painful. Weren't nothin' for the pain 'cept brandy. Owl made up some stuff what helped when healin' but the doctorin' part could hurt a right smart. Me and Dad and Cain would sometimes have to hold folks while Anne was workin' on 'em. Mostly to keep her from gettin' hurt. I saw her get knocked plumb out from a head butt when she was workin' on a man's teeth one time.

"Luther, my friend. Why you got a rag tied around your jaw? You havin' teeth problems?" Dad asked. All Mr. Luther could do was nod. "Well, you're in luck, kinda. Anne is here. She can make you better in just a minute if you'll let her. I'll warn you, though, Luther, we may have to tie you down to get it done. Is that gonna be okay with you, Luther?" Dad asked as he tried not to let Mr. Luther see him grinnin'.

"Tuied duuwn?" Luther near screamed as best he could with his mouth tied up tight and full a' homespun. "Whuut oooh say? NOOO! Don't duu. Nooo."

"Well, now, I ain't sayin' she'll need us to but if we need to tie you off is that okay, Luther? I mean, it looks like you got some painful hurt goin' on in that mouth 'a yours. If you don't want to be tied down, maybe us and the boys can just hold ya. How'd that be, Luther?"

"Yuuu laave ma be, Tuumpy! I'll see ta whuu huuls me duuwn. Joust lut Auune say whut, hare, Tuumpy?"

"Okay, Luther. We'll see what she says. But if you need tyin', I'll oblige it done fer ye. Won't cost you no extra. Wouldn't want Anne to slip cuttin' anything off, don't you see." Luther reached out to try and hit Dad. He really had Luther goin'.

Anne looked in his mouth once we got him in to the cook room. She ordered him laid out on the fixin' table. She gave him the choice of bein' tied off or held, but she didn't tell him what the cure was. He'd a not stayed still if she'd told him.

"Mr. Luther, I hope you can hear me. I'm gonna have to cause you some pain to fix this tooth. It is broken in such a way that I cannot remove it. If we do not fix this tooth, you may get very sick. For sure you will be in severe pain for many days to come. If I doctor this tooth, it will be better tomorrow with only a small amount of pain. Your choice, but if you decide to be worked on, I will require you be tied down or held. I advise you to be tied down. You think while I get what I need. If you decide to let me see to you, drink several swigs of some brandy before I get back. I will do this quickly to cause you the least amount of pain. What say ye?"

We was all holdin' Mr. Luther down flat 'a his back on the fixin' table when Anne come back into Momma's cook room. She was holdin' a small piece 'a antler with a tiny sliver of metal stickin' out from its end. Weren't much bigger than a thick tail hair of a horse 'bout two inches long with a half hook bend on the end. Looked to be part of a nail Dad would use to fix shoes on his stock, but it was smaller around. Anne said later it was something she'd made to help pull sewin' thread up tight for mendin' after she'd sew'd up a cut or what not. It worked out good for what she was fixin' to do to Mr. Luther.

"Mr. Luther, can you hear me?" Anne asked from across the room by the cookstove. "I am fixin' to work on you so open your mouth wide. Be ready when I come your way." She opened the cookstove door. Hot coals lay silent from the morning meal. I never know'd what she was doin' till she come back over. Her hand behind her back.

"Okay boys. Hold tight. Dad, put your left hand over his eyes. Your right on his chin. Keep your hands clear, and for sure, Dad, don't let him shut his mouth. I mean it, Dad. Don't let him shut his mouth. Here we go."

I could not believe what I saw next. It hurt me to my backbone just watchin' it. Out from behind her back, Anne brought the small tool. The sliver of metal was glowin' red hot. She steadied her left hand on top 'a Dad's which was layin' over Luther's chin, then usin' her right to guide the hot steel, she drove that small, red-hot sliver down into the roots of that broke tooth without a slow motion one. Worked it all 'round inside the break burnin' out the roots what was showin'. It took all we had to hold Luther's body down once he went to convulsing from all the serious pain he was feelin'. Dad near lost a thumb tryin' to keep his mouth open. I took an elbow to the side 'a my head what near laid me out. Anne no sooner burnt that hole but what she went back to reheat the metal point. Three times she had to do that. Mr. Luther went out after the second. He didn't wake till the next day. His tooth a little sore but nothin' near the throbbin' he'd been livin' with. He gave Anne three layin' hens for helpin' him out. He was real appreciative. We eat 'em for supper. Dad had plenty what laid eggs, so we didn't need 'em. They eat good.

Elizabeth was drawin' to me as she walked toward where I stopped Peter to dismount. I tried to go on like I'd not seen her, but we'd caught eyes. Weren't no goin' back now. 'Sides, I didn't want to. I never understood why my heart stopped every time she come near. It didn't matter that she wore her farmin' clothes, sun hat and apron. Had sweat leakin' down the sides of her perfect face, across her lips. Her chestnut hair hangin' out from under her hat on both sides of her head callin' to me like one 'a them sirens I'd read about in one 'a Momma's books. Some hangin' down the back made sure I seen her full. She didn't try to hide herself when she seen us. She come straight on over. The knee places on her apron covered in fresh dug earth. Rich, dark Choestoe earth. Her hands dirty. *They'd started plantin'*. Mrs. England grow'd her harvest the same way every year. If it weren't a real wet spring where dropped taters would keep and not rot, she'd plant earlier than most folks. She grow'd a lot 'a different things, but she was know'd for her sour cabbage and peppers. I always liked eatin' with her.

"Hello, Miss Elizabeth," I managed to say after gettin' off Peter's back, removin' my hat and squarin' up to her. I had to lock my knees for fear 'a them foldin' up underneath me when she started talkin' back. "It is good to see you workin' in the . . . I mean . . . not good to see you workin' . . . I mean . . . yeah . . . good you're workin' . . . no . . . uh . . . it's good to see . . . you . . . here . . . in the garden . . . uh . . . here I mean . . . workin' . . . no, uh . . . it's good to see . . . you. Not workin', seein' you . . . uh . . . just good seein' . . . you. In the person. Uh, yeah . . ." *Way to go, stupid, I thought.*

"Hello, Jeb -- Wolf," she giggled out payin' little mind to him. She'd stopped uncomfortable close in front 'a me. Face on. Lookin' me in the eye. I was some taller.

"Good morning to you, Miss Eli-sa-beth," Wolf said back grinnin'. He had trouble sayin' her name. Didn't fit his mouth right. "It is good to see you safe. Your family well. Jebediah, I will take the mules to the barn. Tend to them. You come when you wish."

I heard what he said, but I didn't hear it, neither. Elizabeth had grabbed my left hand in her right while I weren't payin' mind to how she was movin'. The touch of her fingers had dumbed me. Her blue eyes had taken the air straight from my lungs. My heart beat so hard once it got back workin', I figured it to pop like a skillet fried frog leg when you bit into it. How could a maiden do such to a young buck like me. We needed to talk. I had to get set with this goin' on or get from it. Her pull was just too much. She know'd it, too, I believe.

"I've been waiting for you to come, Jeb. I would like to speak with you on matters of private concerns. Will you spend some time with me this evening? Just the two of us -- alone. My mother knows. We will sit where I go to pray. It is near. I will go there after supper. You must find me. If you do, I will speak to you. If you do not, I will not speak with you. What say ye, Jebediah?" She grinned, mockin' Wolf, who was mockin' me.

She was meant for me. I reckon I'd know'd it since the first time I seen her. I remembered she did something to me that time, too, far as breathin' went. We was young then. I would like to speak to her for sure. I allowed it was a good thing Wolf taught me trackin' 'cause I sure wanted to sit with her. But I weren't gonna need none 'a them skills for findin' her prayin' place. I already know'd where it was. Little flat place up the creek a good ways. Nice place near a smooth pool backed up from a beaver's home. It was a good place for prayers or talkin' or for a smoke. It was a quiet place. Me and Wolf had found it a few moons back while out on a walk. We'd looked in on her but she didn't know of it. We was just lookin' out for ours. It was the way.

"You go. I will find you. There is nowhere in these mountains you can hide from me," I said as I moved in a little closer while grabbin' her other hand in mine. That put us near nose-to-nose. Her scent made my muscles go tight. She smelled like dirt soap. The feelin' I pulled from it touched me deep. "To tell it honest, I was aimin' to ask you for some time to talk as well, Miss Elizabeth. I look forward to our sit down later. You can tell Mrs. England I'll be a safe escort for you, if you choose to tell her of our comin' together to talk. She ain't gotta fear you bein' with me. I'll make sure no trouble comes for ya."

I don't know what come over me. My insides kinda took over. It felt like somebody else was movin' for me when I let go her hands, grabbin' her by the shoulders. My eyes was starin' into hers. I couldn't move, but I was movin'. I ain't never in my whole put together tried to stop what I was doin' and try to keep doin' it at the same time, 'cause I didn't want to, yet, I wanted to. What was happenin'? I pulled her gently to my person. Our lips come together near straight on which was just fine with me. The taste of her sweat mixed with her soft lips on mine near made me lose thought. My heart exploded inside my chest. It started painin' me again it was beatin' so hard. I had no control. Never did I have trouble steadyin' myself to shoot folks or game meat with bow or gun, but there weren't no relief from what I was sufferin'. It was the best feelin' pain I ever remember in my life. I did not want it to end.

Mrs. England had a huge spread laid out for us when supper come that evening. Took a bait 'a food to feed everybody. All total they was seven 'a` them kids, not countin' Elizabeth. She was part of a group 'a women livin' there what totaled five, even though she'd just turned thirteen recent, she was still looked out for as a woman. She did a woman's work, they considered her a woman. Three of 'em helped with the place when they was there. Most of the time they was off doin' "the work of the Lord" as "they were called." Could be there stayin' or not. They always said they went where they was told. I understood that. Disobeyin' the Great Creator was dangerous business. They was four originally, but only three had come back. Nobody know'd where the fourth had got off to. The Indians couldn't even find her trail. They figured her for bein' took to the spirit world. Stopped lookin' for her after a time.

The fifth lady I believed to be Momma to one 'a them boys what lived there. He weren't but four years old. She was young enough to be his older sister. It made sense them bein' together. I liked 'em both. She was sweet, but very shy. I know'd enough about her to know her way 'a life weren't by her choosin'. The boy was normal. Curious, with an adventurous side. Reminded me 'a Wolf the way he did. I'd always spend some time with him in the woods when I come, if I had time. He liked bein' out in the woods.

True to her word, not long after supper Elizabeth slipped off. Wolf, too, which made me curious 'cause he know'd what I aimed to do that evening. Her momma give me a couple wanderin' looks while we was eatin' but paid me no mind while cleanin' up afterwards. I eased on out the door without sayin' nothin'. I seen the four-year-old while shuttin' the door. He wore a big grin across his face. His momma standin' over him wore a little one, too. That told me all what lived there know'd where I was headed. I didn't care. It was Elizabeth what needed to hear what I had to say, if I could say it. I didn't know love other than what I'd learned from the Bible. God, others--family. I didn't really know what the word was supposed to mean when it come to speakin' with common folk, other than to look out for their needs, but I know'd I didn't want to be far away from Elizabeth. That was something I was tired 'a worryin' over. She stirred up my thinkin'. Made it where I couldn't reason good when out on trail 'cause my thoughts kept jumpin' over to her side 'a the fence. With all the strangers on the trails lately, losin' thought could slip you into trouble 'fore realizin' trouble was there. As I trailed upstream to her prayin' place, I felt real, gut bindin' fear. That girl scared me.

She had a small fire goin' by the time I got to her prayin' place. Dark was all around. Me knowin' where she was let me go straight to her. She wouldn't be expectin' me as quick as I'd really got there. That give me a little time, so I stood off in the night, watchin'. She moved like smoke driftin' on a day with little breeze. Gone were the clothes for plantin' work. Takin' their place, Cherokee-made skins and settler-knitted homespun. Foot skins what come to her knees. Stitched skin leggings tied off watertight runnin' near seamless down the sides of her legs. For sure done by a very crafty soul whoever made 'em. Her top was a tall in the neck long sleeve, homespun shirt with a wide braided leather belt tied tight over the top of her waist. A bone handled short knife was laced level into that belt just above her left hip. Easy to grab with her right hand if need be. I recognized the work on that handle. Same bone as mine. Come from one 'a the best knife makers in the mountains, George Black Oak. The front of her hair laid pulled back over the back tied with a small leather strap what held several beautiful beads. She was the vision of perfection for my world. We would talk. I needed to find out just how deep into my world she felt like walkin'. I hoped it was to the center of my soul 'cause that's where I felt her most. We was fixin' to find out. I prayed for words as I made myself known. The warmth from her fire offered comfort. It was a good place for a talk.

"Elizabeth, I have found you," I said as I walked out from the north edge of the darkness, stoppin' when I felt the heat from her fire good. I put my hands out over the flames to warm 'em some. "I told you I would. You've built a nice warmin' fire. Should I fetch in some more wood?"

"Welcome, Jebediah. I am glad you found me. No, I keep plenty of wood here for when I come to pray," she said as she moved to the edge of the fire opposite me. It was strange the way she was doin'. Like she was scared or what not. "I knew you would. I've heard stories told of you and Wolf. You are a known woodsman. The Cherokee call you "Spirit Filled One." They speak of how you survived the blue birth. Wolf is the son of Dancing Bear. Brother to Moon Shadow. A keeper of the valley. I had no doubt you would find me. I just wanted a little time to pray before you came. You were watching me. I felt your eyes. You should know. I, too, am very spiritual. A gift given me by Holy Spirit. I praise Him for it."

"Is this why you pray, Elizabeth? Because you search for the things you are to know? It is good to know the will of the Holy One. You would know then, why I am here, yes, Elizabeth?" I asked hopefully.

"No, Jeb. Don't be silly. I don't see all or know all. I feel. Only an Indian can be a true seer. I am as you, Irish. I only feel things that are happening around me, and only sometimes, not always. But, yes, I feel I know why you are here. It scares me. Please talk to me, Jeb. I want to know your heart. Do not fear. I long to hear your words."

She was feared, too. That could be good or bad. What was she feared of? How I felt about her? Or how she hoped I felt about her? I was fixin' to find out.

"Elizabeth," I said as I looked down into the fire then back up at her. We locked eyes. I couldn't speak.

"Yes, Jeb? What is it? Haint got your tongue? Or has something else reached up and grabbed hold of you?" she asked while movin' toward my side 'a the fire. I moved toward her. Both most likely feelin' the same thing. We squared off with our fronts pressed together. Our faces inches apart. I could smell her. Her sweet scent was strong as we draw'd together. The kiss lasted several seconds. I hoped they weren't nobody watchin', but I know'd they was. I didn't care. Kissin' her was the most enjoyable thing I'd ever done. It was easy speakin' after we come apart. That kiss told me all I needed to know. We was meant.

"Elizabeth, I need to know something," I said kinda low so's only we could hear as my heart got to beatin' so hard I near couldn't breathe. "Maybe you can help me understand what I'm sufferin' from. I can't stop it when it starts, . . . and it's you what makes it happen. Every time I see you, my heart begins to pound inside my chest. I can't help it. The air for my lungs is hard to draw. I can't move my legs normal 'cause my knees start wigglin'. That makes me stumble when I walk. How is it you do these things to me? My thoughts always turn to you when I am alone. If I'm not careful, I will think of you all the time. Thinkin' some other boy might be over here scoutin' around gets my mad up. . .. Has there been any bucks over here scoutin' around, Elizabeth? 'Cause I don't like thinkin' they are. Why is it I think about you so much? Wolf gets mad with me about it. It bothers me when out on trail. I gotta get this settled. You gotta tell me something . . . I wanna declare for you, Elizabeth. What say ye, will you be my intended? For marryin' and family makin' when our time comes? I will be a good husband for you. Provide all you will ever need. Protect you. Be there for you. I never want to be without you. That is all I have to say. Please understand why I say these words. I cannot help how I feel."

She stood lookin' me in the eye for what seemed like a long time. She didn't smile. She didn't speak, but the look in her eyes told me my words had touched her deep. Tears got to wettin' her face some 'fore she ever spoke. Even then it was just a little squeak. No more than a slight nod as she dropped her eyes from mine while wrappin' her arms around my middle. She didn't have to speak. I know'd how hard it was to talk with a stuck throat. Her eyes spoke all I needed to hear 'fore she unhugged me, runnin' off into the night quicker than Old Man Bobcat. Wolf would follow her home. She was one of us now. It was his duty. Thompie and Celia had just got them a new future daughter. I was in love with a girl what loved me back. My life had changed for the better. I hit my knees thankin' the Great Creator 'fore leavin' her prayin' place. I would return there many times in my life. It was a special place for me and her. Always will be.

Chapter 12 - Things Ain't Always What They Seem

The vision touched Wind Is Strong. Troubled her so deep she stayed gone from our place three days after the day she woke from dreamin' it. That made it four full days her gone when she come awake her final morning 'fore comin' back home. Unfortunately for her, she'd brought no cover. No food. All she sensed was silence mixed with what wood noises they always are when morning comes. She'd seen her son. Know'd in her heart he was for sure alive. That'd be enough of a feedin' to live on forever if it took that to get him back from the cold lands of her dream. The cold lands of the north. The cold lands she'd flew over when she was Owl. Her heart cried tears. Her soul touched by a love so strong it could travel through time. Connectin' hearts through the spirit world one to the other. Holy Spirit was feelin' her pain. Comfort had to come from the One what only could provide; filled her bein'. Her mind lay scattered from the realness of what she'd seen. Her soul near broken for her boy. Nothing certain to her now but the fact she was soon goin' on a trail to find her son. It was time to have a little talk with Black Oak. She know'd what his answer would be. It was the commitment to her heart she needed to hear. Her goin' meant folks dyin'. That would need to be made clear. Smoked over. Then let him make his mind. She knew his heart, but his soul was of his own charge.

She spent the rest 'a the morning in the quiet, thinkin' on the vision. Studyin' on what was gonna happen over the next several moons. Stayin' till the day grow'd warm enough to wash 'fore comin' on to our place. She wanted to tell Black Oak 'bout her vision. Get his feelin' on what it meant. She loved us like brothers. Trusted us with all kinds 'a questions. Told us things she'd not tell others 'cept for George, but this was something she wanted him to cipher. She'd caught a fondness for Black Oak that kept her by his side most 'a the time. He didn't mind. Weren't much different than havin' another warrior along on trail. She was savvy in the ways 'a fightin'. Strong in body since gettin' full healed. Dad and Black Oak had worked with her some on how to defend your person if attacked. And, of course, how to attack if you felt the call. You'd not want her slippin' a knife out on ya. She'd already proved that.

Four days in the woods alone without washin' can leave one with a heavy scent. That weren't good if you was huntin', sure weren't good if you was plannin' on gettin' close to the one you felt for most. To get George Black Oak to spend time talkin', it took her bein' close to get his full attention. Make him comfortable enough to ask her request. He was a man of deep thought. Always considerin' the goin' on's around him. The needs of others. Her needs. Livin' free. No place of his own. Movin' here or there through the mountains. Stayin' with folks for a time or durin' different seasons like corn pullin' or plantin' time. Settler or Indian didn't matter. He treated all the people he trusted the same. He'd been stayin' in our barn for the whole time Wind Is Strong had been with us. Watchin' out for her while she healed. He'd left for a few days at different times, but mostly he spent his time on our farm close to Wind Is Strong. He'd help Dad with things to pass his time. Seein' to Wind Is Strong all he could, givin'

Momma and Anne a break from their treatin' of her wound. He enjoyed their talks. Walkin' in the woods when the seasons was in change.

As Wind Is Strong neared the pond on the upper side of our farm, she could see there was plenty 'a fire wood layin' by the iron kettle what heated the water for our big ol' hemlock tub. She know'd all the truck she'd need to start a fire includin' pine knot, steel, and flint was covered by a stone layin' in the ground just off to the west. She obliged herself.

Wind Is Strong commenced her washin' chore by gettin' a good-sized water heatin' fire goin' under the iron kettle. She climbed the hill to open the water gate enough to slowly fill the tub. Gettin' it part way full, she then changed the water flow to the kettle. It was already kinda hot from the fire gettin' goin good so it steamed a big cloud when the cool flow hit it. That big puff 'a steam, mixed with the pine knot smoke risin' dark against the sky, ought 'a do what was necessary while she washed. She filled the bamboo trough with hot water till they was plenty heatin' the tub. She eased over to the steps what dropped down into the water, and slowly stripped off her homespun and skins. Takin' her time to fold each piece stackin' 'em against the stone seats. She was in no hurry, so she stood straight for a bit reachin' high as she could to stretch herself out. Enjoyin' the late spring cold air what'd just made her body come alive. Every inch of her skin could feel the cool sting wrappin' itself around her body. That made her arms draw up in front of her chest, made the water feel warmer as she stepped in ever so slowly takin' a seat along the west side. From that seat, she could watch all the four trails what led from our farm to the tub as she made herself comfortable; waiting. A smile come to her face not long after sittin'. She was not disappointed in her plan to signal her bein' home. The sounds were faint, but they were the sounds she was hopin' to hear. Her man was comin'.

"Wind Is Strong," George said as he sat a rock seat next to the tub lookin' across to where she sat. "I saw your smoke. Figured you to be home looking to wash. I hope you have had no trouble while on your journey. Are you well? Did you go far? Did you make this trail alone? I can go for food. You must be hungry. Celia just made some fresh cornbread. The kind you like with the dried peppers. If not, you can eat when you are done here. I will sit with you while you wash. Thompie and me, we thought to go look for your sign. It is good you have returned home to us."

"I have gone nowhere, Black Oak. I was here. Praying. Fasting. Down on the rise where the stone seats are carved. Sometimes I go there to seek wisdom from Holy Spirit. See Old Man Sun light the day. This time was strangely different from any other time I'd gone there. I became so tired I had to stop praying and lay down. A deep sleep come on me not long after Old Man Sun had awakened the valley. I had a vision as I slept, Black Oak. You were a part of this vision, so listen closely. My dreams spoke to me. Holy Spirit has shown me my son. His spirit is calling to me from a land north. In my vision, I went to him. It was cold there in this land. White with snow. I am confused to what it means. I need to tell someone who can help me understand. Can you, my friend, help me with this? But, I will only listen if you come, sit with me in the water. It is warm. We can talk. That is all I have to say." She turned her head slightly to stare at the Big Bald. She almost grinned.

Black Oak wanted to hear what her vision told so he bent from his seat to take his foot skins off settin' 'em back where he'd been sittin' as he stood. Loosed his braided leather belt from around his waist. It held only his short knife what stayed laced into the belt's braids constant. Took the leather bindings from his hair, but left the hawk feather he wore most all the time. A gift from Wind Is Strong. Grabbed the top of his homespun shirt with both hands slippin' it over his head in one smooth motion. Foldin' it neatly, he laid it 'a top his foot skins. His belt a top all that. Knife on the very top for easy grabbin'. He turned to the tub. The sun shinin' on his front, showin' the lines where his muscles come together. His huge, barrel like chest risin' and fallin' as he draw'd air. He was thick from front to back. The scars layin' on his chest and shoulders, from his many near life endin' fights, made shadows on his skin. A slight pull on a simple leather cord allowed his skin leggings to fall to the ground leavin' only his homespun mid-cloth coverin' his personals. He reached to both his sides tightening the knots what held that cloth where it was. He would need to leave that on 'til after they'd vowed 'fore Holy Spirit their love for one another. He was good with that. She was worth it to him. As he stepped into the small pool, Wind Is Strong could not help but notice how grand the man was. Big in body. Strong. Quiet. Very brave. Smooth like the panther when he moved. He filled the tub as he sat next to her. The water risin' to just shy 'a the top edge. She'd learned not to fill it more than three quarters full. If she put more water in than that, it would run over the sides when he sat. There was room 'a plenty seein' how four or five folks could use it a time. It was a most wonderful thing to have. Me and Wolf sat in it all the time.

"I have missed you, Wind Is Strong," Black Oak said as he put the whole of his left arm around her back, layin' it on the top edge of the tub then easin' her toward himself. That little move draw'd her up close, face on. "You should let me go with you when you make these times for prayer. Stand watch while you speak to the Holy One. Many strangers are moving through the valley looking for gold. Some are bad folk. Very greedy. I can protect you. We should speak on this later. But, for now, I will listen to your words. Tell me of your vision. Maybe I can understand what it is saying."

She could only smile at the innocence of such a mountain of a man. Her heart felt his worry. She would make a better effort to let him know her plans. Right now, she was enjoying the closeness of his body. The warmth of the water. The heat from Old Man Sun. She put her hands on the sides of his face. Moved her lips to his, kissin' him full for a bit. Once that was done, they sat in silence. Her head on his shoulder. Listenin' to the woods sounds as Old Man Sun started his trail toward night. Then, without explanation, she broke away from their closeness. Movin' to the opposite side 'a the tub from George. She was ready to talk. He know'd from her movin' it was time for him to listen. He sat with his arms in his lap under the water. His eyes closed. His head slightly bent. His ears listenin' close as she began.

"As you know, Black Oak, I long to hold my son again. I pray for him every day I wake to Old Man Sun. There was a time when my family was whole, together. My husband provided for us. He was a warrior. A good man. Future elder with my clan. You and he would have been friends. I believe this. He was very brave the day the evil ones came. Stood his ground killing what he could before their numbers overtook our village. There were so many on that raid. He sacrificed himself as I carried our son to what I hoped would be a place to hide in the woods, but it was not to be. The evil ones had chased us exactly where they wanted us to go. Knew the direction we would escape when it all began. That is where they set their trap. That is where they caught me and my son. I will never forget how it felt when they ripped him from my arms. I never saw him again . . . until a few days ago when the vision came on me. I need to find him, Black Oak. It is time I went to get him. You know I miss him with all that I am. We have spoken of this many times, you and me. It is part of who I am as a mother."

"My soul hurts for your loss, Wind Is Strong," George said as he raised his head to look at her. "I know you love your son. It is good you want him back. A son needs his mother, father too. Tell me your vision. Let us understand where it is your son is being kept. We will go to him. Bring him to your new home here in Choestoe with us. I know we can do this. Holy Spirit will guide us. Now tell me, I am listening."

"Then listen close, my friend. Help me to understand. As my vision came to life, I could see all four directions at once. Could feel their presence. East was calling to me with a warm embrace, but I knew I should not go east to start my search. It was north, where the cold came from, that I felt in my heart was the direction I should travel, so I went. Walking as far as I could before night came. I wanted to go on even though it was dark, so the Change Spirit made me Owl. I took to the air seeing everything as if it were daylight. I kept flying till I found my son. Killed his holders without mercy. They were all older women just like those who held me captive as a slave of The Lost. As the last of the women fell, I grabbed him up tenderly in my claws taking off into the air. You were on my back, but somehow I could see you. Like I was looking from across the valley. Blood stained your winter skins. I looked to the ground. Many were dead I had no hand in killing. It was you, Black Oak. You killed them to help me rescue my son. I realized this as we kept flying through the night back to Choestoe. Landing on the small rise where the rock seats are carved. You were there. I was there, but my son was not. When I took back to the air, I searched till I could search no more. He was not with us. I need you to help me understand this. Where do I go to find my son? Tell me, Black Oak. Help me to understand."

***

Wolf and me left the England farm 'fore daylight two mornings after we'd got there. Laughing Beaver was about. That made us nervous for folks in the valley keepin' the need to make trail at the first of our thinkin'. We aimed to do our part in keepin' the evil warrior from doin' harm. Hopefully, no other young 'uns like Ruby Smith would get fetched up and killed by him. Elizabeth met us at the garden gate as we made our way out. I'd not seen her since our talk on Wolf Creek the night before. She'd just vanished. Sleep was hard to come by previous 'cause I figured I'd hurt her. My hope was that I'd see her 'fore we left. I guess now I was. Jumpin' off Peter's back, I went over to where she stood. Wolf grabbed Peter's rein leadin' him off a ways. That give us a little private time. I meant to listen more than speak as my heart got to doin' that hard beatin' in my chest thing again. I felt it was gonna pop like a bladder pouch when it gets stretched too full 'a water. I wished she'd stop doin' that to me. Made it hard to breathe, too. But even though it hurt a right smart, made it uncomfortable to draw air, I didn't mind. It was all for her. Fear rose up my back for the words I know'd I was fixin' to hear. I lifted a quick silent prayer for courage.

"Elizabeth, it is good to see you. If I hurt you last night with my words, please forgive me. I meant only to speak my heart."

"Oh, Jeb," she said as she moved in close, starin' me dead in the eye. She laid her hands across the front of my chest. "You did not hurt me with the words you spoke. They were like words of a song to me. You made my soul sing as you spoke your heart to me. It is what my heart has longed to hear from you. It, too, beats so hard in my chest when you are near that it hurts. Many times a day, every day, my thoughts turn to you. It's a condition I've had since the day I first met you five years ago. We were children, but I know how I felt then, and I know how I feel now. The pull you hooked in my heart has not changed. I want you with me all the time. You are a need I can't quit wanting for. Yes, Jeb, I will be your wife when our time comes. No other will do for me. You are the buck I want. I will let all who come, if any, know I'm spoke for. You will build us a farm, and I will help you provide for our family. I will have our children. You will be their father. I will be their mother. It is the way Holy Spirit has cut our trail. We will be one."

With all that said, we passed on by with the kissin'. Just draw'd close in a tight hug for a good while. Long enough so's Wolf had to holler for me to come on 'cause Old Man Sun was showin' already. We'd stood talkin' longer than I thought we had, but I did not want to let go. Our bodies pressin' tight after hearin' her words made it feel like we'd just become one body. Our spirits seemed to 'a wove together like homespun right in the middle where the heart grows. She was now a part 'a me. I was now a part 'a her. My thoughts had cleared. No more confusion. I know'd her heart. She know'd mine. It brought comfort knowin' we was gonna spend the rest of our lives as family. Mine and Wolf's trail to find Laughing Beaver had just become a lot less dangerous. I prayed Holy Spirit would continue to guide us.

Chapter 13 - A Bad Day at the Rock Ridge

I stood on a flat rock holdin' the reins of our mules while Wolf made his way up through the boulders to the top 'a Rock Ridge not long after we'd left the England's. Half my mind was still back with Elizabeth. He weren't totin' no truck 'cept his long knife. Left rifle and bow strapped to his mule. Not carryin' that stuff made it much easier to stay hid while slippin' around scoutin'. We know'd a place where outlaws felt comfortable bein' camped what laid off the top some to the west. He wanted to scout it out. Moon Shadow, Wolf's brother, had run up on it huntin'. We named where we was Rock Ridge back when we first found it. Not sure anybody else called it that other than us and ours. It appeared to be the end of a big top what'd slid off the mountain it was still a part of. Hooked up at the end of the new ridge what was created by the slide through a long flat place with very few rocks on its top. Had a lot 'a near grow'd, first growth trees. Mostly dogwood, poplar, pine and maple. Few acorns along the top for there weren't no oaks much. Beautiful when the leaves got to changin' their colors. At the other end 'a the ridge, huge rocks seemed to have rolled out from inside the big top durin' its slide down into the holler below. Lots of 'em what laid in the shade of the big trees around the edges of where the slide stopped had very little moss growin' on 'em. Many of the big rocks looked to have simply come to rest on the end of the new ridge once the slidin' was done. The ground kinda settlin' around each boulder makin' it easy to walk in among 'em. Near perfect for huntin'. We hunted there a lot. Big tree stumps snapped clean, from bein' rolled over by the slide, stuck up here and there like soldiers guardin' a fort full 'a rock soldiers. It was spooky there in the half-light 'cause 'a the peculiar way the rocks laid. It was one of our favorite places in all the mountains. It's where we met Spirit, the black mountain cat Wolf claimed as a totem. They was lifelong friends. She come to us many times over the years while we was out on trail, then one day she never come no more. Wolf allowed them bein' friends was spiritual. I believed it was.

Half-light in the mountains is near hauntin' if you ain't accustomed to it. Movin' through the woods as light is fadin' or growin' is plumb spiritual. Makes for a whole different world when a body travels through the mountains at dusk or dawn. Things ain't as they are, they are what your eyes see, makin' for a real soulful time. Dangerous if you don't pay mind. As the light grows dim in the evenings or fades to bright in the mornings, you can't help but get your back up. The shadows keep you watchin' for trouble as your eyes search. Your heart beats faster as your mind begins to see the things your eyes tell it are there. Your ears strain so hard listenin' for any sound they move. You can feel 'em when they do that. Feels like small, slow critters with dull claws crawlin' up the side 'a your head. All you see comes to life. Saplings move like silent hunters stalkin' game for meat. Rotting logs look like deer or hogs tryin' to slip by so's not to become a hunter's meat. It's a gift from God the way some critters see in the dark. Old stumps move like the black bear. Huge dark trees stand like giant warrior spirits fullfillin' their duty to the Great Spirit by watchin' over the mountains; watchin'.

Half-light gets a body lookin' close for trouble. Half-light in the mountains of Appalachia makes things different. You'd have to trail it to feel what I'm talkin' about. But trust me, it gets spooky movin' through the mountains in the near dark. Full moon nights durin' the cold time, when a body can see to move without lantern light, is one of my favorite times to be in the woods. Makes you feel alive.

Wolf'd stayed gone so long I got tired 'a waitin' where I was with the mules, so I eased around the ridge's south end to a more comfortable place near the old tree line where the ground was less steep. Tied 'em off in the edge of an ivy thicket out 'a sight while not knowin' for sure why Wolf hadn't made it back, but I had no worry. It weren't uncommon for him to be gone longer than he should be, so I found a nice warm spot in the sun layin' back against a big white oak for some rest. Them was my favorite trees for sittin' leaned back on. Great for nappin' 'cause their bark is slicker than other oaks or poplar. Don't gouge you too bad when you settle in for comfort.

I was near asleep, on past the time Wolf should 'a been back, when what I thought was a squirrel hollerin' brought me 'round. It was a while after Old Man Sun had passed his high point for the day. The call was strange soundin' all the three times I heard it. Sounded unnatural -- just weren't right. Could be, I guess, if the squirrel was feelin' poorly—or dyin'. Most folks I ever heard tryin' to make that call had trouble with it, but my granddad could do it perfect. You'd think you'd done wandered in under one feedin' up a big hickory tree when he got to usin' it. He'd even fooled me and Wolf on occasion. I allowed the call come from Wolf on first thought, but after wakin' some and studyin' on it, that didn't set right. I come to realize that Wolf would never cause such a noise like that out in the woods if he could help it . . . then it hit me like a punch in the gut . . . it weren't Wolf I was hearin'.

It's hard to describe the fear what struck me when I come to understand it weren't Wolf callin' out. Knowin' they was evil folks roamin' the same bunch 'a the woods I was in made fear come on me heavy. I had to think. Come square with my trail savvy. See things for how they laid, not for what my mind was tellin' me they could be. Somebody out there was tryin' to make somebody else out there know where they was, out there . . . close by. Didn't figure they was callin' out to me. That meant they was most likely at least two stirrin' around. I had to calm myself. Catch my mind. Figure what I needed to do if it were strangers I was hearin'. Black Oak done proved I could be snuck up on, so that thinkin' was worryin' me. I figured to be extra tight in my senses 'cause I know'd the next to sneak up on me might not be my friend.

Weren't but a minute till I got hold 'a my thinkin' good and it come to me, if I could hear a body tryin' to make folks think they was a squirrel, then so could Wolf. That meant he'd be doin' something about findin' the signal maker. Not sure what, but I know'd it weren't like him to lay aside waitin' for trouble to find him. No, he'd be goin' to find it. I had no doubt in my mind over that. Whatever it was I had to do to find him, needed to figure that in about him.

The sick squirrel signaled again. It was closer than the first three I'd heard a half hour before. I'd got up from where I'd been layin' against the big white oak, then slipped around behind it quiet as I could for cover. Peter was some twenty paces away in the edge of the woods. Him and Wolf's mule was hid well enough not to be seen. All my possibles was strapped to him. My gun, too, and I needed that bad.

The squirrel was gettin' sicker from the sound of its call, but sicker or not, it was comin' my way. Sounded near like it was trailin' me from the flat rock I'd been standin' on when Wolf first went out. That was a concern for sure, 'cause if it was a body trailin' me, they was most likely Indian. If it was Indian trailin' me, I would need my rifle so I could shoot it, if it be enemy Indian. I made my mind to go fetch it. The ground between me and Peter was open grass with a boulder or two layin' in behind me. I kinda know'd where the caller was, so I used a move smart critters use when they know you're around huntin' 'em. I moved just a bit in my crouch to line up where I thought the sound was comin' from to be straight away from my person to the other side 'a the tree I was hid behind. Soon as I know'd the linin' up was good, I took for the woods and Peter on a straight run. Makin' the distance to my flintlock in about a dozen good runnin' steps. I know'd I was runnin' fast as I could but it felt like I was runnin' 'bout half what I needed. I wanted to move fast so the lead ball I figured was for sure gonna come my way might not hit me too hard. I was in the open. No weapon to fight with 'cept for the long knife Black Oak give me. I needed some protection in the worst way. Wolf's rifle was there, too.

I said a short prayer in silent, thankin' Holy Spirit for watchin' out for me as I made it to the woods without nobody shootin' me -- lead or flint. I didn't know if anybody saw me without time to shoot, or just never saw me 'cause I was movin' behind the tree and through the boulders. I hoped I'd ain't been seen. Peter was actin' skittish when I slipped up to him. Standin' his ground where he'd been tied facin' where I'd been sittin' against the white oak so I could watch him. His big ol' ears had become one of my most trusted warning signs for danger. I depended on 'em a right smart. Trusted him to use 'em proper. As I eased up to his rear, he turned 'em back to me makin' sure I was who he thought I was without ever turnin' his head. Once for sure, he peaked 'em back forward raisin' his head high like he was strainin' to hear danger. Big Jim, our lead mule, he done the same thing when out on trail. Witnessed it many times. Ol' Peter was a good 'un. I thanked Great Creator many times for the comfort he always brung me when we was out on trail. His keen senses kept me safe. Probably saved my life a few times what I didn't even know about. I'd never know 'cause he couldn't tell me, him bein' a mule and all.

I stood behind Peter for a few minutes listenin' to anything I could hear. Nothin' but normal woods noises. With as little movement as possible, the Harpers Ferry flintlock slid from its furry leather home into my eager hands quiet as a snake movin'. A simple wrist flick with my powder horn filled the rifle's pan with fresh powder. That made ready the ball and patch I'd seated in the barrel 'fore we ever left Ben's Knob for the England farm. It was good to always be ready for danger when travelin' the woods, for sure when you was out lookin' for it.

The squirrel was gettin' worse in its sickness. The call was not as close as the last I'd heard, which was good for me and the mules. Seemed it'd moved away from us some. That give me the notion to commence a stalk toward the top. That's where Wolf was headed. That's where I'd heard the squirrel call comin' from first. Didn't really know where the body was doin' the callin' after the first horrible noise they'd made, but once they made a few more I had no doubt exactly where it come from. Wolf might need some help if it was Laughing Beaver or one 'a his bunch doin' the callin'. Bein' careful in your doin's don't always keep a body from trouble. Sometimes in the mountains you find you've wandered in on danger no matter how wise a trail you cut. I'd soon know. The top weren't that far from where I'd been waitin' for Wolf. I was a little troubled 'bout what I was gonna find. I allowed Wolf would 'a been back way 'fore the squirrel call woke me. I hadn't really thought 'a that no more till the top 'a Rock Ridge was in sight.

Me and Wolf named the Rock Ridge proper. There were lots of 'em around the sides of the ridge. All sizes 'a rock. Boulders big as a smokehouse plumb down to them what fit in your hand or smaller. Grass grow'd all through the rock. Trees scattered about. None bigger 'round than a common well water bucket. We didn't hunt up on the top much 'cause it was so open. It had a few places where ivy grow'd but mostly it was just an open, flat ground with a bunch 'a big rocks layin' around the edges. A few on the very top but not near what laid around the edges. I figured the outlaw kind liked it 'cause there was places you could hide a camp and still see a good ways runnin' along both sides of the ridge top. Had a good view 'a the valley, too.

I crouched as I moved down the south side just off the top. The flintlock's rear stock steady in my right hand. The front stock layin' easy in my left. I walked kinda sideways with my front facin' the ridge top. Watchin', listenin', feelin' all I could as I eased from rock to rock. The grassy trail I was followin' mostly soft, quiet. I walked makin' the least movement I could and still be makin' way. I was movin' like an old, fat turtle just over the top from where I figured I'd last heard the squirrel caller. My eyes hawk sharp for anything movin'. My ears strainin' to hear even the slightest of noises. I stayed steady, easin' my way near slow as I could west.

The north end 'a Rock Ridge laid up against the big top it'd slid off from many years before. The lead goin' to the big top above was what was left from where the slide broke off the main mountain original. It was mule face steep. Rocks stickin' out from it, too. The south side looked straight up from where I was squatted. Prob'ly a quarter mile or a little more from where I'd tied our mules. A body had to be careful 'bout leavin' good mules tied alone out in the woods. Some gold lookers would steal 'em. I'd seen by havin' to live with the evil how it changed folks. Chasin' gold could turn a man's well-meant trail for profit into an evil trail 'a greed. Happened for a lot 'a the lookers what come to Choestoe. Made 'em near crazy actin' through bad spirits. After the gold got took, they left the mountains different folk from what they was when they first come. Meaner. Greedier. Cared less for their fellow man. Left a lot 'a mountain folk feelin' that 'a way, too, about them.

The brown I was seein' weren't a natural kinda brown I was used to seein' in the woods. Had a darkness to it that was more red than brown. I moved some closer where I could see the whole of it better. When I finally realized what it was, I felt a sickness in the deepest part of my soul. The gold lookers had left the creeks from below. Now they was diggin' holes like caves back into the base 'a the steep what laid at the north end 'a Rock Ridge. I felt my knees go weak when Wolf come walkin' out 'a one 'a them holes. His face beaten. Both eyes near swole shut. His mouth leakin' blood from the left corner. They was two others with him doin' the same as he. All carryin' two wooden buckets 'a dirt and rock what must 'a weighed near half what Wolf did. I watched as the two come out from the hole behind him. The second one lookin' mighty sickly. My heart sank even deeper when I seen the third one -- Opah. The negro from the slave barn we'd freed years before. How had he come to this? Opah was big, strong. Not near as big and strong as Black Oak, but he weren't grow'd yet. He had a few years a growin' left. This was very bad.

Two hefty guards stood by with whips tellin' 'em what to do as they come from the hole with their buckets. The watchers made all three slaves climb a dirt mound then pour out the fillin's from their buckets on top 'fore turnin' back to the dark hole to fetch more bucket fillin's. Wolf helped the weak boy with his. The feeble young 'un could barely lift it to empty. Both Wolf and Opah helped him back down the mound. He looked to be near dead. Wonderin' if they was more guards posted in places to watch, I moved back south some to settle in behind a rock not quite as tall as I was. This let me stand comfortable while I commenced to search the surroundin's lookin' for more watchers. It didn't take long to spot at least four. All was holdin' flintlocks where they sat. Prob'ly more in the holes diggin' or out in the woods makin' sick squirrel calls. The problem had just gotten impossible for a young 'un 'a my size to solve by his self. I allowed it was gonna take more folks to get Wolf and the other two free. It was time for me to ease back the way I'd come. Go for help. I hated I had to leave my friend, but if I didn't go, nobody might know he was there. I allowed I'd need to be most careful leavin' out. Both our lives depended on it. Stood to reason dark would give me cover soon so I waited to leave. That waitin' let Old Man Moon rise. I could see to walk quiet 'fore leavin'. That helped about not bein' caught. Once out I'd go for Peter, then make my way on back to Cain's. Him and Cooper was there. They'd know what to do about rescuin' Wolf. I said a short prayer that Holy Spirit would care for me on the way. Asked Him to hold Wolf in His hand 'til I got back. The thought come to mind as I was sneakin' back south, I could be Wolf's only hope 'a gettin' loose from these heathens. That thought was unsettling.

Rogues had Wolf . . . and they was settlers. I thought to shoot one of 'em as I was leavin', but the moon just weren't quite bright enough to line up my bead proper. I'm fortunate Old Man Moon was dullin'. They would 'a found me if I'd shot one 'a them takers. Holy Spirit works in some mighty convenient ways sometimes. Never gets old livin' with that kinda work.

It was still dark when I got to Cain's place. Took me most 'a the night to get there. Old Man Sun would be lightin' the sky 'fore too long. Lights was showin' in the windows as I draw'd closer. It was time to start the morning meal. That thought reminded me how hungry I was. I'd not eat since breakfast last 'cause I'd slept through dinner time waitin' on Wolf to come back. No time after realizin' Wolf might be in trouble, then findin' him bein' held slave. The thought 'a biscuits and fry meat made my mouth hurt. Rose had got to be a great cook since Momma learned her how to use the indoor cookstove. The smell 'a ham fryin' in a skillet filled my nose as Cain opened the back door to my knock. His eyes read mine. He know'd there was trouble.

"Little brother. What are you travelin' so early in the day about? I thought you and Wolf had gone to the England's place. Where is Wolf by the way? Everything good with y'all? Come to the fire for some coffee. Cooper is in the barn. Isabelle is still asleep," Cain said as we walked to the rockers by the hearth. Rose come in as I started warmin' my hands over the fire.

"Jebediah," Rose said in a concerned way as she removed the coffee pot from the side coals of the fireplace pourin' our coffee. "Brother. How is that you are here so soon after leaving? Where is my brother? Why is he not with you? Is that why you are here? Because he is not with you? Speak truth, please, so we will know."

"Yes, Rose. That is why I'm here," I said lookin' Cain in the eye while answerin' her question. "There is trouble. Wolf is in a bad way. So bad that I cannot free him alone. Bein' held captive by settlers a'top the Rock Ridge. Bein' made to work hard diggin' holes in the steep. There are at least four watchers around the outside 'a where they got him workin'. Two guards at the hole with whips. Maybe more in the holes. It got dark 'fore I could see everything good. We went there early this morning to do some scoutin' 'fore meanin' to go to his place for a few days, then back home to help Dad get ready to plant. He was off to himself to scout while I stayed with the mules. We don't leave our mules alone no more if we can help it. Too many folks about what'll steal 'em. You know that, Cain, so I was watchin' 'em while he went to look around. I stayed waitin' on him for a time, but he just never come back. When I finally went to look for him, there I found him. Done been made slave to some stout lookin' settlers. I ain't never seen farmers act like they are. Them watchers was right where they should 'a been. Guardin' the place solid. Just don't seem like normal farmin' folk to me."

"They may not be farmin' folk, Jeb. Could be they're Blue Coat soldiers that don't work for the U.S. Government no more. Red Hawk has been watchin' some over on the upper east fork of the river Notla. Not sure these you seen are part 'a that bunch or not, but it don't matter. When Red Hawk gets here, we will smoke and talk over this worry, then go free our little brother. Make some evil folk square up. Now, we gotta eat or Rose is gonna scalp us for lettin' it get cold. Don't worry, Jebediah, it's all gonna be just fine. Ol' Cain's gonna see to it. I ain't never let you down before, have I? I ain't gonna let you, or Wolf, down now. Won't be long 'til he'll be sittin' right here at this table eatin' with us like nothin' ever happened. Now, come on, let's eat."

Cain had never lied to me, 'cept for a time or two when it was best I didn't know somethin'. He sounded for sure we was gonna have no trouble gettin' Wolf clean 'a them old soldiers. I weren't so sure. I'd seen 'em. They looked tough as pine knots to me. But seein' things the way Cain did was different than any other way most folks would 'a seen what was goin' on. It seemed to me he was lookin' forward to meetin' up with them what held Wolf. Thinkin' that eased my soul some. If Cain weren't worried, I'd not be worried. Hot buttermilk biscuits with fried ham meat and honey helped with the worryin' a right smart. Course them kinda eats helped with most anything. I hated Wolf didn't get one 'a them biscuits of Rose's. He'd be proud. They was near as good as Momma's. I prayed in the silent Cain was right about fetchin' Wolf back. I missed my friend.

Chapter 14 - I Lead Red Hawk on a Trail

The ground inside the holes was damp. The air cold and wet. You could feel it when you breathed in. Wolf sat in the dark shiverin', studyin' over what was gonna happen. He was too tired to fight back, even if he got the chance. 'Sides, these was tough men what'd took him. Know'd how to treat prisoners to keep 'em in line, which is what Wolf figured himself to be. Haulin' dirt out was gonna make him too weak to walk if he didn't get some food soon. They'd worked him and the two others all day with only a little water. No food of any kind. He was tired, but sleep would not come. He hoped I was still free. All he could do was pray they'd not caught me, too. *"The Great Creator must have a reason for me being with these evil ones,"* Wolf thought to himself. They got him not long after he'd left me with the mules to go look for sign 'a Laughing Beaver. He never saw 'em 'fore they was on him. Laid for him as he passed by a big rock. Them kinda dangers is hard to catch 'fore you done walked right into 'em. Not even seasoned warriors always made it through folks layin' for 'em. A rifle butt to the back of his head sent him to the ground front first. A couple fist to the face made it where he could do nothin' but obey what they said do. His only strength now was in the fact that Dancing Bear, his father, would soon know of what has happened . . . if I was still free . . . or if the Guard found the diggin's. These men what held him would pay for what they was doin'. A body would not want to be them when Dancing Bear found out what they was doin'. Of that, Wolf had no doubt. He know'd that most likely a runner was already on the way to tell the Tribe Elder, or soon would be. He know'd they pro'bly weren't gonna catch up to me. Know'd I was more savvy than to let a bunch like this find me. That confidence in me give him strength when he could feel little. That made me proud when he told me about all of it later on.

Red Hawk had come to Cain's not long after I'd got there. He learned from me about Wolf bein' took. Sent a runner to fetch Dancing Bear soon as I told him. "Dancing Bear will be to the Rock Ridge soon," Red Hawk said as we all sat the fire pit outside Cain's place smokin'. Well, we was all there except Cooper. He'd slipped off from the barn 'fore we ever finished eatin' breakfast. I seen him through the window. Cain seen him, too. He was totin' full battle truck as he left. His strong bow in its special made pouch across his back next to a quiver full 'a arrows. Smokin', yes, we was all smokin'. A pipe full 'a dried burley tasted good after you'd eat a bite. We was full 'a Rose's biscuits, fried ham, dried apples and red-eye gravy. I felt tired from no sleep. Old Man Sun weren't clear 'a the big ridges to the east yet, so the day was still full on ahead of us. That was good. It would take most of our day gettin' back to the Rock Ridge.

"It is his son who has been taken. It is his son's life that is in danger," Red Hawk continued as he rose to stand while he spoke. His pipe finished. "Dancing Bear will bring warriors. He will have the say on how to move on these evil ones. My hunt for Laughing Beaver will wait for now. Moon Shadow will carry that burden till I am done here. The Guard is surrounding the Rock Ridge. No taker will get out from here unless we say. I will take Jeb back to the diggings. We will watch. Count their numbers so we can tell my brother when he comes. He will need to know. Cain, you will climb the steep above where they are digging. Slip down close. Find a place where you can watch Wolf. Wait for Dancing Bear to come before you shoot any watchers if you can but keep the young ones safe. If you need to shoot, you must shoot. This is all I have to say on this for now. We should speak to Great Creator for guidance."

Red Hawk was senior to all of us, so what he said do was what we did. Unfortunately, Cain had to keep to what the elder said even though Cain couldn't shoot that good. He liked close up fightin', but the need for a friendly watcher was there. Nobody know'd where Cooper was, but we know'd he was near. Red Hawk's standin' in the Guard was one 'a high rank. He had many warriors at his charge, as did Dancing Bear. What was fixin' to happen 'bout gettin' Wolf back would give proof to how folks lived what took care 'a one another. Wouldn't take long to come together neither. It give me a deep feelin' of comfort in my Choestoe clan knowin' what folks would do for one another when they was trouble about. Livin' by way of the Good Book made folks look out for each other without thought. It is the way.

Me and Red Hawk left Peter at Cain's takin' off on foot, usin' the warrior's trot to move back to Rock Ridge. I didn't carry no flintlock to make trottin' easier. I was gonna use Wolf's rifle when we got to his mule. Movin' like that cut trail time near in half if a body was in a hurry to get to where they was needed. Red Hawk could run like we was all day if he needed. Did it often. He know'd I didn't, so he walked the steeper parts to spare me. He figured my body weren't used to runnin' like his was. He seen I was tired, too, from not gettin' any sleep. At least I got to fill up on biscuits, fry meat and coffee 'fore me and Red Hawk left to go back to the diggin' camp. That give me some strength. I still needed sleep.

Red Hawk stopped when we got back to Wolf's mule midway through the afternoon. The trot had gotten us there in a short time. It was needin' a drink from bein' tied all night, but other than that he was fine. I obliged him 'fore I slid Wolf's flintlock from its home. He'd do for a while.

"Jeb, listen close," Red Hawk said as he looked me straight in the eye. "You know where this camp is. Lead us there the same as you went before. I will follow you. Keep your eyes to the front. Go quietly. Make little movement. Keep your rifle at the ready. These men are dangerous, Jebediah. Watch your step. Break no sticks as you walk. Move slowly. Are you ready?"

I couldn't speak. My mind was too full to think on common words right then. Me, Jebediah Collins, fourteen-year-old and a few months, was fixin' to lead a senior warrior of the Cherokee Nation into danger where there might be killin'. And not just any senior warrior, but my uncle, Red Hawk. One 'a the most respected, battle tested of all Indian warriors throughout the southern mountains. I was not ready. No amount 'a trail savvy could 'a got me ready for such as he'd told me to do. I could not lie to him. He'd know if I did. That would not be wise.

"I am not ready, Uncle. It is you who should lead us into this danger. I am but a young one who is only learnin' the ways you live by every day. But sir, I respect your judgment, Red Hawk, and I will do this, if you think it best. I do not fear this trail. I will gladly lead, but you are Red Hawk. I will listen for your words as we move along the ridge top. Tell me the things I need to do as only your wisdom will know it. I am sorry, Uncle, if I let you down, but I will do my best."

"Spirit Filled One," Red Hawk called me by what the old ones did. "It is you who I will trust. You are brave, young one. My nephew, Wolf, tells me of the things he does. You, as well. I know the stories of your courage with the bear. The soldiers. Your love of family. Loyalty to your clan. Your reckoning to manhood. Your heart for the one you love, Miss Elizabeth. I wish you a long life with her. She will make you strong children. And do not be angry, but I know you have taken life. All of these things together are leading you down the trail to being a respected warrior, Jebediah. One day, my life will depend on you. I have seen this in my visions. Ghost Bear has spoken to you. I know this. Told you a secret to keep. When this with Wolf is over, I will want you to tell me of this vision. Yes?"

There it was again right square in my face. Indians knowin' things they'd never been told. Just know'd it somehow. He know'd 'a my vision without me ever tellin' him. Wolf would not 'a told that 'cause it was from a vision I'd had. If he spoke on it without my sayin' he could, and Brother Bear said for us not to, it would bring evil to ruin all the good the vision was tryin' to communicate. The only way Red Hawk know'd about Brother Bear was from bein' told in the spirit world. A dream. Holy Spirit minded him with knowledge to let me know it was time for me to tell Dancing Bear of the secret room only I know'd about. I reasoned the time was comin' when he'd need to know how to get in that room with all the gold lookers and government men bein' seen in the valley. I figured to show Wolf when we got him back. From that, he could show Dancing Bear. For some reason, I felt it best to tell 'em that way. Let Wolf go about tellin' 'em all. Have no doubt, Holy

Spirit would work it the way He wanted it done. Folks had very little control 'a things when the Spirit took to movin'.

"I will, Uncle. I will tell you all that Brother Bear told me in my vision. Uncle, I have seen Brother Bear. He walks Mother Earth. He come to visit me and Wolf on the cliff behind their home. Wolf saw him. He is alive. I know it was him. The bear of my vision had a white star on his chest that looks like the cross where the Peace Child was killed. I promise you, Uncle, that Brother Bear who walks Mother Earth, has this cross star on his chest. I have seen it, twice. Once on Wolf Creek, the other at the cliff. It is the same mark that the spirit bear of my vision had. This bear is my totem. Dancing Bear has seen him, when first I saw him on Wolf Creek camped with my dad, Thompie."

"I know this thing you say is true, Jebediah. Your words are truth. I, too, have seen this bear. I, too, know it to be real. I believe you, young warrior. Now, let us go get Wolf."

Red Hawk was serious when he said I'd be leadin' our way to the diggin' camp, so off I led. I took us near the same way I went when I first went lookin' for Wolf. Stayed just off the top walkin' kinda sideways with my flintlock same as I'd done before. I watched him some as he trailed me. His eyes ever movin' but rarely at the ground. I found it interesting the way he walked with his hand restin' on the handle of his knife. He carried no bow or rifle. How his head moved very little. Movements seasoned from years 'a tryin' to stay hid from folks. Never heard him make a noise the whole time we was walkin' in. I changed our way some, droppin' off from the top so we'd hit the very rock I'd stood behind till dark come on me the day before. We stood together lookin' the camp over. He was some taller than the rock. He seen the same as me first time I was there. The holes. The guards. The watchers. The captives.

Wolf, Opah and the sick one all carryin' buckets 'a dirt out from the holes. Each looked to have their own hole this time. I'd told Red Hawk about Opah. He grinned when he heard Cain set the slavin' barn on fire.

"These watchers," Red Hawk said askin'. "They are the same ones you saw, yes? Is anything different? Look close now, Jeb. I need to know if anything has changed since you first found Wolf."

I looked close as I could just like Red Hawk said. I could see each watcher where they sat. I know'd where to look. They, too, moved very little. Weren't no trouble seein' 'em. What leaves on the trees was young. Not filled out full like they would be later on in the hot time. They provided some cover, but you could see through 'em good enough. Problem was, if we could see through 'em, so could the watchers. That weren't a comfortin' thought seein' how they had flintlocks same as me. I did see a few changes. Didn't mean nothin' to me but might to Red Hawk. I told him straight like I saw it.

"Yes, Uncle, these look to be the same watchers what sat there when I was here before. Their clothes are the same, but I do see things that are different. All three, Wolf, Opah, and the sickly one was carryin' out dirt from the same hole. Now, they each have a hole. Before, they all wore shirts. Now they are all bare from the waist up. I only counted four watchers before. Not five. There was no fire pit, but now there is. There was no tent, but now there is. They've stocked their firewood. Started a new dirt pile. Other than those things, all looks the same. Does that help you, Uncle?"

"It will help, Jeb. What I see now, what you see different, these things talk if you know how to listen. I believe one of the stolen has done something wrong. Might be one tried to get free. I do not know, but I think the watchers feel the three must be kept apart now while working. That means these captors are alert. That makes them dangerous. The tent is someone new, maybe one who tells the others what to do. They likely have come during the day while we traveled. We will see who that is before we move. Keeping them bare from the waist up helps keep them close. The skin being bare makes the whip much more painful. Yes, one of them has done something to require punishment for all. I wonder who that one was?" Red Hawk grinned slightly.

Red Hawk said that meanin' Wolf. His grin told me he was funnin'. That was a Cherokee Warrior for ye. They lived for such as we was in. Nothin' seemed funny to me. I felt like killin' was comin'. I had a right smart 'a concern for what I know'd was gonna happen when Dancing Bear got there. Red Hawk weren't worried none. Seemed to me he was ready to have at them takers what was holdin' Wolf, almost like he was lookin' forward to it. I kinda was too, in a hopefully cheatin' death kinda way. The mountains and their ways had gotten dangerous for the folks what lived there. All of 'em, native and settler.

Cain slipped in amongst a small group 'a boulders. A big stump from a cross-cut stood about knee high on the side toward the camp. He laid his possibles pouch across the top 'a that stump then set his flintlock on top 'a the pouch. The rifle settled in a way, that when he crouched on one knee, the butt plate fit near perfect against his shoulder. Knowin' the watchers was there made it easy for him to find 'em all. Six, what he counted. He wanted to shoot one of 'em just 'cause they'd took Wolf. That kinda evil didn't settle well with Cain. He weren't scared 'a what would happen to his person if he did shoot one of 'em, it was others he had concern for. I'd seen him walk straight into a camp full 'a enemy warriors to challenge one whose name we never say no more. An evil man what did bad things. Murdered Wolf's brother, which just happened to be Cain's good friend, Fox Running. Cain put a stop to that killer's nasty ways. He'd never been whooped, neither. I loved my brother. Know'd I could depend on him for anything. He know'd he could depend on me just the same. That's how it ought 'a be 'tween blood folks. Siblings, for sure. Unfortunately, I would learn later in life that kinda bond was rare.

It was strange to me that Cooper weren't around after we eat earlier that morning. It was important to hear Red Hawk's trail orders. He was there in the barn when I come 'fore daylight. He eat like the rest of us, but then he was just gone. They was somethin' up with that. It weren't like Cooper to dodge a fight; no, it was most natural for him to go find a fight. A more curious soul you'd never meet with courage to go along with his wonderin' ways. He was like family. He'd not leave Wolf to these varmints. I allowed Red Hawk had him doin' somethin' somewhere what would help with gettin' Wolf out from his bondage. Him and Cain was tight.

"Jeb, you need rest. Their watchers only sit," Red Hawk said as he pulled me down behind our rock not long after he'd looked the place over good. I was havin' trouble keepin' my eyes open from bein' awake the last couple days. He must 'a noticed. "It is still a while before Dancing Bear will come here. I know you are tired. Lay yourself down behind this rock. Put your head on your pouch. Close your eyes for rest. You are no good for Wolf if you are too tired to fight. Nothing will happen while you sleep. I will stand watch. Close your eyes now for a time. Do not think of your friend. Think of something that gives you comfort. Sleep for a bit. By then, my brother should be here to make this right. What say, ye? Do you understand?"

"I will do this, Red Hawk. I am very tired. Forgive me, but it's been a long couple days with all we been doin'. Now Wolf has been stole. We've had little time for sleep. I'd say you're right, Uncle. Rest is just what I need right now. Thank you for watchin'. Wake me soon," I said kinda out 'a my head tired. I laid down next to the boulder. Put my head back on my possibles pouch. I was asleep 'fore I got settled good. I slept hard 'cause I know'd I was safe with Red Hawk watchin' out.

Cain found a perfect place with the old stump in the middle of a bunch 'a boulders what was still solid across the top. He laid his flintlock on it, then fired the pan with some powder. Checked his flint to make sure it was bein' held tight 'fore he settled his backside in for a few hours watchin'. He could see all six watchers not fifty 'a Dad's paces away to the closest. He got the pull to shoot one again when he seen Wolf come from his hole like some critter lookin' for Old Man Sun. Made him angry seein' the other two come out 'a their holes. All carryin' their buckets of dirt and rock. This time they was men in close hollerin' out at 'em. The one what come from the tent was the one what hollered the most. He was a good-sized feller. Strong lookin'. Kinda fierce in the face. Mean. The worst thing was . . . he was wearin' a Blue Coat and saber.

Now it all come to reason. The U.S. Government was movin' in on the mountains. The watchers didn't look government, but they could be. We'd find out soon enough. Dancing Bear would be to see this made right. When Old Man Sun rose from his bed the next day, Dancing Bear and his warriors would be there to speak with this Blue Coat.

Chapter 15 - A Blood Trail for the Heathens

Dancing Bear sat his hearth as he and A-Ga-Li-Ha listened to the runner from Red Hawk tell 'a Wolf bein' took. His head bowed in silent prayer to the Great Creator for mercy. He'd already lost one son to evil. His prayer was that he'd not lost another one. If that be so, he'd consider that a fate worse than death. Just as he had once before. Listenin' on, findin' out Wolf was alive, made it where he could draw air again, but learnin' he was bein' worked like a slave made him full on mad. Made his back tighten so that the muscles knotted on both sides of his spine. His fist clinched so hard he felt the sting of fingernails cuttin' his palm meat. Cramps hit him like rope knots in behind his ribs and across his middle. His soul sank from the inside as his mind listened to the news. He wanted to yell out as loud as he could, but he remained calm showin' no emotion.

There was only one choice for Dancing Bear now that an evil deed had been done to his family. He would ready himself to lay a blood trail for the heathens what stole his son. Nobody took his son. Nobody worked him as slave. Nobody! The men what done this would pay with their lives, of that he had no doubt. He was tired 'a strangers comin' to the mountains causin' trouble for his people; the settlers he called friends. These would cause no more. His warriors would meet him along the trail come morning. He held serious concern for Wolf's well bein', but he know'd Red Hawk was there with Cain to take care of him. He needed to prepare his mind for what lay ahead before leaving out at daylight. Wolf would be safe as long as he waited. He should know his father would be there soon.

"You go get our son, Dancing Bear," A-Ga-Li-Ha said with some force. He heard the sadness in her heart. For her son sure, but for those who had done this evil thing as well. Their souls would be without soon. Killin' folks for any reason always bothered her way down deep. "Bring him home to me. I want him here for a time. We will take a walk when he comes. Tell him I have said this."

"I will bring him, and I will tell him, A-Ga-Li-Ha. Soon, you will hold him. The camp is less than a day to the east. My brother will be waiting for me when I get there. I have sent the runner on to tell our warriors what has happened. They will wait for me along the trail. As Old Man Sun wakes a new day, I will leave to make sure these evil ones never take more captive from Cho-E-sto-E. Our trails have become dangerous, but I believe this evil will go. Let us pray the Great Creator gives back to the Cherokee all the peace that has been taken by the gold lookers. I believe this to be His way. If it is not His way, I fear that trail with all that I am. The evil of these coming here could dry up our souls like corn standing in a field that has tasted no rain. Pray the hateful strangers that come here stop coming here. Leave us to our mountain home so we can find our peace again. That will be a good day, when they come here no more."

"That will be a good day, my husband, but until then we must stand guard. I am hearing of visions my sisters are having. Of Blue Coats, swarming our lands like the honey makers. Killing our people. Taking our homes and all that we have. Burning our stores of food. Of our old dying, our young as well. Of soldiers, pushing us toward the land where Old Man Sun goes to bed down at the end of light. Much too far away from the life-giving morning warmth we know here. I fear all we are is moving toward an end, Dancing Bear. Do all that you can to not let these bad things happen to our people. If you do that, if we do that, then we honor our ancestors as best we can. I will pray, husband."

***

Wolf and Opah stayed close when dark come the third night Wolf was bein' held. The takers was makin' 'em stay in the hole they'd help dig the first day. Wolf felt a fool for gettin' caught but learned a very important lesson on how to watch your back trail. At least they'd give 'em food to eat, if you could call it that. Some near rotten goat cheese with green coverin' the whole of it for him and Opah to share. Meat soup what looked to be boiled from old salt saved jerky. Couldn't tell from lookin' what the meat was exactly. Tasted good to a hungry soul, though. Wolf eat two bowls. Would 'a eat a third but they weren't no more after Opah finished eatin'. The sickly one had passed on. Wolf and Opah found him curled up in the back 'a the cave they was bein' made to stay in. Same hole I'd seen 'em totin' dirt from first time I was there. They never really know'd where he come from or what he died from. When I seen him, he was coughin' a lot. Wolf figured north for some reason. He never said much to Wolf. He'd talked some to Opah who'd been there longer. The diggers took him away not sayin' a word. Didn't seem right to Wolf the way they took him out. Like he was just something in the way that needed to be moved. Disrespectful to him and his ancestors for sure. Wolf allowed they'd pay for that when they got called across the river . . . he smiled knowin' that was gonna be soon.

"Opah," Wolf said as they sat back-to-back huddled against the back wall of the cave needin' a blanket for warmin' in the worst way. Opah shiverin' hard. "You must stay strong. My father is coming. He will bring warriors. Many warriors. These heathens that have taken us are going to meet him. You will see. I know this thing will happen. I believe it to be soon. The warriors in my clan do not hold for folks who do such as they have done to us. It is like a sickness that comes to your lodge. Fills all with bad spirits."

"Yes," Opah said in his strange accent. "I prayed you would have people looking for you, here. I am so glad to know this. When they come, we will be free, yes? Wolf? When I am free, I will kill their chief. When your father comes, he will let me do this, yes? For my family. For my ancestors in their graves. For my children, so they will know their father is strong. A mighty warrior."

"Yes, Opah. You may have your revenge. My father will see to it. You may kill the loud one, if that is the one. It is going to be a bad day for these snakes soon, my friend. I can feel it. But, Opah, how is it that you have children when you are so young. I believe us to be about the same age. I have no children. Why do you?"

"I do not have them yet, Wolf of the Cherokee. You are being the funny. I am too much young, yes. But, with me, I have wives waiting for me back in my homeland. They will give me many children, when my father says it is my given time to be in the manhood. I pray it will not be long to wait now, my friend. Soon, I will return to my family across the big waters. I carry many stories to tell them of this great land. I love it here. I want to live here forever once I can come to return here. It will be difficult in time to leave my family with so many of these children who I will have. We will see how God allows. I must get back to home first. Now, with the help of your father, I believe I just might make it. I have toted these evil buckets for too many of the days, Wolf. I am ready for to be free of these that keep us. I long for my family."

***

Dancing Bear laid fire to the top of his pipe, then prayed as the smoke rose to the black of the night sky. Morning was close. You could feel the chill what comes when night breaks to day. It's a cold like no other. Like a haint layin' on your person. Walkin' with you. Makes your skin feel cold like raw bacon 'fore it's fried. Soon, the trail leadin' toward upper Wolf Creek would be lit enough to run on, and Dancing Bear would start his trot to fetch his son. Warriors were waitin' even as he started off not too long 'fore Old Man Sun got to showin' over the tops 'a the big ridges to the east. He weren't wearin' his full battle truck. All he toted was two knives and his short war club made 'a seasoned, smoke dried hickory. Stained dark with blood from years 'a fightin' previous. It belonged to his father, Water Runs Deep, who used it in the war with the Red Coats from across the great water as a scout for General Washington. Dancing Bear hardly ever carried that club. Him carryin' it to save Wolf was a sign he was invitin' the ancestors to make trail with him. His possibles pouch laid across his left shoulder hangin' free under his right arm. A-Ga-Li-Ha packed him enough provisions to last several days. Sun dried jerky with a small pouch 'a dried apples and corn. There were springs along lower sections of the trail where water was plentiful. All that put together was good, but once he got goin', he'd not stop till he was face-to-face with Red Hawk at Rock Ridge. He was eager to make sure his son was safe. He trusted all who were there, know'd not to worry, but it was his son—alive—he needed to see, then his soul would know that Wolf was safe.

The air was cool on Dancing Bear's skin. He ran bare on top to keep from soilin' his homespun shirt what was tied around his waist by the arms. That let him feel the pleasant sting of the cool air as it passed by dryin' him from the sweat of a long run. Spring would be gone 'fore long. The hot time would come. The heat that caused settler skin to burn red and the trees to fill full with leaves, would also make all the cool air go away to a place Dancing Bear had never seen. A place they told in stories is covered in cold white durin' all the seasons of the year. He did not believe such a place could be, given that Old Man Sun warmed Mother Earth in all directions. He would need to see this place to know what he'd heard was true.

Warriors was meetin' him all along the trail to upper Wolf Creek. All wore full battle truck. It did not go unnoticed by them that their leader only toted his war club and knives for fightin'. His cherished eagle feather had been braided into his hair. Only A-Ga-Li-Ha was allowed to do that. All Cherokee who seen it know'd what that meant. I know'd, too, when I seen it. They would cover him, when the time come, with their lives.

By the time he'd made it to the base 'a Rock Ridge, he had seven battle hardened warriors in total. With the experience them Cherokee had fightin', the takers stood no chance 'a defendin' themselves, none. The skill each warrior had made them death to any foe they took after. A bunch like them could easily wipe out four or five dozen common Blue Coat soldiers in a night. Woods fightin' come easy to 'em – natural – like wakin' up in the morning. I feared 'em not, but them what took Wolf better had. I don't believe them evil folk had any notion to the hell on Mother Earth that was comin' their way 'fore it did. I felt for 'em a little as I ciphered on the justice they was fixin' to receive while we slipped back out to meet Dancing Bear and his warriors. It felt like a time the Dark Angel was figurin' to move on our evil visitors. I prayed their souls was ready to meet Jesus . . . 'cause they weren't no doubt they was gonna be seein' Him 'fore dark followin'.

Dancing Bear and his warriors had already made it to Wolf's mule by the time we got back there to meet 'em. They were restin' from the long run they'd just made. It'd taken 'em all day 'cause Old Man Sun was gone by the time we seen 'em. They'd built a small fire and was sittin' around it eatin' a bite. None sayin' a word. They'd lay down after they eat. Go to sleep 'til right before first light still not sayin' nothin' among themselves. Given their thoughts to the fight to come. It was their way 'a clearin' the mind. Makin' the body ready for whatever come. It wouldn't last all night, but what sleep they got made true warriors even more dangerous to their enemies, and these was for sure true Cherokee warriors. You'd find no better in the whole of the mountains.

"My brother," Red Hawk said as he walked up to their fire. "It is good to see you can still cover the same ground as one younger. I, too, am able to do this. We are good stock, you and me. Like fine mules, eh?"

"I am no mule, brother," Dancing Bear replied as he rose with a grin. "But you are right. We are good stock. However, now that I am closer, it may be that you are beginning to smell like a mule, Red Hawk. The Change Spirit may be working on you."

"No, Dancing Bear. It must be you whose scent you have picked up. I have bathed of recent. A bad scent is very dangerous in my world," Red Hawk said, lockin' forearms with his brother. "It is good you are here, scent and all. Wolf is well. Do not worry for his safety. We have been watching him. Cain is here. Others, too."

"Yes, Red Hawk. I am here. The ancestors are here as well," Dancing Bear said while raising their father's war club. Red Hawk bowed his head for a second out 'a respect to the spirit of the club and all who'd fought with it. "We will rest. Then we will move on this camp of evil men. Tell me all you know. Let us smoke. Pray."

"We have counted five watchers. There are three that dig, two that stand guard over the tent, and the one that stays in the tent. Now there are only two that carry the buckets. Wolf and one more. A dark one no older than Wolf. He is strong. I do not know this one, but Jeb does. His name is Opah. It seems Jeb, with the help of a couple others, set him free from being sold south of here in Gaines Town many moons back. They both are being held by a Blue Coat. He is the leader. The one in the tent. It is he that we should speak to about their freedom. The takers know nothing of being watched. Neither does Wolf. We have seen no Indians. None of my scouts have found sign other than the ones we see in the camp. Eleven in all that hold Wolf and Opah."

"Thank you for all you've done, Red Hawk. Jebediah, thank you as well. We will rest for a time. Then you and I will speak on how to move on these that take what they want with no thought for others. This is not the way. May the Great Spirit guide us. Justice for these is coming. Nobody takes one of ours. We will set this right. Now I must rest."

With all that said, he left me and Red Hawk to join his warriors. It's hard to describe how it feels to be in the presence of such a deadly group of Indians, just knowin' some 'a what they'd done. These had lived the life of frontier soldiers for their tribe. Seen and done things only history can tell about. Hard men. Fathers. Killers, every one of 'em. Not for sport or gain, but for life of family, friends. Men who lived by their honor. Died by it if necessary. Who could know? One might die this night workin' to free Wolf and Opah. A person they could die for that I didn't figure any of 'em even know'd. To them, their fate was in the hands of the Great Creator. That settled it for their way 'a thinkin'. From that, they did what felt right in their hearts. Livin' or dyin' never troubled 'em that much. I don't think they even thought on it. Thinkin' that 'a way give 'em great courage what made 'em extremely dangerous men. More so than most folks reckoned on. Unfortunately, it was a world I could see changin'. Not for the better, neither. I believed they know'd it. Could see it for themselves. 'Course, knowin' that made 'em even more dangerous, if that was possible. God help the ones what was fixin' to meet 'em there at the Rock Ridge, or anywhere else they was called on to see to the needs of the clan. Killin' for cause was not a problem for this bunch. It just come as a way 'a life for those that protect.

Cain was sleepin' when he heard the crunch of a half-dried leaf under a heavy foot. It was loud enough to wake him, so he figured it was close. Dark had come while he slept. Old Man Moon was shinin' just a touch more than the night before, which weren't much. He'd fell asleep leaned ag'in his stump as Old Man Sun went home for the night. Couldn't help it. Sittin' like that all day made him tired after what little sleep he'd had. He figured Dancing Bear was there already, but know'd his warriors would not ease out to surround the camp until they could see what little they needed to stay quiet. The dark of the night made it near impossible to travel unless a body know'd the ground where they was tryin' to move. That's how the sound got Cain awake so quick. Somebody, what know'd where they was, had sneaked in close. Cain left his stump easin' slow over to the edge of the small group 'a boulders he was hidin' in. He heard more sound. Not loud, but just loud enough for him to know they was folks about. He reached his right hand over the handle of his long knife drawin' it out while turnin' the sharp edge up. Whoever it was had to be close, but the night was thick like syrup makin' it hard to know what was what. You couldn't see over a pace or two out. That's why the whispered voices out in the darkness made him freeze cold where he stood. Squat to the ground out 'a instinct. He weren't expectin' folks in so close. Yet, there they was. No question. He strained hard, listenin'. Hopin' to understand at least a few of their words . . . nothing. It was voices, but they were no more. A sound caught his ear what told him the voices had moved on. He may never know who it was that come so close to findin' him, but he know'd it was somebody.

Findin' out they was folks wanderin' around, who might be folks other than the takers, brought Cain straight awake for the rest 'a the night. He know'd now they was others prowlin' around, and this was somebody what know'd how to be quiet while movin' in the dark woods. His gut feelin' made him think of Laughing Beaver. He prayed the passin' strangers weren't tied to him. Cain allowed he'd need to keep watch different since hearin' the voices whisperin'. Trouble come in many ways sometimes. It was possible that Wolf weren't the only one in danger anymore. Dependin' on who it was out there, what they was figurin' on, we all could be in danger of a sudden. Cain know'd whisperers bein' there might turn out to be bad, but they weren't nothin' he could do till morning. The night had just become a long, sleepless one. Cain figured it all come with the duty. He got quiet. Said a little prayer for the coming of the light. It was gonna change a lot of folks' lives. He could feel that in his soul. "God help us," he prayed.

Chapter 16 - Seven Warriors of Justice

Major Dennis was an oak of a man. Mean. Crooked. Military all his workin' life. A rule breaker that'd suffered discipline from his senior officers for it. He'd killed plenty. Some of it legal through his service, some of it not so legal. He'd steal if given the chance. Mostly for profit. He'd stole plenty from the soldier supplies he'd handled over the years. Enough to provide camp for 'a dozen or more fightin' men, or a few small camps spread out around if one chose to do that -- like he was doin'. All his campin' truck come from the government, along with his clothes, blankets, cookin' truck, long coats, a couple decent mules, extra boots and, of course, weapons. He'd made sure to come out with plenty 'a them includin' a half dozen crates 'a brand new rifles along with several kegs 'a gun powder and a hundred pounds 'a lead shot molded in .50 caliber. He'd made money from sellin' some 'a what he'd stole. Many hated him 'cause he'd took 'em when tradin', but he was so mean most feared to mess with him for recompense. I know'd a couple who weren't feared had he 'a tricked them. He deceived the bulk of his fellow soldiers when tradin' with them, too. Lied to 'em. Didn't treat 'em straight up. As my granddad would 'a said, "His barrelhead has a hole in it." To him, that said Dennis was a thief. We called that low down in Choestoe. Folks wouldn't trade with that kind. His day would come.

Very few of the men ever servin' under Dennis' charge liked him. Some 'a what did had deserted with him months earlier. A couple dozen in all. Them was the ones watchin' out at the diggin' camp. One 'a the four diggin' camps he had spread out around the mountain. He'd supplied all his hands with them new guns, too. He know'd the diggin' he was doin' would get the attention of the locals. Greed for gold had got to runnin' hot through his heart. No different for his fellow deserters, neither. He promised 'em plenty if they'd go with him. Help get it out. Mountain gold. Told 'em he'd found it. Had a small piece he carried with him to prove what he said true. Claimed an old Indian give it to him after Dennis seen some 'a the gold the old man had found. Chunks with the white quartz still attached. He took Dennis to the Rock Ridge. Show'd him the very line 'a quartz he claimed produced the gold he'd found. It was stickin' out from the side of the mountain where the top had slid from. Showin' Dennis that quartz cost the old Indian his life. His gold. Truth be that Dennis never told nobody he'd made the old Indian take him there. Threatened to kill his next 'a kin if he didn't. Never did figure what made Dennis allow the old man was tellin' the truth after he'd threatened him and all, but for some reason, the Major believed the old one found the gold just where he said he did. After killin' him so he could show no one else, the Major quickly gathered his men and supplies. His plan was to dig mine shafts under the layin' quartz in hopes 'a findin' the main core 'a gold. The "Mother's Load?" Wolf had heard him say. Wolf told me later him and Major Dennis talked when he come to visit with 'em back in the cave on the second night he was bein' held. Wolf hated the man. Had only been around him the one day, but he know'd he hated him. Swore to himself he'd kill him if Opah failed in doin' so. For sure, he figured,

Dancing Bear would want to see this man stopped. Keep him from takin' more folks from Choestoe to do his diggin'.

"You boys' wonderin' why you're havin' to tote the dirt from this ol' dig ain't ye?" Dennis said to 'em while holdin' a lantern in their eyes. He'd been drinkin' hard cider. Wolf could smell it on him as Dennis moved in close. Their noses nearly touchin'. "Well, you see, it's like this. My men are too lazy to do it. 'Sides, I need 'em outside to watch out for the savages what are sure to come, bein' that I'm cuttin' holes in their "Mother Earth" as you say, boy, right? Hey! Indian boy. Ain't it bad what we're doin'? Woundin' your mother. You believe that don't you, boy? Say? You hearin' me, Indian boy? Hmm? Speak, you heathen. Tell me what you believe. I ain't scared 'a the likes 'a you or yours. Y'all ain't nothin' to me. 'Sides, way I hear it, y'all ain't gonna be 'round in these mountains much longer no-how. What say ye, boy? Speak, I said!" he yelled as he straightened up and backhanded Wolf across the left side of his face near knockin' him cold. Then, without reason, he punched Opah in the nose, makin' it start bleedin'. He was strong to go along with his mean.

"My kind will always be here, evil one. I am Wolf. Son of Dancing Bear. You will meet my father soon. I do not care that you make holes in the ground. Mother Earth is much stronger than you. When my father comes, I want to bury you in this very hole. We will cut out your evil heart. Burn it over your own fire. This way, you will never know love when you cross over the Great River. I, Wolf, will see to it. You should sing your death song, soldier man. Let the ancestors know your plans are to join them soon. I can see it. Yours will be a warrior's death. That will bring you honor across the river, but no love will be found there for you. You are evil. I look forward to seeing you die. That is all I have to say to you, dirty man."

Wolf's words got Dennis goin' red hot mad, so he reached over and punched Opah in the nose again. This time Wolf heard it crack. "I ain't gonna die today, young one. Nor tomorrow. I will be gone from here by daylight. Tell your father I look forward to when we meet. I want you to know that, 'cause after I'm done with him, I'll deal with you. But for now, I need you helpin' with the dig. Tote your dirt out like a good little Indian slave. Tomorrow, when your father comes, I will be gone. The men who watch this dig will be here to welcome him and all who come with him. We are soldiers, boy. We ain't gonna be done in by a bunch 'a mountain folk what ain't trained like we are. We've fought many no different than what I expect is comin' here to get you. My men are ready. They will fight. We plan to stay here till we find the Mother Lode. When that is done, and we are rich, we will leave."

"No, evil man," Opah near yelled back at Dennis. His voice muffled from his broken nose. "You will not to be going away from this place where you make us do for your work. I, Opah, will see you buried here. It would be best for you to let us go this night. It could save you your life from judgment that is to fall over you when this day grows older. I feel for your soul, evil one. But, as I see this thing, you have done this death to yourself. If you go, know I will follow when a free man soon."

"Then follow, young one, if you think you can, for I'm leavin'. I got three more digs on this mountain I'm havin' to account for, only I ain't got no slave help diggin' them. Just my men. Y'all keep pullin' the inside to the outside. Diggin' where we tell ya. I'll be back in a few days. Sgt. Baker will keep seein' to you. Don't give him no more trouble, neither. I done told him he could use the whip on ye if you do. He'll do it, too. Y'all done know that," Dennis said with a smile as he turned to leave. Stoppin' when he remembered somethin' he needed to tell 'em. He held the lantern high. "You'll be startin' a new hole when daylight comes. See to it you get the floor leanin' to the front, or I'll take the whip to ye myself when once I'm back."

With all that said, he left. Wolf wondered to himself if Major Dennis had any notion as to the kinda fight headed his way no matter what dig the warriors found him at. Doubted if he ever fought true Cherokee warriors on their own huntin' grounds. Doubted if the Major had any idea what he was fixin' to be put upon by. Wolf grinned in the dark as he and Opah sat shiverin'. He kinda felt for the old soldier, but not really. Hate run through the Major. Wolf said you could feel it when you was near him. Folks like him made it bad for others. It didn't seem to Wolf the man had lived a very good life, seein' how mean he was, so Wolf allowed dyin' might be a relief to him. They was most likely a right smart 'a folks who'd find comfort knowin' he'd been put down. Wolf was one of 'em. I know how he felt. You couldn't help but hold hard feelin's for a soul what'd done as wrong as he'd done so many. It's how you control them feelin's what mattered. Wolf know'd how his father would handle his bein' took.

Their sleepin' done, Dancing Bear talked to his warriors 'fore they moved to surround the camp just before the Great Creator blessed them with life givin' light from Old Man Sun for another day. They all prayed in the silent as they sat waitin' for enough light to see to move quiet, while listenin' to their leader's words.

"My friends. It is good you have come with me on this trail to free my son. Evil ones, like we are seeing come to the valley for our gold, have taken him. We will get him back. The ones who have done this will pay with their lives. Hear my thoughts on how I believe we should settle this. Surround the camp without their watchers knowing we are there. Find them. Get close to where they sit. Be ready to move with me. As we know, there are five watchers. Red Hawk and I will walk into their camp. Talk to the one who leads about Wolf. If he does not say the proper words, I will kill him with my war club. If I do this, kill all the watchers. If by chance they do let him go with us, let us get out from their fire before you kill the watchers. Either way, do not leave a watcher alive. This is how I see this before us. Speak if any of you see wrong in my thinking."

They all sat studyin' on Dancing Bear's words for a few minutes, smokin, 'fore silently gettin' up one-by-one and slippin out into the fresh broken darkness like haints. Not a word said between 'em. A body what was used to movin' in the dark could see to travel 'fore most folks could. Them warriors know'd from years 'a doin's just how to go about findin' their way in circlin' the watchers. Dancing Bear was wise. He'd let 'em find their own trail. Know'd they'd seek out their proper places. Be on 'em 'fore they even realized it when the time come. Huntin' was what these kinda Indians was born to do. They was part 'a the woods. Moved like the mountain cat. Silent. Smooth. Deadly. I reasoned, as I followed the warriors out, that these takers had never experienced what they was fixin' to see, and, of course, would never see again. Trail savvy Cherokee warriors stalkin' in their own homeland weren't something folks like them know'd nothin' about. They sat like they weren't feared 'a nothin', but they should 'a been. Takin' Wolf prisoner to work as a slave would be the last mistake these men made. I said a little prayer for 'em as I moved back toward my rock. Not a big one, for I didn't like what they'd done to my friend. Just a short one to let God know they was comin'.

Dancing Bear sat the fire smokin' his pipe while his warriors took to their trails. His face raised to Old Man Sun. He was prayin'. Listenin' with his heart. Red Hawk squatted beside him. They was still sittin' that way as I topped a short ridge to the west, takin' our little make shift camp with Wolf's mule, Dancing Bear, and Red Hawk out 'a sight. Red Hawk had told me to make my way back to the rock I'd been watchin' from. I know'd his thoughts. He was troubled for his son. He was troubled for his brothers, too. The takers had to be dealt with, for others might suffer on their account. He reasoned, if they were keen enough to get Wolf, then more Cherokee would likely get took as well. He would do all he could to not let that happen, yet his concern went even deeper. Many were comin' to the mountains in search of the yellow rock. He hated their comin'. He know'd they'd keep comin' for a time, too. More just like these what'd taken his son. *Did he have to kill 'em all to keep trouble away? No. He did not want killin'. That would only bring more.* His prayer was for wisdom. To know the right thing to do, when the time to know it come. Life and death is in the palm of the Great Creator. Dancing Bear always listened for His voice. Know'd when he heard it clear as a morning song tellin' him his trail to follow. Most times he was sure what the voice commanded. Like the trail he was on to free Wolf. Keep others safe. He would kill soon. A fight against evil. It would not bother his soul. He was sure of his duty as a father, husband, uncle, and elder. He know'd exactly what the voice was sayin' do. He finished his pipe, then stood raisin' his arms to the morning sky. A soft chant began in his center workin' its way out through his voice. He danced. No more than a gentle circle around a small dyin' warmin' fire, but he danced. Chanted his song 'a thanks to Holy Spirit for givin' him Mother Earth. Closed out his talk with God by droppin' to a knee just as his chant ended. He stood again. Stared Red Hawk in the eye as he stood. This time with a more direct focus 'a thinkin'. It was time to go get their son. He felt no fear. Checkin' his knives and war club to make sure they was still laced to his belt good, he led Red Hawk off toward where the diggin' camp lay. His mind clear. It was a good day for a fight. The trail called to him.

The rock where I'd been watchin' from the day before was just as I'd left it. The camp had changed some. The tent was gone. Morning had come on full. Old Man Sun was lightin' the woods, so you could see. My rifle laid across the top 'a the rock loaded full with powder and ball. I'd rested it on my possibles pouch, pointin' the barrel straight at the new hole where my Blood Brother and Opah was bein' made to dig. That made my blood get up havin' to watch that. They weren't haulin' dirt like before, now they had picks. Bein' made to dig a new hole by some mean lookin' feller what wore the army kinda boots. I figured him for a Blue Coat. Me layin' close by but not bein' able to do nothin' got my back up. I know'd this whole thing was bein' seen to by Dancing Bear, but seein' Wolf's sufferin' for the last couple days made my anger spark of a sudden. For sure when I come to realize him and Opah was havin' to dig a new hole. Weren't right them havin' to do what they was havin' do at the end of a whip. Wolf was bare from the waist up. I could see at least two red lines across his back. His face bruised, bloody, and swollen. I needed to help 'em. I figured a good way to even things up would be to shoot the one with the whip. Close as I was I know'd I'd not miss. Drawin' a bead just in front of his left ear, I started an easy pull on the trigger. I needed to feel my Harpers Ferry .54 caliber come back full. The slammin' of its heavy walnut butt against my shoulder would send a lead ball screamin' at the left side of the evil one's head takin' the right side off complete. That would most likely cool my anger some. Give Wolf and Opah a chance to get away. I'd grow'd tired of all the nasty that gold lookin' was bringin' to my mountain home. This new danger brought worry to all what lived in Choestoe. Changin' things to bad, yet, I know'd I couldn't finish my killin' chore. I let off the pull I was puttin' on my trigger. I couldn't shoot the whipper, not for a time still. I'd been taught better. Out 'a respect to Dancing Bear, I would wait. It was all I could do to hold off droppin' flint to the fresh laid powder in the gun's pan. I wanted that man dead for hurtin' my friend. God forgive me, I did.

Cain watched as Old Man Sun lit the diggin' camp. Things was different. The loud one what stayed in the tent was gone. Wolf and Opah was already havin' to work. Looked to be they was startin' a new hole. A watcher stood close by with a whip in his right hand. Wolf looked to 'a been laid upon by that whip. Cain could see the lines clear across Wolf's back. The bruises on his face from bein' beat by fist. That got his blood boilin' with mad. A fight was comin'. Didn't matter to him if he had to face 'em all, he'd get his brother out from among 'em. He was gonna see Wolf free and venged for 'cause 'a what'd been done to him. He studied the camp as he fought the urge to go kill. Six watchers sat in their chosen places. No different than the day before. *Cain wondered if they'd slept there all night*. He checked his rifle, makin' sure all was still ready to fire, then settled the whole of it good over the stump. The bead pointed direct at the chest of the one holdin' the whip. It was all he could do not to drop flint on the man, but he know'd Dancing Bear was due that act of justice. It would be enough for him to help. Be ready to move on the camp when it was time. He began planning how to advance once he was sure Dancing Bear had got there. Spottin' a small game trail, he figured he'd most likely use that to move though the trees. Slip in silent when the fightin' got goin'. Find the watcher what sat close by 'cause he'd have to shoot him first when the killin' commenced, then he could slip on into the camp. Help free Wolf and Opah. Thinkin' like that was the warrior in him.

My thoughts turned to Elizabeth for a brief moment as I stood my rock watchin' the watchers. I hoped I'd live to see her again. I lifted up a short prayer askin' Holy Spirit to watch over her, and me. I made my mind that I was not gonna die at the Rock Ridge that day. For sure not at the hands of a bunch 'a thieves. That thinkin' cleared my mind. I was ready to do what I could to help free Wolf.

Chapter 17 - It's Always Best to be Wise

Dancing Bear could smell the richness of the forest floor as he walked. Bein' late spring meant the sap was risin' in the trees. He could feel the smoothness of the grass through the beaver tail soles of his knee high foot skins as he wandered the trails between the rocks. Could hear the birds singin' their spring matin' songs in what few trees they was on the Rock Ridge. The green tryin' to grow all around him made the air cool and damp. The colors of the season, comin' through the new growth, turned the woods into a kinda flowering tree garden. It was one of his favorite times of all the seasons. If you found a holler full 'a dogwood in full color, it could near blind a body. Put red, orange, and yellow from other growth in with the white of the dogwood and you could sit in that holler with it all day. Get lost in the beauty of it. A heavy scent laid on 'em when you found a bunch in full bloom. Filled your mouth with a sweet honey taste as you breathed in the air around them trees. Would make you dizzy smellin' 'em after a fresh shower rain. The heavy white colors of the ivy and laurel lit the sides of wet hollers where springheads popped up or branches emptied out. Heavy long leafs rose up on both sides of the valley. It was nice walkin' through all of it. Comfortin'. He wished his present walk was to see his life's mate, Ah-Ga-Li-Ha, for a spring walk through the woods. Not on a trail to rescue his son from evildoers what had him captive.

His thoughts turned to where his trail would end as he followed by memory the way to where Wolf was bein' held. He'd been on the Rock Ridge many times in his life. Wolf had told him of us findin' it when we did a few years back, but he'd been on the ridge when out on walks or hunts before and after we thought we'd found it. It was a good place to pray. A good place to hunt. The bear hide blanket he gifted me at my birthin' come from the Rock Ridge. He know'd to the tree exactly where his son was bein' worked. These woods was his home. Know'd 'em well. Know'd where to go to get a good view 'a the camp without bein' found out. Him and Red Hawk needed a plan on how they'd do once they started into the camp and face to face with the evil ones. How to take the camp without puttin' Wolf's life out for the takin'. It was important they didn't make any mistakes. He led Red Hawk to the small rise overlookin' the diggin' camp, which when comin' from the south was kinda down in a short gap at the base of the big mountain the Rock Ridge was attached to. There they found some cover behind a small stand 'a ivy. Squatted to their knees to watch. It broke his heart seein' his son. Diggin' holes for gold lookers was a most disrespectful thing for a Cherokee to have to go through, for sure hurtin' the way Wolf was. His son had grow'd a sight in body and spirit over the last couple years, that was for sure, but he was still a boy. His manhood was close, and the ceremony would be soon, but he was still a boy. Deadly and mountain savvy to a point, but still a boy, and his momma wanted him home.

"Brother," Red Hawk kinda whispered as they watched the goin' on's of the camp. Spotted the watchers where they sat. "This is an evil place. These men are fools. They have no savvy. I believe death would bring them peace. Let us oblige them. We should go kill all who are in this camp. Be done with these heathens. I will lead. Let us go," he said as he started to rise.

"Wait," Dancing Bear said, quietly grabbing Red Hawk's arm without ever takin' his eyes from the movement in the camp. "I want to watch a while. Give our warriors time. I, too, am eager to wet my blade with their black blood, but as an elder of our tribe, I need to know the why of what is happening here. Steady yourself for a spell, Brother. We will go in time. I am not certain we know all we need to know. We need to scout this camp again. Find anything we do not know about. Make it right before we move on these heathens."

"I understand, Brother. You watch. I will go scout this camp. Move to the other side. Speak with Cain. He is watching from the steep where the woods start back full. It would be good to know what he has learned. I will come back here from the east. But Brother, it will take me a while to do this. I must be careful not to be found out. I do not want to put our warriors in danger where they hide. Dancing Bear -- listen to me. Do not go into this camp until I am back. It is best if we go in as one. I feel as you in my spirit, there may be something here we do not know. Have not seen. Say you will wait until I return. I want to hear it."

"Yes," Dancing Bear said in a deep voice of thought while never takin' his eyes off the camp . . . his son. Watchin' in sorrow as Wolf kept diggin', but feelin' hope as Dancing Bear saw him sneak a peak into the woods. He know'd Wolf was lookin' for his father to come. Wonderin' if he was there to free him yet. "I will wait, Red Hawk. It would be good to know anything Cain has learned. Go quickly. Stay clear of our warriors. Come straight back here once you've finished your looking. I regret as a leader of our people that my need to know these takers evil thoughts is not as heavy on my soul as my need to feel justice for my son. The evil ones must pay for coming here, taking one of ours for slave work, and for doing all the evil things they do to others. I will make what has happened here be a warning to all who think our nation is weak. Men like these should be made to know we look out for our own, settler and Indian. My blood runs hot for this fight, Red Hawk, but yes, I will wait. Only for a time, though, so hurry now. Bring yourself back here soon. I want you with me when I go into their camp to get our son."

Red Hawk left knowin' he needed to not waste time. His trail to the north side 'a the camp come right down by me. We spoke but only for a short minute 'fore I followed him on down his trail. I was always amazed at how quiet true warriors could move in the woods. Red Hawk had come on me with his hand around my mouth pullin' me back behind our rock just as I first heard him comin' up from behind. I felt kinda foolish lettin' him get in close like he did, but then I remembered he was one of the most skilled warriors in the whole of the Cherokee nation. The lead elder of the Cherokee Guard. Had he been enemy, I'd 'a most likely met my maker. That was the second time I'd been caught like that by a warrior in my young life. I made a vow I was gonna learn how they did that, then I'd know what to listen out for when folks come up from behind. 'Cause one day I reasoned, that hand what grabbed me weren't gonna be friendly. If I slipped and let that happen, I'd be in trouble. I would talk to Wolf about it when we got him home. He know'd how to do most everything them warriors know'd how to do. He just weren't skilled in all of it, yet. He would be, of that I had no doubt, but George had snuck up on him before, too, just like he had me.

"Red Hawk," I whispered with much concern after he'd took his hand from my mouth. "I don't mean any disrespect, Uncle, but why are you here? I thought you and Dancing Bear was gettin' ready to set Wolf free, but you're here. You can't set him free if you're here. Why are you here, Uncle? When will we get Wolf out from there? He is in a terrible way. I see that he hurts, Uncle, you must know this. What is it that you are doin' instead of gettin' Wolf?

"Jebediah!" he said while grabbin' my shoulders with his hands. "Calm yourself. We are making to free Wolf. Do not worry. Dancing Bear is being cautious. He thinks we need to know more about this camp. Wants to be sure we know where all the danger is hidden. We must make sure Wolf can escape without getting hurt when the time comes. We have looked the camp over from a rise to the south. Our warriors have it surrounded. Still, my brother is mindful. Things don't seem to be as they should. I am scouting as his eyes. Looking for hidden watchers. Soldiers do this. These men look soldier to me. I believe they might have others watching in secret. It is wise to find out. Tell me, Jeb. Have you seen or heard anything different than what you would have thought to see? Think close, son. Any sounds not recognized? I need to know."

"No sounds, Uncle. I see things are just the way we left them yesterday except now the tent is gone. The loud one and his two guards have left with it. Had to be when it was dark. The watchers are in their same places. Sittin' lookin' the same direction. I count five just like before. I was startin' to think they weren't real folks till the closest one to me got up and left. Little while he come back. At least I believe it was him. Looked to be the same kinda clothes but I'm not sure his hat was the same."

"You have a good eye, Jeb. From what you say, I have a feeling that it was a different soul what came back from the one leaving. You have given me a notion that could help us much. Which way did the watcher go? How long till he returned?"

"He went due east from here. Across the ridge straight away. I figure he was gone a half hour 'fore he come back. I allowed it was nature callin' him to business, but I thought his hat looked kinda different on return. I'm for sure on that, Uncle. What do you think that means?"

"A second camp, Jeb. These men are a little smarter than I'd set them for. If there is a second camp, we will need to find it. Maybe one of our warriors on that side has seen this camp. If so, we will clean out that nest before Dancing Bear goes to call on the whip man in the digging camp. We will go find Cain. He is to the north. We will stalk this second camp. Talk to those who rest there. Dancing Bear is very wise, Jeb. Always listen to his words. Holy Spirit guides him. I have seen this many times in our days. He is touched. I was ready to walk into this camp. Confront their leader. Take Wolf from their hold. This would have been a mistake I believe now."

With all that said, we left headin' north to go get Cain. I listened close as we left. I couldn't hear Red Hawk's movements then, neither. He moved quiet as a haint. Even knowin' he was there in front 'a me, and listenin' hard, I couldn't hear him settin' foot to trail. I could hear myself, but not him. I was movin' quiet, too, for common folk anyway. It was scary how them warriors could move in the woods. I was glad they were my friends; family.

Red Hawk walked right in on the point of Cain's knife as we slipped around the boulder in back 'a where Cain was watchin' the camp from. He should 'a know'd better than to try and sneak up on Cain. He could sense danger just like any other warrior. Red Hawk froze when he felt the tip jab into his middle. Spoke the words that told Cain who he was. Cain weren't happy.

"Red Hawk! Uncle!" Cain whisper-hollered. "You should 'a made a call 'fore you come in on me so close and quick. Forgive me, Uncle. I did not know it was you. They was folks close durin' the night. Didn't know but what you might be one 'a them comin' back this way. I am sorry, Uncle."

"Do not be sorry for defending yourself, Brother. My mind is distracted, or I would have let you know I was close. You acted right, warrior. It was I that made the mistake. Thank you for not killing me when you had every reason it should take. Now, you said you had visitors during the night. As you said, it seems there were more than one. Tell me of this. How did you know they were near?"

"I heard them, Uncle. They whispered out in the dark. Close enough so's I could hear 'em, but not close enough to know what they said. I figure they was standin' maybe a minute or more 'fore they moved on. I heard 'em as they moved west. I don't know who it was. Not sure how they moved so quiet, dark as it was. I wish I could tell you more. Who might that've been, Red Hawk?

"Indians, Cain. No doubts. Only woods folk could move on the trails as dark as it was last night. Indians movin' through here on the quiet would be how I figure it. I believe there is a second camp to the east of here. A hidden camp that holds men to watch the digging camp. More soldier men to take watch at different times during the day. We need to find this camp. Kill the ones who rest from their time of watching out for us. Then Dancing Bear can move to get Wolf. What say ye, Cain? What are your thoughts, Brother?"

"Lead the way, Uncle. What you say sounds straight to me. I need to move some for sure. I ain't sat for so long without doin' nothin' but waitin' since my baby

Isabelle was bein' birthed. That was a day to think on for me. How 'bout you, Jeb? A long day that had my sweet Rose screamin' out from her bed, but a day where a miracle happened. I praise the Great Creator for it. Let us have at these heathens, Red Hawk. They need to be taught we don't tolerate such in our part of the mountains. May Holy Spirit be with us. Watch your top knot, Jebediah."

Red Hawk was gone 'fore Cain ever finished what he was sayin'. He weren't listenin' to Cain. His need to find out what was happenin' around him had his mind fetched. Cain noticed it, too. For sure after he'd caught us sneakin' in on him. Red Hawk weren't movin' right. His walk was too fast. Near careless. Cain seen it right off as we fell in behind him. Me in the rear. That was dangerous for us all. Even I know'd that. Got Cain edgy. As a warrior on a killin' path, Cain figured he needed to speak with his uncle on this. He walked a little faster, catchin' up to him on the trail. A simple touch of Cain's finger to the warrior's back stopped Red Hawk on the spot. They squatted to the ground. The elder never looked back at Cain, keepin' his eyes sharp to what was in front of him. Red Hawk didn't typically make mistakes, but movin' against dangerous men could get bad quick if one got careless. He was know'd for his skills. Mistakes weren't common to him. He was chosen for the Guard 'cause he was sharp to his enemies' doin's. It was uncanny how he could think like they thought. Many stories I'd heard on him told how smart he was when on the stalk for his enemy. Always stayed calm. Never let his thinkin' get to wanderin' off. But with Wolf bein' in trouble, and Laughing Beaver on the prowl, Cain clearly saw his uncle's mind was touched. These things of concern brought Red Hawk worry. Havin' worry was bad. Worry caused mistakes. That is why Cain needed to discuss his thoughts with the elder Guardsman.

Cain felt kinda foolish bringin' Red Hawk to halt for speakin' like he did. It weren't his place to call a warrior like Red Hawk to mind for something Cain believed put them in more danger than they should be. Stalkin' enemy folk was excitin' for warriors like Cain when done properly. Carefully. Dangerous if not. Cain had no choice. He must show disrespect for Red Hawk's lead.

"Red Hawk. Uncle," Cain said lightly as they squatted together in the trail. "Uncle? I need to speak with you. I need to tell you something."

Red Hawk turned lookin' Cain dead in the eye. He was not happy. Cain could feel it. "Do not worry yourself for this trail warrior. I know my mind. It will not be taken from me. Holy Spirit is my guide. I hear His voice clearly. My sight is only for the evil that has come to this place. Trust me, Cain. I know your thoughts. I will not make a mistake."

With that all said, he turned back to the trail, leavin' Cain standin' there with his heart in his stomach. How could he have insulted one of the bravest, wisest of all Cherokee warriors in the mountains? It would take Cain a lifetime to get his respect back if he let this go. He stood his ground. "UNCLE", he near yelled while never movin' a step to follow. Red Hawk was on him like a momma panther scoldin' her young'un. The sharp edge of his knife at Cain's throat within' a second 'a Cain ever openin' his mouth. Cain told me later the look in Red Hawk's eyes when he turned on him near got his back up, but he stayed calm. After all, Red Hawk was a warrior first.

"Take your knife away, Uncle," Cain said in a really calm voice while grabbin' the warrior's arm what held it. Cain never flinched. Stared Red Hawk right back cold in the eye. "You will not kill me today, Red Hawk. I will say my peace. You will listen because you are wise. You know I only want the same as you. That is how it must be between us. You need to hear my heart. I see what you do not. I mean no disrespect, Uncle. I just need you to hear the same as you would be tellin' me if I was lead warrior actin' like you on this trail."

"Yes. I hear your words. I now know your heart, warrior," Red Hawk said as he draw'd back his knife, facin' Cain face on. "No, I will not kill you. There is no fear in your eyes. Your courage shows me your need is strong. For showing no fear, I will respect you once more. For the courage to challenge me, I will listen. Speak, brave one. You have my ear."

Cain, in his self, was a respected tribe member. Red Hawk had to honor his status. Also, he was a warrior. Mixed in with all that, Cain was family. He was married to Dancing Bear's daughter, Rose. Red Hawk and Dancing Bear was birth brothers. Killin' Cain weren't gonna happen 'cause family honor held for both, but a little bleedin' weren't a problem. Bein' in the same clan meant settlin' issues without death to either body. It was the way.

"Uncle, I need to lead us to this second camp. Your eyes are wide with anger. Your feet are not fallin' on the trail where they should. We are makin' way too much noise. I know that Holy Spirit guides your thoughts, as He does mine. Listen close, Uncle. You know as a warrior I must do this. There is too much danger near for us to be found on this trail. I mean no disrespect, Red Hawk, but I will take us to this camp. From there, you will decide what we should do. That is all I have to say to you on this matter, Uncle. You are a great warrior. One of which many should hope to be. But this is a matter of family; revenge, and I feel your anger has dulled your trail savvy. If you study on my words, you will know I am right. What say ye, Red Hawk?"

"I hear your words, husband of Rose. You are wise. In my heart, I know your words are true. I could feel my way was off center. That was careless of me as a warrior. It is good you called me to it. I will follow you to this camp. Forgive my pride, young one. My concern is deep for Wolf. My desire to settle with Laughing Beaver never stronger. I want to go with Dancing Bear into this camp. To do this, we must know all we need to know, but it must be done quickly. Dancing Bear will only wait a short while longer before he goes to get his son. We must be there when he does, or death could be his call. The Black Angel is near. I can feel his spirit. We must go, Cain. Take us to this camp, son of Thompie Collins."

Cain settled for a smoother pace with not so much hurry in it. Even I could feel the difference. I know'd his insides wanted to get on down the trail just like Red Hawk, so I could tell he had to use a lot 'a effort to stay steady. Watch close for any level movements not natural to normal woods travel. He moved smoothly. Listened close. Scented the breeze. Felt the ground under foot. A true warrior sees everything. Spots things most folks would never see -- like the watcher we'd just slipped up on. Squatted tight in behind a thick bunch 'a ivy not near noticeable for a careless one, except Cain had his mind clear. Know'd out 'a habit what to look for. Chances was good Red Hawk might 'a seen him, but Cain for sure did. Cain stopped us. Bent to one knee on the trail quiet as a rabbit easin' through on wet ground. Me and Red Hawk did the same. We'd seen it, too, once we followed his stare after squattin'. Cain had found the second camp. My heart started poundin' in my ears so loud I couldn't hear nothin' else. I found it hard to draw air clean. I prayed for the killin' I know'd was comin'. Out 'a fear and excitement I made myself as unseeable as possible. I was gonna do everything Red Hawk and Cain did to keep from bein' found out. I come to realize my very life would depend on me not makin' any mistakes. This was a little more than I'd figured for. My thoughts turned to Momma. There was a chance I'd never see her again. My soul ached.

Chapter 18 - Sean Gets Hit Hard

Sean watched the Indians 'til they left from his place, slippin' out from the big white pine top just as the light faded. They weren't nothin' for 'em to steal 'cept a small kindling splittin' axe, so he figured 'em moved on to their next thievin'. Sean forgot he'd left it stuck in a wall on the inside of his barn. They'd found it. He liked that little axe, too. Black Oak had made it for him. He made mind to get it back. I seen him kill a squirrel with it once as it ran up the side of a big oak tree. We smoked that critter and two rabbits over our campfire that night for supper. Mixed the meat with some dried fruit pieces we boiled what'd been sun dried the season before. That was some good eatin' for two hungry mountain boys.

They left headin' south, but Sean know'd they could be anywhere. He made his way headin' north ridin' his mule to make better time. He stopped about half a mile away from where he'd been watchin' the trespassers in the white pine top. There would be no fire in his camp this night for fear 'a lettin' 'em know where he was. He'd stay quiet, too. Spent all his wakin' time listenin' close for anything movin'. Weren't long till he heard the call.

Red wolf yelps are ways 'a communicatin' among a family. If they come close to your camp of 'a night, you'll hear 'em yelpin' back-and-forth tellin' one to the other where they are. They're sayin' they know about the thing they've come up on. How to move to attack it or get away from it. Which way to go if escape was due. The sound is different than any other in the woods. Very difficult to make for folks. The wolf yelps Sean heard durin' the night weren't real close, but they weren't real critters, neither. Sounded more like a sick squirrel. He'd never heard nothin' like it. Hoped to never hear nothin' like it again.

Red wolves can see at night near like folks can of 'a day. Can smell food from a mile or more if the wind is right. Nothin' travels the woods like wolves. Nothing natural in the mountains is more deadly to meat critters than a couple 'a red wolves huntin'. Never saw 'em in packs much, maybe a couple times. They did most 'a their huntin' as a family. I loved hearin' 'em call of a night when the moon show'd bright, but it's a fear when a family comes up on your person and you not know they was near. You're standin' there in the woods alone one second, the very next you can be surrounded by 'em. It's 'cause 'a the way they move. Spread out to cover more ground but all headin' in the same direction. Raises the hair on back 'a your neck when you get in close to 'em. Makes the strongest of men wonder their intentions. I never hunted 'em. Never cared for the fur. Had some, just never wore it much. Some folks did. Lots of 'em got took for the hide trade by gold lookers when they come. They'd trap 'em. Sell their hides at market. The last 'a the red wolves all went away not long after the gold did, for the most part, anyway. You'd see one on occasion. Hear one ever once in a while. I hated them lookers comin' in ruinin' my home.

Sean was confused by the sound he'd heard. Couldn't really say what it was. He lay quiet. Flat down on his back just off the top of a small slope covered by ivy thicket. The wind carryin' his scent due north. That would keep anybody headed north from smellin' his person or his mule. He only heard the noise the one time, but it didn't make sense to him. If it was Indian, would there not 'a been more callin'? He thought on it long as he could 'fore his eyes would not stay open. Old Man Sun shinin' was the next thing he remembered hours later. The smell of smoke that weren't simple camp fire smoke sharp in his nose. He grabbed his rifle. Jumped his mule in one stride sinkin' heels to haunches. The mule know'd to run when Sean did that, so he run fast as he could. Mules ain't the fastest critter on four legs but they go as hard as they can when you want 'em to.

Sean rode straight for the smoke. The fear come in knowin' it weren't smellin' like a woods burnin' smoke or a fireplace smoke. No, it was a much heavier smoke than those. Only one thing could smoke like that. Sean know'd as he rode, that what he was gonna find when he got to his place would be bad. He prayed what he could as his mule headed straight for his barn. Sean wondered why they would burn his place? These must be evil folk. He would pay mind to be careful. Log homes and barns can be rebuilt, but scalps and blood cannot without divine intervention. Sean figured to not bother the Holy One over that. He'd been given good sense. He'd try his best to use it.

***

The second camp we found was small. Just a restin' spot for the watchers to use next to a small branch at the bottom of a short holler. They must 'a figured it a place that would keep 'em safe when not guardin' the diggin's. Down low and out 'a the wind so they could rest in comfort. Only four there, countin' the watcher in the woods out from camp. Three sittin' in homemade chairs around a small warmin' fire. At least we didn't see any more, but in the kinda doin's we was in, you always had to figure they might be more comin' or goin'. Be careful for it.

There was two extra chairs around the fire. Red Hawk thought it best to make our way around the camp. Leave it to itself 'cause it weren't a worry, but he couldn't. Cain, neither. They never looked at me, but a quick glance from one to the other told 'em both exactly what they wanted to do. We eased on to start slippin' up on what we thought was a lookout, but as we turned to move on, he was gone. Weren't but a second 'til we seen him. He was already up and walkin' back to camp when the east breeze carried us a clue to what the man was doin'. For good or bad, it brought the scent what told us the watcher was not a lookout. We all smiled while risin' to our feet. We started walkin' toward camp with little care other than makin' square why we was all there in the first place. All of us payin' mind to stay clear 'a where the watcher had been squatted. Warriors would never answer the call of nature that close to camp. That was to be done in private. Away from folks, but never near water, camp or where you aimed to hunt.

As we moved on to talk with the watchers, Cain know'd Red Hawk was still hungry for revenge. His back was up for his nephew. Wolf was in trouble, which made Red Hawk most dangerous to any he come up on. Would be till he got his family out from bein' held. Cain figured to watch him . . . some. Didn't want him doin' somethin' what might let the rest 'a their bunch know they'd been found out. Cain motioned for Red Hawk to go on in. He'd stay hid in the woods with me. Catch any what tried to run off hopin' to warn the others. It was near funny seein' them watchers' faces when Red Hawk come out on 'em. Most likely the only true warrior they'd ever seen, and this 'un was wearin' full battle truck. He was a sight for folks not familiar with seein' his kind. I'd grow'd accustomed to it, but I remembered the first time I ever seen a bunch 'a warriors together. The soldiers in camp weren't scared more than amazed that this creature had just walked into their lives. It took 'em a minute to finally figure it all out 'fore the boss 'a the bunch stood to speak with Red Hawk. He should 'a never left his chair.

"Stop there, Indian. You ain't too smart walkin' in on us all by yourself like this. We don't cotton to your kind. We've heerd 'a y'all. Murderers and thieves the lot 'a ya. I figure I'll just end my trouble with you bein' here in my camp right now. Get gone from here or I'll cut a furrow down the middle 'a your head big enough to see through," he said as he reached a pistol cocked and ready out from his back, levelin' it at Red Hawk's forehead. The elder Indian never moved as the gun's barrel touched cold to his skin just above the bridge of his nose.

Not sure exactly what got the watcher's attention, but something told him they was pain in his chest. The look what come to his eyes told a body he'd just felt the feelin' of death. Could 'a been he felt the sting of cold steel as it sliced through meat and muscle or the beatin' of his heart stoppin' from the sharp edge 'a Red Hawk's knife cuttin' it near in half. Either way, he was dead just a few seconds after he realized he'd been kilt. He never even saw the arm move what ended his life on Mother Earth. Red Hawk's glare into the man's eyes as he slid his long knife from his chest was one of pure hate. A look that came to all Cherokee who had to put up with the newcomers and their evil. Red Hawk was glad that 'un was dead. It was the man's own choice. Now to put the fate of the other three to themselves.

The others never realized their mate had been kilt till they seen him fallin' to the ground limp as a dead body should be, then not gettin' back up. Red Hawk had pushed the dead man off to his left 'fore takin' a couple steps toward their fire. Starin' hard into their eyes searchin' for their next move. His long knife held up in front sightful for 'em as could be. Dark heart blood runnin' from its tip to its handle then down onto his hand. He'd not loosed his grip from the original hold he'd took 'fore killin' the first watcher. Out 'a habit, mostly. Know'd from years 'a fightin' men that if folk blood got between his palm skin and the knife's bone handle it would make the knife uncontrollable slippery for good fightin'. Hard to use. That would turn the fight to bein' more dangerous than it should be for Red Hawk. He didn't mind the blood on his skin. It was warm. A token of revenge for Wolf. He'd make sure to clean the blade and handle good once the second camp fight was over.

Only one was brave enough to stand challengin' the senior warrior after seein' his mate killed. My dad always said "bein' stupid was hard to fix." They's times to stand strong when you have courage, and they's times to sit quiet in wisdom, even for those who have that courage. Listen with your whole bein' 'fore ever sayin' or doin' anything. A wise man holds to this. Keeps his life. Warriors hold to this. I've heard 'em go long minutes 'fore ever sayin' words in conversations of importance. This watcher didn't hold to that smart kinda thinkin'. He started hollerin' revenge talk for his friend at Red Hawk while pullin' his own knife. Red Hawk could see in his eyes he was lookin' to kill. I'm not sure if the watcher ever know'd what actually killed him or not. Probably thought for the short second it took his mind to stop thinkin' that it was some kinda Indian spirit doin's. It weren't -- just pure skill from a practiced hand and a strong bow. The other two never moved after they saw his endin'. I'd not seen anything like it on a person. Hogs yes, but never through a man's person. The only way I know'd what'd happened was I heard the arrow land some twenty paces to the man's right after shootin' plumb through his head. Seen it layin' still on the forest floor after hearin' it land in that direction. Blood and brain coverin' it from flint to tip, all the way down the hickory shaft, then stickin' so thick to the turkey feather fletching it laid the feathers to the shaft like they was covered in syrup. I know'd then where Cooper had gone after our morning meal a couple days earlier. The watcher stood for just a second after bein' hit, then fell limp to the ground just like his friend earlier. It had to appear to the other two watchers that haints had done come in on 'em. Two bein' dead and nothing really to see what killed 'em. The elder of the two never moved from his chair. The younger rolled off from his chair to lose his stomach on the edge of the branch they was camped by. I couldn't blame him. It was a gruesome sight seein' two folks die so sudden. The older watcher seemed to be cryin' but they weren't no tears. Red Hawk spoke to him. I could hear in his voice that his heat for revenge had cooled some.

"Old one. Evil man. You have come to my home. Taken my family to use as a slave. Why have you done this? I did not come to your home to take your sons or steal your worth or burn your homes or stores of food. Why do you do these things, white man? Go away. You are nothing but trouble with your need for the gold rock. Do not come back here. If I see you again, I will kill you. Take your nasty ways. Go from my home. I wish you never to return here, if your trail allows you to make it home alive. Unfortunately for you, my warrior brothers are all around. I will not call them back. You will not see them, but there is hope they will find you. I fear the Black Angel is coming for you this night, but he won't be summoned by my hand. I do not care if you die. It is now in the hands of the Great

Creator. You should never have come here. You are fools. Take what little you have and go from this place, now. This is all I have to say to you."

Bein' done talkin', Red Hawk reached for their coffee pot. Poured its contents all over the little warmin' fire they had goin'. That would tell anybody what passed, camp was finished. No fire or smokin' bed 'a coals meant no folks in woods talk. He moved toward the older watcher while slippin' his long knife back in its leather bed. Stopped short of the man lookin' him square in the eye. He never stood long 'fore his right arm struck out like a rattle maker, backhandin' the watcher so hard to the right side of his face I heard bones crack. That sent the man flyin' out 'a his chair like a pumpkin' what rolled off the harvest wagon accidental, landin' him flat to the ground hard. Blood squirtin' out 'a both nostrils from the broke jaw and nose Red Hawk laid him with. He never touched the younger of the two. Never even looked at him. Must 'a figured he weren't no problem. 'Sides, he know'd me and Cain was holdin' our rifles on the camp ready to drop flint if the need show'd. Cooper was close by, too. We never saw him when happenin's like we was in took place. He favored bein' alone when stalkin' or defendin'. He was more deadly that way. Reminded me 'a Wolf's brother, Moon Shadow.

Me and Cain stood hid back in the woods a ways while Red Hawk done his talkin'. Two was dead. Two more was gonna be dead if Dancing Bear's warriors run up on 'em. They left out from camp on Red Hawk's orders headin' due east carryin' what few possibles they owned. I remember thinkin' it could be good for 'em goin' east. Less likely to cross trails with any Cherokee. They had no choice in leavin'. Their diggin' camp was done. They know'd from meetin' Red Hawk that their head man would be settled with soon, too. Know'd they weren't gonna be no more gold pay for watchin' over the diggin' camp. It was time to move on. Any watcher comin' back would find their friends layin'. The other two gone. Seein' what'd happened would make 'em slip off for cover. Hopefully make 'em wonder if what little gold they was gettin' was worth the risk 'a sufferin' death. Send 'em off at the thought of it. The warriors surroundin' the camp would kill any they caught slippin' off, 'cept maybe for the younger of the bunch. Young ones would return home. Tell folks to leave well enough alone up in them mountains. Weren't nothin' there worth goin' for. Seein' death changes a man when he's mixed up in the happenin' of it. Makes a body feel it could 'a been him.

We followed Red Hawk out from camp maybe a quarter mile 'fore he stopped next to a growth 'a rock what looked like a small cave with its top took off. Had a springhead holed up near two paces across comin' out from the center of it. The whole place was surrounded by laurel. He drank a long, cool drink 'fore movin' down the branch some. There he slid his long knife out from its sheath washin' the blade in the runoff pondin' up below the springhead. Once his blade cleanin' chore was done, he turned to take a seat on a small boulder near the front 'a the rock growth. His back toward the trail we'd come in on. His eyes front. Me and Cain both got us a drink. Thinkin' on how good that water tasted, it come to me I hadn't watered in a while. I fetched an extra swallow or two 'fore I moved to sit a rock next to Red Hawk. Cain did the same, only he sat a little higher up in the rocks than we did. He could see our back trail from there. I figured he was makin' sure them watchers weren't fool enough to follow. As I sat next to him, I seen Red Hawk's look had changed. Gone was the tense squint of anger that worried

Cain so earlier, in its place was a look of concern. More normal for what he was facin' with Wolf bein' took. His voice was calm as he spoke.

"We have awoken their ancestors, Cain, Jeb. I'm not sure the souls of those two dead will be welcomed among those of his that have crossed the Great River. They did not seem like good souls to me. My long knife spoke to them as bad souls. The Great Creator will now decide their fate. They are nothing to me except dead enemy. Cain, take our brother and return to your watch place. There you both will wait until you see Dancing Bear move into the digging camp. I will be with him. Our warriors are all around, so if there is a fight, be watchful of what lays in the woods. I believe there are dangers we still have not seen. Remember, the murderer Laughing Beaver is somewhere near. Forgetting that could cost you your life, if he finds you before you see him. I must go. Dancing Bear will not wait much longer before he moves. His blood runs hot for his son's freedom. Mine does as well. It is time we set Wolf free."

Red Hawk was right. Dancing Bear weren't gonna wait no longer. He'd waited long as his soul would let him suffer his son's pain, but he'd waited long enough. It was clear to the leader in him that Wolf would learn from what was happenin', but the father in him allowed he'd learned enough. His son had grow'd weak. It was noticeable. Dancing Bear could see it. His diggin' efforts were showin' hard as he struggled to raise and drop the pickaxe. He was on the edge 'a breakin'. The one with him, too. The time had come for the son to experience true freedom only his father could provide. Wolf was fixin' to go home. No person near where we was could stop it, neither. Some was gonna die tryin', but none would hold Wolf any longer.

Red Hawk made it back just as his brother turned to leave from his watchin' point. Dancing Bear stopped as they come together face on, drawin' back as their eyes locked. Red Hawk had seen that look on Dancing Bear's face before. Hard. Cold. Angry. Ready for vengeance. Death was on its way for a visit. The Black Angel was comin' to Choestoe. Red Hawk was for sure no enemy would leave the Rock Ridge alive that day.

Chapter 19 - The Rogue's Trail

Sean sat his mule while lookin' his place over. Tears wettin' the corners of his eyes. His heart cut deep from the sight 'a what he'd called home the day before. A place he'd worked hard to build. A place where he dreamed of havin' a future. His own family to tend for. Weren't much left. They'd burned it all. His home, barn, nothing but a heap 'a ash and smoke. All the outbuildings was burnt. Smokehouse and woodshed was still burnin' some. What meat he'd had in stores was gone. They'd most likely took that. Bein' late spring, there was little left so losin' it weren't a big problem. He would need to hunt soon. Only parts of his home still standin' was the stone foundations him and his mule had worked so hard to set just perfect. His rock chimney and hearth stood like a monument to all his time and love. The fireplace, still laid with dried wood for makin' a fire, weren't even smokin'. The wood he'd stacked in it previous still layin' a'top the fire dogs waitin' on a flame to get goin'. That was spooky lookin'. You'd a thought them logs would 'a burned right off but no, not a spark 'a fire had touched 'em. Sean had laid split log floors when building his log home and they was burnt plumb up, but them sticks in the fireplace weren't even charred. Strange how things work.

Tracks said it was the same Indians he'd caught spyin' a couple days before. He recognized the sole print from their foot skins as matchin' the sole prints he'd found at the watchin' place. He allowed these was a bunch out for what they could get. Layin' torch to his home was a purposeful act by what was most likely some deadly Indians. He would find these rogues. Get square with 'em for takin' his home. What he had weren't much, but it was his. He'd worked hard for it. His trail would now be the same as theirs, 'cept his was a trail of vengeance. They'd hurt him to his core by takin' his home. He was gonna make sure they hurt no others . . . and he wanted his little kindlin' axe back. It was a gift from a true friend.

Havin' his mule already packed for travel let him keep walkin' as he rode through lookin' at all they'd done to his place. There was nothin' 'a worth left to rescue. The only remaining survivor was his boilin' kettle sittin' just inside where his front door had been. He remembered settin' it there just as he was leavin', but it weren't full 'a ash then. Didn't seem real watchin' the smoke rise from the black and gray piles that'd been his living quarters the last couple years. He had a deep-down hate for them what burned it. He come to realize, as he kept to the trail away from his little farm, that it was a good thing he weren't there when the evil ones come. He'd 'a been kilt. Pro'bly burnt along with the rest 'a everything he owned. He stopped his mule when the thought struck him deep. Hit his knees on the drop from the mules back. It was time to thank Holy Spirit for his life. Seek protection for the trail ahead. His prayin' took him well into the night. He woke where he'd stopped next to his mule. He was ready to make things right.

The outlaws' trail away from his place was easy for Sean to follow, or anybody else, really. The evil warriors weren't tryin' to hide where they was goin'. They didn't seem worried over whoever owned the farm followin' 'em. Sean know'd when rogues like these got out on trail anything could happen. Weren't no reason to the why, of why they burned his home and barn, 'cept for plain ol' hate and meaness. What they done was just plumb awful. He could feel they weren't feared, neither. It show'd in how fetchin' their trail sign read. Near careless, but purposeful. He made mind to stay a ways back while followin'. Could be they was watchin' out for him. He'd make camp early hopin' it didn't rain to wash away the sign he followed. Their trail led south. Most likely goin' to some place near Wolf Creek. Sean know'd that area well. He'd stayed on Wolf Creek for a while after leavin' out on his own from the soldier camp what brought him to the mountains. He liked it on Wolf Creek.

Laughing Beaver had a big time burnin' the log place. He and his mates did it out 'a spite and hate. He allowed the settlers was how come all the trouble had come to the mountains. One less homeplace made it all better to him. He know'd the owner would be angry, but he cared none. If that settler was fool enough to trail him, he was fool enough to lose his life. It would be a fight Laughing Beaver would welcome, but it was not the fight he'd come to the land of the rabbits for. No, that fight would be with one much more worthy than whatever settler he'd burned out. Red Hawk, of the Choestoe Clan, would fight hard. He'd not want to die at the hands of Laughing Beaver. That comin' together would end badly for one or the other. Laughing Beaver was eager for the time to come 'cause he had no doubt who'd walk away alive. He smiled thinkin' on it, while makin' his trail toward Wolf Creek. Major Dennis would be waiting. The warrior was eager to see how much gold the diggers had found.

***

Dancing Bear was clear of mind as he followed a faint game trail on in to the digging camp. He know'd exactly what he was gonna do. Know'd his warriors would be in their chosen places as he made himself known to all at the camp. Wolf and Opah saw him. Dropped their digging tools on the spot. Sgt. Baker seen 'em do that but paid no mind. He was focused on the two warriors who'd just breached his perimeter . . . and so boldly. The soldier feared little from Dancing Bear and Red Hawk 'cause he had guards out watchin', but the posted watchers held no concern for Dancing Bear as he walked toward Baker. They was havin' their own encounter with certain Cherokee warriors they'd just met.

Holdin' Baker's face with his eyes, Dancing Bear draw'd up close. The only question left to Dancing Bear was how many words would be said 'fore he ended all threats to his son. Baker was the first to speak as Dancing Bear and Red Hawk come to a halt in front of him. The officer's whip in plain view of all who looked. Dancing Bear and Red Hawk did not. The elder's blood boiled on the inside as he listened to the Sergeant's words hearin' the disrespect in his meaning, but you'd not know it. He was calm as deep water on the outside. Full emotional control in a situation most men would be shakin' in their britches over. A true Cherokee warrior. Tried many times by the hot flames of battle. This one would most likely not be his last.

"You two can stop right there, savages," Baker said as Dancing Bear and Red Hawk kinda looked at each other. Actin' like they didn't know what the man was sayin'. 'Sides, they'd done been stopped for a step or two when he commanded 'em. "Don't play dumb with me, now. I know y'all know what I'm sayin'. What business you got with us here? Y'all friends with that crazy Laughing

Beaver? I ain't never seen y'all with him before, but you dress like him. Who are y'all, now? Tell ol' Sgt. Baker or I'm gonna let my whip get y'all to talkin'. Understandin' me, boys? Huh?" he asked as he cracked his whip out in front of his person fast as a rattle maker strikin'. He left the end on the ground ready for another strike. I hardly seen him move.

I could hear every word Baker said. Saw Red Hawk's face draw up as the Sergeant mentioned a familiar name. The officer should 'a been beggin' for mercy instead 'a makin' two ranking Cherokee warriors even more anxious for revenge. I learned after so many intruders had come to our mountain home that most was just greedy, low down souls what most likely would sell their mommas for a gold coin, long as she didn't know it. Some weren't so bad, but most come with greed in their hearts like Baker and his bunch. Takin' folks to make 'em work was just plain evil. This man was livin' his last few seconds on earth and he didn't even know it. With a mere turn of Dancing Bear's head, six watchers screamed out in death one right after the other. The look on Baker's face softened oh so quickly after he heard the last watcher die. He weren't so bold now that he stood alone. His whip layin' limp on the ground still held by his right hand.

"I have come for my son, evil man. You have taken him captive. Put him to doing your digging work because you yourself are too lazy," Dancing Bear said as he looked to his son. "Wolf, bring your digging tool here. Give it to this soldier man. Let us watch him dig for a while. How about it, Blue Coat? I want you to dig like my son has been digging. But first, tell me about this man I dress like. I am curious why you would think we are with him? He must know of these diggings from what you have said. Is this so . . . boy?"

Sgt. Baker didn't know what to do. He was holdin' solid on the outside, but on the inside he was shakin' in his soldier boots. He was gonna die. He had no doubt about that. This thought gave him what little backbone he had left. He weren't gonna be made to dig like some slave. That just weren't gonna happen to him. His reaction was not unexpected by Dancing Bear. He was waitin' for it to come.

"I don't know him, Indian. He come with Major Dennis the other day for the first time. Only been here one time since. Nobody among us ever seen him before. Ain't seen him again since he brought us your boy. That's why I thought you might be one 'a his bunch. You all look alike to me. Heathens the bunch of y'uns."

"We are not of his kind," Red Hawk said calmly. "But once we have freed our son, we will find this Laughing Beaver. He and I will fight. I will kill him same as my brother here will see you dead, foolish one. You should never have come to our valley. Hurt our people. You will pay with your life now. Sing your death prayer, soldier man, before we call your ancestors from across the river."

Sgt. Baker looked like he'd just felt somebody walk over his grave. His insides bust out makin' him scream at the top of his lungs while drawin' back his right arm to loose his fury through his whip. Dancing Bear would have none of that. 'Fore Baker could draw back good for his strike, Dancing Bear stepped in close layin' him out with a blow to the right side of his head with his father's war club. The whip never finishin' its strikin' effort, droppin' soft against the ground. Dancing Bear had struck first. Sgt. Baker was dead. Wolf was now free. We all come to the camp after we seen what Dancing Bear had done. Not sure I could 'a ended it with a single blow to the head, but Dancing Bear know'd this trash weren't the reason Wolf was bein' held. Laughing Beaver was. He would now need to talk to this Major Dennis. He sent his warriors straight away to find him. He hoped Laughing Beaver would be there as well.

***

The outlaws' trail weren't hard to follow even after a day's lapse for fallin' behind the three what burned his place. Sean wanted them to get to wherever it was they was goin' 'fore he let 'em know he'd found 'em. 'Fore he let 'em know he'd trailed 'em from his home. 'Fore he let 'em know he know'd they was the ones what burned him out. He was for sure gonna talk to 'em over it 'cause the further up the trail he'd gone, the more mad he'd got. That kinda mad give a man strength in a fight from knowin' he was in the right. How dare they burn his home and barn. That was wrong. Uncalled for, for certain. We didn't tolerate such in the mountains. This was the stuff we all know'd would happen, too, when the ones what craved gold got to comin'. Sean just never figured it would be Indian doin' it to settler like the three that had turned on him. Indian to gold looker or intruder maybe, but not to other settlers. Only line 'a figurin' what made sense to Sean was -- these Indians weren't from Choestoe. These rogues was visitin' from another place. His figurin' had to be straight. He know'd most all the local folk. Know'd none that would burn a man out for just the feelin' 'a doin' it. Where we lived, you might have a quarrel with a neighbor, but that was settled through peaceful means like a good ol' fist fight, or a sit down with other neighbors lettin' them decide the fate of whatever it was a quarrel was over. Most times folks just worked it out best they could between one another. Didn't wanna be a bother to other folks by involvin' them in their problems. We never had no real issues among those what lived in the Choestoe valley.

All our problems laid with the outside folk what come there.

Laughing Beaver sensed more than know'd someone was followin'. Nothing had shown itself as a sign but he know'd they was there. Years on trail makes a body most trail savvy. That's why he sent one of his warriors back to cross check their backtrail. He needed to know how many was followin'. He figured it for the one who owned the log home and barn they'd burned. If it had been Laughing Beaver's homeplace, he would be trackin' the ones what done it, too. This follower had grit. He felt for the loss of such a worthy settler, but his rule had always been -- anyone who follows Laughing Beaver will be dealt with. This rule had kept him alive many times. The order to his man was to kill and get gone if only one was followin'. The rogue had no problem with that. He would make it personal. Sean had a fight comin'. His fate was now set.

Sean walked his mule as he made his way south toward Wolf Creek. He was thinkin' about all the folks what lived over near the creek. A certain little chesnut haired girl he'd spotted a while back workin' with her momma in the house garden kept comin' to mind ever now and then. He made mind to pay Mrs. England a visit when he got this trail done. He'd never talked to the girl, but their eyes had met. He thought she had the most beautiful blue eyes. He was wonderin' if she'd been declared for as his mule made the slightest movement with his head that weren't common unless she was bein' aggravated by flies. That movement snapped Sean's focus d'rectly back to the trail. Somebody was near. Sean could feel it. If he hadn't been lost in thoughts about a girl, he might 'a picked up on the visitor himself. He allowed his mule must 'a thought he was bein' careless, so she warned him. She was a good mule. Sean know'd just what to do. He acted out 'a instinct.

Sean stopped his trail and tied his mule to a sapling movin' toward her rump away from whoever might be on ahead. Once to her backside, he moved in behind her so's not to be seen from the front. After makin' sure he was hid good, he eased his flintlock out from its leather sleeve and primed a full load 'a strikin' powder. With all that done, he moved into the woods like he was goin' to answer nature's call. He went in far enough to where he couldn't see his mule no more. There he leaned his flintlock against the far side of a huge white oak while droppin' quick to his knees for another prayer. Once he'd asked the Great Spirit for strength, protection, and courage, he hurried back out to his mule. Movin' like he was lacin' his britches back up, he untied his mule and began on down the trail. He hadn't gone a half dozen steps 'til a most feared of all lookin' warriors stepped out in the trail some twenty paces ahead of him. The warrior's right hand held a long knife. Its sharp edge turned up for killin'. Sean seen that knife. Figured it had been used to kill many folk. It was a knife held by a warrior he did not want any part of, but know'd he had killin' on his mind. Sean had no plans of dyin' on his present trail 'a vengeance. Seein' the warrior got his back up, though. He draw'd his own knife, makin' ready to defend himself.

"Warrior," Sean hollered. "You are here to kill me, no? Tell me true, warrior. For that is my plan for you. But tell me first. Why did you burn my home? I have done nothing to you! I will warn you, evil one. I have made peace with my Creator. I have sung my death song. Have you done these things, burner? I hope you have, 'cause I'm aimin' to send you across the Great River to meet your ancestors soon as you figure you're ready. Come on when you are, boy!"

Sean was tauntin' a battle-scarred warrior. He thought silently that he'd lost his mind bein' that he was so young, but he needed the rogue mad. So mad he would do anything to kill Sean. That meant even a chase if it come to it. Sean hoped he lived long enough to make it back to his flintlock. The warrior said nothing. He just charged head on like a crazed boar hog. Sean got ready. His knife out front waitin' for the charge. The wait was short.

Sean felt the sting as their two bodies come together. Somehow, he'd stayed his feet. The top of his left leg commenced to screamin' in pain like he'd never felt. His knife gone from his hand. Sean got the nerve to look down. The slice went from front to back through his skin leggings, sinkin' hard into his thigh. The warrior's knife had cut muscle all across the top of his leg a little below his braided waist belt. The pain he felt was like none he'd ever know'd before. The amount of warm blood runnin' down his leg told him it weren't good. He needed to tie off above the cut with something, but he had to get from there first. He wondered where his knife was. He didn't remember droppin' it. A quick look around show'd him the warrior layin' curled up on the forest floor. He seen he'd done damage in the comin' together as well. The handle of his long knife was showin' stuck full out from the middle of the warrior's gut. He was layin' on the ground pullin' it out as Sean limped off for the woods. He never remembered movin' his arm let alone makin' a stab to the warrior's middle. He realized instinct had saved his life. Thanked the Great Creator for it. He was amazed he'd done that. His hope was just to live through that first runnin' together then get to his gun. Stickin' the rogue solid in the middle had give Sean time to limp away faster than he thought he could. He know'd the warrior would be up and followin' since he was most likely not gonna die for a day or two. Sean ran straight to try and fetch his rifle. He didn't have to look back to know he was bein' followed by evil. He could hear the Indian strugglin' in his effort same as he was. Heard him grunt as an oak sapling knocked him down.

The warrior was gainin' ground as Sean reached the white oak where he'd left his gun. It was a soul sinkin' feelin' when he rounded the tree to find no rifle leanin' up. Had he come to the wrong tree? The outlaw Indian was comin' on fast, makin' it hard to think. Sean needed to find his gun. The warrior was gettin' closer. He could hear him hollerin'. It scared him some hearin' the threats from a dyin' warrior. "I am coming for you, settler. You have hurt a warrior of the Shawnee. I will see you die this day. You say you have made your peace with the Creator, so have I, young one. This will be a good day for you to travel across the Great River. Say your prayers now. I am coming."

Sean could hear the Indian movin' closer as he searched fast as he could for the tree where he'd left his gun. They all looked alike as he went from one to the other bleeding more and more as he went. His mind gettin' fuzzy from the loss 'a blood. His walk staggered. He had to find the tree. It was now a matter of life and death as the warrior was gettin' closer. This tree, no, this one, no, this is not it, wait, yes, no, why couldn't he find it? That one, yes, that one. It had to be there. He rushed around the far side as the warrior moved within' a couple 'a lunges of where Sean disappeared behind a huge white oak. The Indian had no notion there was a loaded flintlock fixin' to slam into his chest. The impact stopped him eye to eye with Sean for the brief second it took for the warrior to realize his fate.

Complete surprise showin' in his eyes as Sean's finger pulled the rifle's trigger. The lead ball blasted the Indian back against the oak tree dead as used leather.

Sean was alive. He had enough strength left in his person to make it back to his mule 'fore workin' on his wound. There was a leather braided cord he could use to tie off above the cut in his leg. He had salve that Anne had give him for cuts and such, but they weren't enough for such a cut as he'd got. He had to doctor himself bein' that he was out on trail alone. If he had less strength, he might bleed out 'fore he could get the flow stopped. His doctorin' done, he made a small warmin' fire, then laid camp. He fasted that night in obedience. Thanked God for his life. His spirit was sad that life had been taken, but it was not Sean's choice. It would 'a been him or the other. He was alive. Now there was only two rogues left to answer for burnin' his home. Once he rested, he'd move on after 'em. He know'd Holy Spirit weren't ready fer him to come home, yet. That was a thought 'a comfort for his trail ahead.

He was curious as to what the other two rogues would do when their mate didn't come back. Would they back trail lookin' for him? No, Sean didn't believe they would. That's how them kinda folks lived. Your life was your life. If you lost it, that was your fault. Nobody you called friend was responsible for it. They would know he was most likely dead, but none would go lookin' for him. They had a trail to finish. Gold was much more important to them than the life of a friend. I praised God daily for my raisin'. I could not live like them awful folk did. Their dark world allowed demons in close. Their persuasion obvious in the fruits of their spirits. Thank you, Great Spirit, for my mother and my father and the raisin' they supplied me with!

Chapter 20 - A Time for Rockin'

Wind Is Strong sat straight backed in her rocker. A rocker George had made custom for her. She was restin' on our back porch late one evening after she and Momma had cleaned up from supper. George Black Oak by her side. Their heads laid back against their rockers while they slowly eased front to back. The cool of the fall air chilling the skin around their necks, on their chest and faces, their arms. You could smell the late fall sweetness of the woods as the evening breeze flowed down the valley. I remember that smell often in my walk even now. Other smells like syrup boilin' fresh from the sorghum mill or late in the season apples bein' cooked for preserves or butter lingered long after all the makin's was done. They was rockin' close enough for her left hand to lay comfortable across his huge forearm. Black Oak liked to sit the evenings on our porch. He'd watch for critters to venture out into the pastures below our home. Sometimes he'd get some meat with Thompie's long gun. That rifle never left the porch. Stayed loaded full constant. A body never know'd when they might need a reliable long gun to shoot something what needed shootin'. It was one of a half dozen spread out around the outside of our home. Neither George nor Wind was talkin' much. Half-light was almost on 'em as Old Man Sun had finished his run across the sky headin' to bed down. He needed rest to make his next day's run to warm Mother Earth.

Her plan was comin' together. It was now late in the time of falling leaves. The harvest was in. She know'd in her heart that it was time they spoke about, seriously spoke over, their upcoming trip to the north land. Harvest bein' done meant the time was proper. She wanted to know for sure the heart of the man she loved. Was he meant for this journey? Did he care for her enough? Once they'd got her son back, only a love from the soul would build a bond strong enough to get them back south with their lives. She had to know his true and deepest feelings for her – her son. She asked Holy Spirit in the silent to guide her words so that she would know without doubt as to the danger Black Oak would confront for her. She felt she know'd him true, but she had to be sure. Her heart pounded as she readied herself to breach the subject of goin' and fetchin' her son back. She didn't know what she'd do if Black Oak weren't true to his promise to help her. Words was easy to say when emotions ran hot, but the heart would speak truth if one listened through their own heart. She would know if he spoke true. Her heart would be listening.

"Black Oak. My friend," she said as she leaned forward in her rocker to catch his eye. Her rocker stopped its front to back. His did not. His face was calm. His eyes lookin' through her into the pasture beyond. His look curious, kinda. Warriors was hard to read. "It is a comfort to be with you on this porch. It is a comfort to walk with you in this valley of the rabbits. It is a comfort to be staying near you while I live with Celia and Thompson for a time. It is a comfort to have you in my heart. It is a comfort . . . that I love you. You make my life almost a full circle, and that makes me happy, but I am out of balance in my spirit. I can't find true joy. My mind has been weakened by the things of my past. The things of my future. A part of my soul has been torn away with the taking of my son. My soul screams when the dreams come at night. It can be torn apart no longer believing my son is alive. It is time I found him. I want you to lead me. I want you to find my son . . . I want you to be his father, Black Oak," she declared as his face turned to her. She squeezed his arm.

Black Oak's rocker quit its front to back. A tear wet the corner of his right eye. His look was one of pain. She kept on, "I know he will love you as much as I do. Will you pray for Holy Spirit to speak direction to you in this matter for me? Will you do this for me, Black Oak? Will you do this for us as the one I will trust my life to? The life of my son? My bidding is from one who needs to know your heart, dear friend. Do you love me, Black Oak? Do you love me enough, Black Oak? Does your soul love me enough, Black Oak? You are a great warrior of the Cherokee Nation. I will fear no living body in your presence. This is my statement of trust from my soul, and my son's life, to you. Answer me, strong one. I need to hear your heart."

Nothing. George give her no response in any notion of givin' somebody, what just poured out their soul to you, would have. He simply stood, got down on one knee while lookin' full into her haunting green eyes sayin' . . . nothin'. He raised her left hand to his lips. Kissed it like he'd seen Thompie do to Momma. He liked doin' that. His eyes told her little as he looked away to stand. Risin' to his whole length, he turned and walked off the porch. His trail was takin' him straight to the woods. His natural home. Without even lookin' back, he took off on a warrior's trot. She looked his back trail for several minutes 'fore finally realizin' -- Black Oak was gone. Her heart sank at the thought of it. She'd got no answer to any of her questions. What was she to do now? Would he come back? When would he come back if he was comin' back? Had he gone to pray, or had he gone to be gone? She had no understandin' of what his walkin' off like that meant. He didn't speak a word when leavin', which left her no clear message as to what his behavior meant. It was near more'n she could stand. Her insides jerked as she figured her journey to find her son had ended before it started. That she could 'a just drove her man away. *She didn't think he was that soft. No, not Black Oak.* Trottin' off into the mountains without speakin' a single word was the last thing she expected as an answer from him. Why had he left her? She wanted to be mad, needed to be something, but she was too confused to think on it. She sat her rocker 'til Old Man Sun woke the next day hopin' he'd be back -- he weren't. She went upstairs to bed down for a while. She needed sleep. Maybe he'd be back 'fore she woke.

***

Wolf never moved when Dancing Bear told him to bring the pick to Sgt. Baker. He know'd that was just something said to get the work 'a killin' over with. This Baker had hurt Wolf. That cost him his life. Dancing Bear would not allow folks to hurt his family. But that Major Dennis and that rogue Indian Laughing Beaver, their behavior would cost them more. The seven warriors with Dancing Bear would see to it. Wolf adored his father. He saw courage and wisdom in him most folks never was gifted with by the Great Creator. His father was a mighty warrior in the nation's eyes. Movin' on the diggin' camp was more proof 'a that. Wolf respected his father greatly.

"My son," Dancing Bear said as he moved to wrap his arms around Wolf. His embrace so strong it hurt the cuts on his back. Wolf cared none. It was his father that had him. Not the evil what took him. Not the evil what kept him doin' the work. He was finally safe. The pain he felt from his father's hug a reminder of what'd happened to him over the last few days. He must thank his father, but vengeance was still to be had.

"Father, I knew in my heart you would come. I searched the woods every morning hoping to see you. Now you are here. I want to go home, Father. I want to see Mother. Can you take me there this day? I don't think I can go much longer. These evil ones have hurt me, Father. I am hungry. The cuts on my back are hurting from the evil of the whip. I hope Owl is home when we . . . Father meet my friend . . . Opah . . . ."

That was all Wolf spoke 'fore he blacked plumb out. Stayed that way while me and Opah carried him and made camp at the south end 'a the Rock Ridge. Opah weren't trailin' much better, but he was more awake than Wolf. He'd been at the diggin' camp for a time longer. He'd grow'd more used to it. They both needed rest, water, and food 'fore takin' on the trip back to Slaughter Mountain. We only had the one mule, so we'd need to take our time. Weren't no hurry no how. Dancing Bear demanded Opah stay with them until his strength come back. Opah had no problem with that. He was weak from his time as a captive. He was welcomed by all when we did get him to Wolf's home. Dancing Bear respected Opah for what he'd been through in his young life. It was strange how God let us free him from the slave tradin' barn, then brought us back together many moons later. In all my days, I never ceased in bein' amazed at how Holy Spirit works in our lives. Saw it many times. Felt it hundreds more. I learned from my father that it was best to follow God's will. If you try it through your own person, a body just makes a mess 'a things. Folks ain't smart enough to tell God how to do. That's a good thing, too. I've tried it. The outcome is not good.

"Opah," I said as we sat the warmin' fire cross legged drinkin' us a cup 'a hot, black coffee. I was smokin' my pipe thinkin' on what all had just happened durin' the daylight previous. What led up to all of it. Wolf was layin' asleep on a folded quilt. Another folded under his head. His dreams was talkin' through the night. We was waitin' word from Dancing Bear. Him and his warriors was out huntin' for Major Dennis and Laughing Beaver. Red Hawk and Cain was runnin' scout for 'em. That was a big responsibility to lay on Cain. Runnin' scout for a pack 'a warriors means you can make no mistakes. I said a quick prayer for him. No tellin' where Cooper was, only that he'd be wherever Cain needed him to be to try and catch Laughing Beaver.

"Opah, my friend, I don't understand how my Blood Brother, Wolf of the Choestoe Clan, come to be in that diggin' hole. We'd just left the England place to look for sign on the Rock Ridge. Once we got here, he went up toward the top to scout a camp place we know'd about. I waited with the mules. After he'd not come back for a while, I moved to the south end of the ridge figurin' that'd be the way he'd come out if it was late when he got done with his scout. He never come back. I waited 'til late in the afternoon to leave the mules and go search for him. That's when I come to find what y'all was bein' made to do. I waited in the rocks 'til dark, then sneaked out to tell Red Hawk what'd happened. He sent a runner from the Guard right off to fetch Dancing Bear. That is how we are here, but how is it that y'all come to be here? Somebody with savvy caught up to Wolf. He's near as woods wise as a true warrior. Tell me friend. How did you and Wolf get took?"

"It is very strange how we were taken, Jebediah, my friend. It was a call in the woods you see. I call like no other I have heard since coming to this land. It sounded like sick animal that needed help. My brothers and I, we went to search for this animal. We found only soldier men. Two of my brothers escape. One is killed. I was taken. There was an Indian. He made this noise. If you ever hear it, run from that place which you are. It is no good, this call. Wolf, same as me. Only he never saw the Indian. He said he knew of his person. A name which means happy beaver. I wish to revenge this man for taking the life of my brother, my people. Jebediah, we found much gold."

"I know this sound, Opah. I heard it clear not long after Wolf left me to go scout the outlaw camp we know'd about. That must 'a been when they got him. He's got a wound on the left side of his head. That's where they most likely hit him when they took him. I know this Indian, Opah. He is not kin to happy beavers. He is called after a beaver. His name is Laughing Beaver. He holds much danger for those he crosses in his travels. My uncle, Red Hawk, had a run in with him several moons ago. Wolf's brother, Moon Shadow, was near killed by his trail mate. I believe he and Red Hawk will fight now that the heathen is back in Choestoe. He will die here in the valley. I know this. Red Hawk will be ready when that fight comes."

As we talked, Wolf come awake. He sat right up leanin' on his elbow, then lookin' straight to the treetops he started speakin' out of his head. It was near funny listenin' to it. His body was low on water. Bein' without for days at a time can cause you to go near crazy 'til you get filled back up.

"Jebediah," Wolf said kinda quiet like while lookin' to the treetops. "There is a squirrel here we must hunt. It makes a terrible sound when it barks. Have you heard it? If you do, look to the trees. It's big enough to eat small folks like us. I never saw it, but it knocked me flat to the ground from behind with its huge tail. You weren't there to watch my back trail, Jeb. Where was you? How come . . . you . . . not . . . being there . . . brother?" he slowly asked as he laid back flat to sleep. His mind near crazed. I did feel bad about not bein' up on the ridge with him, but one couldn't leave his mule unguarded with all the gold lookers about. That threat caused us problems. A body only left 'em tied alone if you had too.

Red Hawk come to camp later in the night. Wolf had woke some by then. He was sittin' up drinkin' the juice from some dried fruit I'd boiled when the warrior slipped in near unseen. He never did get close to the fire the whole time he was there. Stayed fifteen or more paces away. His back to it constant. Never lookin' direct into the flames. The word he brought was less than we'd all hoped for, but it was settlin' all the same. After hearin' it, I was most thankful me and Opah had been made to stay in camp with Wolf.

We was livin' durin' a rough period of time. The Southern Appalachian Mountains of 1829 was havin' many visitors. Government folk got to comin' 'round more that year, too. Soldiers was heard to be botherin' Indian folk; some settlers. The streams and hollers was full 'a all kinds 'a different type folks. Most lookin' for gold while mindin' to their own business. Their work was hard. They'd only stop their searchin' to eat and rest. Many had no time to worry over takin' what belonged to others, but then you had those like what took Wolf. Them kind that was out to take advantage 'a folks. I hated that all them gold lookers was roamin' around where I lived, messin' up our lives, fillin' us with worry and anger and regret. The lookers made our way 'a life more dangerous to live than necessary. We all prayed for it to end so our world would go back to the way it was before gold was found. Seemed to me puttin' an egg yolk back in its shell might be more likely. I believe I'd come to realize after a time . . . the life I know'd was comin to a draw'd out end now that word had got out about Choestoe. More and more folks would come lookin' to stay. Nobody was gonna stop 'em. I wondered for Wolf and his clan. He would suffer from all the U. S. Government would do to the Cherokee through the 1830's. The Black Angel would be a constant companion to his nation after the Indian Removal Act was passed, and Andrew Jackson is the one what called for it.

"Jebediah," Red Hawk began. "Dancing Bear has sent me to give you word. Major Dennis and his men are not something any of you will need to worry over again. They have gone from this place never to return. Our warriors found their other digs with little trouble. Dennis was there as well. I apologize to you, Nephew, and to you, O-pa, I know your honor was due. You wanted vengeance, but these were dangerous men. As mean as any I've fought that have come here through these times of change. Know that their punishment was just. That should give you comfort. The Great Creator delivered them to us. Their fate set the day they made their minds to take young ones from Choestoe. Taking Wolf just brought judgment to their fate sooner rather than later. Wolf, as we know, is the son of a tribal elder. The one who took him, Laughing Beaver, did not know our clan, or he would have let Wolf be. He knows now. He carries that knowledge with him as he travels alone. His mates no longer with him. Wolf, Jeb, listen close. Dancing Bear and the other warriors are on the trail home. Some are injured. Unfortunately, one will be carried back to his home. Your father is unharmed. You will leave here at Old Man Sun's first light. Make your way back to Thompie's farm. Anne will be there to see to Wolf. Jebediah will lead. O-pa is welcome. Do you understand what I have told you concerning what Dancing Bear wants you to do? Answer, young ones."

No one answered right off. We was chewin' on what we'd been told. I was hurt that a warrior had been killed. That knowledge distracted me some. I come to realize after a minute of nobody talkin' that Wolf was too weak to talk, Opah too unfamiliar with Red Hawk to be comfortable speakin', so it was up to me to make sure Uncle know'd I had it square in my mind. He was a wise man. He know'd he was mostly talkin' to me anyhow, since I was gonna be leadin' our trail. I know'd the warrior's mind after studyin' on things for a bit.

"Uncle. Do not worry. I hear your words and understand. I will take my brother and our friend to our home to see Anne. We will stay there with Anne until she says it is a good time to travel, then we will go on to Slaughter Mountain. We will do this. Do not worry over us. But Uncle, what about Laughing Beaver? If he still lives, won't we need to keep an eye out as we trail?"

"You will, Jebediah. But the last sign we found of him said he was headed back through the low gap toward Yonah. Cain and Cooper are following him. We will know his path soon. I leave now to go find Cain. Our concern is for Wolf. Get him home safe, Spirit Filled One. He needs rest. I will come to see him soon. My trail is for Laughing Beaver. It is time to put an end to his way of life. Too many have been hurt by it."

Chapter 21 - Cain and the Warrior

After doctorin' his leg best he could, Sean followed the rogue's tracks for over a mile 'fore he found sign in a place where it was obvious folks had been hurt fightin'. He rode his mule 'cause his leg was still leakin' some. He was weak. He'd been to the Rock Ridge with me and Wolf so he know'd his way around. The tracks he'd been followin' led him to a holler east of the main ridge. The little camp he was lookin' at show'd signs 'a killin' recent. Early morning from the looks of it. The wet fire meant somebody had to leave while the fire was still hot. No bodies there to show for sure, but the two places he saw blood most likely meant two folks had been kilt. He'd seen them big spots stain the ground in other places where he know'd killin' had happened. Yep, two folks dead with the others run off. That's what the sign told. Was it the ones he was followin' what did the killin'? Could 'a been. There was a lot 'a sign in the camp so it was hard to say exactly. Where did the bodies go if there had been killin'? He was for sure they didn't get up and walk off on their own. Most likely other folks with 'em took care to bury 'em? Hard to know exactly.

The voice what broke the silence nearly made him jump scared from his mule. After his calm come back, he turned to face what he hoped weren't his death. How had anybody got in as close as that voice was without him knowin' they was there? He allowed he must 'a rode in on 'em while they was watchin' the small camp. Only figurin' he could come to what stood to reason. Sean was crafty as they come. Few could 'a slipped up close like the voice was without him knowin' they was there.

"Boy," come the voice again from just a few paces away. Sean saw nobody as he turned his mule lookin' in the direction he thought the sound was comin' from. Where was he? "Boy," come the voice again. "Look up, boy," the voice said. Sean obeyed. "You see me, boy? You're lookin' right at me. Look close now. Tell me you see me. We still got a couple hours 'fore dark. They's plenty 'a light. Surely you see me. Say, boy?"

Sean looked as hard as he could from treetop to treetop but saw absolutely nothing. It weren't 'til Cooper moved his right arm did Sean see him certain. He was covered in oak leaves sittin' a limb not twenty paces away. Sean was right in his thinking. He'd walked right in under Cooper Whint. But why was he hidin' in a tree?

"Boy . . . you sure are careless walkin' in under me like that. Had you been that evil Laughing Beaver, I'd a had you dead and to the ancestors 'fore supper tonight. You're askin' yourself why I'm up in this ol' tree for, huh? Well, I'm up here on account."

"What do you mean on account, Cooper? And why didn't you make yourself known to me that you was up in that tree watchin'? Near scared a year's livin' out 'a my hide soundin' off like that. How you been, anyway?

"Good. Always good, Sean. Yep, I'm up here on account, on account 'a Cain told me to. I ain't never gonna argue with him for no reason. 'Sides, I like movin' alone. You know that. Me and him started out to trail the evil one you're followin' . . . uh . . . why you followin' ol' Laughing Beaver, Sean? That ain't too smart by your lonesome. -- Anyhow, me and Cain started out together to trail

Laughing Beaver after all the fightin' was done here, on Red Hawk's orders, but Cain figured it better if one of us stayed behind to watch this camp. He thought Laughing Beaver might circle 'round and come back here. Maybe try and meet up with any of his mates we didn't know about. How you been, Sean? Have you lost your mind? Why would anybody like us wanna track this heathen? He's death walkin', Sean. Has fate been kind to ya? I see you still got your mule. I'm savin' up for mine. Got near four dollars already. Should have four more by next year. Thompie's keepin' me one he said he'd take eight dollars for. I aim to get me that mule, Sean. I want him bad."

"I hope you get this mule, my friend. I am well, but my place ain't. Thanks for askin'. You won't need to be stoppin' by there no more. These heathens I'm followin' burned my house, barn, corral and all my sheds to the ground. They was three when I first got on 'em, but now they're down to two. One laid their back trail watchin' for me. He showed himself this morning not long after I'd got to followin' 'em good. I got a bad cut to my leg from when I fought him, but he lays about a mile from here, and I lay not, my friend. He won't be botherin' no more folks. That leaves only the two what made it to here. Not sure my leg is gonna let me go on for now, though. It might be good if I went to see Miss Anne. Get her to doctor it fer me. I'm feelin' kinda weak, don't you know. My minds gettin' to where it ain't workin' quite right, but I need to see my chore to the end, Cooper. This Laughing Beaver needs to be settled with. He took all I had."

"You go on to see Anne, Sean. Get your wound tended to. Do not worry over these varmints you're followin'. One ain't with us no more and Red Hawk will see to the worst of the three soon enough. Sign he's left says he's headed out from the valley, but Cain don't trust that.

This Laughing Beaver has much cunning. He is evil, no question. Red Hawk will see it squared for all the outlaw has done. Maybe he will come back here. Let me put one of my special arrows in him, like I did his friend earlier. He will not like that. I am certain of this."

"Mind to be careful with yourself, Coop," Sean kinda mumbled out while startin' to sway side to side some while sittin' his mule. "I believe I'll turn the trail . . . toward . . . Thomp . . . ie's now . . . Coop . . . be . . . to you . . . see you . . .why . . . you . . . what doin' . . . Coop . . . here after . . .

Cooper could tell by the way Sean was goin' on he weren't doin' too good. Could see the blood on his leg what run down the side of his mule as Sean turned to leave out for Thompie's. There was a right smart of it. His hair and face was soaked with sweat. He'd lost his hat. The color on his face was kinda grayish mixed with white. He didn't look like he was gonna make it sittin' his mule much longer. Cooper come down from his tree just as Sean leaned forward 'fore fallin' off complete head first to the ground from his mule. Coop would need to take him on to see Anne. That thought was most pleasant in his mind. It would be good to see her again.

***

Laughing Beaver know'd folks was after him. They weren't close on his trail, and he'd not seen 'em yet, but he know'd they'd be there. You didn't kill a senior warrior of the Cherokee Nation and get clear from it. His only hope to stay alive now was to leave the valley of rabbits. Go west to where other Indians had already gone. Find places where nobody know'd him. He could get lost out there in the vastness of the western wilderness. He'd talked to other low lifes what'd come from there. They spoke of lands where no man had been. Rivers so wide a body could only cross on boats. Grass patches layin' as far as a man with good eyes could see. Mountains so tall they stayed froze on top year 'round. Settlements scattered here and there with riches right for the takin'. He wanted to see these places. Feel their treasures. But first he had a fight to finish. Red Hawk, of the Choestoe clan, had caused him dishonor among his people. Didn't matter that it was a bunch 'a thieves and murderers and cutthroats what thought less of him, it was still his people. Red Hawk would need to pay with his life for such embarrassment to his respected reputation. Then he would be feared again.

Dancing Bear and his warriors took turns carryin' the body of their brother warrior. He'd fought with courage 'til bein' overcome by Laughing Beaver and his evil mate. He'd fought hard killin' the Shawnee what run with Laughing Beaver but was stabbed from behind as Laughing Beaver used his friend as bait to trick the warrior. He was a brave soul. The nation would miss him in the comin' years. Dancing Bear called a halt at a place on the Keowee Path where several main trails come together. He would go to his home until time for the burial.

"Mighty warriors of the Cherokee Nation. Thank you for standing with me against the evil that invades our mountains – our home. We have lost a brother today. He is with the ancestors now, but we have freed one who was taken from us. Made our home a safer place for all our families. It has been a good day. I will miss our brother being with us in body. We can look forward to seeing him again when we cross the Great River to be with the Peace Child. Tell the wife of our lost one that I will be to her home at the end of two suns. We will bury her husband as the third sun rises. Go quickly now. Watch your trail close. We have many visitors in the valley." With that said,

Dancing Bear left for Slaughter Mountain. He needed to talk to his wife. Wolf was safe with Anne or would be soon. She needed to know that.

Cain know'd he was right when he figured Laughing Beaver might double back. Slip in to the soldier camp for whatever reason. He'd gone through the low gap but did a switch back not a half mile in toward Yonah. Cain doubted the outlaw was welcome there, either. His kind weren't welcome most places they'd come from.

The outlaw's trail was more fresh once Cain hit the switchback. Laughing Beaver must 'a stopped to eat or rest for a bit while Cain kept to it. He weren't as far ahead as he was on the way from the diggin' camp. Cain felt the cold go across the back of his neck when he realized Laughing Beaver was close. He know'd Red Hawk was due the fight, but he wanted it in his spirit. Longed for it deep down. Dark was near on him. His would be a cold, dark camp since Old Man Moon had gone to get more light. He'd be back in a couple days but that would help Cain none that night. Laughing Beaver got Cain's back up. He would sleep half-awake knowin' the warrior was movin' about. He prayed Red Hawk would come soon. It was time he'd be gettin' back.

The sound was faint, but it was sound enough to bring Cain full awake from his half asleepness. Made him sit right up cross legged. His hand on the bone handle of his long knife. Cain weren't sure what the noise was exactly. It sounded like scratchin' or what not similar. Whatever it was, he was awake full listenin' for it. Strainin' so hard to hear he felt his ears wiggle. He needn't have wasted his effort. The sound never come another time. It didn't need to. It was sittin' close enough for Cain to scent in the pure dark, then see a bit once his eyes come awake good. How had the warrior done that? He was close enough to touch. Cain felt a fine, cold edge ease into his neck meat as no more sound was made at all. He froze as he felt a slight sting what stopped just shy of the main blood line in the side of his neck. The knife holder's scent told Cain how close to death he was. His instinct of the evil he was facin' told him he'd best stay perfectly still. Why had the intruder not killed when he could 'a? The question that was asked would provide the answer. He thanked Holy Spirit for his life, again.

"I know what you think, blue eyed one. Why has he not killed me? I am asking myself the same question as I hold your life in my hand. Think, lad, before you move as a fool would move with that buck horn handle you got in your right hand. My knife is sharper than one you would use to shave the hair from your head. Its edge will find your life's flow quicker than a rattle maker striking if I feel one wrong muscle move. Are we understanding, Mr. Cain?"

"We are," Cain managed to squeak out. The sting becomin' a little worse by tryin' to speak. He could not believe he was sittin' in his own camp bein' held by a murderin', thievin', slave tradin', low life what called himself a warrior. One who was so much a part of the woods he made no sound when he traveled. His scent that of a rotting stump. Cain had never been so took. The warrior held his life. This was one woods savvy Indian. Cain allowed havin' to hide all the time, or look out for folks tryin' to kill you, made you more sensitive to your surroundings. That would explain how he could see in the dark to know Cain had his hand on the handle of his long knife.

"It is not you who I mean to square with, settler. Go home to your new wife and young one. Leave this matter to me and the elder. If I see you again on this trail, I will send you across the Great River to meet with the ancestors. Take my words as truth. I will leave this rabbit place and never return once Red Hawk and I have finished our trade. You will need worry no more about me. My trail is done here . . . when Red Hawk is dead."

The cold of the knife at his throat went away as the warrior slipped soundlessly into the night. Cain heard nothin' as he slipped from their comin' together to the woods beyond. *How had he come in on me like that?* Cain asked himself. Never had he been so had. Laughing Beaver was without a doubt the most silent Indian he'd ever come across. He hoped he'd never meet up with another like him. Owl the Wise One explained it to Cain on one of her visits to see Izzy a while after Wolf had healed complete.

"Warriors that hold the evil of Laughing Beaver can walk on the breeze, my son," Old Mother told Cain as they talked over what'd happened to him moons later. "The demons that hold their soul give them powers others do not have. I believe this. I've seen hurt warriors that should pass on heal overnight. Old fire stories that are told no more speak of the ones who could move from place to place without ever leaving their body. It is not something of this world that gives them this unholy way, it is the evil one that slips around like the fox. The father of lies. I have no medicine that will protect a body from their demands. Only the Holy One can give protection to those the evil means to take. It is a spiritual battle going on around us both day and night. Rare is the time that I have visions of the battles now that my old body can no longer tolerate knowledge of spirit sight, but sometimes I do. A vision of the spirit world is not something common folk need to see."

If Owl's words was truth, and he believed they was, a new kinda caution would need be learned. One taught by those who understood the workin's of the unholy. He would pray for answers. They would come.

Cain's world had just changed with what Laughing Beaver had done to him. Before the visit, he felt he could hold his own with any man. Laughing Beaver had shown him this weren't truth. Evil had took on a whole new meaning to Cain. He know'd they was bad spirits and good spirits, but never had he know'd the particulars of how them demons come on folks 'til meetin' Laughing Beaver.

Red Hawk found Cain after pickin' up his back trail out 'a the low gap. They both know'd Laughing Beaver would leave the valley through there. Red Hawk wanted to talk with Cain. He found him still sittin' in camp long after mid-day, his fire near out. That told Red Hawk something was wrong. As he studied Cain a little closer, he saw the slice on Cain's neck swollen red with a dried blood trail runnin' down from it. Red Hawk sat without sayin' a word to his nephew. Laid a few nearby sticks on what coals they was left to get a few small flames jumpin'. Lit a pipe 'a Weaver, offerin' it to Cain. He took it. Commenced to tellin' Red Hawk in perfect Cherokee what'd happened. Red Hawk listened to the pain in Cain's words. Know'd just how he felt while listenin'. He'd had the near same thing happen to him on different occasions. He could sense the confusion Cain was feelin', so he chose his words carefully. He understood that even though Cain was a warrior, he was still bein' introduced to a way not common to settler folk. Indians was comfortable with nearly all the goin's on when spirits got to movin'. They seen it often in their raisin', but settlers only believed in the Spirit of God. Holy Spirit the Bible calls Him. I believe he controls our trails into the spirit world. I cared to go no deeper into any world I couldn't see full or touch with my hand that Holy Spirit weren't charge over. I left all my spiritin' up to Him.

Indians went a little deeper. Scared me when I'd hear Wolf talk about some of the things he'd seen. I went to some 'a that spirit talkin', but it didn't feel right to me. I never worried Wolf about it. He was my friend.

"It is a difficult time in our lives when we face certain death and Holy Spirit spares us. No reason a body would make it through 'cept for His hand. It is most humbling," Red Hawk explained. "I myself have known certain death -- only to live as we speak. It is all we must do to give our thanks to the One who created us. He watches over our souls from morning to morning every day. Without Him, we would have no hope. Cain, you must think of this. Thank the Great Creator for giving you life. For sparing your life. Do not question why Laughing Beaver did not harm you. Go from this place to your home. Take care of your family. I will be there in time. I know how you feel, my son. Moon Shadow saved me from certain death with Laughing Beaver when he was wounded a few moons ago. The demons in this life are real. They walk in Laughing Beaver when he is in need the most. It is a terrible life to live. I will save him from his misery. Send him to the land where the evil ones go. I do not know this land, but I know it is defeated by the blood of the Peace Child. I thank him for this. Now, go home. I will finish this with the one they call Laughing Beaver. It is time he stopped hurting folks. Take care, Cain. Thank you for being who you are. You make our tribe hold honor. I am proud that you are family."

With that all said, and it was a lot for the elder warrior, Red Hawk disappeared into the woods like a haint movin' over water. Cain allowed that might be the last time he'd see his uncle alive knowin' what Red Hawk was headed in to. He moved to a safe spot between a boulder and a huge blow down. Dark nights made it hard to move in the woods . . . for most folks. There he found a flat place to bed down. Figured his dreams would not be good. His thoughts turned to Rose and Isabelle. He'd nearly left 'em forsaken by gettin' himself killed. He just couldn't come to settle with the fact he was almost gone. Should 'a been gone. He would take Red Hawk's advice as the morning come, he'd go home to Rose. She always provided him with love comfort. He know'd Laughing Beaver had bested him, but he would not best Red Hawk. That thought give Cain satisfaction. Sleep soon took him. There weren't no dreams. His spirit was calm.

Chapter 22 - George Returns to Wind Is Strong

Black Oak was headed east as he made his way up to Wolf Pen Gap. Not sure no wolf was ever penned there in that gap, but that's what I always heard it called. I think maybe somebody lived there by that name. I've heard different tales as to why the name, so I ain't gonna repeat none of 'em for gospel.

It was just 'fore dark, the fourth night after he'd left Wind Is Strong in her rocker on the porch at our place. George was buildin' a small heatin' fire to warm himself 'fore sleepin'. He was one camp away from bein' back. Been gone three full days, but his walk had proved worth the effort. The words Wind Is Strong spoke to him after supper the three days previous made his soul come alive. He was a mile from our place that evening 'fore he ever realized he'd not said anything back to her. That bothered him some 'cause it was disrespectful to the person he cared for most in all the nation. He know'd she was strong. Mostly thought things through 'fore actin'. He hoped she'd figure it best to wait for him to return. When he saw her, he would tell her what his heart was sayin' about what she'd asked. Yes, he would be her husband. The honor was his. Yes, he would be the father of her son. That honor he would share by adopting the boy. It changed his world thinkin' on all of it, so he asked in his prayers each day for Holy Spirit to guide him. Matters of the heart weren't common for him.

His three days on trail had been used in a fast for the trip ahead, but more importantly, the time had been spent on a walk to get some answers from the evil that'd took Wind Is Strong's family. Black Oak would get bound up with mad each time he thought on the story Wind Is Strong told concernin' the raid what took her son, killed her man, and made her a slave. She never know'd exactly where they took the boy. Was never able to learn durin' her time as a captive. The only thing she'd learned was that they'd gone north. She had few answers to give when he asked, but George's recent walk had gotten the answers he needed. It cost him little; The Lost . . . more. A small, kinda deep cut to his upper left arm what hurt more than it looked like it should, for some reason. A shallow poke to his right thigh from the short knife of a warrior he'd thought were dead. Brother to the one who'd stole the boy. Those pains he could live with. Common to him if one thought on it, but the pain his beloved was feelin' for the part of her soul that'd been torn away, that was pain he would not tolerate.

His life would now be for her. He would make this known when he returned to Thompie's next morning. For the night, he needed rest and food. The rest he would get as sleep come quick. The food would be a while in the tastin' 'cause he'd taken none for his walk. He know'd Celia would have food cookin' for breakfast by the time he got there next morning. His belly cramped thinkin' on it as he forced his eyes to close in sleep. A trick all warriors used. They know'd how important sleep was to their ability to stay alive. He'd made camp on the north end 'a Wolf Pen. His spirit achin' to speak with Wind Is Strong. It would comfort her to know he'd found where her son was taken. All they need do was go and get him.

His vision durin' the night put truth to his thinkin'. The meaning clear to him like Old Man Moon shinin' full durin' the cold time. It told George Black Oak's spirit the things he needed to understand 'fore goin' north to face those what owned Wind Is Strong's son. He awoke next morning confused. Still, he was certain beyond doubt what the vision meant. It was time for him and Wind Is Strong to go north . . . and he meant for me and Wolf to go with 'em. That would be four travelers takin' the trail north to find Wind Is Strong's son. In all the Appalachian Mountains, we were to find where he was, settle for him, then bring him home. This was a trail me and Wolf would hate to miss, whether we was invited or not. We'd done proved we kinda went where we wanted. George told us later of the vision. It didn't bother him much that we was goin' with, 'cause he trusted our woods savvy, but, only to a point. We weren't warrior yet, after all.

Wind Is Strong rose early the fourth morning of Black Oak bein' gone. She was now full on mad. She stomped around the cook room fixin' breakfast to let everybody know she weren't happy. Least that's how it seemed. Momma heard her stompin' and bangin' from the back bedroom while startin' breakfast. Decided not to get up. She'd just let Wind Is Strong do the cookin' that morning by herself. Momma would stay right where she was, in a warm bed with Dad. She know'd Wind Is Strong could get feisty when her blood got up, dangerous even, and we all know'd her blood was up. It was up on account 'a George haulin' off to the woods all strange like he did. Not tellin' her for certain any answers to her feelings. The hurt was deep, but not soul deep. She loved George. We felt for her bein' worried the way she was, but we all know'd to stay clear when she was moodin'. She carried a little knife George had made her. She could whoop that thing out on ye 'fore sayin' scat cat, too. I'd seen her do it. She never went nowhere without it, neither. Slept with it for comfort. We didn't figure she'd ever pull it on us, but you had to be careful around her if she was angered up. For sure if she had cookin' truck in her hands.

The confusion she'd held over Black Oak leavin' without answerin' her questions was gone. Anger takin' its place. George left her without a word. She did not understand why he did that. It was rude behavior from a man what show'd most all folks respect constant. If he come back that morning, she would . . . she would . . . she would . . . cry, . . . then hug his big ol' neck so hard it might just kill him. She ached inside for the man she'd gotten used to havin' around. She loved him. He loved her. *"No wonder it was all so frustratin'" she thought*. She was mad on the outside, but the loneliness she was feelin' on the inside come from her soul. She'd learned from her past sorrows that bein' lonely cut deeper than bein' mad. She missed her man. Maybe if she know'd where he was, and that he was safe, her anger would not have risen so, maybe. She didn't know. Didn't care, really. She'd done taken her mad out on the skillet fried scrambled eggs that was supposed to be eggs with runny yolks. She'd cooked George some runny yolk eggs every morning he'd been gone thinkin' that might be the morning he'd be back. Messin' up the eggs for purpose made her feel some better. *George didn't like his eggs scrambled. Ha! But she know'd he'd not say nothin'*. She prayed in the silent for his safe return . . . 'cause she wanted to kill him when he got back! . . . After she squeezed on him for a while. Love had her tied up in a knot she couldn't . . . didn't want . . . to untie. She cried some.

George Black Oak eased through Calf Stomp Gap makin' his way to Ben's Knob where we lived. The feeling he was havin' weren't common to his way 'a thinkin' when out on trail. He'd sensed somethin'. The scent he'd caught 'fore he come into the gap was strange. Made him stop his trail to take notice. *What was that smell?* It was none like he'd ever smelled before, but it was gone quick as it come. He would remember this smell in his spirit. It might mean something later. Right then, he needed food. Needed to talk to Wind Is Strong. Needed to talk to me and Wolf. He needed to talk with Thompie . . . he would have to do.

Old Man Sun was barely showin' light you could see by as Black Oak neared our place from the south. All that direction was uphill from our home, so the morning breeze was liftin' right to him as he got closer and closer. The crisp smell 'a fry meat cookin' caught Black Oak in mid-stride makin' his legs go weak. His mouth shoot water out from the insides. He followed the south trail nearly to our back pasture, then walked the edge 'a the woods on down to our back porch. The scent what laid low in the back yard smelled of delicious fry meat sizzlin', near done biscuits bakin' in the oven, and that wood smoke. Oh, the smoke from a cookstove smells like no other smoke you'll find in the mountains, for sure if you was as hungry as George. Made your soul feel warm. Barn smells was mixed in with all of it. Critters and barn doin's made stink what smelled like home to George. He was happy to be there. Soon he would walk in the back door of our log home to the waiting arms of his future wife. The mother of a son he'd never met. It was a good feelin' knowin' folks loved him for who he was.

A peek in the back-window show'd Wind Is Strong doin' the morning cookin'. Her back to the door. Celia was not in sight. It would be a good time for him to sneak in while no one was lookin'. He smiled thinkin' how he was gonna surprise Wind Is Strong, and how she would be glad to see him. He would surprise Wind Is Strong. She would be happy to see him. It was a great plan, or so he figured. He'd not took to consideration the irrational thoughts of a body in love. His soul was anxious.

The latch string was out. That meant the folks inside was expectin' company or not mindin' visitors. George figured it for him bein' missin' like he'd been. He pulled the small braided thread out from its hole real slow like raisin' the latch on the inside quiet as he could. He watched Wind Is Strong through the back window to make sure she didn't jump scared. He know'd she kept a short knife on her person constant. He didn't care to be leakin' from any more places than the two he had at present. She never turned as he quietly slipped in the back door makin' sure to shut it quick and quiet as he could. He know'd she'd feel the cool morning air on the back of her neck as it drafted in if he didn't. Well, he must not 'a closed it quick enough, 'cause when he turned toward her from his door closin' chore, she was standin' face on to him. Her eyes opened full like she'd just seen a bolt 'a lightnin' up close. In her left hand, she held a skillet packed full 'a cathead biscuits. The handle covered with thick homespun. Her right gripped tight to the handle of the long blade knife she'd carved the morning breakfast meat with -- from the fryin' scent he figured it for bacon. She had a temper. He'd seen it a time or two when talkin' about the ones what took her boy. The look on her face as she tried to command that temper let him know he was fetched up in her mad. It was not the look he'd hoped to see after three tough days in the wilderness without food. Her look weren't hard to cipher, though. She founded it when she stayed put at the stove. Weren't runnin' to see him like he thought she would. It seemed she might be happy to see him, maybe, but also mad as a hen caught in the rain, and, then, a kinda hurt showin' through all of it what grabbed at his heart. George allowed it had to be a difficult face for a body to make, but it looked easy on her at that moment in time.

He read from all the sign she was showin' that her feisty was on. He allowed it might be a little bit 'fore he got the hugs he was hopin' for, if he got one at all that night. Her blood was up, too. He could tell by how red her face was. How the bloodlines in her neck was poppin' out each time her heart would beat. Her reaction weren't what he thought it would be. It come to him that him leavin' like he did hadn't settled with her too good. He spoke gently to try and calm her mind. His voice low and slow as he made his words.

"Wind Is Strong. It is good to see you. I have missed you these days that I have been gone. I hope you are well. Maybe you are angry with me? I sense that you hurt. You have that right. I was rude to you. I left you on the porch without telling you where I was going, forgive me, but your words were as sharp to me as pointed flint. Confusion made me lose understanding of how I should think, so I left this place to follow my commitment to you. I went to thinking days down the trail you and I are to make. I followed my instincts. I want you to be safe when we hunt for your child. Know that your heart has spoken to me all the time that I have been gone. I should have told you the answers you wanted to hear, yes. Your heart required answers. Your spirit required answers. I understand that now. I am sorry. I am here for you. I will give you the answers you seek. Speak your heart. I will not leave you again."

Wind Is Strong still stood just as she was when he come in. Biscuits in one hand. Knife in the other. She listened to his words while her heart pounded in her ears.

Her insides wanted to scream at him. When she first saw him, her fingers itched to scratch blood from his face, but her heart spoke different. Made her arms want to hold him. Squeeze him tight as she could . . . her lips wanted his. All she was feelin' circled in her mind like fish in a creek. She didn't know what to do, what to say or how to act, so she just let go. All the emotion she held inside come out like water over a steep fall. She began to quiver. Turnin' back to the stove she dropped the skillet down hard, then turned back quick as a spider strikin', slingin' her arm at George. That move sent the long knife end over end with the skill of any warrior stickin' it flush in our back door just over Black Oak's right shoulder. He hardly saw it in time to move so he just stood his ground while it thunked less than a foot's length from his right ear in the hard, oak slab what formed our back door. Followin' that she ran at him straight out commencin' to pound on his chest with both fists hard as she could for near as long as she could. Screamin' out words the whole time what didn't make much sense. George just stood there. He felt the stingin' pain as the cut on his arm opened up with each blow Wind Is Strong landed. The blood flow got Wind's attention. She felt the warmth on her own arm 'fore she ever saw what caused it. She looked to his eyes as she ended her beatin'. Her mind rightin' itself some. He had the warmest eyes of any man she'd ever known.

She felt her heart sink to the lowest part of her middle as their eyes locked into each other. She near dropped to the floor 'fore George caught her up. His arms felt like life to her as his strength gave her cause. She crossed her forearms behind his head. Commenced to huggin' as tight as she could. Her tears ran like rain on a windowpane as she jumped full into his arms wrappin' her legs tight around his lower back. That got the blood to flowin' out from the poke on his leg. She didn't see that one 'til later. She wrapped her body around his so hard George found it hard to breathe. Reminded him of how strong she was. He did not say a word. He know'd Wind Is Strong was lettin' go all the frustration and counfusion she'd been doin' battle with since his leavin'. Mostly 'cause 'a him. He know'd it best to just let her get it all out. When that was done, they could talk.

"Black Oak," she managed to whisper in his ear while holdin' tight to his neck. "Why did you leave me? Why did you not say something that I could hold on to while you were gone? I thought I'd scared you off from being a part of my family. I feared you didn't love me. I feared you had changed your mind about helping me find my son. I do want the things I told you. Please, Black Oak, tell me we are one. Tell me we are going to find my son. Tell me now . . ." her words faded as she kissed him hard with a kinda kiss only true love could create. He responded in kind. Her soul rested.

"Wind Is Strong," he said weakly as they draw'd apart slow like. Her feet findin' the plank floor as their eyes locked again. She longed for his words. "I must eat. I've been without food since I saw you last. My mind will clear as I feed. I need to wash. Wait for me here while I go to the well. I will explain all to you when I sit to eat." With that said, he left out the back door, leavin' her standin' there to chew on all he'd said. The knife still stuck solid. He did not remove it. That would be for the one what throw'd it.

Wind Is Strong come back to herself full as George left to go wash. She remembered little of throwing the knife. It was the one she'd been slicin' bacon with, so she know'd it was her what slung it, she just didn't remember the loosenin' of it. Her heart sank thinkin' on what she'd done. She scolded herself for near hurtin' her future husband. Felt terrible for it. After gettin' the long knife out from bein' stuck in the oak slab, she went back to the cookstove to fetch what she'd cooked earlier. The biscuits was perfect even though she'd left 'em in the skillet longer than she should have. The bacon was done 'fore George ever got there so that weren't a problem. The gravy peppered. Layin' warm on the stove top in the same skillet what cooked the bacon. All was right except the eggs, they was wrong. Black Oak didn't like 'em cooked all scrambled up, but it was too late now. He'd have to eat 'em or wait for more to be cooked. She would learn something of his nature with how he handled the eggs bein' cooked in a way he didn't like. That kinda stuff would be important when they was married. He was a man she wanted to please.

She'd been too thought provoked the last half hour to do anything but sit and listen to George as he come back in from washin'. Her soul smiled at the thought of bein' Mrs. Black Oak. She could feel his spirit talkin' in the words he'd spoke to her since gettin' back. She could sense spendin' the rest of her life with Black Oak. That was just fine with her. HIs coming words would be nice, but in her heart she know'd their meaning. . . . at least she thought she did. His words completely changed the way she was feelin' deep inside. It was the words she'd longed for. Her soul cried out in the silent.

"Wind Is Strong," George said matter 'a fact as he took a seat at the table. His food layin' out ready to eat. "I know where to find your son. I have found the ones who took him. They told me who traded for him. I know the place where he was taken. We can go there. Find out who has him. It is a place of Indians, only most are outlaw, and," he said as he looked her in the eye, "most are women. The boy would be taken there to be traded. These women will know where to find him. The ones I spoke with were certain of this. They had no doubt. Swore to it before I made sure they would take no more for trade. We must find these women. Ask them where the boy has been taken. Go get him. It is a terrible trading place. It lies to the north many suns from here. We will take Jebediah and Wolf. When the harvest is in, we will go. I must eat now. We will talk later. I am . . . sorry for hurting you. This is all I have to say." He tucked his head commencin' to eat.

She said nothing. No words would have come if she'd tried. Just left him to his eatin' as she rose from the table to go sit the hearth in the main room for a smoke. Some good Weaver tobacco would be just right. She needed to think on all she wanted to take on the comin' trail. Most of it she had figured out moons before. Kinda had it all layin' out in expectation, ready for when the time come to load her possibles pouch for the trail she was now gonna take come winter. It was good she'd thought it all out ahead 'a time 'cause her thinkin' had just become all about her son. What would she say to him? How would she let him know who she was? What words would she use to tell him who he was? He'd only be five years of age, so it would have to be handled gently. She hoped the whole of the takin' him away part weren't gonna be any trouble. She had no gold coin that would buy him back, so they weren't but one thing she could do if the ones what had him didn't want to part with him. Her vision had told her to be prepared to kill. The dead women in her vision come to mind when Black Oak said the place her son had been taken was run by women. Most likely the same kinda women what held her for a year. She did not want killin', but she would have her son when we found him. Not one person on earth would keep her from bringin' him home.

She hadn't fallen in love with George because of this, but as her husband, the whole Cherokee nation would defend her right to take back her son. Slaves was common in the Indian world, but the takin' 'a folks against their will weren't tolerated amongst the Nation, for sure if murder was done to forge the takin'. Unless it was enemy of course, that was different.

***

Anne was home when Cooper got Sean there for her to doctor. We come in not long after. His leg had festered some but weren't bad enough for her to have to worry over takin' it off or nothin'. Sean was out when they got to our place, so Cooper had to explain to Anne what all had happened. She understood his meaning, but she wondered why his talkin' was a little confusin'. She smiled as she asked him to stay for a while . . . she'd never been courted.

Chapter 23 - The Death of a Warrior

The cool of the morning air woke Red Hawk. He could feel rain comin'. Sensed it in his bones as he paid call to his morning constitution. He'd brought no sleepin' truck. His bed was piled up mast from the forest floor. The trail he was on sought vengeance, so his pack was light. Only battle truck and jerky. The rest of his possibles lay hid in the dry. He'd fetch 'em back after his duty was done. He looked forward to that time, when the evil one was ended. His thoughts turned to the things what brought him to the trail he was on. Family . . . family was important to Red Hawk. He would do anything needed for what family he had. He couldn't understand folks what didn't. He found comfort knowin' Wolf was with Anne. Know'd she'd take care seein' to him. It was common for clan folk to watch a body close after they'd been around folks held by evil spirits. They wanted to make sure none had got draw'd into their person from bein' too close to 'em for a while. He know'd Anne would look Wolf over for that, which give him peace. Red Hawk know'd the only real protection from true evil was the Blood. Wolf was fine. Jesus covered him with His Blood years before. The old timers would tell ya, no evil spirit could hold a body if they truly are protected by the Peace of Jesus. Bad spirits can influence, but they can't get through the crimson flow.

He'd bedded down for the night on the south end 'a the Frozen Top not far from the Mitchel place. Trail sign said Laughing Beaver had come through there recent. He was alone. It was Red Hawk's plan to pick up on the outlaw's trail the next morning as Old Man Sun made it where a body could see to walk quiet. He reasoned there was no tellin' where the evil might be hidin'. He'd need to pay close mind to his surroundin's while on trail. Red Hawk figured Laughing Beaver back in Choestoe to settle their wills. In a way, it was revenge that drove both warriors to the comin' fight. Red Hawk was keen to that. He just didn't want 'a get crippled or kilt by the ambush he know'd Laughing Beaver would have planned.

It was late morning as Red Hawk made his way north. Laughing Beaver was leavin' an easy trail to follow. The elder warrior know'd by such an easy trail to read that he was expected to be followin'. It told him the outlaw weren't feared. Red Hawk slipped on as careful as one could. Listenin' hard while watchin' everything what moved. His senses sharp as they'd ever been. He know'd killin' was in the air. Could feel the Black Angel circlin' like buzzards over a dead carcass. Felt the ancestors givin' him warning. He obliged 'em by bein' extra careful. The one he was after was most likely the worst enemy he'd ever faced. Dancing Bear had warned him of the warrior's known treachery in battle. Red Hawk would watch Laughing Beaver for that treachery once confronted. Would not trust anything Laughing Beaver said or did. He stopped his trail to pray for a bit as his thoughts turned to the fight he would soon face. He would need all his skills to defeat this enemy.

His back got up as he skirted the north end of the Frozen Top still followin' the evil one's trail. The warrior had turned down into the valley movin' on north toward the river. The slight hint of camp smoke told him exactly where his foe was. He weren't hidin' -- he was waitin', but why so near to Sean's place, and why was it camp smoke instead 'a chimney smoke he smelled? If Sean was alive, and if he weren't out on trail, they'd be heavy chimney smoke trailin' up the holler. His concern come knowin' it weren't the proper time 'a year for folks to be out travelin' or visitin' or takin' a new trail. Most stayed close to home in the spring to get their fields ready for plantin'. Red Hawk allowed something weren't right. Sean should be home. The thought that he might 'a been murdered by Laughing Beaver quickened the elder warrior's pace. He had to stay calm. Hold the anger that was trailin' up his back or he might get careless. Make a mistake that could cost him his life. Figurin' all that made his fightin' instincts take hold of his bein'. He had no fear.

Red Hawk went straight on in to Sean's place, figurin' him for possible dead. He found the outlaw sittin' the stone hearth next to a small fire in what was Sean's home a few suns before. He was bare from the waist up. Strong showin' in his muscles. Battle truck hangin' off his left side. Red Hawk didn't know Sean had been burned out. He wondered for him. Was he near or had he been kilt in the burning? Weren't no doubtin' who'd done it. Why else would he be there? It was clear as creek water in a drought that he wanted Red Hawk to hurt for Sean's loss, so he picked this ground for their fight. He hoped seein' all the burnin' would make Red Hawk weak in spirit, but Red Hawk was stronger than that. Battle had hardened the warrior beyond simple compassion. Laughing Beaver just didn't know it. Yes, it bothered him about Sean bein' burned out, but his body weren't laid out nowhere. If the evil had killed him, the body would 'a been put out for Red Hawk to see. Try and make him lose focus. It weren't showin', so he figured Sean alive somewhere. He cared none about the burned-up home and barns, other than he was facin' the outlaw what'd done it. Built things could be replaced if a body chose. Thinkin' Sean was still with the livin' give Red Hawk strength.

"I have come for you, evil one," Red Hawk said as he stopped a few paces shy 'a where Laughing Beaver sat the hearth. "I aim to end your murdering, stealing ways in this valley. Take revenge for Ruby Smith. You remember her. You killed her for no reason up on the Blood just a few moons back. I will take your heart the same as you took hers. Revenge for my nephew, Wolf, too, who you made to dig your holes of greed."

Hearin' that about Wolf got Laughing Beaver's attention. He never realized the boy was so important. He'd a kept him for sale to the north had he know'd who Wolf was. Folks around Choestoe would 'a never seen him again. Laughing Beaver quivered thinkin' that was good fortune for the boy.

"Search your soul, black hearted one. Know that I am speaking truth. Now fill your hand, you murdering dog. Make ready to die," Red Hawk said while pullin' his long knife, then slappin' his left palm with the flat of the blade. That made a sick flesh slappin' sound that was heard up the holler a ways. Laughing Beaver took notice. There was anger in Red Hawk. Anger could be made a weakness.

"I am here, Red Hawk," Laughing Beaver said as he stood, drawin' his long knife in the same way, only he didn't slap his hand. "I was hoping you'd find me. How do you like what I've done to this place? I believe all settlers should be burned out. Keep the mountains to us and the ancestors. You choose to live with these settlers that come to our mountains. They are not of us, warrior. Why do you respect them so? Are they not bringing the very things to our home we want kept away? I say they are. That is why I steal them. That is why I burn them out. That is why I kill them. You should join me, Red Hawk. Together we could kill them all, you and me. What say ye, Elder?"

"You are a fool. Do you think those that come will stop coming? No, that will not happen. There will be more upon more as our time comes to an end here, false one. It is not what I want, but it is coming. You could kill them all. That would only bring more. It is you and your kind that have brought this trouble here with your greed for want. You know only hate and death and profit. Love has no hold on your spirit. It is a sad life you live with no hope but only unto death. You see all who come here as bad. I do not share this belief. Many settlers that I know are good people. The one you killed was good people. Her family are good people. They will see your hair hanging from the door of their barn when I am done with you here. I hope you said your death prayer before lighting that fire, Laughing One, for you will leave Mother Earth this day. I am going to end your being trouble for my people."

With all their talk said, the two come together in a slamming of bodies that landed them both square in a pile 'a burnt ash from the logs that'd been Sean's home recent. They commenced to fightin' like their lives depended on it, 'cause they did. One warrior would walk away from this fight, one would lay dead. It was the only option for either soul. After several minutes 'a wrestlin' around tryin' to kill one another, they come out lookin' like black haints what done wandered into the valley. The black cloud they brewed up while rollin' around fightin' surrounded them as they pitched out from the burnt house into the yard. Both had cuts in places that would come back to hurt later on, but neither had made any killin' blows as they faced off to catch some air 'fore knockin' heads again. Both their eyes shinin' like stars on a dark night they was so covered in black.

"Elder," Laughing Beaver said as he stood bent over, his hands on his knees. He draw'd air hard. "I'd figured you for dead by now. You are a mighty foe. I've fought none more skilled. It will be a shame to end your life on Mother Earth, but it is a chore I must see to the end. I am sorry, my friend. I have no honor."

The shock on Red Hawk's face from the words he'd just heard was none the surprise for Laughing Beaver. He'd seen it on many different men he'd betrayed. The outlaw merely squatted with a slight nod that brought a sharp flint point from the woods right at Red Hawk. Fortunately, the elder warrior was payin' close mind to bein' wary of any treachery 'cause Dancing Bear had give him warning. The moment he heard the slightest bit 'a deceit in Laughing Beaver's voice he made for the ground like he'd been shot. The arrow passin' clean over his body as his back slammed flat to the ground. That slammin' near knocked the wind from his lungs. The speed at which Red Hawk moved startled the one who'd denied him rightful honor. That split second was all Red Hawk needed. With his left arm he pushed up from the ground hard, while his right drove the long knife edge up through the bottom of Laughing Beaver's middle. He worked his way up from there as he stood to his feet liftin' the dyin' warrior with the knife as he went. Jerkin' it free, he switched the handle to his left hand, then jabbed his right deep into Laughing Beaver's chest. Red Hawk ripped the heart clean out with one hard tug same as the outlaw had done Ruby. Stuck it in Laughing Beaver's face so the dying warrior could see it beat its last few thumps. Red Hawk figured what was fair for Ruby Smith was fair for the one what done it to her. Laughing Beaver fell to the ground dead. Red Hawk took for the woods where the arrow come from -- nobody there. He figured whoever it was allowed they'd not be gettin' paid since their boss was now to be with the ancestors. Red Hawk did not sense any more danger from Laughing Beaver's mates. He would like to know who it was shot at him, though. They'd made a good shot. Red Hawk should 'a been hit. He just had the jump from bein' wise for deceit. His brother's warning had saved his life.

He built a small fire out 'a dried pine then dropped some green on top after it got hot enough to burn it. That green wood made a hot bed 'a coals that glowed red-hot orange after the wood burned up. The tore out organ singed 'fore lightin' up and burnin' when he dropped the warrior's heart on that bed 'a coals. The smoke from the meat was black as night, tellin' Red Hawk the evil was now ended. He would tell the old timers of what he saw in the black smoke. They would know what it meant.

***

We was home. We'd got to our place as dark was comin' on us. Cooper was there with Sean. He told us about Sean gettin' cut bad in a fight with one of the rogues what run with Laughing Beaver. Anne allowed he was gonna be fine. She started tendin' to Wolf. He'd not been awake enough to ride alone on our way home, so Opah rode front on Wolf's mule while Wolf rode tied in behind. A braided leather rope wrapped twice around Wolf's back and Opah's middle, tied off on the ends with a hard knot, kept him from fallin' to the ground. Him bein' tied on like he was made for a sight, but he never woke more than to grumble about all of it a little. Anne put Wolf upstairs to bed straight away when we got him inside. He weren't awake enough to eat. Black Oak come to see him. We would tell him all about what happened later. Me and Opah needed to eat. We followed Wolf to bed once we was done with our supper. I chose the bed next to Wolf.

Opah next to me. We both fell to sleep quick we was so tired. Wolf woke me later in the night. He couldn't help it. His soul was troubled.

"Jebediah," he whispered, payin' mind not to wake Opah while sittin' the edge of his bed. "Are you awake, brother? I need to speak with you about a vision that has come to me. Jebediah? Wake, boy. I need to tell you some things we need to remember. I have seen the trail our fate will be taking us on soon. We must speak with Black Oak. Jeb? Are you hearing me, Jeb? Say if you are."

"I'm hearin' ye, Wolf," I whispered back half asleep. "Black Oak is on a trail. Good for him, brother. I am tired. We will talk when Old Man Sun wakes us in the morning. Now go back to sleep, Wolf," I said as I rolled over away from him.

It didn't matter what I said to him. He was rested, had something to say, so we was gonna talk. He grabbed my shoulder, rollin' me back over to face him. Started tellin' me about what he allowed was fixin' to happen to us. I had no choice but to wake some. Listen to his words, so I did. He weren't gonna have it no other way no how. It was his feelin' that I needed to know what he know'd right then. That was fine. He was usually right in matters of the spirit. I did best I could to hear what he said, but I heard nothing 'cept we was gonna speak with George at daylight. That settled it to my understandin'. I was just too tired to hear what all he was sayin' so I fell back asleep. When I woke, Wolf sat his bed just as he did while talkin' to me earlier in the night. He'd not moved. Had the same curiously concerned look on his face. He'd sat there the rest of the night waitin' on me to wake. He was most determined. When I did finally wake, we went to find George straight away. I reasoned the knowledge Wolf had was important enough that even breakfast was gonna have to wait. I wished, after realizin' that, that I'd listened a little closer to what he was sayin' earlier in the night, but I was tired from the last few days 'a rescuin' so I'd slept durin' most 'a what he said. I got curious thinkin' on it as we went to find George. I had a notion what it concerned . . . but why us?

George was kinda waitin' on us when we reached the barn. He was sittin' the bench outside the mule corral workin' the blade of a long knife he'd built recent on his favorite whetstone. He'd traded for that stone with some Indians from the west. It was about the size 'a Dad's hand laid out flat, mostly white in color. Weren't a bright white like snow, but more a buttermilk kinda white. My goodness it'd lay an edge on a knife like no other stone any of us had. Anne used it for sharpin' all her doctorin' knives. Needed 'em to be sharp as could be 'cause she had to cut on folks a right smart in the seein' to of their doctorin' needs. Many wounds had to have the bad flesh took off as they'd heal. Flint points would have to be cut out on ocassion. Deep splinters or slivers of wood what'd got shoved in a body while workin' or fightin' would have to be sliced out. Burns had to be scraped. Anne handled all that just fine. She was plumb good at it. Me and Wolf would help hold folks down when she needed. It sounds strange, but she cut off a right smart 'a fingers, toes, ears, hands and feet. Most was hurt in some way then turned 'fectious. Had to be removed 'fore the bad blood got to movin' through the person's blood trail. I'd seen that happen before. You'd not wish that on a bad somebody. Dyin' by blood posion weren't easy.

"Black Oak," Wolf said with much respect sittin' the ground in front 'a George. I sat with him. That was strange us doin' that. "I have been many days with little food or water. Made to work to the near end where I felt I would see death. Deep sleep found me last night. While there, I had a vision. In my sight, I was with you in a land where the white cold lays on the ground for many moons. I have never been to this land, so I know only what my dream has told me. Can you tell me what it is that I have seen, Black Oak? Have I seen what it is I needed to see? Tell me, Uncle. I am most interested."

"You are not alone in your vision, Wolf," George said lookin' me square in the eye. I wondered why he didn't look Wolf in the eye 'cause he was talkin' in answer to him. "I have had this vision. Wind Is Strong as well. I waited here for you and Jebediah to come out from the house after you woke this morning. It is important for you to understand, what it is Wind Is Strong and I will ask of you. Here, take my pouch of Weaver tobacco. Go start a fire in the pit. Pack a fresh pipe each. I will go check on Wind Is Strong, then return soon. Do not leave."

With that said, me and Wolf moved to the fire pit to start a smokin' fire. Once it was goin' good, we packed us a bowl each 'a Weaver, then sat back on the rock seats to enjoy a cool morning smoke. All the while wonderin' just what it was they needed us to do. Wolf allowed from his dream we was goin' with 'em. I couldn't figure that since we weren't warrior, but George did sound like they wanted us to go. I allowed our little conversation was gonna be interestin' for sure. I enjoyed my smoke as I waited for George to come back to the fire. We didn't have to wait long. George come back, but Wind Is Strong was not with him. She had gone on a walk when she woke. No tellin' when she'd be back. She had a lot on her mind. It had turned common for her to seek peace in the quiet of the woods when morning come. Not sure she know'd we was there or not. We never saw her the night before.

Pro'bly wouldn't a mattered. She was hurtin'. It was her way 'a findin' comfort. She prayed a lot.

George packed himself a bowl 'a Weaver after I give him his pouch back. We all smoked some 'fore the talkin' got goin'. Nobody said nothin' for a while after we'd finished our pipes. Weren't in no hurry. I'd seen these kinda talks take all day or longer. Sometimes all night if needed. Conversin' on serious matters with Indians meant thinkin' things through from every different way 'a thinkin'. Missin' some little somethin' of importance could cost you or your fellow trail mates their life. Talk had to be made with a lot 'a thought. Not payin' mind to the dangers one might face was just plain careless. Some didn't live long in the mountains when they got lazy and careless out on trail, so a body had to watch. The wise ones of the Cherokee thought things through 'fore actin' one way or another, or 'fore tellin' warriors how to do. I always honored that wisdom in my dealin's with folks. Saved me from hardship many times.

"Jebediah," George said while lookin' into the fire. I figured him to be deep in thought. "Myself, and Wind Is Strong, we are leaving when the harvest is in. She carries a heavy soul being apart from her son. I will go north with her to fetch him. I have fasted three days. Prayed to the Holy One. My vision was clear. You are to come with us on this trail, Spirit Filled One. Wolf was not there but I see no reason he should not go with us. He has seen in his own vision, but you are to be there for reasons I was not told. I believe this to be a true warrior's vision of protection. I ask you now. Will you go with us to the north lands to gather her son? Bring him back here to live. As a future warrior of the clan, do you understand what we ask?"

Well, there it was then. He'd used my Indian name. Weren't no gettin' out of it after that, even if I'd 'a wanted to. Me and Wolf was goin' on a trail north to fetch back the son of our sister. Those lands would be cold if we went far enough. I know'd that. Bein' that it would be early in the winter, it might not be too cold if we was lucky. If not, it'd be cold like I'd never really know'd cold. Sounded like just the trail for me and Wolf. I could see in his eyes he was beggin' me to say yes. I don't know why he was so anxious. No way I'd say no to goin' with Wind Is Strong and George on her quest. I could feel Holy Spirit talkin'. No doubt in my mind He meant for us to go. It would be interestin' to see what was gonna happen on the long walk we'd be takin'. I grow'd eager with each passin' moment near shoutin' at George: "Yes, Black Oak. I understand. We will go. Just let us know when."

His look never changed when I answered his question. He simply beat out his pipe in the palm of his left hand, then blew the ash into the fire. He rose from where he sat, turnin' for the house. Without a word said, he walked across the yard and through the back door of our home. His mind was settled.

Real hunger pangs caught Wolf as we sat the rock seats thinkin' on the words that had just been spoken. When you have talks like what we'd just had with Black Oak, you tried to remember every word 'cause most times each word had a particular thought to communicate. I turned it all over in my mind. I had no question as to the understandin' of what we was gettin' in to. We'd be risking our lives goin' out of territory to try and find a missin' young 'un nobody'd seen for many years, but it weren't our fate to judge. Wind Is Strong needed us. We was gonna do all we could to oblige her.

"Jebediah," Wolf said as he grabbed his middle with both hands. "I must eat. I was so full of my vision that I did not feel the hunger when I woke. I feel it now. We should go in for breakfast. Mother Celia will be looking for us. I would not let her down. We can speak on what our duty will be when once we have eaten. What say ye, Jeb?"

"I'm ready to eat myself, Wolf. You been without for a couple days. I know you're hurtin'. I wanna hear what happened to you at the Rock Ridge. How them outlaws come to have ya. Are you okay? Do you have any hurts other than needin' food? I saw you bein' made to tote dirt. I wanted to shoot the whip man, but I know'd I needed to get help 'fore doin' that. I went for Red Hawk, Wolf. I hated to leave you there, I did, but what was happenin' to you required more folks to help settle. You understand that don't ye, Wolf?"

"Jebediah. My brother. I am fine. My body hurts, but it will heal. Do not concern yourself with how you chose to get me free. You did just as I would have done. Just as any wise warrior would have done. It is my honor to have you as my Blood Brother. When you chose to go for my uncle, you saved my life, Jeb. I will always remember this time. My uncle will honor you. I know he will. You are on the trail to becoming a full seated warrior. I am proud for you, Jebediah Collins. That is something few outside of Cherokee ever receive." With that said, Wolf turned for the back door of our home. The cook room was there. You could smell fry meat cookin'. I needed it, too. My concern turned to Opah. He was asleep last I saw him.

When I entered the cook room, Opah, Wolf, Dad, Anne, Cooper and Black Oak was all sittin' at the Lazy Susan eatin' table. Food was spread all over. Most everybody had commenced to fillin' their plates since Dad was done sayin' the prayer. I took a seat by Wolf straight across from Opah. Wolf'd done filled his plate with ham, biscuits and gravy, two scoops of scrambled eggs and a spoon full 'a Momma's blackberry jam. I did likewise. Opah ate mostly eggs with a biscuit and some jam. He didn't favor fry meat. Only person I ever met what didn't eat thick-sliced, salt cured bacon or ham. He said they didn't eat such where he come from. Not havin' fry meat for breakfast made me not want to go there. Me and Wolf never did understand his thinkin' on morning fry meat. We allowed we couldn't live without it. He laughed about that.

"Jebediah, I think you would like of my home though we do not eat the fry meat like you. Our meat is different . . . eh . . . is from different where I come from. I do like the goats here. Their meat is too much like the what I am used to. We eat of the fruit for our morning meal. Bread fresh baked with strong tea and milk from much cows. Many like you have here in your home only different in the color. We eat of eggs, but for ours are bigger from much larger chicken. No, not chicken, but . . . eh . . . bigger, uh, bigger not chicken but like chicken, yet to be bigger. You know bird? I don't see here in this land. It does not matter. I say thank you to all here. It is nice to be here with you as family. I miss my family. I will go soon to see them. A big boat waits in the south that will take me there. It will be nice to go for home." Everybody smiled at what Opah had said. We all liked him.

Opah liked bein' in our home, but you could tell he wanted his family. He'd done made clear to me they was women folk waitin' to marry him once he'd got back home. He never said how he come to be caught up in the slave tradin' world, but I know he stayed free after we'd freed him in Gaines Town right up till them gold lookers took him. He never talked about that much, neither. I couldn't blame him. What's done is done. Let it lie.

He loved my momma. He said she reminded him of his momma. She'd fixed him up with some 'a Dad's homespun clothes and foot skins. His tops was a little big but hung well enough on him. The leggings fit near perfect. He spent the rest of the night talkin' to her after cleanin' up from supper. They stayed up late rockin' after we'd all bedded down. Momma felt for him. I reckon that's how mommas are. He missed his home, though. He'd made that clear. I couldn't blame him for that, neither.

He was gone next morning when me and Wolf woke. We had no sign he meant to go so soon, but he said he was goin'. It was clear he meant sooner rather than later. His bed was made back like it'd never been slept in. Maybe it hadn't? Nothing there to show he'd ever been in our lives 'cept a small nugget of gold stuck solid in a piece 'a white quartz laid purposeful on Wolf's possibles pouch. Wolf said it was a nugget like what they'd been made to dig. I guess it was Opah's way 'a sayin' goodbye and to not forget him. We never saw him again. If he made it back to America with his many children, I never know'd of it. I always thought it strange how he come into our lives twice. I was a better person from knowin' him.

Chapter 24 - The North Trail Begins

The cold time come early that followin' season after Black Oak asked us to go on trail with 'em. Set in just as the leaves got to fallin' good. Winter would be long for all who lived in the valley. That was not good for us, bein' we was preparin' to make trail to even colder land to the north. The harvest was done. Our family's food stores was in the dry. It was time for us to go. God had blessed us with a bountiful crop from everything Dad planted. We'd have food 'a plenty if the cold time did go too long. Wind Is Strong made sure we had a full stock 'a sustenance to last us for the many days we'd be gone. At least we'd eat good while we froze near to death. I could feel in my bones, it was gonna be a cold trail.

Me and Wolf was packin' our campin' truck, makin' sure all we had would be dry for when it rained or snowed. It bein' the cold time, we'd get one or the other durin' our time out on trail. You could know that would happen. Our canvas slips would make sure we all stayed dry. Them things was handy when the rain come. Wind Is Strong found us in the barn. Asked if we could meet her out by the fire pit later after supper. She needed to talk to me. I agreed, even though it seemed out 'a sorts her wantin' to plan a sit-down talk. I was eager to hear her words, so me and Wolf headed to the outside pit once we'd all eat and cleaned up from supper. I was sittin' the stone seats smokin' with him and Black Oak when she come from the house. I'd forgotten just how beautiful she was. Some women was just handsome creatures. That's all you could say.

Wind Is Strong sat by me on the stone seats when she come from the house to the fire. I don't mean beside me like you'd sit beside your friend, rather, beside me tight. Side-by-side up close to my left side. I liked her bein' close like she was. Her warmth give me comfort. When she got settled, she was leaned up in front 'a me some. I could see the full of her back. The blackness of her hair laid down between her shoulders. It followed the length of her spine across her homespun top bound by a single braided leather cord 'bout half way down. That cord was laced to the tail feather of what must 'a been a huge red-tailed hawk. I could smell her 'cause she'd washed recent. I caught the rich scent 'a Momma's spring flower soap. She turned her head toward me as she leaned back a little, lookin' me di'rect in the eye. The feelin' she stared into me froze my soul like a rattle maker freezes its prey 'fore strikin', only my freezin' weren't from fear. Mine was from attraction.

My soul quit breathin' the moment her green eyes locked into mine. I could feel her. She had a pull to her like I'd only felt once in my young life. My heart took to skippin' what made the muscles in my chest cramp. No wonder George loved this creature. I remember thinkin', *she was what women folk ought 'a be.* I was took. She'd hooked me like a starvin' brookie after a summer rain. Her words felt like a heavy quilt your momma puts over you on extra cold nights when she comes in late to make sure you're sleepin'. Oh, she touched a body with her bein'. Wolf allowed it was spiritual when we talked about it later, but she weren't sittin' up close to him like she was me. The way I was sweatin', I figured it for physical. I liked it. Bein' around Elizabeth, my beloved, made me feel the same. I liked that more. It become knowledge to me as I got older, some women just have a certain pull to their bein'. There ain't no explainin' it. It just is.

"Jebediah Collins, my brother," she said almost in a whisper while placing her right hand on my forearm where it lay in my lap. I felt a stirrin'. "Spirit Filled One. You have spoken to Black Oak. He has told you of our needs. Your eyes tell me what Black Oak has said is truth. You are with us to find my son. I am glad, but I am curious. Tell me, Spirit Filled One," she moved even closer while squeezin' my arm, lookin' deeper into my bein'. "Tell me true, Jeb," I could smell the sweet scent of her breath. Felt its warmth on my cheek. "Do you take this trail for yourself . . . and for Wolf . . . or for my son and me . . . or . . . to honor your uncle, Black Oak? Know this, your answer is important to me. I can feel your spirit, Brother. I am a seer. I think you know this. Let your spirit understand my hurt, and I know the answer you speak will come from within. From the place inside us where only truth is known. Speak when you are certain, then I will hear from your heart. I must be sure of who I know you to be. This trail to the north has become a matter for Holy Spirit. He will be our guide. Our visions are proving true . . . except for you. I did not see you in my dream, so I am wary of the father of lies. I saw only myself and Black Oak. I need to know that no evil has come to you. That I can trust your spirit. I need to know that your spirit is still pure, for my son's sake, that no evil has touched you down deep. This is why my soul is concerned for your intentions. I mean no disrespect, young warrior, but you were not a part of my vision. Only, Black Oak did see you. This is strange. Tell me, Jebediah, why do you help me in this quest to right what was made wrong in my family? Why are you willing to die for someone you may never meet? You don't even know his name. Speak, future warrior. Let me listen."

In my natural days, I'd never been spoke to from the depth of emotion I could feel she was speakin' from. I know'd that to be spiritual. I short prayed to Jesus that He would comfort her. It struck me to the core, tryin' to figure what answer I could think of that would give her the confidence in me she needed to let us go on trail with 'em. George had made it clear he wanted me and Wolf along, but I know'd inside if Wind didn't trust us bein' there, we'd not be goin'. I had to think for a few minutes 'fore answerin'. I got up and moved over to the pit. Fetched a small flame to fire my pipe fresh while searchin' for words that would let her know how I felt. Her concerns was serious. She loved her boy and missed him awful. Wanted him back in the worst possible way 'a wantin'. My answer would need to be clear. It had to be truth spoken straight from my heart or she'd think I weren't serious about helpin' her. I loved Wind Is Strong. I'd do anything for her and hers. She had to know I was true. I had to make her know. My answer needed to give her spirit comfort. I said a silent prayer while finishin' my pipe. I felt better after that. God give me words as I went and squatted in front of where she sat. Stared her in the eye like she'd done me. Her eyes was nice.

"Sister, Wind Is Strong, hear me. Listen with your heart. Do not be fooled by the trickery of the liar maker. He is our worst enemy. I believe this. Know that you are a part of my life. You are my family. Of all the things you ask, yes is my answer. My life would be of little use if my faith were as shallow as the hope of a vision. Holy Spirit has brought us to this place. We will be protected. No different than when Wolf and me risked all for you. Your life is important to us. We will trail together to save one of our own. It is no less than I would do, or any of us would do, to help one of our folks. You are a part of me because I love you. I am a part of you because you love me. There is nothing as powerful as love. God is love. That is why I look forward to meeting my new brother. It is good the Great Spirit is guiding us. Let us listen for His voice, from that you will know in your heart I am true."

Once I was done with my answerin', it was a minute or more 'fore she spoke anything to me. She'd dropped her head as I finished but she weren't cryin'. She was heart listenin'. Thinkin' back on everything I'd said. Searchin' the words I'd spoke for any influences of evil. She'd not find any. I weren't concerned. My heart couldn't deceive her in any way. She would know if she listened proper. She raised her head after a short time. Spoke to me with the same emotion she'd spoke to me with earlier. I seen I was wrong. She had cried a bit. The corners of her eyes show'd wet. I wanted to hug her hard. Make it all better, but I dared not move. I had to know for sure she believed what I'd told her. Her words made it all better.

"There are times in all our lives when we find ourselves certain of truth, Jebediah. I feel I am in that place with you. I do feel the bond of family. My son will be a better man having you as his uncle while he grows. Your words have touched my soul. Your spirit is pure as I knew it would be. Forgive me, Brother, but I had to know from you whose thoughts held in your mind. The evil one has not bothered you. I'm sure of that now. We will leave at Old Man Sun's first light. Make ready what you will need for several moons on a cold trail. My things have been ready for some time. I have been gathering my pack for many moons. Black Oak is ready as well. I feel we will see the white cold fall before we return, so plan your clothing wisely. We will take mules to ride and for carrying our truck. Make sure to pack all your needed weapons. Plenty of shot and powder. You will need to take your bows. Bring a whole quiver of hunting arrows. We do not know what we are walking in to. We must make ready with careful intent. Be prepared as warriors always are. Thank you, Brothers, for doing this. I pray the Great Creator watches over us. I pray we find my son."

She kissed me 'fore she left. Not the on the mouth special kinda kissin' but the on the face kinda kissin'. Still, it was just as feelin' as any kisses me and Elizabeth ever shared. I loved my beloved in a way that made me feel like a part of her bein'. My love for Wind Is Strong was a different kinda feelin' love, just as strong and pullin', but different. Most likely the kinda love God feels for us. Fetchin' for sure.

Momma was sad when I told her of my plans. We was sittin' the rockers at the hearth later that night. Neither one of us could sleep. She already know'd what was happenin'. She just hadn't heard it from me. She spoke wisdom while we talked about it all.

"Jebediah, this trip will be a long one. You will be gone many moons. It is important that you remember your father when you are gone. He will need you in the spring to make ready the fields for planting. I pray you are back long before then, but you may not be. Christmas is in a few weeks. I know I will be missing you then, if you are not back. Remember, on Christmas night, I will lift up a special prayer for you. That will be my gift until I see you again. Now, you listen to Black Oak and Wind Is Strong. Your trail could get dangerous. You and Wolf watch out for each other. Use all your wisdom and make no mistakes if danger does find you. I know all will be fine. Black Oak holds much respect among all Indians. He will protect you if evil comes your way. Pray each morning and each night.

Listen in your heart for the words of our Master. He will be with you always. Pull strength from that if fear comes on you. I love you, Jeb. Remember that on the cold nights, it will help keep you warm." She hugged me as she left for bed. I cried.

Dad didn't say near as much next morning while we was packin' the mules as what Momma had the night before. He'd taught me near all I know'd about trail travelin', other than what I'd learned from Cain and Wolf's family, so they weren't much for him to say other than goodbye. Momma was still bedded down in the house. She'd said her goodbyes to all after supper evening last. Dad's aim was to make sure we got everything we'd need. It was easy to forget something when your mind had already gone to trail, and the mules was still in the barn. He was always up 'fore Old Man Sun anyhow. He cooked breakfast a lot 'a times lettin' Momma sleep in. He was a good cook, but not near what Momma was. You could eat his food, even if sometimes it was hard to know what'n all was in it. He give me and Wolf some warnings as we was leavin'. Told us to make sure to keep our powder dry. Make sure the flint in our rifles was set proper every morning 'fore headin' out. To watch our feet and keep 'em dry. To pay mind to our mules for signs 'a danger. They'd pick up on it every time 'fore folks would, if you had a good one. I trusted Peter with that. He was a good mule. I felt for Dad. He wanted to go but couldn't leave the farm for that long of a time with Black Oak goin'. One of 'em had to stay the farm. Take care 'a the stock since Cain had got married and moved off. He was sad I was leavin'. I could see it in his eyes. I understood how he felt when I thought on it later that day while ridin' Peter. Me and Dad spent a lot 'a time together durin' the cold months. We worked the farm, cut firewood for the house, tended to the mules, coon hunted with Ol' Stripe, hunted game meat, picked up rocks from the fields 'fore burnin' off the old growth gettin' ready for plowin', and all the other busy things folks did durin' the cold time. I felt the pang of sadness at not gettin' to do those things with him for a time. For knowin' I'd not see him and Momma for a while. We'd catch up when I got back. That would be a good day.

We had three mules and one pack animal loaded for our trip north. Them was all Dad could spare. George's mule was at Dancing Bear's. Had been ever since Wind Is Strong had come to stay with us. He didn't like ridin', preferrin' to walk most places. We all had to leave our bear skin blankets. They was just too heavy. Our pack animal couldn't tote all we needed and them too. We would miss those. Black Oak would walk or trot while leadin' the trail, whichever he felt was needed. I rode Peter with all my weapons and possibles. Wolf rode his mule packin' all his truck. Wind Is Strong had her own mule. Dad gifted her one after takin' her into the family. Her mule was black mostly with some spots of white. It was a good mule. She carried all her personals same as me and Wolf 'cept she paid mind to leave seat room for her son on the return trip. Hers was a draft horse mix, so it was a big mule like ours and Big Jim. I wished many times on that trail Big Jim had been with us. He give comfort when the trail got tough. He was savvy to trail life. The fourth critter to our train was for provisions, both mule and human, so he carried everything else that weren't packed on our own mules. All our campin' and cookin' truck rode on him. It weren't no mule like the others. It was one 'a Dad's old jack's what didn't breed no more. He was a good donkey. Strong in his legs right up 'til Dad had to put him down a couple years later. We'd took him on trail a lot, so he was used to haulin'. A body'd not look to him for sign, though. He couldn't hear good or smell good or see good, neither, but he was honest at followin' the lead mules. Come natural for him. You could trust him not to run off. I allowed he was smart enough to stay with all the other stock 'cause he know'd if he got shed 'a them he'd not find his way back. No different than folks, really. Old Timers quit huntin' when their eyes got dull. Sad to watch when it happened to folks. Hard to go through as one grows older.

The trail north sounded simple enough. Black Oak told us all 'fore we left, Dad included, how he planned to get us to the tradin' place where we hoped to find Wind's son, or at least his whereabouts. We'd follow the Keowee Path for a few days north, then turn east on the main east-to-west trail the Cherokee used for trade. The tradin' place lay close to that trail. We were going to a land only George know'd about. He'd seen it when he went there with Old Mother many years before to fetch a young 'un she was told had been stolen then took there. The girl could not be found when Black Oak went askin' about her. The information Old Mother was told weren't right. The girl had never been taken to the tradin' house. Black Oak said they never found her, neither. The girl was a child of a friend of Old Mother's. She was very sad when they had to return to Choestoe without the girl. I'd heard the stories of it from years back. The home where they was supposed to 'a took the girl was a tradin' business run by Indians, and from the stories I'd heard, they'd trade with anybody, legal or not. George said when he went there it was mostly run by one Indian woman, but there was another settler kinda woman what told everybody what to do. She had friends like her. He said she and her kind wore black robes what hung to the ground with strange lookin' hats on their heads coverin' everything but their faces. They'd not let you see their hair. Carved wooden crosses hung around their necks. He allowed they was mostly nice 'cept for the leader. She felt evil to him. It was not a good place from the way he told it. Evil seemed to 'a set in on it for purpose. A major junction for outlaw slave tradin', really. He told us about it the third night on trail. All was goin' well.

"I must tell you of the place we are going, Jeb, Wolf. Wind Is Strong knows this," George said as we all settled in by our campfire after cleanin' up from supper. Hung our meat in a tree. "It is a bad place, this house of trade we go to. Many young ones stolen in the south are taken there. Ruby Smith would have been taken there had Laughing Beaver been able to make his trade for her as he wanted. Few know where it is, or even that it is. Wind Is Strong's son was left to this evil place after he was taken. The warriors I spoke with of The Lost have told me this. I know the trails that will take us there. We are still a few suns away. It is dangerous to enter as strangers. We must take care. When we come to the end of the trail north, I will go in to see what I can learn. Jeb, you will come with me. Wolf, you, and Wind Is Strong are to stay with the mules. Keep them hid from any travelers. Most in these woods will be outlaw. Watch for each other. Do not speak with any. Do you hear, Wolf?"

"I hear you, Uncle," Wolf answered. "I will do as you have said. I know my duty to these things. Stay with the mules. Protect them and our stores until you and Jeb come back from the trading house. Keep them hid. Protect Wind Is Strong. Watch out for her well-being. Do not worry, she will be safe with me. I will watch close for any who travel. We will not be seen. Is this correct, Uncle?"

Wolf said that part about protectin' Wind Is Strong to show her his courage. She didn't need me or Wolf or

Black Oak, for that matter, protectin' her. Wolf know'd that. She was warrior strong. Savvy on trail as any wise Indian I'd ever met. She made the trip safer for us with her talents. She felt it nice Wolf thinkin' of her, though. I seen her smile when he said them words about protectin' her. She loved Wolf. He made her feel wanted. That was a good thing since she felt responsible that we was all walkin' into a possible fight on her account. She would have her son, though, if we found him. She and us alike figured no different. A fight could be comin'. Me and Wolf know'd it. We made sure to keep our knives skin slicin' sharp each night after supper. Neither one of us wanted to do any stabbin' or cuttin' 'a folks in particular, but we both know'd a sharp knife does a better job defendin' than a dull one. No arguin' that.

"You have so said, young warrior," George answered. "I know our provisions will be safe with you on watch. Wind Is Strong will have no fear with a warrior of your skill to guard her. I will not worry. You have given my mind peace," George finished with a grin. Wolf grinned back.

Sleep was long in comin' that night. I lay awake wonderin' why George wanted me to go with him to the tradin' place and not Wolf. I allowed, as sleep took me over, that it was because of his vision. I would do as I was told. His judgment was the rule on our trail. I would show him the due respect he deserved. He was George Black Oak. A mighty warrior of the Cherokee. I was a part of his clan. My duty was to do exactly what he needed me do. Mindin' orders was easy for me. It's just that sometimes the tasks he needed weren't all that easy.

It was the last day of our trail north to the tradin' place. The white cold had started to fall a couple days before. Snow was everywhere. Thick like cake icin' layin' deep on the ground. That gave clout to Wind Is Strong's vision. Made us feel more confident in findin' the one we was lookin' for. George didn't mind walkin' in the snow. He'd changed into his knee-high foot skins with beaver tail soles when the snow first started. His feet was warm and dry. For that matter, his whole put together was warm. So warm in fact, that as he walked, he took off his homespun under top and winter skin shirt with the hair turned in. Walked bare from the waist up with snow fallin' for most 'a that afternoon the snowin' commenced. I couldn't believe it 'cause I was shakin' cold ridin' Peter. Camp that last night on the north trail was cold, too. I know'd it would be. I allowed Momma's heavy quilts was the only reason I didn't freeze plumb solid. I thanked God for those quilts. I swear to this day, I believe I'd a near froze to my death had I not had 'em. Good, heavy quilts on a cold night are a gift from the Great Creator from the talents He gives to women what can make 'em. I promise you they are. I thought about my bear skin many times when I woke up cold, though. Them things is warm when the cold comes on your person in camp. Soft for sleepin'. I slept under it many nights in the woods when not keepin' a fire for warmth. Stayed comfortable most all those times. Them skins would 'a been nice to 'a had for us, but I understood. Our jack could only haul so much and they was heavy.

Chapter 25 - The Feel of Evil Come

Wolf woke me the morning after we'd made it where we was headed goin' north. It was still snowin' a right smart but the sky was showin' more gray with light than the days previous. He wanted to talk 'fore me and George headed out for the tradin' place -- without him. He was sensitive about that. Hadn't spoke to me near the whole day before, only when we was makin' camp. A little jibberish about how cold he was or somethin'.

We was camped less than a half mile from the tradin' grounds. A good two hundred paces or more off the main east-to-west trail. Our camp was hid good behind a thicket of old growth ivy thick enough to hide our heatin' fire. Our trip up had been just as I expected, cold and lonely, which made for a long trail 'a travelin'. The cutting cold kept it impossible to stay asleep once sleep did come. We was all tired because of it. Weren't much to do after supper on long winter nights like we was travelin' in neither, 'cept talk or sleep or smoke your pipe or sharpen knife blades. I found it hard to keep my hands warm enough to do much when not sleepin'. We faced uncomfortable cold constant. Never got full warm. Always seemed like the fire was a long way away when you tried gettin' close to it for warmth. One side 'a your person froze while the other near burned. You'd have to turn yourself like you was on a standin' cook spit when warmin'. We'd bed down early 'cause it was warmer under cover. Weren't no gettin' true warm, though. Some part 'a your person or another froze constant.

I was glad we'd finally made it where we was headed. Seven nights we'd camped makin' it that far north. The last five 'a them nights was pure cold with snow all around the last two. I missed sittin' the hearth with a big fire burnin' in the fireplace surrounded by log walls. Hot stew constant straight from the cast iron soup kettle what hung over the edge of the coals. Truth be told, I was ready to go on back home. I had to keep tellin' my spirit what we come for. That thought made it all bearable. I wanted Wind Is Strong to find her joy for livin' again and her son needed to know his momma. She needed the boy to know who his daddy was. Who his true folks was. What blood run through him. It held important to her. It was something she needed to do. Her spirit grow'd dark because of it.

"My brother, Jebediah," Wolf said kinda slow like. Sorrowful even as we stood alone by the morning fire he'd got goin' 'fore daylight. "I long to be going with you. I know what I do here is important. We must not lose our mules or provisions. I know this, but I want to see the trading place. I want to be there as you are. I fear for you without me there to watch your back. We have heard the stories from those who have seen it. It is a place like one will never see again. It is a bad place. I can feel the evil that lives there from here. Be careful, future warrior. Stay wise. Follow Black Oak close. Do not get away from him. Listen to what he says. Follow what he tells you exact. Feel everything around your person as you move. See everything. Sense what it is that should not be where it is. See others before they are near, but do not look into any of their eyes. They will know you if you do. Be aware. Stay clear of all unless Black Oak knows them. Rely on your own feelings if you think danger is near. Tell Black Oak if you are concerned. We are savvy, you and me. We have been on many trails. Remember all we have seen together. Remember all we have learned. Use these things to stay alive, Jeb. Do not let any of them poke a hole in your body with their knife. If they do, stick two fingers in as deep as you can. Feel where the blood is pumping from and hold down. Stay calm if trouble does find you. Keep the handle of your long knife close to your side. I will pray for you constant. May Holy Spirit guide your thoughts."

My goodness but that was a mouthful for him. He was bothered to the core for not bein' able to go with us to what turned out to be more of a stockade than a tradin' house. I felt for him, but at the same time, his warning give me worry. I could tell by the way he went on about it all that there was something he know'd I didn't feel I was privy to. I wondered what that was. Could be he couldn't tell me without makin' me fearful. He know'd if my spirit held fear that would make what I was doin' even more dangerous. That'd not do. We both know'd I had all I could chew for the time.

"Wolf, you are my best friend in the whole put together. My Blood Brother. Nothin' can ever happen that will change what that means. I may be goin' into this village at Black Oak's commandin', but next time it might be you. We never know the Will of Holy Spirit 'til we know It. For some reason or another, accordin' to Black Oak's vision, I was chosen to go, not you. I hope he knows his mind, 'cause from the way he tells it, most everybody around the place is Indian 'cept for the black robe women. I hope to not meet up with them ladies. They sounded hauntin' to me. I wish you was goin' with us, but I understand somebody needs to watch our belongings. I trust you with all of it, Wolf. It steadies my soul knowin' our provisions is safe. But remember – they ain't worth dyin' over. Get clear 'a here if keepin' our truck demands you gettin' killed to stay. Wind Is Strong should understand that as well. Explain it to her when we are gone. Watch out for her, Wolf. Guard her just as you guard the stock. She is careless in her pain. I can feel her spirit cry when I pray for her in the mornings. We must get this thing done. She needs her son to become whole again, and I grow homesick for the comfort of a warm hearth. Keep your senses about you. Wind Is Strong is a seer. She has a pull to her I cannot explain. Take care of Peter for me. I will listen to your words and watch my doin's close. It will be wise if we both keep our senses about us." We locked forearms 'fore partin', but no more words was said between us. We know'd each other's hearts.

Black Oak was ready. We was gonna walk on in to where folks made trade. Leave the mules in the woods with Wolf and Wind Is Strong. We toted our knives and possible pouches. A flintlock each slung over our shoulders by a braided leather strap. Powder and ball in smaller pouches laced to our belts. I was surprised to see George packin' a short gun in his waist belt. He hardly ever toted that gun. I'd seen it, but not recent. Seein' it again told me he was figurin' our quest was a serious thing. I figured after layin' eyes on that I'd better stick to Black Oak like we was tied up tight with a rope. Wolf and Wind Is Strong would stay put with the mules and provisions. That was a most important job 'cause Black Oak didn't wanna spend no time fillin' our stores for the trip back. We'd brought enough to last both ways figurin' everything went the way we all hoped it would. Knowin' mine and Wolf's lives to that point in time made me ask myself, "Why would we figure it for that?" Hardly ever did our plans work out like we figured 'em. Most times they'd turn out for good either by our plans or not, but, I had hope we'd stick to this 'un. Wind Is Strong did say the Holy One was leadin' our trail. That's a powerful reckoning to believe in. Gives a body confidence in what they're aimin' to achieve. I allowed her son was as good as had thinkin' the Holy One was helpin' us di'rect.

The snowin' had stopped when I finally laid eyes on the tradin' place. I weren't struck by the way it looked from the outside. It was just a plain ol' fort lookin' thing with sharp topped poles standin' side-by-side on end all around it in a circle. Inside the walls was some log houses. Three in all sittin' alongside a woodshed, smokehouse and small barn. The building in the middle was the largest of the three. Looked kinda like a Cherokee longhouse, just not near as big. A springhouse sat inside the wall to the west. That give the ones inside fresh water constant. They'd built a privy to the north. Maybe fifty paces clear 'a the wall. They was a worn trail to it from the main gate which they'd built directly opposite the privy to the south. It was that gate me and Black Oak went in once reachin' the place. I weren't ready for what I seen. Still troubles me when I think on it.

If there ever was such a place as a God forsaken place, we was walkin' through it. I never allowed folks would live in a place what smelled so nasty. I wanted to turn around and leave just from the stink. It hit you square in the face the moment you breached the main gate. Made it hard to breathe. Smelled like death rot. The folks we seen looked alive enough, seemed clean enough, but somethin' smelled. I'd smelled that kinda stink before. Couldn't remember from where, though, and that took to botherin' me. Put me even more on edge knowin' that smell should most likely be took as a warning. I couldn't call to mind just what, or where, the scent made come to mind. I wished I hadn't, later on when it did come to mind . . . it was the scent of evil.

"Jebediah," George said as we stopped a few paces inside the gate to look around. His words would seem slow to come by. It didn't help that everybody we could see had stopped what they was doin' to stare at us; at George Black Oak, rather. He was a rare sight for sure.

"This place is worse than when I was here with Owl. When we visited, there were only the two small buildings. No logs for outside walls. No gate to come and go. I do not like being here. It smells of evil. Come, let us go to the main lodge. We will ask about the boy there. Keep your eyes open for warriors, Jeb. We may need friends. More men are here now than I remember. I do not see the Cherokee women who were here before. I do not like this. Steady your mind as we search for answers, Spirit Filled One. Listen to your senses. Trust your thoughts. Know where every person is around you. What they are doing. Feel as we walk. My spirit tells me there is something dark working its evil here. Let us beware."

"I will," was about all I could whisper, as I looked around at a couple dozen or more folks starin' at us. I was wishin' Wolf had come. I saw no warriors, and them I was lookin' at had to be the hardest livin' bunch I'd ever been near. A mix 'a rough lookin' settlers and what was most likely rogue Cherokee and Creek. These was the evil folks you looked out for on trail when you was hopin' not to see evil folks while out on trail. We was in their hive. Not sure we needed to be there, but we'd walked right in. Most of 'em was men, too, which was a surprise to us. George allowed most 'a the folks there when he went previous was women. Allowed the place was run by women. Probably was when he'd gone before. Weren't that way no more. Rogue traders the lot of 'em looked to me. Probably killed or run off any that was there previous. Black Oak was right. Your spirit could feel the darkness as you walked through it. Something was bad dark all around. Made me near lose my stomach. Pro'bly would have, had I eaten much the last few days. I'd not been able to for some reason. We had plenty, I just weren't hungry. I allowed it was the cold keepin' me from bein' hungry, but I weren't so sure after feelin' what I was feelin' inside them fort walls. It was more of a sickness in my spirit. Stange feelin'. I would need to remember to ask Wolf about it when we got back to camp.

I was anxious to get inside the middle building. I wanted to get away from all the stares from them on the outside, and, I hadn't been inside nothin' but a tent for several days. I was lookin' forward to gettin' warm near a fireplace and not havin' wind blowin' cold across my face near constant. That would be nice for a change.

We followed the path stomped into the snow where others had walked. Took the front steps up, then crossed the porch to a single oak door what led inside. There was barefoot tracks in the snow on the porch. A single woman's track. Some of the tracks had a little dirt in 'em, meanin' she'd been there recent. The storm what brought the snow was a bad one. Hit the tradin' fort hard. The cold white had blow'd in coverin' the porch boards complete. We suffered in camp because of it. Lots 'a wind. Seein' them tracks made me shiver as George pulled the end of the latch string what was hangin' out from the door. *"What kinda woman would walk barefoot on a snow-covered porch?"*

The oak door eased open as we slipped through. Squeaked like a mouse when George went to close it back. It was near dark inside. Smelled like fireplace smoke mixed with folk stink. My recollect come to me when I scented that odor. That was the evil smell I couldn't place before. It was slave stink. The air was full of it inside the main lodge. It weren't quite as bad as it was inside the slave barn Cain near burned down that time we went to Gaines Town for market, but it was the same stink. You'd not confuse that stink with nothin' of the like. The fire was out with only a bed 'a coals still heatin' what little it could. It was colder inside than it should 'a been. Hard to see full on right in front 'a your face, but I know'd from the faint sounds I was hearin', they was other folks in the room along with us. Didn't have but two windows in the whole building. They was small openin's not lettin' in much light. A solid back door smaller than the front laid to one corner. A lone oil lantern hung from the ceiling. It burned bright enough to see around once our eyes corrected to the dark some, but it weren't much light. It looked to be hung dead center the single room house, direct in front 'a the fireplace.

Below the lantern, closer to the door, was a simple four-legged desk, or small table lookin' thing. It stood out on the edge of what light shown from the latern to the floor. Sitting at that desk readin' a small book was a black robed woman. Her back as straight as I'd ever seen a body sit. Looked to be near painful havin' to sit that straight. I was cold with my winter skins on standin' in that room, but all she wore was a black robe dress kinda thing. A look to her feet show'd she wore no shoes. That explained the barefoot tracks we'd seen out on the porch when comin' in. She had no hat coverin' her hair. It was showin' full while hangin' down over her shoulders and bosom. It was long, stringy lookin' brown stuff near matted full from not bein' washed in a while. No beads or feathers was wove in it. The black robe stopped where her head fit to her shoulders. It had no collar to button closed around her neck, so her throat show'd full. The skin on her neck was dirty. Her face glow'd candle white against what light was shinin' off her book. Her skin young with few wrinkles. The book was layin' flat on the table turned bottom up makin' the words upside down. Weren't no way she was readin' it proper. Both hands lay flat, palms down, to the side of either page facin'. She wore no rings or bracelets. Her fingernails was long and dirty. Sharp on the ends like they'd been worked over a whetstone. Raisin' her eyes when we come in, she commenced to starin' at us one to the other. Same as all the folks outside had done. I didn't trust her the moment we met eyes. You could feel from her look she was evil. I somehow know'd her soul was touched. I figured she was most likely possessed 'cause they weren't a doubt in my bein' she was the source of the evil what held that place. I could feel it. I promise you I could. Not sure how that was happenin', but I couldn't stop knowin' what I was feelin' to be true. I figured that was what Black Oak meant by listenin' to my senses.

The look on Black Oak's face told me he was feelin' the evil as well. I sensed my spirit was losin' its stomach from the disgust 'a bein' near the evil what held this woman. She had black eyes what made my skin turn cold. I'd seen a few Indians with black eyes, but never a settler. I didn't wanna be anywhere near this woman, but Black Oak had to be, so I stayed with him as he walked up to her. Her eyes narrowed when we draw'd closer. I swear to this day she growled at me. Black Oak never took on like he noticed. Her face was dirty like all the other parts of her skin that was showin'. I had no trust for this being. The black robe wearin' just weren't right to my way 'a thinkin'. Why would a body wear such while livin' in the mountains? Made no sense to me. Had to be hard to trail in. Skins held a whole lot more purpose than long black robes when movin' through the woods or stalkin' food meat. I allowed her mind was gone. I did not know at the time how right my figurin' was.

Black Oak stood in front of her for a good minute or more, neither one speakin'. Made me most uncomfortable. She never moved. Just kept starin' at me, then at him, then back at me. A crazy little grin formed at the edges of her mouth while she did that. A look come in her eye I'd never seen from a body. Like it weren't her -- but somebody else -- but really her. That was spooky. All the lookin' back and forth got to be more'n Black Oak wanted to stand around for. He started askin' her some questions. It become clear to me, the longer I stood there, that we'd walked into danger, weren't no doubtin' that. Just how much was hard to figure. Two others come in with their arms full 'a firewood 'bout the time George got to askin' what he wanted. They went to stokin' the fire. I was proud 'a that. Cold filled that room thick.

"Woman, I have need for knowledge of one who was brought here some time back. It is a boy we seek. A boy from the south brought here by the clan we all know as The Lost. Tell me woman, have you seen this boy? Did they bring him here? Do you know where I will find him? I need this knowledge, dark one. Tell us if you know."

Black Oak spoke plain. If she answered, we'd know all we needed to know, then we could go fetch him and leave. I prayed in the silent for her answers. He'd called her "dark one." I wondered if he'd picked up on something I didn't catch? Made me curious.

"The Lost, yes. I know of them," the woman said as she looked over to me, then dropped her head back to her book. She said no more. Only kinda growled again after she said she know'd 'em. I figured them growls was meant for me, but I didn't understand the why of it all. Black Oak took to her again.

"You know of them. That is good," Black Oak told her. "Think back to the days many moons ago. Did they bring a young boy to trade? A Cherokee from the land of Yonah. Think woman. Tell me if you know of this trade. Were you here then?"

"Oh yes, mighty warrior . . . Black Oak," she barked back with a snarl while raisin' her head again to stare at him, then over at me. That lookin' back and forth was gettin' aggravating. Her teeth was near rotten lookin'. Her tongue black. "I was here. I had just come when that raiding party brought their plunder for trade. The black robes took care of those that were property. Queen made sure all for sale were ready when folks come to trade. The little one had to be carried around the sale ring. It could not walk for itself. I wanted to kill it. Blood Moon would not have it, so we sold it. Queen knows who got it. You will need to talk to her. I do not know where it went. I want it back if you find it. I will talk no more on this matter. Leave now while you can. Do not be inside these walls when darkness comes." She bowed her head like she was prayin'. She was a strange creature.

"How is it that you know my name, woman? I have not told you of who I am. It is not common for one such as you to know things they should not. This tells me who knows your spirit. You are of the evil one. Answer me now in the name of the Peace Child, this boy with me, do you know his name? Tell me, for I now know the truth of you . . . witch."

Witch? Wait, what? She was a witch? How did he know? How'd that happen? What was she to do now? Oh, what kinda world was this? I'd had relations with the spirit world but that was all with mostly good spirits in familiar surroundings. This was my first run-in with the evil kind in their own surroundings. I didn't know what to say, what to do, or if there was anything I could do. It seemed by the way she looked at me that she know'd who I was just like she know'd George. I moved a little closer in behind his huge body. I wanted to hide.

"Oh yes, warrior of the Choestoe Clan, I know this one with you. I have seen him in my visions many times. He is powerful in spirit. He is the Spirit Filled One. Yes, yes, yes, we know of this one. He lives where the rabbits dance. I have been to this place. Owl the Wise One lives there. I know her well when I travel in the spirit world. Now tell me, warrior, how much for this young one? I want him. He will fetch the purist of gold when I take him for sale to my sisters. How much? Tell me now!" she kinda hollered while slammin' her palms down on the table. One on either side of the book.

Her voice was like that of a mountain cat screamin'. It hurt your ears bein' up close like we was. I allowed she really was a witch after hearin' what she screamed. How else would she know who we was? Who the Cherokee thought I was. I'd heard there was witches in places hid, but never had I for sure met one 'til now. Wished I weren't meetin' that one. She was scary, but, for some strange reason, I weren't scared. I should 'a been, but I weren't. I soon learned why.

"Witch," Black Oak said kinda nasty. "I know your fear. You will answer me, or I will let him to you. Now, tell me how you know these things of us. I have not told you who I am. I have not told you who he is. Tell me now, wicked one. Holy Spirit will come on you if you make false words. Know this before you speak. I would not want this one to hurt you for being took by evil." He looked at me kinda serious. I didn't get what was goin' on. It was like Black Oak was threatening her with me. How was that possible?

"Do not let him move me, warrior. Keep him to yourself if that is how it is to be. He will not be sold today. I fear he brings trouble to this place. I want him to leave. Go now, or I will let my friends take you out."

She'd no more said that than both them heathens what was tendin' the fire pulled short guns from their waist belts, then aimed 'em both at me and Black Oak. That made me fearful. I hoped Black Oak was ready to leave. I know'd I was. These doin's was trouble I wanted no part of, but, unfortunately, I was laid in the middle of it like a fat hog stuck in a waller. I couldn't get shed of it all if I'd 'a wanted. I would need to act accordingly.

"What is this woman? I need only to know what has happened to the one I search for. We've done you no harm. Now you have your men pull weapons on us. This will not do." Black Oak near screamed as he moved like a cat into the darkness to our left. Disappearin' from sight like a haint into the dark room. Gone so quick the men had no time to fire at him. I stood alone with two short guns pointed at me. I was near shakin' it had me troubled so.

I could hear him movin' in the darkness, but the men didn't shoot. I wondered at that. You couldn't see him, though, so maybe they had no target. He'd moved to the darkest part of the room out 'a sight. I heard him no more. The next I saw him he'd grabbed both them heathens by the side of their heads and smashed 'em together. Sounded like an oak maul hittin' a locust wedge when me and Dad would split fence rails. Their arms went limp. The short guns fell to the plank floor. I know'd both them outlaws weren't trouble for us no more. The witch would be next. She know'd it, too. Took for the door straight away. Black Oak stopped her with one word: "Queen!"

Chapter 26 - The Benefit of Truth Can Be Painful

Wind Is Strong saw to it that she and Wolf had a proper camp to guard. We'd made it sleep worthy the evening prior, but that was all we'd got done 'fore dark set in. George was eager to go seek word next morning, so we left the settin' up camp chore for them to finish while we was gone. Wind figured we'd be stayin' a few days, so camp needed to be comfortable as could be. They obliged their chore by sheddin' the donkey of its load, then puttin' all our campin' truck to use. Stored our provisions in the dry under a canvas stretched like a tent cover. Took down all the truck we'd put up night before puttin' it all back up in better places we couldn't see in the half light. The meat they hung in a tree. George shot a young buck while scoutin' the trail the fifth day out. The fresh meat was a gift from the Creator. No doubtin' that. Them critters didn't move much in the white cold. Hardly ever seen one. Still had half 'a that in a meat pouch to hang as well. Me and Black Oak was expected back 'fore dark. Nobody know'd for sure if that was gonna happen. A body could reason Black Oak pro'bly had it figured.

***

"Sit, witch," she did as Black Oak said quick as a cat poucin'. She was fearful, turnin' to look at me as she moved from the door to go sit. I could see it in the look she give me. Her face seemed to change but then still look the same once it'd changed. Strangest thing I ever saw. "We will show you mercy. I have told you. I only seek word on a missing boy. You are of no interest to me, demon. Jebediah, come lay hands on this witch. Stand behind where she sits. Put one hand on each shoulder. Pray the Blood over her. Do not stop until she is still. Now, Jeb! Do it now!"

The voice what commenced to comin' from her mouth when I moved toward her weren't common to nothin' I'd ever heard. Whatever it was had her did not want me comin' near it. Black Oak meant for me to hurry. I understood why when I touched her. No sooner had my hands squeezed the woman's shoulders did the voice stop. Her body jerked straight like she was sittin' when we first come in. I could not see her face. I was proud 'a that. Her eyes bothered me. She felt cold as I began prayin' Jesus over her. I didn't know what to say, so I just asked Him to cover her with His Spirit. It turned out to be the proper thing to say, but when I first said it, I didn't think it was. It weren't 'til she went hostile on me did I fully understand what exactly Black Oak was havin' me do. I near couldn't hold my grip on her shoulders my words bothered her so, but I held on 'til she quieted, then kept holdin' like I'd been told. She turned her head toward Black Oak. It was a different voice what come out from her mouth that second time she spoke.

"Warrior," the woman cried with a sound I know'd was straight out 'a hell. Scared me something awful, but my mind said, "hold on." "You spoke words that I would not be harmed. Now you have this one trying to send me away. What is this you are doing, Cherokee? I will not forget your disrespect when your day comes to cross the Great River. You will know I wait for you when you see me in your visions -- if this one is victorious. Tell me what you intend of me. I am losing this fight. Your fate will be decided if I am driven from my home. Make him stop praying to the Son. Make him stop touching me with those hands of fire."

"Silence, evil one. I will not listen to any more of your lies. You are Queen. I know this. Tell me, Queen. Where will I find this boy I seek? You know the truth. Let it be known and I will have the Spirit Filled One remove his hands. You can have your black hearted life here as you know it. We will go, and not return to harm you. Tell me what I seek to know. We will leave you here to your evil. Tell me now, low one," Black Oak hollered.

"Warrior," she replied in that same awful growly kinda voice. Reminded me of a dog gone mad. "There are times we do not need to know the whole truth. Times when the pain of truth cannot be made to bear. I will tell you the truth, but first you must know where you are." With a wave of her hand, the lantern above the desk went to full light. I removed my hands from her shoulders, leavin' her to kinda slump down in the chair. She was weak. The sight was more than I could bear.

It was the source of the foul stench what filled the tradin' fort then flowed out the main gate. It's what I smelled when we first got there. Little ones. Lot's of 'em. Kids not older than four or five. All were gagged, bound and harnessed together with braided rope. Their heads laid to the side like they was restin', but they weren't restin'. They was just so weak they couldn't move. Appeared to be tied in a way that kept 'em all from fallin' over. What was this place? Why all the kids? She told us after lowerin' the light again with another wave of her hand. That time it looked like she could barely raise her arm.

"You see, warrior. This place holds the lives of many. I do not think you know what these young souls are for. Men will come. They will take these to places I never know. Yes, I am Queen. You are wise to understand this. You ask me to tell you where one child has gone that came here many moons back when all we do here is children. No one knows who they are. No one knows where they go. The ones who do not go are sent down a much darker path than these that are pure. I will not tell you more. I know no more. To find the one you seek, one must know who bought him. I cannot tell you. I do not know."

"Again you lie, witch," Black Oak hollered at the woman loud enough that I felt his voice in my chest. "You know the truth. You know Blood Moon. I killed him many moons ago. Do not fear him. Now, you will tell me the truth." I'm sure they heard him outside he was hollerin' so loud.

He motioned with his chin for me to put my hands back on her shoulders as he moved over closer to where she sat. I did as I was told. It jerked her straight up again. She grunted in pain. I liked hurtin' her. I allowed she'd hurt lots 'a folks her own self. She was evil.

"Begin your prayer again, Jeb, and they will speak. We will hear them speak." Black Oak said while gettin' close to stare the woman in the eye. He put his left hand on top of her head. "Tell me the truth. I demand it through the power of Holy Spirit. I will speak to the one you are torturing, demons. Let her go now."

I weren't for sure why Black Oak called the woman "they" or "them", but I had a notion. There was more'n one demon caught up in her possesion. That's all that made reason to me. I figured I was right about that, so in my prayer I asked Jesus to bind them. He did. I felt her body become warm again. George then got his answers. It weren't what we wanted to hear. Far from it. Unfortunately for us, it turned out to be the truth.

"Warrior," the woman said in her normal but noticeably weak voice. The bad spirits had become silent. "I am sorry for what has happened to you . . . to the boy you seek. I will tell you the truth, if it is what you want to hear. I would not want to know this truth, but I will speak it while I can if you truly want to know. I was not a part of it, but I know it to be true. Tell me, brave one. Do you want to know this truth?"

"The child is to be my son," Black Oak said softly. "I must know who has him. His mother needs to find rest in his life. Yes, I do want . . . no . . . need . . . to know. Our family will not be whole without him. I will go to where he is. We will take him if we must. Yes, woman, tell me. I am eager to find him."

"The seasons change, warrior, and with those changes come things we cannot reason," the woman began real slow like. Speakin' in a near whisper she was strainin' so. "Why life is so fragile for many, but yet, those who are weak become strong . . . if they live. I am sorry, warrior. The one you seek does not live. In his weakness, the cold was stronger. I remember the one you speak of. He was one of many that died that season. I saw this. Now, you have heard. Release me to my fate. The demon Queen will never leave me. Death is the only rest for me. I would accept it for my peace, warrior."

I heard her words, but I didn't understand it all. I think she'd said that Wind Is Strong's son had died in the cold. That stood to reason figurin' it cold like it was there, and him bein' so small at the time they took him. My soul sank inside. I never thought the child would be passed on. You'd think the stealin' folks would make sure their profit stayed in the land of the living. Worth nothin' to 'em dead.

The ways of life just didn't make sense sometimes. This was one 'a them times. I could not figure why this had to 'a happened. The Great Creator knows all. One day I'll ask Him.

"Again, you lie, heathen!" Black Oak shouted back. "The woman is lying for you. Pray harder, Jeb. Make it speak truth! Kill it if you must!"

"No," come the soft voice from the woman again. It was the same voice as the last we'd heard. She spoke as her head slumped down restin' her chin to her chest. It was a strain for her to make words.

"I am weak, warrior. I will die the evil death if you let this young one keep praying over me. The Holy One lives in him. I am but a woman weakened by the evil that lives in me. The words you have heard are words of truth. The child died after he was sold. You can trust me. This is how you may know it is about the child you seek. A woman of The Lost told me this about the boy. She believed it would make him worth more gold.

"The warriors of The Lost bragged about killing the father. Claimed he was a mighty warrior that fought to the death to save his wife and son. They took the mother for a slave, but they feared her. They believed her a seer. Kept her tied with the dogs away from the rest of the clan. She escaped by killin' the chief when he called for her about a vision. A warrior, Blood Moon, searched for her seeking revenge because the chief was his brother. The slave was the mother of the one boy from the south they brought. It may be that she is dead now. I know not. The mother is the only true seer I ever heard of, so I remember the lot. Most of the young ones of that time were too weak for the cold. They are buried not far from here. Please, I am done with this life. These spirits tell me what to say, what to do, where to go. I am too near death to lie. The truth has been spoken. You must believe me. I am sorry. I beg you to forgive me for the bad spirits. Warrior, please . . . show mercy. Give my soul peace while they are afraid of the Spirit Filled One. It is time to rest."

"What are you called, woman? George asked as he moved back to the fire. The two men were startin' to wake up some. He lifted both their heads one at a time slittin' their throats clean with his long knife. They never finished their wakin'. I did not care he done that. I just wanted to get shed 'a the place. Be done with all the spirit talk. It made a body weak.

"I am called Simone. I come from across the great water. On the boat to here was a witch, she filled me with these evil ones. I have known no peace since I came to this land. This place was once better, not proper, but better. These things inside me killed all the black robed women. The locals make me wear their robes to let everyone know I did it. They fear me, or rather, what is inside me. Your boy, he has powers. Does he know this, warrior? Have you told him, warrior?" She turned to look at me about the time Black Oak run his long knife clean through her heart and out the back toward me. The woman never moved. Just slumped forward even more, finally comin' to rest on the plank floor. Her life leakin' out around her. He had given her rest. Me and Black Oak hit our knees prayin'. We wanted no part 'a them demons what would be leavin' her.

They weren't a soul in sight when we come from the door of the lodge. Dark was comin' on. It hit me of a sudden that we'd been with that witch for a time 'cause it was morning when we come to her. That thought give me chills. It didn't feel like we was there for that long. Hunger weren't painin' me or nothin' like I'd missed eatin'. I figured it for witch time. I just wanted to get out from the whole put together. I'd had enough of my spirit feelin' sick.

Black Oak was leadin' with me followin' close behind. I did not want to get away from him. I'd a rode his big ol' back if he'd a let me. All the folks what'd been busy outside when we first come was gone in or maybe left for the woods. I said a little prayer to the Great Creator to keep any and all from goin' west. Wolf and Wind is strong was in camp to the west. We left the fort on the same trail we come in on. It must 'a snowed all day 'cause it laid a sight deeper than when we'd come that morning. Everybody was forced to walk the same path to keep from havin' to high step everywhere, made foot travel a sight easier. Problem was, most everybody used the same path. The pack 'a woodsmen what come on us in the woods just outside the stockade was usin' it same as us, too. Only they weren't travelin', their intentions was to come on us to keep us from movin' on. Their buckskins covered in snow from the knee down. I allowed they'd made their own trails gettin' out ahead of us so's to stop us. They wanted to talk, but Black Oak was in no mood to talk. He squared off at 'em drawin' his long knife. He'd failed to clean the fresh blood off. They saw that. His look was near crazy when he draw'd that knife. They seen that, too. It seemed to me his soul was hurtin' so deep from the pain he was feelin' that his mind was touched. I'd never known that depth of pain in my young life. The biggest one did the talkin'. The others just stood there lookin' cold.

"We mean you no harm, Cherokee. We just aim to make sure all is settled with you in this place. Bad as it is, we live here. That woman you just met . . . she is the devil. She holds us here. Are you the devil, mister?"

No sooner had he said that, than ten flintlock rifles cocked almost all at once. It was a sound I never forgot.

Black Oak never flinched. He spoke plain when he wanted to make sure folks heard him. Not so much when speakin' common conversation. I could tell by the way he spoke to them folks he wanted them, and all what listened around that place, to hear him. I wished Wolf would 'a been with us. He'd 'a been proud of his uncle.

"Let all within the hearing of my voice remember these words," Black Oak boomed up into the air as he stood tall as he could while raisin' his long knife straight up over his head. "Tell them to your families. Know I spoke truth when you tell it. The evil that has held you is dead. It is time for you to make this a better place. You will stop selling the little ones. I, Black Oak, of the Choestoe Clan, will come back here soon to make sure this trade has stopped. If one of you is hurting children when I come, your blood will cry out from the ground for mercy. Hear me when I say this to you. I speak for many that will be with me. I would begin now. Go look to those in the long house."

He looked straight at the big fella what stopped us to talk. He was a big man, too. I allowed he must 'a had a look to him Black Oak didn't care for 'cause he draw'd back his right fist full hittin' the man square in the mouth. I heard bones or teeth or something crack as Black Oak's huge right arm drove that man back into the snow to our left. He disappeared whole into the deep, white cold. A couple of his mates sprung to help him. He was out. Blood leakin' from his mouth and nose. A single bloody tooth fell from his mouth when they lifted him, layin' him out flat in the path. He could 'a been dead for all he looked like. Black Oak never checked. He just marched on from our run-in like it never happened. I know'd he had a harder chore on his mind than killin' settlers. I would not want to be the one responsible for telling Wind Is Strong the terrible news about her son. Hearin' it straight from the witch woman, I believed it to be true. Black Oak obviously did as well.

I could smell the campfire as we come to it from the north. We'd circled the camp makin' sure nobody'd found us. Air was movin' up from the south makin' it warmer. The snow was kinda startin' to melt off the trees and in the high places on the ground. I didn't like it when that happened. Seems like it was wet everywhere you went. The only dry place would be around the fire out for a couple paces. You could get dry next to the fire there in that ring. That's where Wolf was when we finally got to camp. Dark had near come. He was sittin' a piece 'a wood what laid solid on top of a big rock. I wondered how he got such a rock to the fire by himself. Wind Is Strong had to 'a helped him. She was not in sight. Black Oak went to her tent. She was not there. He asked Wolf, but he didn't know for sure just that she'd went for a walk and had not come back yet. With some quick scoutin', Black Oak found her tracks in the snow leadin' up the ridge from where we'd camped. He followed 'em in a hurry 'cause dark was settlin' in. Found her sittin' a flat rock prayin'. His heart sank as he went to her. What words could he say that would make what he had to say the least painful. He could not answer his own thoughts. He prayed in the silent that Holy Spirit would speak to him about it 'fore he had to tell Wind Is Strong what he know'd to be the truth. Her son would not be going home with them.

She heard him moving toward her in the snow. He was close. It always amazed her how quiet he could be. He had word. She know'd he did. Could feel in her soul he was hurtin' from what he'd come to tell her. Her soul cried from what she know'd he had to say to her. She felt for him. She would make it easy for his efforts. She loved him.

She didn't want him sufferin' any more than she know'd he was from losin' his future son. But, what he didn't know, and what she pulled comfort from, was knowin' he'd still be a father. She'd see to it once they was hitched proper.

"My brave warrior. Do you think you can sneak up on me? What kind of wife would I be if I didn't know my husband was near?"

She said this as she reached deep inside herself for the strength to stand and meet him in mid-stride. His head held low. His usually broad shoulders slumped in pain. He didn't know yet, but he would never have to speak. She'd seen the bad news as she rested earlier in the day. The meaning of her original vision had suddenly become clear in her mind. The reason she didn't have her son in her claws when she got back to Choestoe in her dream . . . he was not there to bring back. His journey across the river had been made many moons before. She understood that as she woke from her sleep. It broke her heart, but she was comforted knowin' the boy was with his father. Her heart know'd it for the ancestors had come to visit her.

"It is hard for you to find the words for what you must tell me. I know this, Black Oak. I am a seer. The vision I had before we made trail has been made clear to me this day. I fell asleep in my tent while praying for you and Jeb this morning. Holy Spirit visited my dreams, Black Oak. I have seen the truth. The cold was too much. My son is dead. The Black Robed women are dead from something I feel is evil. I know this. I have known this all afternoon. Do not hurt for me, Black Oak. I have settled with the ancestors. My son is where he should be . . . with his father. One day I will join them . . . and you will be a part of us as well. My husband will welcome us. I promise you this. You . . . and the children I will bear for you. Let us go from this place to our home in Choestoe. Become the ones we both want to be. I love you, George Black Oak. I always will. I will not mourn for my son as is custom. His crossing was many moons ago. All is in balance. My loss is his gain. He is with Jesus. He is with his father. That makes him, and his parents, very happy. We will look for our comfort in that."

Chapter 27 - My Special Life Gone with the Times

Me and Wolf know'd about witches. Know'd some was rumored to live in the mountains near Choestoe at one time or another. We'd heard of 'em durin' our growin' up years. Nobody we know'd was for sure ever caught as one, but folks didn't want 'em around. We'd heard tales 'a their shacks bein' found hidden in the backwoods and hollers where it was hard for Old Man Sun to shine through, but no souls had ever been brought to bare. No fire stories we ever heard told of any bein' caught. The old timers said they liked to live away from folks, so you'd never seen 'em when travelin' or out on trail. Wolf allowed if they was any near us, they must move of a night. Maybe they did? It was curious that witch know'd Old Mother, though. Weren't sure what that meant, our grandmother knowin' true witches. Real possessed witches like I'd just tangled with. That woman, Simone, who them demons was holdin', she didn't need to be around folks. You could see when first meetin' her she was wrong. I figured that's why all the stories we heard had 'em livin' out where the ground was poor for farmin' or comfortable livin'. Long way from flowin' water like Wolf Creek or the river Notla. The old timers believed witches is feared 'a running water in the mountains. Reminds 'em who Jesus is, the Living Water. The demons what hold a witch's spirit fear Jesus and His bunch with their whole put together. Superstition run deep in the immigrant mountain folk. They brung their thinkin' from their homelands.

True witches, and their kind, are not of the good things in life like one could be led to believe through false visions. I know'd after facin' a real one they weren't nothin' but nasty bein's. Smelled like death rot. Looked like death walkin'. You could tell at one time Simone was most likely a nice lookin' woman, 'til them demons started feedin' on her. The light on the inside had gone out. Them evil things just lived through her body, keepin' her takin' in food and breathin' air.

She'd asked George if I know'd I had powers. No, I didn't know. Didn't know after she asked that, neither. Nobody confirmed it to me. No matter to my way 'a thinkin'. Havin' powers weren't something I cared about. Not sure I wanted powers. I would pray askin' Holy Spirit to take 'em away so I wouldn't be bothered with 'em, if He would. I'd never heard it mentioned around my person that I had anything more than what most common folk did, but somehow, the witch know'd I had some, or rather the spirit what was in me that day sure had some. At least over whatever it was holdin' Simone.

Old Mother explained it to me a time later, after we'd been back a season or so. She told it so I understood exactly what I'd been messed up in. She was near to passin' on the day I spoke with her about witches. Her mind still sharp, even as old age had broken her body. She rarely left Dancing Bear's log home after a while. Sat by the fire rockin', mostly, tryin' to keep warm. That was sad to me. Our talk about witches was the last I ever had with her about anything. She crossed over a moon or so later. Her words that day made it clear to me that witches was nothin' but tools of the devil. Souls used for his purpose. I stayed clear 'a folks like the one I'd met when I could. Unfortunately for us later on, Wolf didn't.

"The woman you met was named Simone," Old Mother said near whisperin' from weakness. Wheeezin' from a bad lung she claimed was caused by an evil something. "She is, was, a being who is took. I saw she was lived in from the first time I met her. She was here years ago when I was the age of Anne. I stayed at her camp for a time. She wanted me to learn her ways, but I did not trust her. I tried to help her understand Holy Spirit, His ways, but she fought me. I did not like the demons what held her, so I made them leave. I never saw her again. It is good she is at rest. I only saw her for a short spell, but her eyes held much sadness. I felt for her. Yes, it is good she is passed.

"Understand what I tell you, Jebediah. It is not the body, of the one that is a witch, that has power. It is the one who holds the body. The evil one makes sure they do as he wishes. It is a stolen life, but the devil's strength keeps those outside the Blood from meddling. Without change from the Holy One, death is the end for all who walk this trail. Know them by their fruits, my son. Be careful of their treachery. The one you met was the same age as me, but I am sure she looked much younger. You have the spirit to understand. To know when you are among these witches, Jebediah. Remember what it feels like to be near them. Mind that next time you feel one is near. I have known only a few, both Cherokee and settler. Be watchful, Spirit Filled One. They will not like you when once they meet you."

Wolf was curious when we come back from the tradin' place. He asked no questions with words, but his face pleaded for the tellin' of what went on. Did we know where the boy'd been took? Was he there? Black Oak settled his mind some when he told what'd happened after supper that night. Wolf had more questions about the goin's on after the tellin' than before he know'd any of it. He was sad for Wind Is Strong, but he was still his curious self.

I had questions for Black Oak myself, once he was done tellin' Wolf what'd happened at the tradin' fort as I called it. That's what it looked like, a fort. Weren't no soldiers watchin' it for livin' purposes, but it looked like a fort all the same. He answered my questions honest. Weren't nothin' I didn't figure for.

"No, Jebediah, I did not know the danger of what we faced once inside the long house. Only when I saw darkness about the woman, did I know she was a tool of the evil one. You call them witch, so I used your word for her. I knew she was held when the two helpers brought the wood. Their eyes set with the far away evil look. Their scent was wrong. They will hurt no others. You, Spirit Filled One, you made the demons angry. You drove out the evil when you spoke your prayer. You have a gift, young one. It is not my place to tell it, but you have been given special favor by the Holy One. He will teach you as you gain in years. Trust Him. Keep Him in your thoughts. He is your strength."

He left to go lay under the quilts with Wind Is Strong in her tent a couple paces away from the fire. Our tents was staked close together to help block the wind that seemed to blow constant. The ends turned toward the fire for catchin' what heat we could when the flaps was open. He left one side open for decency. They weren't married official, but it was cold. He slept with her every night to keep both of 'em warm. I couldn't blame him for such. I'd do it for my beloved if she was there and cold. We was all cold. Hurtin' cold.

Me and Wolf got a chance to talk about the tradin' place now that he know'd what'd happened. We took out our tobacco pouches, movin' to the far side of the fire from the tents for private talk. It was cold. We huddled close while sharin' two heavy quilts. We was warm enough.

"My heart is heavy for our sister, Jebediah," Wolf said as we smoked. "I hurt in my spirit like I have lost family. I did not know this boy. One day I will. I love Wind Is Strong. I know she will see him again in the land of the Peace Child. I hope she knows this. It will give her comfort. I found peace in this understanding when my brother left us to pass on. The pain is hard. Sharp like a fine blade. You feel the hurt of death, but you sense peace. I know I will one day see him again in the land of our ancestors. We will hunt. You will go with us, Jeb. Fox Running would want you there."

"I would be honored to go on this hunt with you, Wolf, if I'm there when you take mind to go. If I'm not, don't wait around. Go on and enjoy the freedom of paradise. The Bible says we are but a wisp of smoke on this rock we call Mother Earth. I'll be along 'fore too long, if you're plannin' to go ahead of me. I reckon I'd like to stick around down here long as I can. I'm founded here. Folks is tolerable for the most part. I reckon we'll just have to live with the change our ways are takin', but I worry for our family, Wolf. Seems like Indians is gettin' put upon by the intruders more'n settler folks are. Trouble might be on the way for us. Maybe it is already here? If the tradin' place is anything like what we stand to see, the deep mountains may be our only way 'a makin' it. They's places our families can go won't nobody find us. We'll be fine. You and I can make it through anything, Wolf. We done proved that. Whatever the future brings, we will be fine."

"Of that you speak truth, brother. We have come far in our learning as future warriors. We know the way to where it is we need to go. The way of our ancestors. Our families will depend on us more in the coming times now that this season of change is on us. But, if there comes a time to fight, a time when the changes are not right, I will fight. I do not want this fight, but I will accept it for my duty to family – our home. My fear is the Blue Coats. I believe they will come in numbers I would not want to see. I fear my home is going to be a memory to the children of my children. It was not this way in my father's day or his father's day or any of the old ones' days. This is a time of change, and with it will be bloodshed. I know this will happen. The old ones speak of it. We will go home from this long trip north, Jeb. Our families miss us. Let us stay close to them for a while when once we return. It seems times are growing dark. Our kind may need us."

None of us felt like travelin' that next day, so we stayed camp one more day and night takin' our time to pack everything on our stock proper. It was important to get loads bound correctly when bein' toted by a mule or what not. If you packed a critter in careless fashion, your animal could give out too soon each day, for sure on such a long trail as we was headin' back on. It give Wind Is Strong plenty 'a time to get herself together as well. George know'd she needed some time. Wolf and me talked all the way back after he'd heard what happened with the witch. His questions passed the time. Made the day trip shorter. The nights was long and cold. No way to make them pass no faster. Wind Is Strong was just real quiet most 'a the trip back. She'd talked all the way north 'bout how she expected life would be different once we got her son home to Choestoe. I know'd she was hurtin' deep. She stayed to her tent wrapped up in quilts near constant when camp was made of a night. I felt for her.

I thought about things a lot durin' those long, cold nights comin' back home. It was even cold in the Cherokee nation once we breached the boundary. Wind Is Strong was near back to her old self by the end of our homeward trail. She'd stayed up with us the last two nights around the fire smokin' and tellin' tales 'til we all bedded down for the night. It was clear she missed her son, but she would go on with her life. The Great Creator had been kind in givin' it back durin' her escape from slavery. She would not disrespect that. She'd found love. Black Oak would make her a perfect husband and father. She considered him humble. A man who lived his life to serve his people, and those he called family. He had courage and strength like no other. She feared nothing when with him. She wanted it to be that way the rest of their lives. He would oblige her. She would give him sons.

Elizabeth stayed on my mind constant. I couldn't help thinkin' on her most all the time. I missed her bein' near on the long north trail. Longed for her warmth on the cold nights under Momma's heavy quilts. Thinkin' on her while tryin' to go to sleep kept my mind from studyin' about how cold I was. I think we all near froze. It was strange for me to think on, as I lay cold of a night not sleepin', but me and her would be weddin' the following spring. Weddings in the mountains durin' the spring are a thing of beauty. Colors all over the sides 'a the mountains turn everything into a paintin' by God Himself. Mix in all the festivities of a special comin' together and me and Elizabeth was gonna have us one grand time 'a gettin' married. I looked forward to it in a most anxious way.

It felt good to be back in Choestoe after our trail north and back had ended. I slept by the fireplace that first night back. Kept the fire goin' big till morning, enjoyin' the warmth I'd been longing for the last few days. Everybody was sad to hear what we'd found out about Wind Is Strong's son. She was comforted by Momma and the lady folk from the valley for more'n a month once word got out of us bein' home. Losin' a child was a strong pang among mountain women folk. This one required a pourin' out 'a love like none I ever saw in my whole put together. I don't think one family missed comin' to let Wind Is Strong know they was feelin' for her. All in the valley had got to know her. Liked her a sight. All was amazed at her gettin' free story when it was told around the story fires. She know'd it fortunate she'd found such a place as ours to live. God was good. She'd lost her husband, her son, her life, but she'd been given a second chance at all that evil had took. This time no raid would get her family. With Black Oak as her husband, she would not let that happen again.

We did just what Wolf said when we got home. I stayed the farm all the growin' and harvest time that year. Made sure to check up on my beloved several times. I looked forward to those trips to see her all the long workin' hours durin' growin' season. We took turns stayin' at each other's home durin' harvest. Didn't see Wolf but a couple times 'fore Killin' Time in the fall, when folks butchered their winter meat. He was different the last of those times I saw him. I found out from speakin' with Dancing Bear that Wolf had been to see that hog jumpin' maiden. That told me straight away what his problem was. He would understand my need to be with Elizabeth better after he come to understand the comfort a woman can provide, if she chooses. He never mentioned it to me. I expected no less. Worryin' over a woman weren't something Cherokee warriors spoke about. They just lived the life. Woman or no woman.

She and Elizabeth got to be close in the years followin'. All our kids grow'd up together, even with the changes that made our lives more confined. I never grow'd use to mountain life after it was all made different. The mountains weren't never the same once outside folks found out about all there was to have. We lost our freedom when the greedy ones realized how special a place Choestoe is. Brung their nasty ways to bear on us. The U.S. Government seen to that by takin' what was owned by the Indians. Givin' it to folks what didn't understand the way. It was selfish of me to think on, 'cause a lot 'a folks prospered, but I wished many times that the gold had never been found near our home. Maybe we could 'a kept our lives as adults the way they was all our growin' up years. That would 'a been nice. Still, those times are gone, never to be lived again. I was proud to 'a been a part of 'em.

My time on the farm the rest 'a that year was a special time for me. I would have many fond memories of mine and Dad's and Momma's time together. Memories of all the talks we had in the cool of the evening while rockin' on the porch. I loved doin' that. Anne was gone as much as she was home, seein' to folks' needs. I went with her on occasion. Them trips created memories for sure. I visited with Cain, Rose and Isabelle more than I should 'a. Left Dad waitin' on me a couple days at different times from bein' late gettin' back from their place. That little girl hooked me hard. She was something else. Fiesty like her mom, but not feared 'a nothin' like her dad. She would grow up to be a strong, beautiful woman. She and Wind Is Strong become good friends over the years. That was special, but the changes what kept comin' to the mountains made her hard in her emotions for others. I understood that. I felt the same every once in a while.

Mountain folks and the Indians just suffered with all the greed flowin' in to the valley. It was hard to accept. Hard for a body to not fight back at every turn, but you had to be careful. Many of the invaders was dangerous.

I thank the Great Creator for my parents, every time they come to mind. I'm proud of 'em raisin' me the way they did – for teachin' me the way of our faith -- about the Blood and what it means to my soul. They loved us kids. Raised us proper because of that love. Taught us to respect others the way we'd wanna be respected. Not because most others had done anything special to respect 'em for, but because it's the way. The Bible says Jesus come to serve, not to be served. That truth holds a special light in my life. I learned it from Dad as he read to us from the Good Book of a night 'fore beddin' down. I never forgot his teaching us from the word. Those things I learned was the unspoken rule in old Choestoe, not really so in the new. It's a shame that special times have to end. Fortunately, I held on to the truth we all lived by in the valley of the rabbits and will 'til I cross the Great River: Treat folks how you want to be treated. Be someone all folks can depend on. Be responsible for your own doin's, considerin' others first. Take care of the old ones, the widows, and keep the young ones safe. If we all did that, our world would be a better place . . . much like our time in the Choestoe me and Wolf grow'd up in. A time that is now lost, in the land where rabbits dance.

The End

Meet Our Author

J. R. Collins

J. R. Collins was raised in the valley he so passionately writes about. A descendant of the first pilgrims to the area, he proudly claims heritage and roots through the people of the Appalachian Mountains that settled in the Choestoe Valley sometime in the latter part of the 1700's early 1800's. Born and raised in North Georgia, he grew up like Jeb, hunting and running the ridges of Choestoe.

Collins is a graduate of Young Harris College in the North Georgia Mountains. His first novel of young Jeb Collins, *The Boy Who Danced with Rabbits* introduces a folksy method of storytelling much in the style of another famous American author, Louis L'Amour. The second book in the best-selling series, Home From

Choestoe, *Living Where the Rabbits Dance,* continues the saga of Jeb Collins as he matures into adulthood along with his best friend, a young Indian boy, Wolf.

The third book in the trilogy, *Spirit of the Rabbit Place,* follows Jeb as he becomes a mature adult man who finds trouble, excitement, action, adventure and romance in this finale.

Watch for additional books by J.R. Collins from A-Argus Books.

Made in the USA
Columbia, SC
03 August 2021

42573827R00178